"YOU'RE SAFE HERE, AURORA," ETHAN WHISPERED.

His fingertips lightly touched her along the slant of her jaw. His fingers slid behind her head, and steadied her under the fierce taste of his passion. Stunned, she offered no resistance. His mouth was ardent in its claim, and Aurora was aware of her own simmering response, of a like spark of desire quickening within her. Her hands lifted and gently roved the contours of his face. Oh, how she wanted this, wanted him. She knew time would grant them no favors, that they had to grab greedily for all they could have of this fleeting moment. Her arms stole about the breadth of his shoulders, and she buried her face in the warm hollow of his throat.

"Aurora," he groaned.

"Shh," she murmured, hushing him with the light press of her mouth. Slowly, his hands slid up her back, and she felt his breathing quicken. . . .

DANA RANSOM'S RED-HOT HEARTFIRES!

ALEXANDRA'S ECSTASY (2773, $3.75)

Alexandra had known Tucker for all her seventeen years, but all at once she realized her childhood friend was the man capable of tempting her to leave innocence behind!

LIAR'S PROMISE (2881, $4.25)

Kathryn Mallory's sincere questions about her father's ship to the disreputable Captain Brady Rogan were met with mocking indifference. Then he noticed her trim waist, angelic face and Kathryn won the wrong kind of attention!

LOVE'S GLORIOUS GAMBLE (2497, $3.75)

Nothing could match the true thrill that coursed through Gloria Daniels when she first spotted the gambler, Sterling Caulder. Experiencing his embrace, feeling his lips against hers would be a risk, but she was willing to chance it all!

WILD, SAVAGE LOVE (3055, $4.25)

Evangeline, set free from Indians, discovered liberty had its price to pay when her uncle sold her into marriage to Royce Tanner. Dreaming of her return to the people she loved, she vowed never to submit to her husband's caress.

WILD WYOMING LOVE (3427, $4.25)

Lucille Blessing had no time for the new marshal Sam Zachary. His mocking and arrogant manner grated her nerves, yet she longed to ease the tension she knew he held inside. She knew that if he wanted her, she could never say no!

DANA RANSOM
DAKOTA DAWN

ZEBRA BOOKS
KENSINGTON PUBLISHING CORP.

For Irene Goodman
To the start of a long and
successful partnership.
Thanks for the encouragement
and the insight
that made
DAKOTA DAWN
and
DAKOTA DESIRE
possible.

ZEBRA BOOKS

are published by

Kensington Publishing Corp.
475 Park Avenue South
New York, NY 10016

First printing: November, 1991

Printed in the United States of America

Chapter One

Had the horse not stumbled, he never would have seen her.

Snow whipped and swirled about the figure of Ethan Prescott as he hunched within the heavy warmth of his buffalo coat. Even with his hat tilted forward and his collar turned up to shield his cheeks, his face felt fair to frozen beneath his thick beard. It was going to be a doozy. No doubt about it. The frigid wind was screaming down from Saskatchewan and Manitoba, the air filled with stinging pellets driven by a knifing force. Within the hour, the hills of the Dakota Territory would be a place not fit for man nor beast, and Ethan meant to see both safe at the end of the trail before the path closed in around him. Nothing could survive unprotected when the ill-tempered blizzards settled in, sometimes for days at a time. It was best to cozy up close to a fire and wait for the savage winds to blow themselves to a calm. Then the digging out would commence.

At least he'd managed to clear his trap lines. Behind him, wrapped securely in a tarp of duck cloth, was the means of his next year's sustenance, the lush beaver pelts he would trade for supplies and the necessities of his solitary existence. He could live off the land if he had to, and at times he'd had to, but Ethan

5

liked his comforts when he could get them. He could forgo companionship much more easily than he could the full-bodied smell of fresh ground coffee beans. An acorn substitute just wasn't the same steaming in his morning tin. And so, he would disregard the danger to have his precious coffee and whatever else he could barter from the value of the furs.

He hadn't been to the post for nearly a year, hadn't heard a white man's voice or seen skin not bronzed and hair not greased into a glossy black sheen. Though he would tell himself he didn't miss it, Ethan found he was cussing the turn of weather that would delay his seasonal journey down from the Hills. And it wasn't just because he was perilously close to being out of coffee. Sometimes, when the howl of wolves was the only accompaniment to the incessant wind, he found himself simply aching for the sound of a human voice. He got the lonelies so bad it was near to a fever raging out of control, consuming him, almost to the point of forgetting his circumstances. Almost. But like these merciless snows, the feeling would lessen in time. All he could do was wait it out.

Mostly, he enjoyed the life he'd been forced to lead. He knew an absolute freedom, a kind of pure independence not found in cities or settlements. There, someone was always on hand to be answered to. There were responsibilities and obligations, wanted or not, rules to abide by, right or wrong, just or unjust. And there was always someone needy, someone seeking, someone dependent who would take advantage of even the most guarded heart. He'd had enough. He'd seen enough of civilization to know that here was where he belonged. Here there was only nature to answer to. A body could step out into the day stark naked and let up a howl if he was of a mind to, and no one, save a few startled woodland creatures, would be about to see or care. A man could survive on his wits, on his strength, on his primal instincts, which could only be honed away from the blunting social strictures of humanity. And he had only himself to worry over, to care for, to think of. No one to "tsk" if he chose not to shave, no one to chide him for his moodiness, no one to call him from his occasional dark studies. No unasked-for opinions, no guides or graces to maintain. Freedom. It spread above with the proud majesty of the mountains and waved below in the calm ripples of prairie grasses. There was a sweet acceptance in the tang of pine carried on soft breezes and a balm for a troubled heart in the deep-starred, silent nights . . . and nothing to interfere with the slow, careful piecing together of a shattered life.

Ordinarily, Ethan wouldn't mind a week or so of solitude buried in his cabin. He had traps to ready for spring. He'd been working some fine red maple into a rocking chair. After the thaws, he planned to attach a bigger porch to the front of his cabin. There, he would rock and smoke his pipe and think on the dreams of his youth, as if he were a man beyond his prime instead of this side of his thirty-third year. But before he could consider mending traps or smoothing wood or rocking and smoking, he had to escape the uncertain present with which nature was confronting him.

Already, there was precious little left of the trail ahead. Ethan was guiding his big sorrel more from instinct than actual sight, as the whirl of snow led to near-blindness. He had to rely on the horse's sense of direction, that its wish to be snug in its lean-to was as great as his own desire to be basking at his hearth. He wasn't unaware of the precariousness of his situation. He'd heard of man and horse found yards away from the shelter of cabin and barn frozen stiff beneath engulfing drifts. Skill and luck alone couldn't always keep a man alive. Sometimes, it was just a matter of timing, even seconds. And Ethan meant to beat out that unsympathetic clock of mortality at least once more.

The snow was wet, melting when it hit bare skin, and then, almost at once, becoming crystalline again. Swipes from his ice-encrusted sleeve provided no relief when cold threatened to seal upper to lower lashes and end his limited sight altogether. He was in the process of rubbing at his eyes when the gelding took a misstep on the uneven, snow-covered path and shied violently away from the trail's edge. The abrupt movement nearly cost him his seat.

"Whoa, son. Easy now, boy," Ethan soothed out of habit. He took a more masterful hold on the reins and looked to see what had startled the big horse.

There, on the side of the trail, nearly obscured by the snows drifting up on three sides, was a huddled shape. He squinted hard against the slice of sleety dampness, at first disbelieving. A human shape.

Ethan, who was as surprised as his mount had been, had no choice but to rein in and risk loosing valuable minutes in his trek toward home. Who in God's name would be foolish enough to be caught afoot with a winter storm abrewing? Impatient with the decision to stop, the big horse snorted and tossed its head. Smokelike plumes shot from flared nostrils. It was anxious to continue toward shelter but obeyed the command to stand when its reins hung down.

As he stepped from the high gelding Ethan sank into snow over the tops of his high boots. Wading, floundering, he struggled the few feet to where the figure lay immobile. Probably too late anyway, he told himself, but he had to check. He couldn't imagine one of Yellow Bear's braves being so careless. Catching

8

hold of one stiffened contour of the buffalo robe left exposed, he rolled the equally and alarmingly stiff body face up.

At first, Ethan thought his vision played him false. He blinked hard and struck at his doubting eyes with the back of a gloved hand, hoping to clarify what they showed him.

A woman.

A *white* woman.

He wasn't sure which sight stunned him more. He sat back on his heels, while his backside grew chilled in the snow, and stared. And stared, as if he'd never seen a fair-skinned female before. What was a white woman doing up in the Hills? Alone. On foot. Trust a female to place herself in the most troublesome spot. Wrestling one heavy glove off with the tug of his teeth, Ethan put fingertips against lips that were cold — so cold. He waited. Then, almost like a warm spring breeze, he felt her breath blow faintly upon his flesh.

She was still alive.

Not for long, he knew, if he didn't get her out of the harsh elements and inside where he could force some heat back into her fairly rigid body. There was no time to consider the complications of what he was about to do. He'd no choice but to take the woman to his cabin. It was that or leave her to die. Neither a difficult choice nor, at the moment, a conscious one. Carefully, he bent and began to gather her into his arms. Weighted down with sodden robe and heavy with unconsciousness, she created quite a burden as he wallowed through the drifts to where his sorrel pawed restlessly at the frozen ground. It was his luck that the woman was as round and heavy as a barrel of salt pork, instead of slender and feather-light. Staggering under her bulk, he faced another dilemma.

9

There was no room on the gelding's back for two riders and the large pack of furs. Nor could he lead the animal along the rapidly filling trail. The snow was too deep. There wasn't time. They both had to ride and that meant discarding an accumulation of fur worth a year of supplies and comforts.

Ethan settled the sagging woman into the saddle, shifting her until sure she wouldn't slip. Then he drew a long blade from his boot and regretfully slit the lacings that held the bounty of peltry to his mount. He tried not to think too much about what he was doing, about what he was losing in this instinctive act of charity. Even in the wilds he wasn't free of the demanding price womankind would place upon him. Trust the weakness of the fairer sex to again cost him all that he owned. Hang it, he could well starve as a result of helping this crazy unknown female. Well, he wouldn't exactly starve, but how he'd yearned for that coffee and fresh tobacco. He tried not to scowl and grumble as he lugged the pack off the trail and into the trees. Maybe, just maybe, the covering of snow would keep the wealth of furs safe until he could return for them. Maybe no animal would come upon them, no Sioux hunting party. He let them drop, knowing they'd be just another mound of white in seconds, then, just in case, he notched one of the pines to mark the spot.

As he boosted himself into the saddle and gathered the limp, costly burden to his chest in order to handle the reins, he forced himself to mentally discard the furs and concentrate on keeping them both alive in the swirling world of white. And he forced himself not to think of what he was bringing to the silent sanctum of his home. A female companion. A *white* female companion.

His thoughts brewing as bitterly as the wind from

10

the north, Ethan nudged the horse forward. Toward home.

First things first. When he reined up his sorrel in the clearing he'd carved out of wilderness, Ethan knew what a tight race he'd run against the rapidly piling snow. Already, he had to wade through waist-deep accumulations with the woman in his arms dragging across the fresh white surface to get to the door of his cabin. For just such eventualities, he'd built his home with a door which opened inward. The fire lay cold in the grate, and the single room was only slightly warmer than the outside. Not much he could do about that for the moment. Gently, though he gave no thought to the instinctive care, he deposited the unresisting form upon his bed, and then he went to do what he knew must be done.

It was snowing too hard for the lean-to to offer enough protection for his horse. Determinedly, he wrestled open the door to the smokehouse and urged his gelding within. The animal snorted and balked at the heavy odors hovering thickly inside the small room, but Ethan paid it no mind as he secured the reins to an overhead ring beside a haunch of venison. Knowing it might well be days before he could venture this far from the house again, he dragged in a bundle of hay and topped a barrel of water so the animal would not go wanting. Then, after he'd secured the door, he strung a heavy gauge of wire between the smoke house and his own front door. That way, if he had to, he could find his way across the yard. In a Dakota blizzard, a man could get lost and perish the moment he left his porch. He had no desire to wander to his death in his own front yard, nor to lose his precious mount. The wire would be a lifeline if need be. He only hoped it wouldn't come to that. However, seeing how the drifts were already to the tops of his cabin windows, he knew it was a foolish hope. Before nightfall, the snow would cover his little cabin as if it were of insignificant size.

Ethan closed the cabin door, sealing it in darkness though it was yet midday. With an ease of familiarity, he crossed to the yawning fireplace and dropped down on one knee. He didn't bother to remove hat or coat as he arranged kindling and used a lucifer to coax a steady flame. He crouched there, feeding the blaze, feeling its heat thaw the ice from his whiskers and tie string while his thoughts leapt and flared like that waking fire.

Who was she, this white woman? Even without turning back toward her, he could see her features vividly as captured by a stunned, half-starving mind. He added another log and listened to the snap and pop of hot sap as he imagined the sound of her soft breathing from his bed. And suddenly, his warming body went all over cold again with a chill of uneasiness. Already her presence seemed to fill his small home and his every thought with a powerful, disconcerting force. He jerked his hand back, his fingers nearly singed from lingering too long while he negligently woolgathered. Sucking on those abused fingertips, he made himself pay attention to the task before him. Only when the room was permeated with a welcoming flicker of warmth and light and a kettle of water was set to boil did Ethan Prescott turn to his uninvited guest. To the woman who had invaded his lonely sanctuary in the woods.

She hadn't moved within the swaddling of buffalo hide. Melting snow formed dark, wet patches upon his bedding after making runnels through the shaggy mat. Quickly, he disentangled her from the cold embrace of the robe and tossed it to dry over a fireside chair. Only then did he get his first clear look at the

12

woman he'd rescued from winter's wrath.

The friendly fire effused a glow of liquid gold upon features bronzed by sun and burned by cold, features that didn't need artificial tricks of tender light to appear beautiful. Whoever this wilderness wanderer was, she was as lovely as any woman, North or South, that Ethan had ever seen. Fine bones arranged her eyes, nose and mouth into a pleasing symmetry beneath a tousle of hair the reddest natural shade he could imagine. Her brows were arched in delicate crescents, the bridge of her nose thin and straight above a pair of well-drawn lips. Lips so rosy, so lush they sold the promise of sweetness better than any confectioner's window. Lips that invited—no, demanded kissing. And for the first time in his five years of isolation, Ethan was shaken by the desire to know lips like these again. Would they taste as soft and yielding as those that tormented his dreams? Would they bring heartache just as easily?

He studied the featherlike fringe of lashes that were swept against those burnished cheeks in unmoving arcs. What color were her eyes, he wondered with a distracted curiosity. With that riot of red hair they would be green, he guessed. Maybe blue. Or brown, like his own. Then he gave himself a harsh mental shake. Here he was wondering about her lips and closed eyes, and neither would open to reveal the answer to either question if he didn't see to the state of her health. He forced his bemused gaze to leave the intent evaluation of her face, and immediately he was beset by more provoking questions.

Beneath the well-worn buffalo robe, the woman was a batch of confusing contrasts. Her form was inadequately and perplexingly gowned in fine back-East fashion. Ethan had no notion of the prevailing style in women's clothes but he would venture the ru-

13

ined silk had been all the rage, with its series of frills and bows. A tight smile took his generous mouth. Just like a silly, irresponsible city-bred girl to go awandering off, heedless to consequence, unmindful of who might suffer in her absence. It had been a long time since he'd felt such luxurious fabric in his calloused hands. It was a tactile torture to his memory, as he eased her from a curled-up huddle on her side over onto her back. And abruptly he knew why it had been such a struggle to carry her.

"Oh, my God," he breathed hoarsely into the cabin's stillness.

She was not shaped by ungainly fat, as he had at first assumed. The woman was obviously, very, very pregnant.

"Oh, my God," he repeated, half in awe, half in horror. At no time in his lonely male fantasies had he asked the good Lord to provide him with a female made frustratingly unavailable by the swelling of another man's child!

Well, here she was and there was no denying her state. Slowly, other considerations crept in to prompt his stunned thinking. She was very pregnant and the snows outside were sealing them in together for what could be weeks. Did she have that much time?

Cautiously, he placed a large hand upon her ripe abdomen, feeling a curious stirring of nostalgic delight at the smooth, rounded contour of life beneath palm and silk. He waited, scarcely chancing a breath. There. A hard, vigorous punch of impatient humanity just below his hand. The child was healthy and rearing to know its surroundings. Now, it was up to him to see the mother strong enough to give birth. Who she was and how she'd come to be wandering in a storm in her condition ceased to be important. Seeing that she survived was. He'd no way of knowing how long she'd lain beside the path, but he guessed it was long enough to endanger her life.

In contrast to the cut of the gown, the woman's feet were clad in fur-lined Miniconjou moccasins. Not exactly the footgear an Eastern belle would wear to accent the silken ensemble. Quickly, he unlaced the moccasins to check her extremities. Bare toes showed high color, not the dangerous dead-white of fatal exposure, and so did her fingertips when he looked there. Mild frostbite. He kept her hand in his huge palm for a long moment. It was a delicate hand with long fine fingers. The kind that would have a man at beck and call. The kind a lady in a stylish silk gown would have. Not the kind of hand to sport hard ridges of callous and ragged nails. He let his thumb trace over those tough reminders of toil, and the wondering returned. What the devil had this fashionable woman been doing to earn this evidence of grueling work?

Spurred by the need to have these perplexing questions answered, Ethan began to purposefully tend his guest. The silk gown was wet and cloying, more a danger than a protective covering. It would have to go lest she become chilled. By now, the cabin's small interior was pleasantly warmed by the fire. Ethan shifted her slightly to one side to find his duty made easier by the fact that the back of the dress was open to the waist. It had obviously been cut to skim a trim figure, not one burgeoning with child. Why she would chose to wear it—yet another puzzle. Carefully, he eased the damp fabric from fair shoulders, shoulders gently sloping and white, so gleaming white. Ethan felt a fierce tightening inside himself, winding notch upon notch into a painful binding as the gown slipped lower, exposing more of the same pale flesh.

She wore nothing beneath the inappropriate dress. She was a slender woman, built with long, fragile-looking bones. There was none of the soft fleshiness along her limbs that he'd expect to find on the wearer of an expensive gown. Her arms were lean, shaped by arduous labor and sleek muscle . . . not the arms of a female tending her needlepoint and tea parties. Her figure hinted at strength and a certain degree of deprivation, as if she'd known hunger as well as hard work. For all her sinew and near-gauntness, he could see the coming child had lent a fullness to her creamy breasts, as the fabric came away from them. Ethan's ravening gaze was held by their perfect beauty: heavy, succulent, tipped with a beckoning tease of coral. Hills a man could lose himself in, inviting mounds meant to be explored. His hands gripped the damp material. They shook with the control he exerted, wanting to glide up those tempting white swells rather than helplessly knead the length of sodden silk. His palms grew damp. What would it be like to have that pink flesh fill them? He heard a low, rumbling sound rasp though the silence and realized with some surprise that it was the sound of his own long-denied need.

He tore his stare down from the womanly roundness to a greater swell. One that spoke of motherhood, one that made him ashamed he had entertained such lustful thoughts. He tugged the useless gown from around slender hips, averting his eyes to avoid further hot fancies. However, the sight of her long, shapely legs provided an equal provocation.

Heaven above, what could he be thinking?

Almost angrily, he jerked a softly tanned hide from the foot of the bed and flung it over her ripe nakedness. A breeding woman and he as randy as a bull moose in rut. Imaginings, vile and indecent to a man of his upbringing, forced him to move away from the bedside, away from the temptation of this vulnerable woman a cruel God had thrust upon him.

Before the heat of the fire, Ethan stripped off his heavy coat and draped it where it would dry. Steam rose above the water he poured into a basin from the fireplace kettle. After testing it with his wrist, he soaked a rough towel in the heated liquid and wrung it thoroughly. He turned back the robe at the bottom of his bed and wound the towel compress-fashion about the woman's chilled feet. It would serve to bring up the body temperature and restore sluggish circulation. They were small feet, barely filling the length of his hand. The dainty feet of a lady, meant for kid slippers, not crude native moccasins. Bare feet. As bare as the rest of her. He pulled down the robe and tucked it in with fierce movements. There was nothing wrong with *his* circulation. Then, he prodded himself to become busy with the fixing of his meal. His visitor would need nourishment when she woke, whether he wanted to offer the hospitality or not, and he needed something to occupy a feverish mind distracted by thoughts of woman and soft skin.

With a stew of minced elk meat and root vegetables simmering on the trammel, Ethan packed his pipe with some of his soon-to-be depleted supply of tobacco and commenced to smoking while he observed the rounded silhouette on his bed. A baffling mystery, one that gnawed at his mind the way the woman's beauty gnawed at lower regions. There was no trace of civilization for distant miles, no traveled roads, no homesteads, no settlements. No place she could have wandered from. So how had she come to the woods, into the far reaches of the hills where the last of the Sioux and Ethan Prescott roamed free?

And that evoked deeper, more urgent questions. What on earth was he going to do with her? She was in no condition to travel the rough and rocky miles into the valley alone once the snows were gone. It would be safer for both mother and child if she delivered in the snug cabin. But then, he would have mother and child to contend with and all the complicating agonies of heart and mind. Still no easy solution. What was he going to do with them? He knew the impossibility of escorting them to the ranches or town below.

And now that he'd brought her to his wilderness sanctuary, how safe was he? He could well have been better off getting lost in the snows outside.

If only his horse hadn't stumbled.

Pain. Terrible, ceaseless pain.

It needled through her feet, stinging her toes, jabbing mercilessly at their tender arches. She tried shifting them to alleviate the torment, but, oddly, she could not. Her feet wouldn't budge. She worked them back and forth a moment, but movement was restricted.

They were bound.

Dear Lord, they'd caught up to her!

Eyes wild with panic flashed open then blinked in confusion at the sight of framed walls. There was a moment of relief followed by wariness. Where was she? And why did she hurt so? Fright gave a hurried rhythm to her breathing and her heart began to bump frantically against her ribs as the details of her flight returned. She remembered the snow, the terrible, dragging exhaustion. The discomfort in her belly. Alarmed, she shifted her hands to the swell below her breasts. The feel of life stirring beneath her palms brought a familiar calm. Then, another mystery. Where was her gown?

In a cautious terror, she turned her head slightly to see who had made a prisoner of her, keeping her bound, vulnerable and naked. Peering through a

18

fringe of heavy lashes, she observed the perimeters of a small room built of rounded logs. It was furnished sparsely with crude table, wash stand and chairs. A great stone fireplace occupied one wall, its carefully banked fire sending refractions of light off the metal traps hanging from the ceiling beams; their vicious jaws gleamed with use and care.

A trapper's cabin. Dear God!

At that moment, she felt like some small and helpless creature caught within a wicked grasp of steel. She wouldn't be foolishly lulled again. She was far from safety. Her teeth clenched to seal in a moan. Why did her feet ache so? Had they been tied too tightly?

Something savory simmered in a pot, tempting the empty cavern of her stomach into giving an echoing call. The sound seemed unnaturally loud, and she bit her lip, fearing it had given her away. Silence gave her the courage to continue her study of the surroundings. She twisted even further on the bed to allow a greater view. And froze when she saw him — the huge, still man before the fire.

With shadows playing behind the wide spread of shoulders, he had the appearance of a giant whose great head nodded upon a broad expanse of chest. Clad in thick beard and rough woolens, he gave an immediate impression of raw, primitive power, and a responsive fear shot through her. Whoever he was, he looked at one with the wilds. Not the sort to give shelter and sympathy. Her wide gaze fell to where huge hands splayed upon thighs the size of sturdy oaks, hands that could wring the life from her with a single twist. Hands that would have no trouble in subduing one frail woman great with child. Her mouth went dry in fear.

It was a sudden kick from within her massive belly

that forced her from her apprehensions. Her hands went protectively to that rounded girth where an innocent life depended upon her to think and act. Though not yet a mother, she felt all the fierce instincts of parenthood flood through her. She must protect her child. She had to escape from the slumbering giant whose steel traps glittered menacingly overhead.

Slowly, she sat up, no easy task given her unwieldy condition. Clutching the hide covering to her bare breasts, she reached down to see what imprisoned her ankles and knew a degree of confusion.

A towel, not ropes.

She pulled it free and awoke a shimmer of prickly discomfort from yet-numbed toes. It was then she remembered the cold seeping into her feet as she trudged determinedly through the snow. Frostbite. How severe, she wondered, as the memory of horror stories and amputated limbs tortured her mind. She gently rubbed her feet until the pain grew too much for her to bear. Would she be able to walk? To outrun this new danger? She'd have to. She set her jaw to endure what she must and swung bare legs from the bed.

She knew a moment of pure panic as the groan of the rope bed caused the giant figure to stir restlessly. She sat paralyzed, scarcely daring to breathe until her captor quieted. Then a furtive desperation had her gaze sweeping the floor around the bed. There, she found her damp moccasins but not her dress. Quickly she pulled on the snug fitting hide slippers, gritting her teeth against the protesting agony from her abused feet. The knowledge that she would have worse to bear should she not escape gave her the bravery to continue. Wrapping the bed robe more securely about her shoulders, she placed her feet on the planked floor and stood.

Oh, God, it hurt! Bolts of sharp torment ravaged

20

her, seizing her feet like tearing jaws; biting, shredding, crushing. It would have been so easy to fall back upon the bed, to succumb to whimpers of distress and agonized sobbings. But she couldn't. Biting her lower lip until her mouth filled with the salty tang of her own blood, she forced one step, then two from her throbbing feet. Her face was wet with the dampness of pain. Her jaw ached from the effort of containing her cries. Still, determinedly, she stumped across the rough flooring with only the robe to conceal her nakedness, with only her anxiety to be free propelling each excruciating step.

She paused at the door, breathing heavily, shaking as if in the throes of a consuming illness. She dashed an unsteady hand across her eyes to clear them of sweat and tears and braced herself to face the cruelty of the weather. She'd no idea where she was or how far she would be forced to travel before shelter could be found. But she knew the direction. Down. Down out of these merciless hills. Once she reached the valley, she would find safety. Safety for herself and her unborn child. And to obtain that, she would conquer the weakness of body and the harshness of nature. Purposeful, she pulled on the latch string.

But all her gritty courage, all her fierce resolution, could not overcome what she confronted upon easing open the door. An entire world of cold, stark white. No trees, no sky, no nothing. Just a wall of white.

A small sound of anguished despair escaped her surprise-slackened lips. There was no place to run.

Before she could accept this abrupt end to her flight and think of what to do, huge hands as rough as bark and as strong as steel caught at her shoulders, and her moan of dismay rose into a wail of terror.

Chapter Two

"Let me go!"

The shriek tore from her as the large hands compelled her to turn. Horrifying memories and her captor's sheer size made her feel menace in his intent. Rounded eyes flashed upward in panic. She was all too well aware of her position, snared in the trapper's cabin, of her nudity beneath the robe, and of her own helplessness. She wouldn't endure it over again. She couldn't. That desperate determination gave strength to her struggle when her exhausted body would relent. There was nothing to gain in surrender, no mercy to be sought from this huge, shadowy stranger. Only a cruel certainty she'd learned ten short months ago. And it would not be borne without a fight.

"Let me go!"

"Where?" came a quiet, calming voice. "Where would you go?"

His eyes were brown, she noticed then, deep in color, rich in sincerity. Kind eyes, was her first impression. That in itself was enough of a surprise to subdue her frantic and ineffectual wriggling. And inexplicably, the terror began to wane, freeing her from her fear long enough to consider what he said. Where, indeed. Her glance returned to the impenetrable wall of snow. No way out. Nature, like circumstance, had trapped her with this man.

"You're safe here," he continued. As if to prove it was so, his hands gentled on her arms, becoming instruments of support rather than restriction. "You've nothing to fear. I can't allow that I've ever harmed a guest beneath my own roof. Not mannerly."

"Then where are my clothes?" She threw that up at him, daring him to pretend there was no implication of threat, while all the while her body began to tremble with her knowledge of it. She'd seen enough in the past few days to make her leery of any man's motive. A glazing of lust that yet played with nightmare intensity upon her frantic mind. Recalling it, her bravado was nearly reduced by the humbling helplessness of her situation. But one thing she'd learned was never to show fear.

The burly trapper regarded her for a long moment, and, to his credit, his dark eyes never dropped from the challenge of hers to consider what was concealed beneath the robe. His smile was wry, his words as bity as vinegar. "I thought you might prefer a little lack of modesty to pneumonia. The things you had on were soaked through. The dress is there, under the bed, all dry and folded but I can allow, t'weren't much in the way of a good fit. 'Bout as much good as that scrap of hide you got on against the wind and cold outside."

She regarded him for a long moment, gauging his words and their possible truth. Imperceptibly, her tension began to ease. In its place, the shock of what her body had already suffered rose with a vicious trembling. Yet, stubbornly, she refused to be subdued by circumstance or logic.

"Why are you keeping me here?" Her voice was frail with fatigue but threaded with an underlying fiber of strength.

"It's not me, little lady. That's Mother Nature's doing, and only a fool would think to challenge her when she's this het up."

His tone was mild but his gaze chided. So, he thinks me a fool, she surmised in irritation. Better that than the truth. She could see the questions lurking in his eyes and knew she was in no state to fend them off. A staunch will could not best the feebleness of form, and she was close to collapse.

Sensing her unsteadiness, the giant suggested, "Let's get you off your feet. They need to heal up some after being fair to froze."

She couldn't argue that. As she took a wobbling step, a soft cry of pain escaped before compressed lips could catch it. Without leave, the huge stranger swept her up with the ease of thistledown and carried her, not to the bed where she might have mistaken his intent, but to the fireside chair. There, he settled her and with an almost unconscious thoughtfulness, drew the robe up to shield her modesty more fully in what was a most immodest situation. She'd no doubt that he had unclothed her before her awareness had returned. He'd had ample time to learn of all the mysteries covered by that length of hide, yet now he sought to put her more at ease. Circumstances that should have brought a stain of shame to cheeks were tactfully sidestepped by that simple gesture.

The fire was wonderfully warm. She stretched her toes toward it and endured the prickly sensations that foretold of life restored. A life undoubtedly saved by the man regarding her with a curiosity not to be denied. What else would he not be denied before the snows abated and she was allowed to continue on her way? What reward would he deem sufficient for her rescue? Her lips thinned. Her chilled fingers tightened on the robe as if it had the power to protect more than

24

her nakedness. Nervously, she glanced toward the fire, seeking to forestall his questions with ones of her own.

"How did I get here?"

"Why ma'am it certainly weren't by my invitation," the big man drawled as he bent down near the fire. There was no mistaking the displeasure in his tone. "Couldn't very well leave you out there on the trail, though it cost me a winter's worth of furs to tote you here."

That surly admission raised a flicker of temper from a soul she'd thought too worn to respond. It wasn't as though she'd demanded he make the sacrifice or had purposefully fallen in his path to freeze, although his annoyance would suggest he believed it was so. His sullenness required a reply, one she returned with a brittle snap of pride.

"I am sorry you do not feel a human life worth the exchange, but I'm glad for your momentary lapse. I'll see you're remunerated for the loss as soon as I—as soon as I am able."

Remunerated. A fine five-dollar word if he ever heard one. Ethan looked at the bedraggled female, who by right shouldn't possess such a fiery temperament after all she'd been through, and was moved to a sketchy smile. A feisty little thing for all her finery and fancy words. She was afraid of him, of being shut up with him as the weather howled outside, yet she dared display such uncommon spunk, like a mild field mouse rearing up to seize the snout of a timber rattler before it struck. Instead of being grateful for just being alive, she was railing at him for his lack of hospitality, forced though she knew it was.

Gold. Her eyes were gold. Not green or blue or brown. A pure prairie gold, as rich as the grasses ripening in the fall, as rare as the metal sought in the

25

Hills. Basked in firelight, the combination of hair and eyes quickened the image of something molten, running hot like liquid flame. Something tempting but ready to scorch the unwise. What a beauty she was, rare and wild and full of mystery, this wilderness woman. And suddenly, he looked ahead with a feeling of panic to the days and nights they'd be forced to keep such close quarters. Thank God for her burgeoning state, or in his daze of long suppressed desires he might have been tempted to risk the heat and snatch for the riches she possessed. That knowledge shocked him no little bit, for he always considered himself a gentleman, even in this place that lay beyond the reach of civilization. To find a vein of primitive emotion wending beneath his acceptable decency shook him to the core. Had living alone in his near-primal state so changed him that the woman's breeding condition rather than his own moral code would have him hold his passions at bay? The man he'd once been would have never considered taking a woman against her will, yet here in the woods, his needs rolling as violently as the unseen winds, he might have used her helplessness to his advantage. What manner of beast did that make him?

She sat quietly, watching the plays of passion move over his face the way seething storm clouds boiled over the mountain peaks above. And she was frightened by what she saw there. They predicted something dark and dangerous on the rise, and she had no means of shelter should they gather to unleash their fury. She clutched at the robe, hiding her fears behind an impassive face, just as she'd been schooled to do. Had she gone from one desperate situation to another? What she knew of mountain men gave her no sense of security. They were a wild breed, as unpredictable as a cunning cougar, as surly as a silver-tipped grizzly, and known for their scorn of polite standards and humanity in general. Hadn't she learned that brutal truth firsthand? She was an intruder here in this cozy cabin. His cool stare told her that all too plainly. Whatever kindness had moved him to bring her in from certain death was fast fading. She was familiar with the trickles of apprehension, with having her hope torn cruelly from her, leaving only her wits and will as the means to survive. And she would survive. She'd come too far to fail now. She would do whatever needed doing to see her child to safety. If this giant of a man thought her at his mercy, he was sorely mistaken.

She cast a covert glance about the room, seeking a means to turn things in her favor. Over the crude mantel, an old Sharps rifle rested in a cradle of deer horns. Was it loaded? He would know but she did not. Too great a gamble. Propped up beside the hand-piled stones was a Henry repeater. Loaded? Again, she had no way of knowing for sure. An empty gun was no threat. On his hip, he wore an Army Colt with the casual ease of one well-acquainted with its use. It was doubtful she could get the drop on him with his own sidearm. Then she looked overhead to the heavy metal traps hung upon the low ceiling beams. If she could grasp one of them and swing it with enough force, she could stun him and take his gun. Her mind spun ahead, seizing on the crazy plan with a desperate sense of purpose. Then she could bind him hand and foot and bide her time until the trail reopened. Yes, that's what she would do.

Secure in her secret knowledge, she returned her attention to the man kneeling at the hearth. A bit of her confidence failed as she followed his large hands as they fed the fire. Such a big, powerful man. Would ropes hold him? Fear and a cold resolution curled with her as she looked again to the six-shot revolver. Could she use it? Her heart hammered anxiously within her breast as she entertained the question.

Then, as if to provide an answer, she felt a twinge of movement in her belly.

Yes. Yes. She knew then that she could kill if it was the only way to protect her unborn child. And she could kill without remorse.

"How did you come to be out on that trail?"

His words intruded upon her grim thoughts, startling her. Her wide-eyed gaze jerked up from the study of his firearm to meet his steady stare. Did he know what she was planning? If he guessed she meant him harm, she might never get the chance to escape. Cleverly, she sought to distract him from both her intent and his question.

"What are you cooking? It smells wonderful and I've not eaten since yesterday."

He was not so easily led. "And just where did you take your last meal?"

She fought back the frown of aggravation and plied him with a hopeful smile. "Might I have something to eat?"

Ethan knew she was being evasive. He also sensed something akin to mischief working behind those golden eyes. However, the memory of her gauntness, of the hunger displayed in each contour of her ribcage kept him from refusing her request. Silently, he dished up a steaming plate of the fragrant stew, then watched as she devoured it with a ravenous gusto. The fervor with which she wielded her fork was due to more than a day's deprivation. She ate like a half-starved hound, gulping portions with scarcely the benefit of chewing.

She continued to ply her fork without an interruption of rhythm as she watched him draw a broad-bladed Green River knife from his left boot. The

28

well-honed metal glinted as he poked at the logs in the fire grate, using the tip to roll them so the flame would burn evenly. Then, he set the wicked-looking weapon upon the hearth as he reached for another piece of wood.

"Could I have some water?" she requested softly.

He rose without comment to fetch her some from the bucket by the door. As soon as his massive back was turned, her hand shot out to snatch up the knife, quickly secreting it in the folds of the robe. Then, she went on to finish the last of the stew.

"Here you go."

She took the tin from him with the offer of a small smile and drank greedily. When he knelt down before the fire, it was all she could do not to choke. What if he noticed the missing blade?

"Could I have some more stew? If it's no trouble," she added that last with an unaccustomed meekness and extended her plate.

"No trouble," he remarked with a contrary grumble, as if begrudging her every bite. Still, he spooned up an ample helping.

She ate more slowly this time, savoring the taste and the comfort of a full stomach. At last, she set the plate aside with a contented sigh. "Have you any coffee?" she asked of her reluctant host. "I'd dearly love a cup."

"Sorry," he growled sourly. "And no after dinner tea cakes either. Be glad for what you got."

She nodded somberly and was glad — for both the meal and for the fact that he seemed to have forgotten his knife.

With the warmth from the fire seeping through her and the chill of the blade resting against her thigh to provide a sense of security, she allowed herself to relax in the chair. Her companion dismissed her presence, making no further attempt to draw information from her as he pulled another chair up before the uneven firelight. With a large slab of wood clamped between his knees, he pulled a draw knife toward him in sure, confident strokes, exposing a warm, reddish grain beneath rough bark. Drowsily, she wondered what he was making. The scent of fresh wood shavings was pungent and somehow comfortingly familiar. Beneath the heavy sag of her eyelids, she let her gaze detail the features of the man opposite. For all his size and gruffness, he no longer had the power to frighten her. She was holding the knife as protection and believed that to be the reason. But as she studied him, she realized that was not all together true.

Burnished by the glowing embers, his brown hair took on rich auburn highlights, not a fiery red like her own, but deep and luxurious like the wood he pared. It was poorly cut, probably with his own hand, aided by the knife she concealed. Wisps of it strayed over the collar of his rough woolen shirt in unruly curls. His heavy beard was of a darker shade. It appeared soft rather than bristly in the gentle light. From what she could see of his features, they were strong and fine, more like the Southern-bred gentlemen his quiet accent suggested, than a burly mountain man. She had only to think of that truly frightful breed to know the difference. Memories swirled up with a dark, desperate panic. Unwashed flesh, the stink of hides, clothing stiff with the filth of the profession. And the feel of coarse, hurting hands. Hot, foul breath upon her face. And eyes, eyes burning with all the promise of a soulless, ruthless hell.

She shuddered violently and thrust the memories behind her. It took a moment for the uneven jerks of horror to leave her breathing. Her fingers tightened on the knife. Never again would she be helpless.

Her "host" hadn't noticed her fleeting distress. His dark eyes studied the wood he held with no less intensity than they'd regarded her moments ago. Concentrated, cautious, controlled. The directness of his stare, the steadiness of his hands, and the brevity of his speech all suggested those same things. What manner of man was he to retreat from the world in preference of his own company?

The slow, compelling strokes of the cutting blade enticed her eyes to follow, lulling them with the repetitious movement, quieting her with their sameness. Sleep—deep, dreamless, healing, was upon her before she knew it. She didn't awake when he gathered her up and carried her to the bed. Nor was she aware of his wry smile when he beheld the glitter of his Green River knife as it clattered from her strengthless grip. All she knew was the safety of a warm, dark oblivion.

Only once he'd resumed his whittling away at the gentle curve of maple did Ethan realize she'd never answered any of his questions.

Not even that of her name.

It was an impatient call of nature that finally roused her from a comfortable sleep. With the baby crowding inside her and disrespectfully poking, she woke with the urgent need to seek relief. Her eyes opened groggily to a scene of confusion. Then, slowly, it returned to her, the cabin, the snow, the big sullen stranger. And with that knowledge came the embarrassment of her situation.

He'd been turning slabs of bacon in an iron skillet when he caught sight of her movement upon his bed. With a nod of acknowledgment in her direction, he was quick to avert his attention back to his cooking. She felt the heat of awkward color climb into her face when forced to voice her needs.

31

"Excuse me," she put forth hesitantly, surprised to find she knew no name to call him. There had been few formalities exchanged during their first meeting. When his dark gaze lifted in question, her cheeks grew that much hotter, nearly warm enough to cook that breakfast he was tending. "I was wondering if — I need to know where I might — Is there some sort of convenience I could use?"

When at last she blurted it out, he stared at her as if she'd struck him a sharp rap between the eyes with the wooden spoon he was holding. Then he blinked in understanding, and a warm ruddy tinge filtered up above his beard. He stood, wiping his palms distractedly upon his denim pants and glanced about in search of an answer to this unexpected problem. There was no leaving the cabin. They were snowed in tighter than a matron's corset. Within the small, single room, with himself as the sole occupant, he'd never seen the need for privacy. Until now. While his guest shifted in obvious discomfort, he wracked his brain for a solution, then abruptly brightened.

She watched as he rummaged through several cups set on the shelf of an open-fronted cabinet. With two nails tucked between his lips and a handful of heavy twine, he strode to the head of the bed. Three firm blows from a hammer sunk a nail at his eye level. About its exposed head, he knotted one end of the cording. Then he crossed the room and placed the other nail at approximately the same height.

"I don't know why I didn't think of it," he murmured with hammer poised. "When my wife was carrying, she couldn't drink no more than a thimbleful before she — "

His sentence stopped, cut clean by the pain of memory. What made him speak of his wife to a stranger when he'd forbidden all thought of her within his own mind? Jaw clamped shut to prevent any further sentimental blunders into the past, he smacked the hammer down with unnecessary force, once, then again.

"Damn!"

His thumb went reflexively into his mouth where he nursed its throbbing in ill humor. Deftly, he wound the other end of the twine about the second nail and drew it into a taut line with his right hand. Over that bisecting cord he tossed a course woolen blanket to form a partitioning screen. Then, he passed a basin behind it with the mutter of, "Best I can do under the circumstances."

Necessity overcame modesty. The blanket would do for the moment. Once she'd tended the demands of a compressed bladder, she considered his words. A wife? The knowledge that he'd had one somehow lessened her fear of him. It meant that at one time he'd known civility, even if he turned from it now. Where was she now, this wife of his? Abandoned? She didn't think so. There'd been so much warmth in his voice as he spoke of her, such heavy loss in his silence. His expression had closed up like the jaws of his steel traps. She'd seen that face of fierce denial before, worn on her father's beloved features as they put her mother to rest. Was that why this man with his cultured drawl had seen fit to withdraw from the world? She wondered but could not ask. One question would lead to another, and he'd be prying into her own circumstances. That she couldn't allow. She didn't want to know any more about this stranger than she meant to reveal to him. Everything would be much simpler that way.

"Here."

She gave a slight jump as a swirl of plaid flannel was tossed over the blanket curtain. She picked up the garment. Obviously one of his shirts from its big proportions. Not much but better than the buffalo robe. Gratefully, she slipped it on, pleased to find it easily encompassed her girth and came almost to her knees. As she was rolling back the engulfing sleeves, her gaze caught upon a glint of steel upon the edge of the bed. The knife. She'd forgotten all about it. She'd no doubt he'd placed her in the bed after she'd fallen asleep. Had he also placed the blade beside her in an attempt to still her fears? Or was it that he felt even the heavy blade would be no threat wielded by a pregnant woman? Was she foolish to feel relieved when she donned her heat-stiffened moccasins and slipped the knife through one cuff in a makeshift sheath?

He was doling out the crispy strips of bacon onto two plates when she stepped from behind the curtain. He glanced up, and she could feel the heat of his gaze as it scorched up the length of her bare legs to stop uncomfortably at the swell of her belly. He looked quickly back to the table he'd set with the twin plates, a platterful of biscuits and a pot of indescribably aromatic coffee. Those wonderful scents drew her to one of the chairs in a slow hobbling walk, her wariness not forgotten but effectively overcome. She helped herself to half of the offering and was intent upon gobbling her meal even before he poured the coffee. She remembered he'd denied her a cup the night before and felt honored that he would part with what he obviously did not want to share.

He settled upon his chair with a bemused look as the immense quantity of food was consumed. As her tableware moved from plate to mouth in a hurried tempo, her big golden eyes watched him cautiously, as if she expected his hospitality to be jerked away on a whim. That distrustful gaze, as well as the hollow between shoulder blades and slender throat exposed by

34

the open collar of his shirt, made him again consider her circumstances. Where had she known such hunger?

"Has the snow let up yet?" she asked thickly through a mouthful of biscuit.

"Hard to tell. Wouldn't matter though. Be a day or two before we can start digging out." Did he imagine it, or did her face pale significantly? "I got plenty of wood, food and water, so you don't need to worry over it. If that's what you're worried about."

Her eyes dropped quickly to her plate. Ethan could see her thin shoulders square into a defensive line of tension beneath the bulky drape of his shirt. He knew it was none of his business, whatever her reasons for being stranded in the hills. And normally he was all for minding his business, but something in the mystery she presented provoked a nagging curiosity. It was more than idle boredom or the desire for conversation in a tongue other than Teton. It was more than just to satisfy the twists of his imagination that had kept him sleepless most of the night. His questions made an intriguing Chinese puzzle. There was only one way to solve it but he couldn't make the pieces fit. He hated to walk away from a challenge.

"How are your feet this morning?" He would start slow and ease his way into her confidence. But when her gaze lifted and he saw its guarded gleam, he knew it would be no simple task.

"Better, thank you. Thank you for all that you've done." That was added stiffly, as if she was waiting for him to levy an impossible fee for his aid. "You saved my life."

A more ungracious thank you he couldn't imagine. Ethan settled back in his chair to regard her thoughtfully and was rewarded by a suspicious posture. There was nothing meek or helpless in her stare.

"You were ill-prepared for a walk in the woods," he noted mildly, then watched the flickers of alarm and deliberation skirt her impassive expression. What was she so afraid of giving away?

"The storm blew up so fast I had no time to seek shelter," was her bland reply.

"Shelter from whom?"

"From a scruffy trapper who asks too many questions."

That bit of clever evasion won her a begrudging smile. "Can I at least know what to call you?"

She hesitated even at that little thing then said, "Aurora."

He said it to himself, slowly, feeling the sound of it roll sweetly over his tongue. "Pretty name. Bit unusual."

"It means 'dawn'. I was born at daybreak with this head of red hair. My mother said it was like watching the sun rise."

"Your mother?" he prompted smoothly.

"She's dead." The blunt answer halted that line of questions. The slight quiver of her soft lips before they set into a firm compression told him that that occurrence, though no longer fresh, was yet painful. He didn't pursue it.

After a moment's awkward silence, the fiery Aurora asked, "And you? What do I call you?"

"Ethan Pres—" He choked up on his surname and she knew immediately that he wished he hadn't spoken it. Seeing he'd made her all the more curious by the delay, he finished tightly, "Ethan Prescott."

He waited as if he expected the name to mean something to her. It didn't. Instead, it furthered the sense of wariness weighing her every word. This man was a stranger. He could be anyone, anything. Though she felt reasonably sure she was safe for the

36

moment, there was no guarantee how long that respite would last. The danger was far from over. She had to remember that, so her answers would be guarded, so she would be ever alert for the chance to escape. She couldn't afford to gamble on whether this big man would prove a help or hindrance to her plan. She'd learned to trust only herself. The same color skin and a pot of brewed coffee did not make him her friend. Harsh memory reminded once again of the folly of trust. Why increase the threat of being returned to face her possible death? She knew nothing of this man to make her comfortable with placing her future in his hands. No, silence was best.

With renewed suspicion lumping the food in her belly into a hard, unsettled knot, Aurora stood to gather the emptied plates, carrying them with her halting steps to the basin used for washing. When he realized her intent, Ethan was quick to stand and protest.

"Here now. You don't have to do that."

"You've made it clear I'm not a welcomed guest. I mean to work for my board. It's not my wish to be beholden."

There was so much pride, so much stubborn dignity in those curtly spoken words it pricked his conscience for being an ungracious host. To challenge her would bring further slight. So Ethan sipped his precious coffee as the lovely enigma clad only in his shirt saw to the scrubbing of his pots. He was more than merely aware of how each movement caused the plaid flannel to sway against the trim and curiously tanned backs of her legs. From behind, there was no hint of the plumping pregnancy to keep his thoughts in line. There was only sleek, agonizingly evident femininity.

Aurora stiffened at the abrupt sound of chair legs scraping on floorboards. She didn't turn but held every muscle tense in wary readiness for flight or fight. She heard him move to the fire then there was the spit and sigh of logs being shifted. Her posture eased. Her breath resumed. And she returned to the scouring of the iron skillet.

The day stretched out into long silent seconds. There was no shift of sunlight to tell of the passing from dawn to dusk, only the flicker of firelight, warm and even. Another meal was eaten, this time with no attempt at conversation. For what could two strangers say to one another without the use of questions? Neither was willing to begin the domino effect beginning with harmless inquiry and building to awkward secrets. There were no safe topics, no idle talk that wouldn't lead toward sensitive and best unspoken subjects. The questions were there, burning beneath the surface, playing behind gazes bronze and brown, but neither wanted to reveal too much by beginning innocent conversation. And so there was silence. Deep as the snows. Impenetrable as the trails. Chill as the outside air. Drifting, settling, covering potential danger.

A low, disturbing ache seeped through Aurora's spine. She shifted on the fireside chair but could find no comfort in its hard contours. Restlessly, she rose, pressing her palms to the gentle curve of her back to rub at the tension gathered there. Movement eased the discomfort, so she walked aimlessly about the cabin, feeling, but unwilling to acknowledge, her host's gaze upon her. Neat, orderly, efficient. It wasn't the interior she'd expect in a trapper's transient home carved from the wilds. There was no settling of dust, no coating of neglectful cobwebs in distant corners and far crannies. Nor did Ethan Prescott's appearance, aside from the bushy whiskers, show any sign of unkept indifference. His clothing was worn but clean. His hands and face were weather-harsh yet tended — signs of a civilized existence he'd chosen to ignore yet couldn't entirely abandon. His soft speech had the slow drawl of a son of the Lone Star state, like many of the wranglers and cowpunchers her father employed. So far from home, yet comfortable in this northern wilderness.

Reluctantly, she crossed to the corner bed—it was such a small space and Ethan Prescott occupied so much of it—and drew the curtain to see to her body's impatient needs. Then, as she pushed the basin beneath the rope-rigged bed-frame, she found the way blocked and moved the obstruction. It was a heavy leather bag. Even before she peered inside to see the tools of the profession, she knew what it was. A surgeon's satchel.

A healer? A man of medicine, not menace. The questions swelled into an irresistible tide. Why was a man of skill now a creature of primal subsistence? Why would he hide in the Hills when men of his trade were direly needed in every boomtown in the territory? What had he done to make him hesitate to give his name, to conceal his calling behind a bristle of beard and cautious eyes? Frustratingly, she couldn't ask without a willingness to give answers of her own. What he once was didn't assure that he was still a man of noble intent.

Regardless, as Aurora settled down upon the borrowed bed to seek her rest, her palms sought her distended middle, and she was calmed. One of her greatest fears eased. Though desperation prodded her to flight, she'd been consumed by the terror of giving birth unattended. As familiar as the life had become stirring regularly within her, bringing that child into the world was a vast and frightening unknown. Her time was near. She knew instinctively. Her body was readying and to this point, she'd been resistant. Now,

Aurora relaxed. Whoever he was, whatever he was, Ethan Prescott had the knowledge to coax her child from the security of her womb into the longing emptiness of her arms. And for the first time in many, many months, she slept easy.

After sound and movement ceased behind the curtain, and Ethan was sure she slumbered, he rose to draw back the blanket, letting the fire's heat into the chilly nook. He meant to withdraw quickly but the sight of her curled upon his bed beneath his blankets held him for a long, uncomfortable moment. Having a woman bang about his pots and plates stirred an odd wistfulness within him. Thoughts of soft curves fitted against his hard angles provoked an even greater restlessness. How long it had been since he'd enjoyed the feel of a woman's skin, since he'd snuggled in companionable warmth to another figure, had seen to desires banked and left to smolder. The need of those things growled through him. Only the sight of her profile where her cheek nestled into palm checked those rumbling wants. There was a vulnerable trust in the way she curled in sleep. There was an innocence in her soft breaths, a sweetness in the gentle sweep of lashes and tangle of bright hair.

Silently, he retreated to the fireside and to his uneasy thoughts.

Chapter Three

It was cold, bitterly cold, and just what Ethan Prescott needed to temper the dangerous heat within him. Cold and distance: the safest cure for the weakening of control.

For three long days he'd chafed inside the tiny cabin, deviled by what he knew better than to seek again, tormented by what he desired and could not have. For three tortuous nights he'd forced himself to remain by the fire while the intriguing stranger's quiet breathing teased him from across the room. Every rustle of the bedding, every sleepy sigh rubbed raw upon his imaginings, seducing his will, wearing on him until morning found him as surly as a bear. Then he endured the sight of her moving about his chaste surroundings, his shirttail dancing sassily above her knees, her braid of fiery hair swinging along her shoulders, always so temptingly near, with only the swell of the child and the fraying remains of his honor to hold him at bay.

They'd come to an unspoken truce to make the situation bearable. Both agreed to act as if neither had a past or future. It was simply day to day. Questions that simmered and sparked were not allowed to flame, and the suspense lent a palpable tension to the confines of the snugly chinked logs.

He would ask how she was feeling when he meant, *Who are you and where is the father of your child?*

She would compliment the satiny sheen of the wood he worked while she wondered, *Why are you hiding in the wilderness, tending a length of maple instead of the ailing with those large, capable hands?*

He would find himself purposefully ignoring her rounded middle to appreciate the delicate structure of her face and slender curve of her calves. *What would it be like to share this room, that bed, with such a lovely woman?*

She would gather up the dishes, pretending not to notice the sudden change in his stare from wariness to want. *How long will I be safe ever within reach? How long will he be content to remain before the fire?*

Minutes, hours crept along, feeding the uneasy friction.

And then, after they'd finished last evening's meal and Aurora stood drying his dented tinware, he'd reached over her shoulder for the can of tobacco on the shelf. She swung around in panic, a gasp catching in her throat. Her big belly bumped him as they came face to face. The hand that had been reaching for the makings of a smoke found a tendril of soft hair wisping from her temple. And for an instant, time stopped. The taste of tobacco was no longer what he craved, not when ripe, parted lips were so near. Terror—and more surprisingly, anger—brightened eyes lifted to his. That golden gaze called him to his senses, and he snatched up the can with a hastily muttered, "Excuse me."

She'd turned back to the dishes but the tautness never left her shoulders. She'd seen the naked gleam in his stare, and it had frightened her from her tentative sense of safety. He didn't draw back the curtain that night to warm her in her slumber, for he knew she wasn't sleeping. She lay stiff and waiting until the early hours of dawn. And that's why he'd tugged on his heaviest clothes and burrowed out. Because he was perilously close to becoming exactly what she feared.

The brilliance of the day made him blink like a groundhog in the spring. Around him lay a world of perfect white. Only the rear slope of his roof and chimney cap were visible. Sunlight glistened upon the surface crust of snow. Once tested, he found it was thick enough to support his weight. Cautiously, he made his way to the smoke house, identifiable only because he recognized the trees on either side of it. He spent better than a half hour digging down to the door and was welcomed by the low wicker of his horse.

"Howdy, son," he murmured and the animal responded to his familiar tones by butting its head against Ethan's chest. The scent of horse, leather and smoke was comforting, as was conversation with the big sorrel. He was used to expressing his opinions to the attentive gelding when there was no other company around for miles. And now that he had companionship, he found the silent intelligence of his mount refreshing. The horse, much less testy than the secretive female inside his cabin, answered his ramblings with affectionate nudges.

"Maybe I should just bed down out here with you," he muttered as he rubbed down the rough coat of winter hair. "You're a dang sight more friendly. But not near as pretty." He thought of the fiery hair spun like raw silk and the slope of tempting shoulders, and he sighed heavily. "At least I'd get a little shut-eye."

Finding ample fodder remained, Ethan secured the door and crawled back up to the dazzling wonderland. It was so cold that breathing frosted the insides of his lungs and burnt his nose in a purifying ache. Behind him, wisps of smoke curled up from the fire he'd stoked inside his cabin. Returning there so soon would only stoke a different kind of heat. He needed the crisp, frigid air to clear his thinking. He needed to work up a sweat of exhaustion rather than soak in a sweat of self-denial. The trail disappeared into a blind of trees, presenting an inviting challenge and an escape from his inner conflicts. Just what he needed.

The way was just difficult enough to require full concentration and just far enough to expend energies balled tight from restraint. At the sign of a knife-scored wedge, he began to dig in the heavy snow, deeper and deeper until he struck a solid object. Panting and grinning, he dragged his pack of furs to the surface. He could smell the freshly ground coffee beans already. After a short breather, he shouldered the weighty bundle and began the trudge back to the cabin. The extra burden made passage all the harder. Several times he floundered and sank waist-deep and nearly helpless. Each time, he managed to struggle for a foothold, spurred on by thoughts of coffee beans and tobacco and perhaps a few new clothes — maybe even a length of dainty calico and soft swaddling fabric fit for diapering.. Then, he shook off those thoughts. He wouldn't be providing for Aurora and her child. That would be up to another, to the one who'd been foolish enough to lose her to the blizzard.

And what if there was no other man?

That thought crept in along with the seeping cold to work just as paralyzingly within his system.

What if she had no one?

Where was she running? He was more obsessed than ever with finding out that answer. Could he let her go if there was no one waiting to welcome her and the babe? Or was he just plain crazy to think he might have something to offer? Something for a woman and a child that wasn't his. It hadn't been enough the first time. Why should this be any different?

Hardened by that knowledge, he waded the last hundred yards into the clearing he'd wrought with his own two hands. Why should he think she'd want to stay with a bearded stranger who frightened her with the very thought of passion? Moreover, why in God's name would he even consider asking? There was no place in his guarded life, within his guarded heart, for a woman and her child. He'd been alone too long. That must be the reason for his whimsy. Maybe this year he'd spend a little more time at the trading post amongst his own kind. Maybe he'd use a bit of his hard-earned profits and visit one of the agency whores. Better than fouling up his future with improbable hopes. Far better than risking all for an impossible dream. Those dreams had died in Texas. He thought he'd buried them deep in the dusty ground. Why he should want to exhume them now, only to suffer anew, was as baffling as the mysteries surrounding the woman sharing his humble home. Better he forget about both. If he could.

Almost immediately, he knew something was wrong. At the bottom of the opening he'd tunneled through the snow, the door to his cabin stood open. His heart crashed against his ribs. Had she been fool enough to strike out on her own, thinking she could battle the sucking drifts and plunging temperatures? Had she seen his absence as a chance to escape? Surely not—not in her condition. Then, he remembered the look of terror in her eyes. Had his improper lusts sent her and her child to meet their deaths?

In a numbing panic, he slid down the bank of snow right through the open doorway. The room was cold; the small fire was no match for the penetrating chill

45

of winter. He saw in a glance the discarded firewood scattered about the hearth where it had tumbled. A puddle of dampness. What—? Pushing the door closed against the seeping drift of snow, he glanced about, almost afraid of what he would find.

Aurora hadn't fled the cabin. She lay curled upon the bed, knees clutched to her massive belly. Her golden gaze flew up to his. In a voice raw with anxiety and meaning, she managed to gasp, "Ethan, the baby."

Aurora had been relieved to find the cabin empty when she awoke. The desire she'd seen burning in Ethan Prescott's gaze when he'd trapped her against the cupboard with the huge, hard wall of his body made her all too aware of him as a vital man. A man with needs and wants strained to their very limit. She'd watched it build and smolder and had seen the evidence of his strong control each night as he sat before the fire while she had his bed. The sudden contact had taken her by surprise, frightening her with a reminder of her helpless, isolated position, angering her because she'd just begun to trust him and respect him for his honorable restraint. And then, more complex, was the way her pulse was startled into a hurried thrumming when he touched her hair. She had wondered, crazily, impossibly how that big, roughened hand would feel moving gently upon her skin. Crazily because she knew that was not the way of men, impossibly because she'd already known too much harshness to believe in a tender touch. So she'd lain awake, fearing what she knew quickened within him, chiding herself for what stirred within her own breast.

And so she'd been happy to find him gone. It was a respite from tension. It meant she could soon be on her way. If the trail was open, she couldn't afford to linger. She had to go. Then, she could put those strange quicksilver shivers of anticipation she'd experienced at his touch far behind her, to concentrate on the life she would have with her child.

Her child. She thought of it that way, as hers alone. For it would have no one else when it came into the world. Protectiveness swelled within her. Her child. The thought of its birth occasioned both anticipation and anxiety. Would it be a child of her body, all gold and fair and fiery? Or its father's child? Long ago she'd determined to love it regardless, for it was innocent of the sins of its conception. As she'd felt the first stirrings move within her, she'd known such incredible joy, such awe. Her child. Hers alone to love and shelter.

She knew the moment she stood that something was different. The baby had shifted down to rest upon her hips, making the simplest movements difficult. The familiar ache in her back intensified to a relentless pressure. And she began to wish she was not alone in the snowbound cabin.

To take her mind off the grinding discomfort and suppress her increasing fears, Aurora busied herself with mundane chores. She made coffee and biscuits. She had no appetite, but Ethan would be hungry and cold when he returned.

What if he didn't come back? What if something happened to him on the snowy trail? What would become of her then?

She forced those panicky thoughts away. Of course he would be back. He was used to the hills and their temperamental ways. She could imagine the big Texan in his adopted element, striding through the trees, tall and powerful among them. The picture she called to mind comforted her and she clung to it. Still, her movements quickened with mounting agitation as the

47

morning stretched out into lonely hours. And so did her body's distress.

The fire had burned low, its flames guttering in the grate. Aurora bent to gather an armload of wood, then struggled up with her burden. She gasped as an intense cramping seized her middle. Firewood tumbled as she gripped her tortured belly. About her feet, a pool of birthing water stained the puncheon floor. She stared at it through wide, dazed eyes until comprehension crushed her in its inexorable hand.

The baby was coming!

Her first thoughts were ones of total panic. Not now, she wanted to scream. Not while she was alone. But the vicious twisting returned, refusing to wait. The time was now.

Sobbing in distress and dismay, Aurora staggered to the door. Unthinkingly, she flung it open, her terrorized mind focused on one thing alone. Ethan. If she could call to him, to let him know she needed him, he would come. She knew he would. Cold air assaulted her like a brutal blow, cutting through the shirt she wore, freezing her lungs as she drew a helpless gasp. It turned the desperate dampness on her cheeks and lashes into stinging crystals. It forced her frightened cry for help to strangle in her throat as she fought against the pain and numbing cold. Forgetting the door, for there was no help there, she stumbled toward the warmth of the fire until another wrenching pang drove her to her knees. There she huddled, whimpering miserably. That wretched sound of weakness and defeat goaded a deep inner strength.

Get up, it demanded of her. *Bring this child into the world with dignity, not cowering like a frightened camp cur. Introduce this child with courage, a courage you'll need to sustain you and the babe. More difficult times lie ahead. Don't fail before the battle begins. You're all this baby has. Your strength will be its own.*

Slowly, Aurora gained her feet. She panted hard and brushed at the perspiration chilling her face and neck. Warmth. She needed warmth. And rest, too, so she could endure the long trial ahead. She shuffled to the bed and eased her spasm-wracked body down upon it. She moaned into the next sharp, contorting pain then gathered a calming strength when, at last, it left her. If the child was determined to come now, she would deliver it herself. What other choice was there? There was no time for fears or doubts, as both would crowd and confuse the clarity she needed were they both to survive. Women had been having babies for centuries and not always with the convenience of having their doctors present. If they could do it, so could she. After all, what was a more natural event in a woman's life? Her body knew what to do. All she had to do was wait and prepare.

Her child. Her child was about to be born. She smiled grimly into the next contraction, viewing its rending power with anticipation. The pains were strong and regular, urging the child on its way to meet her. She rode with them as best she could and used the time in between to rest and revive. It was hard work, harder than any demanded of her before, but when it was done, oh, when it was done . . .

But what if everything wasn't all right? What if what she'd suffered on the trail had somehow marred the baby? The wrenching pangs suddenly contained an element of threat. Was everything proceeding as it should? How could she know? What could she do if it was not? She writhed beneath the image of the baby turned inside her, its air blocked by its birthing cord. She drew a dark vision of herself bleeding to a slow death in the cold cabin. All alone. No. Fiercely, she blocked those weakening thoughts. Everything had to be fine. She wanted this child. Oh, how she wanted this child.

Then, she saw him, standing like a snowy mountain, his broad shoulders seeming to span the small space like the supporting beams above. And she knew everything would be fine. Her panic crested and ebbed in a wash of relief. She called to him, using his given name for the first time as another cramping spasm gripped her.

"I'm here."

Those two words, spoken near, so firm, so confident, embraced her with their confidence. Gratefully, she surrendered control to him and concentrated upon her own body's responses until they quieted in an ever-shortening lull. She watched through half-shuttered eyes as he flung off his snow-covered hat, pack and coat and tossed more wood on the fire. When he came to kneel at the bedside, she managed a weary smile.

"I thought I was going to have to do this alone. We're glad to see you."

His big hand engulfed hers, supplying a squeeze of encouragement. He continued to hold it while her fingers bit deep into his palm then relaxed.

"How close are they coming?" he asked in a voice that exuded a calm knowledge.

"A minute, maybe a little more." She looked up at him, drawing strength and composure from his steadying presence. "Have you done this before?"

This time, he smiled. "In theory. It'll be a pleasure to bring new life into the world after seeing so much of it on its way out." His words were tinged with a moment of melancholy but her expectant gaze brought him out of it. There was no time to wonder what his shadowed gaze saw when he looked inward.

"What should I do?

He rubbed her knuckles with his other hand. "Looks like you've done most of it without me. Let's take a look see." Trustingly, she let him shift her onto her back and urge her knees up and apart. His big hands moved over the trembling muscles of her thighs, easing the tension from them with the steady ply of his fingers. Gentle. She'd known his hands would be gentle.

"Quite a head of hair on this little fella."

She gave a breathless little laugh of excitement. Before she could ask him what color it was, a new, urgent tightness clamped through her middle. "I have to push," she groaned.

"No. Not yet," he ordered with a quiet authority. "Blow. Blow hard until the need passes and I'll get things ready."

Obediently, she began to huff and puff and amazingly, the overwhelming pressure ebbed. She sagged with relief, vaguely aware of him tucking towels beneath her hips and draping her bared legs with a warm robe. How had he known how cold she'd become?

Ethan reached beneath the bed for his satchel. The moment his hand closed upon the worn leather, a terrible reluctance seized him. He shut his eyes, forcing his shaking fingers to retain their grip. The feel of the bag, the sound of the instruments clattering inside it—instruments of healing that had turned into instruments of torture. Sickness rose up in his belly and the sound of anguish, inhuman, excruciating anguish, beat inside his head.

Don't take it off, Doc. Swear you won't take it off! The pain! I gots to have something for the pain!

They're coming in by the wagonload. Slop off the tables and get ready.

But there's no morphine. There's no more quinine.

51

No more clean bandages. No time for stitching. Just hack it off and close out the screams.

He couldn't breathe. A sweat of remembrance broke out on his forehead — cold, as icy as death. His heartbeats were as loud and regular as cannonfire, shattering, shaking through him. He wanted to release the bag and the memories that it held for him. He wanted to shove it back out of sight and pretend that he had pushed aside all that it represented.

But Aurora moaned.

And the cycle of death became a cycle of life.

Ethan jerked out the satchel and dashed a sleeve across his damp forehead. He couldn't heighten the woman's fear by looking as though he didn't know what he was doing. Or as if he were afraid of doing it. Awaiting him was the reason he'd gone into medicine, not the reason he'd run from it. He moved back up beside her and smiled when her big eyes turned to him for encouragement. Her features were taut and pinched, dampened by her pain. But she, too, managed a smile. And her calm, courageous beauty strengthened him.

"I can give you something for the pain," he offered softly but she shook her head upon its pillow of tangled red hair.

"No. I want to see my baby."

Again he smiled, she thought in admiration. "All right, then. We'll do it together." With one arm curving beneath her shoulders, he lifted her up to fit a bolster of blankets behind her back, holding her in a half-reclined position. Pressure eased in her spine and a sense of control returned. The forceful compression began once more and she blew like a locomotive gathering steam. Ethan moved around to check the baby's position, and gave the welcome report, "Fine, you're doing fine. The next one should do it. When it comes,

I want you to push for all you're worth."

She wanted to plead exhaustion. Her limbs were trembling fitfully and felt bereft of strength. She was tired, so horribly tired, she wanted to forget the whole thing in favor of sleep. But the baby wouldn't wait, and Ethan was regarding her with such a proud, approving stare that all she could do was nod and try to gather the last of her reserves. She couldn't disappoint either of them. Her eyes slid shut, seeking sanctuary, seeking comfort, and it was supplied by the light stroke of his fingertips along her sweat-spangled cheek. She turned into his palm, covering his hand with her own to hold it there so she might rest within its strong, rough contour. Then the moment was upon her. Tension clenched inside her, surging in a great compelling tide. Her fingers gripped his, and, in panic, she sought to forestall the inevitable.

"No," he instructed firmly. "Don't blow. Push. Push into it."

"I can't," she moaned, puffing hard, trying to give her drained body an instant of respite.

"Yes, you can. Come on, Ora. You can do anything you put your mind to. You're one hell of a lady. Come on. Push, Ora."

He curled her fingers over her upraised knees and she clung, straining, groaning with effort.

"Yell out if you need to," he urged.

"No," she argued stubbornly through gritted teeth. "I won't welcome my baby with screams and pain."

"Then get ready," he advised. "You're about to be a mama."

With a sound that was half wail, half shout of exultation, she gave a mighty heave and expelled the child from the sheltering darkness of her body into the brightness of the world. It responded with a howl of displeasure from the bloody cradle of Ethan's hands.

"We did it," she sobbed happily, sinking back in spent accomplishment. "Ethan, we did it."

Looking down at the wiggling bit of humanity delivered into his grasp, Ethan felt a wondrous tightening about his heart. The feeling swelled until it crowded his throat, permitting only a raspy speech. "We did. Yes, we did." Carefully, he lifted the mewling infant over the tented knees and into its mother's waiting arms. " 'Fraid he's not much to look at yet." Was that his voice, so husky and prone to shaking?

"He," Aurora echoed faintly as she enfolded the babe in an instinctive embrace. "A son. My son. He's beautiful."

No, he thought distractedly as he stared at them both through a wavering gaze. She was beautiful. She looked like a radiant Madonna there upon his bed, cooing at the newborn. Her bright hair streamed down to spill over her shoulders, a waterfall of flame. Tendrils clung to the moisture of her brow and he longed to brush them back with a gentle gesture. He watched her expression as she regarded the child, the way her soft skin flushed with delight, the caring smile curving her lips, the tender devotion brightening her gaze. He watched mother and son, feeling a choking pride and a humbling awe as if he'd somehow taken part in the miracle of life, as if he had some claim to the pair of them. And suddenly he was taken with a second of insanity; he wished the beautiful Aurora would lift her gaze and bestow the same melting look of love upon him.

It was crazy. He knew it. Yet, deep within the empty recesses of his soul, he yearned for it to be so, for this woman and her child to belong to him, for them to fill the cavern of loss inside him and give him purpose once more. A purpose denied him once before. The chance to participate in this unique event had been stolen from him that time; it seemed only right that he should claim this moment as his own. For five long years, his ears were deaf, deprived of that wail of discovered life. For five empty years, his hands waited to receive delivery of a precious bundle. His heart had lain as cold ash all those long, aching years, waiting for a chance to well with masculine pride. Tears he'd wanted to shed in wonder and joy had gone dry in a well of sorrow, but now he felt them collect behind his shimmering gaze. What an ironic justice that fate should supply all those missing elements with the coincidental stumbling of his horse.

He'd saved her, he'd brought her here so he could have the opportunity to experience those joys lacking in his life. Aurora and her child would replace the agony of loss with the fullness of family.

Then she looked up at him, and though that gaze was filled with warmth and thanks, there was no tender intimacy, no invitation for him to share in her joy. Feelings of proud possession chilled and faded within his heart. They weren't his. This was a stranger passing through his life, taunting him with what he would never have or hold. He had no claim upon her parental pleasure, no right to demand one. He was an outsider. And he recoiled from it as if unfairly wounded.

Aurora puzzled over the subtle change in Ethan Prescott. She could have sworn they'd breached all the unknowns to enjoy a binding closeness at the birth of her son. Never had she trusted anyone so completely. She'd suffered no embarrassment, no discomfort, no hesitation in placing herself into his big, capable hands. Gentle hands, she remembered. The experience they shared was incredibly personal, yet there'd been no sense of awkwardness between them as two near-strangers. It was if suddenly they'd known each other forever, as if the creation of this child was something special wrought between them. When he'd brought her son into her arms, a host of emotions had gathered within her heart—a love so great it encompassed both the red, wrinkled child and the bearded man who held him. She wanted to hug them both in her happiness, to draw Ethan into this poignant bonding as the tiny figure wriggled at her breast.

Then the moment was gone. And she felt bereft, somehow unfairly cheated of his regard. It was an empty feeling even as her arms enjoyed the special fullness of her child's form. He was again the guarded stranger whose wary eyes both warned and watched. So thin and impersonal was his smile that she wondered if she'd imagined the link between them, a product of a needy mind clutching for security. But no, she knew she hadn't. Confused, she wanted to asked what had caused the change in his mood. She wanted to call him back into the charmed circle of her delight. But he wouldn't be drawn.

He looked away from her gaze and began firmly to knead her soft belly to complete the birthing cycle. When that was done and she was dozing with the aftereffects of fatigue, he lifted the child from her arms to sever the cord and wrap its waving legs in swaddling. She tried to cling to the comforting image of Ethan Prescott with her child in his hands. It was somehow so right, so appealing to the woman in her, to the mother in her. This man and her child. A wistful smile shaped her lips as heavy eyelids slipped downward.

While Aurora drifted toward slumber, Ethan gently bathed the child. It was a tender task, one that tugged upon instincts and emotions he thought best denied. The baby was so small and helpless, yet it wriggled with determined energy. Stubborn. Like its mother. He observed its tiny perfection through proud eyes.

Eyes that stung then abruptly cleared in surprise. It was then the baby's mottled skin took on a healthy bronze color and the clean shocks of hair gleamed raven's black. It was then he understood part of the mystery of Aurora's silence.

The child he'd helped deliver was half Indian.

Chapter Four

"Is there something wrong?"

Aurora's anxious question was prompted by Ethan's intense study of the child in his arms. A totally unfamiliar panic jarred her from her search of sleep, a sense of responsibility for the new little life she'd created. Had her late stage travels somehow harmed the babe? Had her state of fear affected him in some way? Guilt clutched at her as fiercely as she gripped the blankets. If she had in any way damaged her precious child . . .

"Ethan?" It was a hoarse whisper.

His gaze came up slowly and for a moment, he stared at her with the same piercing scrutiny. Finally, recognizing the sharp lines of anxiety etched upon her features, he extended a close lipped smile. "Nothing's wrong. All the right number of fingers and toes. He's—perfect."

Then she knew.

Aurora raised her head high with a defiant pride. If he was waiting for a display of shame or regret, he would be sorely disappointed. Never, she vowed, never would she dishonor her child with either disloyal expression. He was a child of her body. She'd felt him grow and wriggle within her for nine months, dependent upon her strength, her care. That would not change now. If anything, those protective instincts were greater, more vibrant, more intense. He was more vulnerable now, exposed to the unfair harshness of the world, and she must be ready to defend against each perplexed look questioning his appearance. She owed no explanation and would give no apology, not to Ethan Prescott, not to any of the curious who would regard her son with prejudiced suspicion.

"He has your eyes," Ethan said softly, and Aurora knew a moment of uncertainty. There was no censure in his steady gaze, no demand for answers to her son's parentage. He knew, and he didn't care. And for that unconditional acceptance of her past and of her half-breed child, Aurora would be ever grateful. She felt the hostility ebb from her starched posture and allowed a relieved weariness to take its place. *Bless you, Ethan Prescott, for forcing no cruel conclusions.*

"He has your appetite, too." He laughed as the babe rooted at his shirt front. It was a low, pleasing sound, as calming and gently musical as summer rain. " 'Fraid I can't help you there, partner. You'd best be asking your mama if she can delay her nap long enough to rustle up some lunch."

She held out her arms and received the hungry child with a tender smile. Excluded from the maternal chore and uncomfortable with the quiet scene of contentment, Ethan drew the curtain to afford her privacy and went to tend his improperly discarded garments.

After a moment of inadequate fumbling on her part and impatience from her son, Aurora established herself as nourishing mother. With the child tugging and suckling noisily at her breast, she languished back upon the blankets, reveling in the sensation. For the moment, she allowed herself to absorb the feeling of complete rightness. Nothing could intrude upon it, nothing could shadow it. And the sense of peace healed an anxious mind the way the luxury of rest worked upon an exhausted body. With her child curled upon her chest, sated and silent, she slept.

She wasn't sure how long she had drifted in heavy slumber but the sense of serenity was still upon her when she finally woke. The dividing curtain had been drawn back so the heat of the fire would reach her. She had been bathed and dressed in a pair of clean flannel long johns. She didn't mind that Ethan had taken the liberty. Deliciously warm and lazy, she lingered with eyes yet closed, allowing her other senses to explore unhurriedly. Two wonderfully melodious sounds reached her, lulling and intriguing at the same time. One was the quiet fussing of her son and the other, a tune she recognized as "The Streets of Laredo" hummed in a resonant baritone.

Coaxed from her lethargy, Aurora opened her eyes to greet a scene that warmed more glowingly than the fire. Ethan Prescott sat before the hearth, methodically shaping a piece of wood. A booted toe was propped against one of a newly finished pair of rockers, slowly swaying a box he'd nailed upon them. Above the sides of the makeshift cradle, she could see blankets wiggling and the protrusion of one tiny, imperious fist waving for attention. It was a tranquil setting, one befitting father and son. A stinging dampness rose in her eyes and she was forced to blink it away when Ethan glanced up.

For a time, they exchanged a silent, communicative gaze, rich with meanings neither understood from the other. Then, he set aside his woodworking and bent over the child.

"Mama's awake," he crooned to the fretting babe. "Now, you can scold her proper for neglecting your supper."

He brought the baby to her but didn't withdraw. Instead, he placed the back of his hand against her brow and cheek and throat to test the temperature of her skin. A bit overly warm but not alarmingly so.

"How you feeling, Ora?"

Ora. She remembered him calling her by that shortened version of her name. It suggested a familiarity, a fondness, a private link, and she didn't protest. She liked it and the casual way he said it. There was no use pretending formality after what they'd been through together.

"Tired," she admitted in answer to his question. "Sore. Like I could sleep for a month but I guess there's not much hope of that."

"Not unless I grow udders." They exchanged a smile.

She patted her son's bottom, wondering at the thick padding there. Where had he found diapering material? And why hadn't she thought of that, herself? "What's this?"

"A piece of some old long johns. Best I could do. I wasn't exactly set up for a nursery, you know. I can keep the little fella covered for a while but I don't have an endless supply of clothes."

"Sorry," she said lamely, feeling helpless to offer anything else.

Ethan shrugged it off. "I've got some stew simmering. You best eat to keep your strength up, too."

She nodded, obediently, willing to follow this particular doctor's orders. When he moved across the room and set up a rattling clatter of plates and pans, she opened the red flannels. Her swarthy son was a quick learner. With no trouble at all, he found the source of satisfaction and saw greedily to his dinner.

Aurora watched the tall displaced Texan ready their meal, aware of how he kept his gaze averted so as not

61

to intrude upon her scant privacy. How had she ever felt threatened by him? She'd never known such kindness, such considerate, capable care as within this unlikely haven. Beneath the bushy beard and rough clothing, Ethan Prescott was the perfect Southern gentleman, regardless of where he now resided and how he chose to live. She felt not the slightest qualm about sharing these close quarters or the care and safety of her son. She thought of him now as healer, not surly hermit, and she wondered, again, how he'd come to this life in the woods. Would he tell her if she asked directly? Would he leave her with her secrets if she pried into his?

With a regretful tug of conscience, she still felt it best to withhold all the truth about her circumstance. While she could trust him with her life, she would not yet surrender the details of her situation. She knew he understood her reservations. He had his own shadowed secrets gathered close to the heart. Because he had taken her into his guarded existence, had saved her from her desperate folly and had helped bring her son into the world, she owed him his right to secrets, and because he was a gentleman and because he feared if he pushed too hard, she would flee him, he would not press her, either. So they would respect one another's privacy and chafe at the distance silence wrought.

"I've decided to name him Scotty," she said suddenly. "Short for Prescott. After his guardian godfather." Ethan stiffened before the fire and she gave a slight frown. His lack of response pricked at her. She'd done it as a way to thank him. She'd expected him to be pleased. Did he object to having a stranger's half-caste child as namesake? She added with a trace of tightness, "If it's all right with you."

Thickly, his heart crowded with the honor, his

memory aching with another who might have borne that name, Ethan murmured, "It's fine by me."

That was all he would say aloud, but as he held the tiny infant while she ate her stew, a softening stole over his expression, clouding his dark eyes, wringing a small smile from reluctant lips. She knew, then, how much she'd pleased him and was content. No matter what questions he might have about the babe, there was no unkind judgement in his wistful downcast gaze. How fragile Scotty appeared in his careful embrace, scarcely spanning the length of his sturdy forearm. Something about the contrast of the child's tender innocence and the man's massive strength opened her heart to a new vision. She saw beauty in the big, powerful hands and a curious sensitivity in features cloaked by burly whiskers. Truly a gentle giant where the baby was concerned.

And in that deferent light, she viewed him as a woman did a man and was not displeased. There was a rugged handsomeness to his face, though he would disguise it behind a glowering countenance and defensive bristle of beard. His lips were generous when coaxed from their somber line into an appealing smile. She was no longer put off by his abrupt and sullen gruffness, but was intrigued instead by his drawling speech and quiet manner. His sheer size failed to intimidate, not after she'd seen it humbled by the frail coos of a child. In that compelling collection of muscle and command there was an aura of security, like a forbidding mountainside giving shelter from a ravaging wind. Upon that seeming impregnable front were niches offering safety and comfort. And like that rocky facade, there was a constancy to him, a sense of permanence that one could depend upon as she had in her time of need.

Aurora found herself studying a stray lock of deep

auburn hair that fell curling upon his brow. She found herself mesmerized by the taut pull of wool across the broad chest giving a sleepy Scotty refuge. She detailed the swelling forearms exposed by pushed-up sleeves, seeing corded strength and, at the same time, tender support where they formed a cradle for her child. And when she thought of the smoldering hunger in his gaze when he considered her as a woman, not a mother to the babe in his arms, she felt a responsive heat spark deep inside her, fanned by this new awareness of him as attractive host rather than threatening captor. She wanted to deem these warming tendrils of emotion as gratitude, for she was thankful for the care and comfort she'd found within his wilderness home. However, gratitude couldn't explain away the curling tension she experienced when she thought of his big, gentle hand pressed against her cheek, stroking along her thighs. Nor did it provide an answer to the intense yearning stirred by the sight of Scotty in his arms or the poignant wish that such a man had fathered her child.

Those feelings matured as the days passed in quiet, endless hours. Time was filled with the routine care of Scotty, with the sight of Ethan shaping wood before the fire, with the sound of his husky humming as he rocked her son at his feet in the completed maple cradle. In such a situation it was impossible not to feel safe and cared for, and Aurora thrived upon it, as did Scotty. Both gathered strength, confidence, and a sense of belonging within that rustic setting, to the big, enigmatic Texan. He doted on the little boy, and there were times Aurora would catch him staring down at the tiny figure asleep in his cradle with a heart-tearing sadness steeping in his gaze. And she wondered again over his pregnant wife and whether or not he'd ever held his own child at his breast.

With Scotty slumbering and the fire creating an intimate glow, she and Ethan would sit on opposite sides of the hearth each evening, sometimes sharing weak coffee, sometimes sharing vague conversation. He'd talk of his native Texas, of its sprawling miles and the rough life it spawned; she'd speak of her finishing school back East, with its cool civility and proper priggishness. That was as close as they'd come to revealing anything personal, in those isolated snippets of the past. Both were teased by the unsatisfactory glimpses into one another's lives but stood fast behind the pact they'd made not to probe or pry. Those unexplained gaps aside, they lived much like a married couple, sharing responsibility for Scotty, enjoying each other's company while the winter winds whipped outside. That illusion strengthened throughout the day, but as the fire burnt low in the grate and time slowed into the waning hours, they each retreated to their separate quarters, Aurora to the rope bed, Ethan to his makeshift pallet of furs, with the length of the room and Scotty's cradle between them.

But during those long winter nights, their thoughts began to creep across that chaste distance to where the other lay awake and aware. How much quicker and more comfortably the cold nights would pass snugged close to another's warmth. How simple it would be to put an end to the taut edge of tension thrumming between them, to ease the incessant ache of loneliness in an embrace. It grew harder and harder to define reasons for staying apart.

Aurora found it easy to be seduced by the wonderfully monotonous days and by the restless, expectant nights. There was no difficulty in developing an attachment to Ethan Prescott that bordered upon desire. She'd surrendered all hope of finding a normal family life, of a good man who'd cherish her and accept her copper-skinned son. There was no question of giving up her child to seek personal happiness, and so she'd resigned herself to doing without those selfish pleasures. Until Ethan Prescott. He wanted her, his every glance spoke it plain, and he loved Scotty. The life the three of them led within the cozy cabin was a perfect idyll, simple, comfortable. But she would be deluding herself if she thought it safe or lasting.

On the morning she awoke to find sunlight streaming through the uncovered windows, the pretty bubble burst. The snow was melting. Time to leave this deceptive haven before her heart, likewise, began to thaw.

Ethan was pouring the last of the coffee into two tins at the table when he glanced up and had his senses summarily arrested. Aurora stood at the window in a shaft of golden light. It gleamed in a fiery halo about the tendrils escaping her loose braid and warmed her lovely features like a kiss of spring. She'd taken to wearing a pair of his red long johns beneath a voluminous flannel shirt. The fabric pooled and sagged but somehow managed to look utterly enticing just the same. With her piquant face and the subtle hint of her womanly curves, she was more devastatingly gorgeous in the rough mannish clothes than most females would be in their finest fripperies. And the man in him rumbled in response.

"Breakfast is ready."

She turned at his gruff announcement and he felt a touch of warning. Her gaze held a distinct sadness. There was a silent plea in her golden eyes and a sharp-edged pang of regret that sliced through his insides with the well-honed quickness of his Green River blade. Why so melancholy, he wanted to ask, but out of habit he held his tongue. Had he asked, he might have been surprised by her reply. Much of what was going on behind that molten gaze would have angered and, contrarily, thrilled him. But they were practiced in keeping to their own counsel, too much so to let even vital questions intrude.

"The trail's almost clear," she said softly and she could have meant anything by that bland observation. Again Ethan felt that prickle of alarm. What wasn't she telling him? Hell, she'd never told him anything. He was growing fast intolerant of her vague references and hoarded secrets. He already knew she had a half-cast child. What else could there be? He'd gone out of his way to prove to her that Scotty's heritage didn't matter to him. What did she hide with her evasive castdown gaze and her furtive glances toward the world outside the door. A world that, for a while, they'd managed to exclude.

Feeling the raw chafe of his longing for the woman cloaked in mystery and a gathering shortness of temper at being denied both his body's needs and his mind's curiosity, Ethan seized on the first available solution.

"I'm going out to check my trap lines," he said abruptly. "Most of them will probably have to be reset after the blast we took. While I'm gone, I'll see if I can rustle up something fresh for the pot."

Aurora was silent for a long, significant minute, but he was unable to interpret the pause. He was familiar with her hesitations, but not with their meaning. Then, in an inflectionless voice, she said, "I'll have supper waiting."

Waiting. Lord, how good that sounded. The image of her at his hearth, tending his meal while Scotty gurgled contentedly at her side, would bring him home with a sense of domestic anticipation. Like family. As if they were his wife and child. Sentiment swelled to crowd his chest, creating a heaviness and a buoyancy all at once. The image was as troubling as it was tempting. Aurora and Scotty weren't his to come home to. They were guests, not residents, and he was beginning to blur that line with the intensity of his wish to change it. His attachment to the boy was deep-rooted, almost paternal. His passion for the child's mother was nearing obsession. And still, by means of their secrets and silences, they eluded him. That would change, he decided, as he bundled into his heavy coat. When he returned, he would sit the red-headed enigma before the fire and he would learn what she had kept from him.

"Don't forget your—hat."

That last word nearly died on her lips as Ethan turned abruptly and they came face to face. He stood so close the shaggy nap of his generously over-lapped lapels brushed her suddenly sensitized breasts. She froze, her uplifted gaze lost in the heat of his. Slowly, drawn by the wants they felt but could not express aloud, his hand rose until blunt fingertips grazed her jaw and the sweet curve of her cheek. Her breath trembled against his palm but she didn't move away. A sudden fear leapt in her eyes but there was a lambent warmth there to overcome it. By increments, those golden eyes began to close, luring him as they did, nearer, nearer, until his mouth touched lightly upon hers.

It was an exquisite taste of tender passion, but nowhere close to satisfying what had simmered for long, longing weeks. When Aurora felt him begin to withdraw, she leaned forward just far enough to continue the pressure, to encourage him to linger. Inexorably, the kiss deepened and still, he made no move to catch her up in a possessive embrace. The heat of his mouth held her, the stirring of her own emotions imprisoned

68

her. A soft sound intruded upon their tentative search, a quiet moan from deep within her throat.

Ethan stepped away.

"I'd better go."

He didn't want to.

"Yes."

She didn't want him to, either.

Clapping the molded Stetson upon his head, Ethan started for the door. If he tarried, he'd end up staying and he wasn't sure he should. Nor was he convinced he shouldn't. There was no mistaking her response to him but he could tell by her hurried breaths that it had taken her by surprise. He wasn't all that steady, either. A little distance would allow them time to think, to get perspective and hopefully, to decide to pursue that promising kiss.

"Ethan?" Her trembling voice set up a resounding quiver inside him. "Take care."

"Don't you worry none about me. I'll be back in time for supper." He pulled open the door and felt the wind snatch his breath as vigorously as Aurora and her son had his heart.

"Good bye, Ethan."

He started out on foot, sucking in the clean, frigid air and expelling it forcefully on an icy plume. Already he missed them, already he was anxious to return. He shook his head to discourage those fanciful notions. One quick kiss settled nothing. Contrarily, he knew inside, it had settled quite a bit. Aurora and Scotty had twined about his solitary soul and were squeezing tightly. It wasn't panic or suffocation he was feeling, it was a constrictive joy. Dare he hope for happiness? A future without the flame-haired beauty and her copper-skinned son seemed unendurable. He couldn't imagine not waking to the child's hungry burbles or the evening firelight reflected back within a liquid gold gaze. When he'd brought her into his life, he'd altered it irreversibly. He no longer yearned for silence, but for a soft, female voice. He no longer craved privacy, but the chance to share. He no longer wished to wrap himself in solitude, but in the slender tangle of Aurora's arms.

He trudged on through the drifts and melting snows, shivering with cold, quaking with possibilities. Would she be content to live with him in the isolation of the woods? He couldn't come down from the hills, nor could he tell her the reason why. She seemed happy enough in the single room, clad in his rough woolens, surrounded by the barest of necessities. For now, anyway. He couldn't dismiss the significance of the dress she'd been wearing when he found her. The fabric was expensive, the tailoring of the finest quality. She was a woman of wealth. She was well-schooled and well-bred. Regardless of how she'd come upon her current situation, that part of her past wouldn't change. Would she come to look upon his crude cabin with contempt? Would she grow to loathe the daily labor required for their isolated existence? Would she begin to hate him for keeping her from her kind and from creature comforts? All he could offer, she'd already seen. Well, not all but enough. Would it be enough to satisfy her?

And what of Scotty? What kind of future could he guarantee her son? Given his mixed heritage, perhaps the world he offered would be the kindest. Yet, he couldn't deny her if she wanted more for him, indeed, the very best. And the very best wasn't hidden on a mountainside, miles from the nearest hint of civilization.

A soft noise distracted him from his thoughts. It was the call of the owl but he knew in an instant of dread it was not made by that winged predator of the night. The low hoot resounded through the trees. An owl's call wouldn't echo. Only man's voice returned to him that way. Ethan continued to walk but his tread lightened and his heavy Sharps rifle eased up at ready. Though he was expecting them, he was startled when three Sioux braves materialized from the trees without a whisper of warning. Knowing them to be Miniconjou, Ethan assumed a nonthreatening posture, although he was alert to the slightest sign of danger. The three braves were renegades from the Teton reservation at the Cheyenne River, traveling without the trappings of the hunt, yet not painted for raiding. All wore eagle feathers in their glossy black hair: one upright, signifying four coups upon his enemy; one hanging downward indicating he counted coup and was wounded; one marked and painted red, the sign of scalps taken. These were warriors, and Ethan was not lulled by the stoic expressions upon their strongly sculpted faces.

"Ho, mita koda!" he called out in welcome. "I am *Wasichu Wakan* and I bid you go in peace."

They made no move closer nor gave sign that they recognized his name. He reckoned they did or they would be wearing his hair and toting off his rifle.

"You roam far from your camp," he continued. "Has your *tiyospaye's itancan,* Yellow Bear, sent you to find me? Have your people need of my medicine once more?" Ethan chose his words carefully, citing the tribal chief to impress them, mentioning his link to medicine to gain their awe. Suitable reactions flickered in their dark eyes as they gauged him as a man of importance. Finally, one stepped forward to address him in broken English.

"Ho, Wasichu Wakan. It is not you we seek. We trail the runaway wife of one of our own. She is of the *wasachu,* like you, and heavy with child. The winds

71

of the Moon of Sore Eyes have hidden her from us."

Ethan was careful to let no quirk of expression betray him. The wife of a Miniconjou. They spoke of Aurora, of course but the fact that they pursued her was unusual. He questioned them as if from curiosity. "Is it not the way of your people to let a wife leave a husband who displeases her?"

Another of the three spoke up, his awkward words harsh with anger. "She did not *wicasaihpeyapi*—throw away the man. She slew her husband. We go to return her to our people's justice."

No trace of his shock was displayed upon Ethan's face. He held to his outward calm while struggling to control the emotions surging up inside. She'd killed a man, the father of her child. No wonder she'd kept so tightly to her secrets. Had she feared he'd turn her over to the Sioux to protect his own scalp?

She'd killed a man.

"Have you seen this woman, *Wadutah?*

Scarlet. A fitting name for his Aurora of the flaming hair. Ethan knew to lie was to endanger all the trust he'd earned from the suspicious Sioux. He'd found them to be a scrupulously honest people who justifiably had little faith in the invading white man's word, yet his had come to be respected. To be caught in a lie would jeopardize his life in the hills. Still, there was no way in hell he would turn Aurora and Scotty over to this trio of hard-eyed renegades.

"I have not seen such a woman. Most likely, you will find her after the thaws, already punished for her crime."

They grunted that it was probable. No white woman could have survived the cruelty of *Maka Ina,* their name for Mother Nature.

"If I should come across this woman, heavy with child, I will send word to your camp."

Satisfied by the sincerity in his tone and by the reputation of his name, the braves nodded and without a word, blended back into the snowy forest.

Confusion reigned in his head and heart when Ethan finally slogged back to the cabin. He had some of the answers — terrible, grim answers — but none yet from Aurora. He wouldn't judge her until he'd heard her side of it. He remembered the knife she'd stolen from his hearth. Had she planned to slay him with it on that first night? Was he alive only because she hadn't the strength to carry out that plan? If the Sioux were on a blood trail, he could credit her fears. No hunter stalked more relentlessly. No vengeance struck more mercilessly. And he knew right then that he would protect her and the child to the very limits of his life.

Even from the yard, he could scent the delicious aroma from his cook-fire and a deep abiding warmth kindled in his soul to war with his agitation. God, it was good to come home to someone. Protectiveness surged within him. He pushed open the door, meaning to demand the truth from her. Then, he would assure her of his support. But there was no need for either.

A pot bubbled invitingly upon its hook. Scotty's cradle sat before the hearth, unmoving. The curtain was drawn back to show his neatly made bed. Ethan blinked slowly, unwilling to register what his eyes told him.

His house was empty.

Chapter Five

Aurora forced herself to take one more step, then another and another, through the knee-deep snow. With each planted foot, icy melt dribbled down inside her moccasins to torment numbed calves and toes. With each lifted foot, the snow clung mirelike, dragging, heavy, making her struggle up over the glistening surface to plunge down and onward again. Her determined strides became a floundering stagger as she fought her way out of the hills. However, as long as she was moving, she wasn't thinking beyond the challenge of each step, and that was infinitely easier to bear than the rush of doubts and dreams crouched in ready assault the moment she paused to rest and feed Scotty. She didn't want to think, not until it was closer to go on than to go back. Though she knew there was no return, the lure of the tiny cabin and the big man within it was as draining on her will as the sucking snows were to her strength.

The moment Ethan closed the door that morning, she'd hurried her plans of flight. Even as her heart beat with passion's impatient rhythm and her lips ached with longing for the memory of their first kiss, she was hardening her resolve against those treasured sensations. Relentlessly, she crushed down those tender feelings with a desperate truth. She'd allowed herself to linger in the beautiful realm of dreams for far too long. Now, the danger closed upon her, threatening Scotty—and Ethan, as well. She couldn't let them come to harm, not even at the expense of all she desired. It was time to go.

Quickly, she fashioned a cradleboard, padding it with Ethan's precious pelts. For that, she felt only the slightest remorse. It would be a long, cold walk and Scotty must be kept warm. She had to think of him foremost. With a buffalo robe tied about her poncho-style, a hastily assembled stew simmering on the hearth as she'd promised and the cradleboard strapped upon her back, Aurora left the cabin and staunchly refused to look back.

Winter sun dazzled each snow crystal into a scattering of precious gems. Clean-cut shadows from every branch and bush stretched out in lacy etchings, first from her left, then from her right, as the day wore on. Had she paused to admire the crisp, bracing beauty of the day, she would have noted with awe the way the wind had sculpted delicate drifts against the merest stem of grass. Her heart was too heavy to find pleasure in nature's wonderworks, her legs too weary, as she trampled over the delicate display of winter art. She was leaving the only scene of perfection she had ever known to travel doggedly through danger into doubt. Each step carried her farther from the hope of happiness. Each moment stripped her of security. But there was no other way she knew to save them all. Save them for what, she didn't know nor care to dwell upon. Ethan would be safe in his mountain hideaway; Scotty would be protected by her father's bounty, once she'd crossed the treacherous miles of white and left the cruel hills behind, along with the burden of her dreams.

A miserable dampness seeped through the heavy furs. Aurora was trembling with fatigue and from a fierce chill. She'd fallen no less than a dozen times, tripped by buried roots and stumps to plunge face-first into the breath-stealing cold of the melting snow. She was soaked through from those frigid dunkings and from the steady trickle of her own sweat of effort. After the first upsetting tumble, Scotty began to cry. His wails rose steadily, protesting the discomfort of winter cold, angry at the binding cradleboard preventing him from movement, frightened beneath the protective robe that swaddled him in darkness. He quieted only while she paused to feed him. They both took comfort from those moments of closeness and shared body warmth.

His fussing cries had echoed through the denuded forest the moment she began to walk, and they were loud enough to carry a dangerous distance. Her pursuers would recognize the distressed sound as human. He was cold, he was wet, and she couldn't blame him for shouting his complaints. She, too, wished she could wail aloud to ease the ache in her heart and the exhaustion of body and spirit. But they were still too deep in the hills for safety, and silence was a necessity if they were to reach the valley below.

"A wa wa wa Inila istinma na."

Unthinkingly, she began a quiet chant, the unstructured lullaby of the Sioux women.

"A wa wa wa Inila istinma na." Be still. Sleep.

She'd heard the Miniconjou mothers's *hoksikigna,* soothing their children when silence on the hunt or on the trail became a simple matter of life and death. As was her situation, now.

"A wa wa wa Inila istinma na."

Gradually, miraculously, Scotty's betraying howls eased to a soft whimpering, then into the stillness of sleep. Aurora staggered onward, wishing she knew some chant to quiet her own internal terrors. Was she going the right way? The only direction she knew was down. She'd been to her father's ranch only once — and not under these conditions. She'd traveled in a well-sprung wagon with a parasol to shade her from the sun. No such comfort was afforded to her now. She had only the sign of the shadows to guide her, only the flagging strength of her legs and will to sustain her. And it would have to be enough. Had Scotty's loud laments been heard? She tried to listen for sounds of pursuit, realizing, as she did, the futility of it. She would see her Sioux pursuers before she'd ever hear them. However, other predators could be stalking them — large cats, wolves, and bears — that wouldn't be so concerned with stealth when tracking a weary human female who was helpless save her wits and one broad Green River blade.

Dusk was nearing, and Aurora realized in some dismay that she would not reach shelter before nightfall. The thought of huddling in the darkness, exposing herself and Scotty to unseen threats prowling the wintry eve, increased the force of the tremors shaking through her. She hadn't known it would be so far. The hills were reluctant to surrender her. If they did at all.

She steeled her mind from bringing forth images of a friendly fire, from the soothing strains of a Texas melody, from the secure feel of Ethan's presence just the distance of a room away. He'd have discovered her gone hours ago. Had it distressed him? Or was he relieved to have his solitude returned? She knew in her heart that he would forget the mysterious wanderer and her half-caste son long before the memory of him would fade and cease to be a torment in her mind. He would be sitting down to the stew she'd prepared, feasting in silence off a dented tin plate while warming flames danced within the big stone fireplace. She could see the rich auburn highlights gleaming through his poorly tended curls. She could hear his husky chuckle as he lifted Scotty from the handmade cradle. She could feel the lingering heat and molding strength of his mouth pressed longingly upon hers.

Sudden dampness welled, blurring her sight, causing her to stumble. She gave a broken sob as her toe caught upon a concealed vine, tumbling her headlong into an icy reality. Scotty, jarred from his slumber, began a lusty wail. Aurora lifted herself to hands and knees, then sat back into the chilling slush, weeping wearily as she cleared the sleety snow and debilitating tears with a trembling hand. This fresh misery soaked through, adding to her ever-mounting sorrow. Soon, she would have to pull herself up and seriously seek shelter for the night, but for now she lacked the energy needed to crawl from the punishing slump of uncertainty. It felt good to cry, venting her helplessness and fear, giving voice to her anger over circumstances that would deny her right to happiness. Her muscles ached with strain, her head throbbed with stress, her heart pulsed in a grieving agony of loss. There seemed no reason to get up or go on — until the whimpering of her son cut through her self-pitying dejection. For Scotty she would go on.

She wished fervently that conscience hadn't prevented her from taking Ethan's horse. She could now be well-mounted, dry and at the threshold of her father's ranch. Instead, she was afoot and wet. And the threat of darkness was gathering. Had she to do it again, she would have pushed her reservations aside. She could have returned the horse to him. It would have given her a reason to go back. To see him again. That thought lingered enticingly. Then she dismissed it with a weary resignation. If she'd stolen his horse, he would most likely meet her with a shot from his Henry.

With frozen fingers she loosened the straps and shrugged tired shoulders to free herself of the cradleboard. For a moment she just sat and rocked the fretful baby while gathering her last reserves of strength. She would find them shelter and continue the arduous journey downward in the morning. One step at a time. That was all she could handle for now.

"Hush now, Scotty," she crooned. "Tomorrow we'll be safe and warm."

As if he'd understood, the baby quieted.

In the ensuing stillness came a disturbing sound, a rhythmic churning, thudding, jingling. The sound of powerful movement through the coating snows. Of branches bending and snapping at some mighty passing. A horse.

Clutching Scotty to her frantically pounding breast, Aurora surged to her feet and cast about for means of concealment. She began to run, a panicked flight toward the shadows where she might find safety from the danger fast approaching in the dusk. The snow dragged at her, making her desperate dash into a languid slow-motion.

A cry of terror escaped her as a huge animal sent up a shower of snow with its plunging hooves, cutting off her retreat and blinding her with its hot, pluming breath. She stood trembling, mind too frozen with fear and exhaustion to urge a posture of defense; as if one blade wielded by a female near collapse could pose a threat. Her air-starved lungs permitted one croaking sound as her gaze lifted to seek the form of her demise.

"Ethan."

It was a prayer, it was a sob, as he flung himself down from the back of his mighty sorrel in a swirl of hide capes. Just as her knees surrendered, his arm was there to provide support. She must have swooned from shock and fatigue, for her next awareness was of an easy rolling motion and enfolding strength. She was riding perched upon Ethan's powerful thighs, wrapped tight in the circle of one crushing arm. Scotty was wedged in the protective hollow between them, as silent as the big man who guided his horse with the pressure of his knees.

Realizing his direction, Aurora managed a feeble, "No. No, we can't go back," but his embrace seized up, effectively overcoming any protest. It was then she knew that she had no true objection. Not now. Not tonight, when cold and damp was no comfort. Weariness made surrender acceptable. Nothing could ease the burden of her fears better than the knowledge of a snug night inside Ethan Prescott's cabin. Better than freezing in an inhospitable blackness, shivering with cold and dread. Nothing could warm through her deadened heart like the awareness that he'd come after them, had come to carry them home.

She let her head rest against his solid shoulder, relying upon his arms to keep her in the saddle while her consciousness waned. She drifted in that comforting circle, without a notion of the turmoil seething beneath her slumped form. Trust allowed her to sleep, then, as innocently as her child.

Ethan was furious.

Even as he clutched her tight, he fumed. How dare she curl against him in oblivious contentment after putting him through such hellish worry? How could she now nestle upon his chest, as if he were some rescuing hero, when she'd fled him like a horrid villain? Upon finding her gone, his world had crumbled. He'd driven his horse recklessly through the snow, torturing himself over every mile with pictures of her and the baby torn apart by wolves. Of them at the ruthless hands of the Sioux. Of mother and child wandering in hopeless circles until exhaustion finished them. She'd put a nameless fear inside him, one that yet quaked and refused to be stilled by the reality of her in his arms. Why in God's name had she fled? Where had she thought to go on foot, through the heavy snows? Why had she crept off while he was away rather than asking for his help to her destination? Hadn't he proven he wasn't the enemy?

As for the reason for her sudden flight, he had no clue. He searched his mind laboriously but could come to no conclusion. She'd given no hint of dissatisfaction. No indication she thought to travel. She'd simply slipped away. Without warning. Without reason. And that scared him. Had she told she him, she meant to go, he would have understood and aided her. He would have seen her safely and with provisions to wherever she would go. Or at least as close to it as possible. She wouldn't have had to struggle through the cold and damp. She wouldn't have been a prospective morsel for the wolves.

Why hadn't she said anything to him? What had caused her to run? The only thing he kept coming back to was the kiss.

Had the thought of his desire so terrified her?

He knew little of women except they were not to be trusted once your back was turned. And this one had fled him. He'd almost lost her as he'd lost another, once before. His reaction had no logic. He should have let her go and good riddance. He should have been glad to be spared an uncomfortable parting. He should have minded his own business.

But what had he done? He'd flown into an incredible panic. He'd pursued her as if she was his runaway wife making off with his child. He'd gone after her fully intending to bring her back with him, dragging her if necessary. To what purpose? To keep her prisoner in his cabin? To hold her against her will? To force himself upon her when her fear of his attentions had caused her to run in the first place?

None of it made sense. No more so than the relief he felt when he saw her floundering in the snow, unharmed. No more so than the thread of longing twining through him at the feel of her gently curved hip upon his thighs. And not so great as the flood of possessiveness controlling conscious thought. He wanted her. He'd gone after her. He was bringing her back.

Now what?

Aurora woke to the welcoming glow of the cabin's windows ahead. The horse was still and Ethan gone from behind her. Just as she was about to protest his absence, she saw his arms reaching up, felt his big hands close about her waist—gently, as if she was something precious and breakable. She turned and slid, stiff and cold, down from the high saddle against the indescribable pleasure of Ethan's broad chest. From their numbness, she feared her legs lacked the strength to carry her even the short distance to the door, but that doubt was never tested. As if he could not bear to relinquish his hold upon her and Scotty, Ethan bore them into the baking heat of the cabin's single room, surrendering them there with reluctance and a murmur that he must see to his horse.

Strange. Somehow, Aurora expected things to appear different since her flight that morning. Nothing had changed. All was warm and wonderfully inviting, from the scent of stew to the fur-covered bed against the wall. This was no prison from which she'd desired to flee; it was a haven in which she'd recouped her strength and summarily lost her will. Ignoring the contentment settling inside, she quickly saw to Scotty's needs, washing him and swaddling him in dry squares of flannel. For once, he showed no interest in eating, his eyes sagging and little body relaxing into the slackness of sleep, as if glad the whole ordeal was over. He gave a sigh as she placed him in the maple cradle, but Aurora felt no such relief. Things were far from settled or over. She knew that the moment Ethan returned and closed the door behind him.

Without a word, he shrugged out of his multicaped coat and draped it by the fire to dry. There was no clue to his mood in the craggy surface of his features. They might as well been of native stone, softening only slightly when he peered down at the slumbering child. Aurora wasn't given to irrational fits of apprehension, but one raking glance from him set her body quaking. It was exhaustion, mostly, that and the frustration of dealing with a heart eager to yield to what the mind couldn't accept. This was not her home. She had no reason to feel so grateful to be back in its rustic fold. She'd set out with a purpose that morning only to be toted back like a disobedient child. Ethan Prescott had no right to track her down, like a man pursuing wayward chattel, or to express any opinion over what she'd done. She and Scotty were not his business. He had no say in when they could come or go. Yet his dark, dire gaze told her he believed he did. She braced for a confrontation, ready to back her actions with haughty claims of independence, but she nearly dissolved into tears at the utterance of his first cross word.

"What the hell were you thinking?"

Aurora sniffed stubbornly and lifted her chin to a mulish angle.

"You foolish female, you could well have died out there, as unprepared as you were. And you've had taken Scotty with you. Didn't you stop to consider that before lighting out on foot without a morsel of food, without a gun, without the means to keep him dry and comfortable?"

Her determined jaw trembled. Dampness trailed down her flushed and frozen cheeks as she searched for an argument and could find none. It had been a foolish and impulsive act. He struck instinctively where she was the weakest. She had placed Scotty at risk and now the desperation that drove her seemed so minute in comparison. Dear God, if anything had happened to Scotty . . .

Her shoulders jerked convulsively but Ethan refused to give over to compassion. Inside, he still shook with the shock of finding them gone. He could still feel that terrible black emptiness and responded to that fear with anger. She'd put him through hell and had the nerve to sit there sniveling, waiting for him to forgive and comfort her. Well no, he wouldn't. Not yet. Not until she fully understood what might have befallen her had he not been in time. Not until he'd managed some control over his shattered emotions.

"Twice now I've saved you from your damn-fool craziness. What if I hadn't happened along? How did you plan to spend the night with no fire, no shelter, no food? With nothing to keep off the animals and Indians? Hell, there might have been nothing but bones left to tell the tale by morning."

She was nearly choking on her silent sobs, swallowing great gulps of breath in an effort not to wail aloud. Horror brightening in her eyes at the image his words created. She looked down at the tender figure curled in a protective nest of blankets, at the trusting innocence of her child. Her features contorted with guilt, and Ethan felt his heart lunge painfully against his ribs. God in Heaven, how dear they'd become to him. If he'd been too late . . .

"Put this on," he growled, flinging her a dry shirt and turning away before she could witness his struggle to hold firm against her hapless tears. He heard her wiggling, the sodden sound of her wet things hitting the floor, the rustle of coarse wool sliding over clammy skin. His eyes closed in the sheer agony of the images those sounds encouraged. For a moment, there was silence, then her soft entreaty.

"Ethan . . ."

"Go to sleep. You're nearly dead on your feet. We'll talk in the morning."

He stood taut and tense listening to the lengthy pause then to the seductive creak of knotted webbing as it gave beneath her weight. Before he could begin to breathe again, her voice came quietly from the corner, stronger now, more certain in that strength.

"Ethan, we have to go."

"I know." Dammit, he knew. She didn't have to tell him. She didn't have to force him to deal with it so soon, while his nerves were yet raw, while his passions yet quivered.

"You know?" How breathless and stunned those words sounded, disbelieving and yet, afraid of understanding.

He heaved a heavy sigh, letting his shoulders roll with the weight of it. Then, he explained. "I meet up with a couple of Lakotas on the trail. They were tracking a runaway squaw who killed her husband." How harsh and judgemental that came out. He couldn't temper the facts unless she chose to deny them. And he prayed she would. He didn't want to believe her capable of such fatal violence, not when he'd worked so hard to preserve the frailty of life.

There was another long, stilted silence. However, when she spoke, it was not, as he'd expected, an apology or in defense of what she had or hadn't done.

"What did you tell them?"

He whirled, facing her with a head full of fury and a heart clenched in confusion. "What the hell do you think I told them?" His voice snapped like the jaws of a steel trap. "I lied. I said I hadn't seen such a woman, this *Wadutah* they were hunting."

She sat up, clutching the covers beneath her chin. Her eyes were huge, golden orbs, as bright as two newly minted eagles. "Did they believe you?"

He gave a derisive snort. "I'm known as a man of my word."

Aurora didn't respond to that. Her thoughts were hurrying ahead, to a danger much closer than she'd imagined. A danger nearly at their door. She should have kept going. She'd made it better than half way down the mountainside, nearly to safety. Then, he'd brought her back, right into the midst of those who threatened her.

She gave a start when he settled beside her on the edge of the bed. She was jerked from her frantic mental scramblings by his compelling presence. Aurora stared at him wordlessly, wanting to blame him yet unable to. He'd rescued her for the moment, and for that she should be grateful.

"You're safe here," he rumbled with sincerity. "I'll see to it."

Those bold, beautiful words were followed by the light touch of his fingertips along the slant of her jaw. Oh, how she wanted to believe him. If anyone could make it so, it was Ethan Prescott. But, no matter how much she might want it, it was impossible.

"For the moment," she said quietly. "Then what? What happens when they cross my trail? They'll follow it right to your door."

He shook his head. He'd taken precautions, guiding his big horse along the path she'd taken. It's hooves had churned up all evidence of her passing.

"Even if they don't," she persisted, "how long before they hear Scotty crying? And if they discover you've lied to them, what do you think they'll do? The Sioux are not a forgiving people. They'd burn you out and kill you to take Scotty and me away. You wouldn't be able to stop them. I wouldn't let you try. Ethan, I can't stay. You know what I'm saying is true."

"No!"

With that roar of denial his fingers slid behind her head, anchoring in the thick, fiery braid, snatching her up to meet the fierce plunder of his mouth. Stunned, she offered no resistance. She let him brand his grinding kisses upon her unsuspecting lips until the cut of his teeth raised a whimper. Helplessly, she opened for the plunging conquest of his tongue within her mouth's moist cavern. His other hand rose to trap her chin between the vee of thumb and forefinger, steadying her beneath the fierce taste of his passion. There was nothing in this sensory assault even vaguely reminiscent of his early overture. This was hard, hot desire, and she quivered in its possessing thrall. His mouth was ardent, angry and aggressive in its claim, almost as if by controlling her will, he could likewise alter fact and fate.

Slowly, when the startled shock of his abrupt kisses ebbed, Aurora was aware of her own simmering response. His urgency quickened a like spark of desire. Oh, how she wanted this—wanted him—wanted to believe that desperate need could command time to stop and give them the chance to explore the incredible potential of what they had between them. But since time would grant them no special favors, they had to grab greedily for all they could have and hold of this fleeting moment.

"Ethan."

It was a sigh, a whisper of sound that vibrated along his every nerve like the pluck of a taut guitar string. The melody was sweet and seductive, yet so poignant it gentled his passions with the merest stroke. It was then he realized how tightly his hand was cramped in the glory of her tangled hair. He relaxed the bite of his fingers impressing her soft skin. And he withdrew from the throbbing swell of her lips with a hoarse mumble of, "Ora, I'm sorry."

He expected her to be repulsed by his crude demands. He braced for the sight of fear or contempt in her golden gaze. Instead, he found a daze of dewy desire in her eyes and a pout of yearning upon her tender lips. Overwhelmed, he remained still as stone, while her hands lifted and gently roved the contours of his face. Breathing quickened into a labored effort. He found himself thoroughly charmed by her innocent inquiry and torn with the agony that he might never again experience her guileless touch. It was too much for the slender threads of his composure.

"Ora," he groaned.

"Shhh," she whispered, then hushed him with the light press of her mouth. Her arms stole about the breadth of his shoulders, and her face shifted, burying in the warm hollow of his throat. By then, his heart was thrusting so hard against the wall of his chest, he feared he would bruise her where she fit snug to his shirt front. Gradually, his big hands came up, at first just to rest upon the graceful fan of her shoulderblades, then sliding, rubbing in small circles.

Kneading.

Needing.

Aurora meant to luxuriate in the feel of him, to enjoy and remark upon every ridge of rolling muscle, upon every breath that rocked her, while his palms worked their soothing magic upon her tired frame. Unfortunately, she was as vulnerable as a babe to the lulling rhythm. Her eyes began to slip and sag. The ability of movement fled her limbs. And she sighed, as sweetly and as trustingly as Scotty in his cradle.

That weary sound wreaked havoc upon Ethan's intentions. How could he court and claim a woman so exhausted that she found his lovemaking overtures as calming as a lullaby? He smiled ruefully into the glossy mass of red hair and dismissed thoughts of waking her with more aggressive suit. Just as well. She wasn't prepared, either physically or mentally, for the furtherance of his plan. Nor was he.

Carefully, he began to ease her down upon the blankets, only to be thwarted by the convulsive tightening of her grasp.

"Stay with me," she pleaded sleepily and burrowed into the security of his embrace. If she only knew what she asked of him. He settled close, letting her shift and snuggle until satisfied with the degree of comfort he afforded. And then she slept.

There was no comfort or sleep for Ethan Prescott through those long hours until dawn. They were the only hours he might ever have to claim her in his arms. And he vowed not to be cheated of a single minute.

Chapter Six

Aurora woke with soft cry. The shadowy vestiges of her nightmare still clung with icy fingers, reminiscent of her futile trek through yesterday's snows. The menacing growls from the wolves—closing a hungry ring about her and Scotty as she huddled helplessly in the cold—became the welcomed rumble of a familiar voice.

"Ora?"

With a moan of relief, Aurora turned into Ethan's arms as if it was the most natural place in the world to seek comfort. And she found it, there against the broad, steadily rocking plain of his chest, there in the secure fold of his embrace. She held to him instinctively. It didn't matter how or why he was there. It was where she needed him at that moment and he hadn't failed her.

Her rapid breaths drew in the warm scents of wood chips and tobacco from where her face pressed into the open vee of Ethan's shirt front. Beneath a springy mat of hair, his flesh was hot and pulsing with the sure rhythm of his life's blood. That tempo increased into a hard, expectant throb as her fingers clutched and curled in the scratchy wool covering his corded upper arm and shoulder. The coarse fabric grew taut under her palms. She could feel his muscles flow like

90

a mighty river current as he moved to gather her closer. Those samples of his strength, those snatches of intimate awareness of him as a man, quickly overcame the vague traces of her bad dream, encouraging one far sweeter but just as intangible. Ethan Prescott was something she could hold to only for the moment.

"I didn't kill him," she said quietly into that warm hollow of flesh and male furring. "It was an accident but they'd never believe that. Not after I ran away."

She felt his breathing still against the tousle of hair crowning her head, then the heavy weight of his cheek resting there. "You don't owe me an explanation."

"I think I do." She owed him much more. Her life, Scotty's. The truth was all she could give in return. Little enough to repay him but not an easy price to surrender. Looking back stirred a long repressed terror, a vulnerability that was harder to suffer than a swift, sure death. It seemed so long ago, as if recounting the events of another's life. She had been someone else altogether then. She'd been the daughter of a wealthy rancher returning from years of enviable schooling in Boston. She'd been sheltered for all her twenty-two years, innocent of mind and body. Then, all of that was gone as she plunged into the cruelty of a life that was a world apart from everything she'd ever known.

She spoke simply of a hot May afternoon when, without a sound of warning, the bluffs before their westbound coach were covered with a party of close to fifty Indians, painted and equipped for war. Uttering wild war-whoops and firing volleys into the air, they swarmed down with unexpected swiftness. The seven men in her group were ineffective in halting that swamping red tide. The smoke of discharged arms was thick in the air. She recalled with a sickening horror the sight of Mr. Jones, their driver, falling slow-motion from the high seat, pierced by countless arrows. The high-pitched shrieks of the other female passenger—a bawdy girl seeking employment in the gold camps—were severed by a bullet to one silk-clad breast. One by one, the five brave men inside the coach were mortally wounded, and in their death throes they toppled over her where she crouched on the floor.

The Indians sprang upon the coach, tearing the cover off the baggage lashed to its top, smashing their way into the trunks with the heavy ends of their tomahawks. The air was filled with their fearful whoops and victorious shouts. Through the windows, she could see the satins and laces of her clothing as it floated down from where her bags were ravaged. Determination to survive stilled her quaking terror. Her fingers curled around the yet-warm revolver of one of the fallen as she meant to fight or die for her freedom. Then, the doors of the coach were wrenched open. Before she could manage a shot beneath the crushing weight of the dead and dying, her wrists were gripped and used to haul her struggling and screaming onto the dusty ground.

"I knew they meant to kill me. There wasn't a shred of mercy in their faces so I vowed not to resort to useless begging. It was a hard promise to keep when I could hear the cries of the wounded being scalped behind me. Then, one of the braves rushed toward me. His face was slashed with white paint down either side in a call for vengeance against the whites who murdered his family. His blade was raised and I could see my death in his hand. And suddenly, one of the others moved his horse into his path, saving my life. I'd been told a white woman in my position should long for death rather than the prospect of capture by the Sioux. But I didn't want to die, Ethan."

She felt his lips brush through her hair and his arms tightened in agreement. His heartbeats were a crashing echo of her own, registering her terror, affirming her courage. The fear, the danger seemed so far removed from the surrounding safety of the big Texan's embrace.

"And so the brave on horseback took you for his own." Ethan spoke that somberly and she nearly wept in relief for the lack of condemnation in his voice.

"It was my red hair. He claimed he'd seen it in a dream and I was to fulfill his destiny. There's no tampering with an Miniconjou's dreams. They're a direct command from their gods."

Ethan nodded, knowing that much of the Lakota religion.

"It was a hard life, a cruel one, not because of the treatment of the Sioux but from the brutality of their existence. They're starving, Ethan, struggling to survive. That's something I could understand, for I was doing the same thing. I had to survive until I had the chance to escape. That meant I had no choice but to submit to Far Winds."

Ethan recoiled from her words. She could feel his body stiffen and his offer of comfort subtly withdraw. Aurora's heart and soul constricted. Had the blunt facts of her capture, stained her in his eyes? He knew, of course, of her half-Sioux child but was facing the fact of Scotty's creation too repugnant for him, as a white man, to endure? The thought that he considered her spoiled by the necessities of survival wounded with unexpected viciousness.

Never, until now, had she felt ashamed of what had happened. She'd done what she'd had to and had learned to accept it with a stoic sense of reality. But now, feeling the bitter brunt of Ethan's silent disgust,

93

she wondered if perhaps she should have let them kill her first. What was left her if not the respect of this man of tender passion?

Oh, Ethan, she wailed within, *Don't blame me. I'm no different because of it.*

But she was different. She'd dared to compromise honor for survival and had borne proof of that decision. Her pride splintered at the knowledge of his censure. A feeling of impurity crawled over her skin, embedding in flesh that had known an Indian's touch — flesh that now repelled Ethan. After struggling so long to hold to life, knowing he despised her for what she'd allowed made her die inside, a slow, agonizing death of undeserved disgrace.

Aurora wanted to cling to him, to plead for the return of his attentive care. She wanted to seize his hands and force them to consider the aching curves and hollows of her body, where, in her heart, she was yet untried and innocent. The flame had extinguished in his veins. The urgent pulse for her was gone. She would rekindle it, if she could, for its heat gave purpose to the woman inside, who had struggled so and yearned to know the healing sweetness of his desire. He was her reward for enduring all she had and now, it seemed, she would lose that, too, because of the price she'd thought not too high to pay. That damnable price. That irrefundable price. Her eyes welled with achy moisture, with the tears collecting in her heart since she'd refused to shed them at her attackers's feet. Throughout her capture, she'd never wept for herself. She'd clung to pride and hope in order to suppress weakness, knowing she'd never recover should she succumb. Ironic, that it was love, not fear, which finally shattered her strength.

She loved Ethan Prescott; for his goodness, for his sacrifice, for his care, for the desire burning within him that sparked a responsive blaze. She wanted to give him, with all her heart, what she had once bartered out of desperation. She wanted to share with him the soul she'd held zealously inside, locked tight against taint, preserved in hopes it could twine freely about the one she loved. But her love brought no comfort. His rejection crushed her heart. His withdrawal shredded her soul. And there was nothing left save tears.

Yet as her sorrow gathered to overflowing, Ethan was unaware of its cause. While her misery dampened his chest, what bound his emotions into a cold internal knot wasn't, as she assumed, her bargained innocence. He had nothing but admiration for her choice, for the courage she'd displayed. What gave him dreadful pause was not the content of what she'd spoken but, rather, the name.

"Far Winds? Son of Yellow Bear?"

Totally unprepared for the snag of torment in his tone, Aurora lifted her head, her anguish forgotten as she searched out the reason for his. Dark eyes glistened with disbelief, with the hope she would tell him it was not so. Having gone so far, she could not spare him that truth.

"You knew him?" Incredulity softened her question; the etch of pain in his face, her answer.

It tortured him to place the noble, loyal, and often laughing son of the chief into the role of the savage who raped the woman he held in his arms. He more than knew Far Winds, he'd considered him a friend. The Lakota brave had taught him how to hunt the woods, how to read the signs of nature. The son of the chief had given him an insight into a desperate people seeking a way to hold to their right to live as their father's before them had lived, proudly, off the land — not out of the hand of their enemy. Ethan couldn't grasp the notion that such a vital life force was gone, extinguished in an instant. Nor could he fathom his friend abusing a frightened woman. It burned his conscience to think he would grieve for such a man. Yet, grieve, he did, bringing an unforgiving lump of betrayal to lodge chokingly within his chest.

"Did he hurt you, Ora?" The need to know tore at him.

"No."

That single word released him.

"I can't say he was kind but I was not mistreated. I believe he cared for me in his own fashion, perhaps he even loved me. It wasn't a feeling I could return. I could respect the man he was but I couldn't think of him as more than my captor."

There was more she could say, yet she locked it way from even this man who might have understood. She didn't speak of her terror at being thrust into a foreign world, of the long nights she'd lain awake, stripped naked so she couldn't run away, expecting to be slain at any minute, over any inconsequential act. The fear and isolation had been her sole companions until, after a ritual she half understood, Far Winds had taken her as his second wife.

In a ceremonial tipi, the bold, bronze Miniconjou brave had claimed her. There was no tender courtship, no consideration for her ignorance or innocence. He'd pressed her down upon the mat of willow rods and robes, using strength, not force, to teach her obedience to his will. Features she'd thought cruel, while screams from the slain members of her party echoed in her ears, appeared sharply handsome in the half light. She struggled in fear of the unknown about to happen and he'd struck her cheek, firmly but without malice. She learned a valuable lesson then. Resistance would yield nothing. She couldn't fight a much greater force physically but she could wage that battle within. She could submit without surrendering; realizing that, she was able to endure what ensued as he pushed up the dress of hide she wore and pressed home his claim within her.

Each night he came to her, and though there was no pain as in that first time, neither was there any joy. She lie still beneath his glistening copper body, blanking her mind as he moved above her in the throes of elemental mating. The only response he demanded was that she receive the seed of their passionless union. Though she was frightened and a bit repelled by the purpose of his visit, it no longer held the terror it once had. She allowed him the use of her young body; he provided for her care and protection — a necessary exchange until she had the chance for freedom.

That chance didn't come. Far Winds shared her mat at night, and during the day, she was supervised by his first wife. Uncheedah was small and pretty. Her lustrous black hair gleamed with blue tinges. Her skin was dark copper. Her eyes were obsidian — and as cold as that flat, black stone. Because she was Far Winds's primary wife, the one he wed as a young warrior, she was in charge of all others he might take into his tipi. Aurora learned a brave could take two or three if he had the means to support them. And though the petite Uncheedah, who was herself swollen with her husband's child, called Aurora *teya,* her co-wife, it was plain the scarlet-haired white woman was resented for warming the bed Uncheedah could no longer share. Upon finding a wife with child, her husband would abstain from commerce with her often for up to two years after the child's birth, or as long as she nursed his babe. The flame-tressed *Wadutah* now claimed those favors, and Uncheedah, used to being the source of much attention as daughter of the camp's medicine woman, sought a subtle vengeance.

Aurora was schooled in the ways of a Sioux wife, and, as her teacher, Uncheedah was generous with her criticism of the impossibly slow, lazy *washichu* squaw. She was also generous with her instructing switch. Beneath the sting of both, Aurora struggled through the language barrier to learn their strange customs. She was taught to dress robes and to bring in the hunter's meat. She overcame her modesty to enjoy the freedom allowed within her elkskin dress and soft moccasins. She developed a taste for the food of the wild, which was often scarce and never wasted; the porcupine, beaver, muskrat, elk, antelope, chokeberries, buffalo berries, currants and plums. No one needed to instruct her in *wistelkiciyapi* when in the presence of her austere father-in-law. It wasn't from respect that she kept her eyes canted down and held her tongue. She was as awed by the hard-eyed chief with his war bonnet of trailing plumes as he was wary of his son's choice of wife. Aurora absorbed what she could to make her life easier and lessen the bite of Uncheedah's stick, but always she was alert, watching for a means to flee.

That sustaining hope faded when September arrived. It was during The-Time-When-the-Wild-Plums-Ripen that their *tiyospaye,* a band of about two hundred, sought a higher timbered riverbend to make their winter camp. Horse-drawn travois laden with great bags and blocks of pemmican, mounted warriors carrying colorful pennoned lances, pack animals heaped high with camp supplies, old men, women and children afoot, and a great herd of horses formed an orderly pageant that spread for miles. Each camp they made was farther from her father's valley below, until Aurora was hopelessly lost. It looked as though she would never return to the world she knew. And then she discovered she was pregnant. Far Winds was puffed with pride, and Uncheedah, who had lost her own child during the long days of travel, smoldered in hatred.

"We wintered in the hills," she continued softly, encouraged by the steady pull of Ethan's fingers through the bright luxury of her hair. His solid heat beside her formed a wall which kept the bitter memories at bay and allowed her to speak with a reasonable calm. Those days of forage and near-starvation had been anything but calm. "By then, I was accepted in the camp by all but Uncheedah, who would lie with Far Winds each night and fill him full of my imagined misdeeds. I think he knew her talk stemmed from jealousy and from the pain of losing her child, so he paid her little mind, at least until two months ago when we began to trickle out of the hills. We came upon some trappers who showed an interest in me. Far Winds was furious and kept me hidden from sight. When they passed by, I thought I had lost my last chance to return home.

"And then, one night when Far Winds was out on a hunt, Uncheedah bent over me with a bared blade. I knew she meant to kill or maim me. She told me to put on the dress I'd worn on the day of my capture. I'd kept it safe all those months and the feel of it gave me hope. With the blade at my throat, she took me from our tipi to the darkness at the edge of the camp. The trappers were there, waiting for me. I thought they were going to take me home."

"And Far Winds came after you," Ethan guessed quietly. What man would not? He could imagine the warrior's distress at finding she and his growing child had escaped him. He remembered well that sense of loss bordering on madness when he'd discovered his cabin empty. "And he paid for it with his life."

"Not at my hand. Please believe that, Ethan." And to further entreat him, she put one slender palm over his heart so he might see how fragile it was, so he might read sincerity in that gesture.

"Tell me what happened, Ora." His tone was noncommittal, waiting to be convinced.

She never reached safety. Her first night on the trail, she found out the truth. Her joy at being among her own kind was quickly tempered. These men were not of her kind, or any kind above the meanest of vicious animals. She'd known a terror more stark and all-encompassing then any that had ever visited her at the hands of the Sioux. When she spoke of the lurid light heating their hungry stares, a hard shudder took her slim frame. And Ethan's arms were there to protect her from the image.

"Uncheedah had not bartered with them to supply my freedom. She had sold me to them for their pleasure. Whatever they planned for me, I would not have survived it," she said hoarsely, through the bile that gathered thick and metallic-tasting in her throat. "They meant to use me then trade me for the highest price. I was so afraid, not so much for myself as for my child." She held back the memory of them talking over the fire, of the one who'd casually claimed he would beat the baby out of her so it would not interfere with their plans. She shuddered and he must have guessed at her horror for his arms squeezed tight. It was a moment before she could continue in a strained voice.

"And then, Far Winds was there. He swooped down from nowhere, catching them off guard. His first two shots were true but the third was not in time to save him. The trappers were dead and I held Far Winds's head upon my lap as he breathed his last. He told me that Uncheedah claimed I fled with the help of the trappers and he had come to fetch me back. He never heard me speak the truth and I knew if returned to his people, they would never hear it, either. All were dead. It would look to them as if my accomplices had slain the son of their chief at my encouragement. I had to run. The storm was brewing but I had no choice. The snows promised to be kinder than Uncheedah's lies. And then you found me, Ethan and for a time, I felt truly safe."

And loved. She didn't add that but she felt it as surely as if she'd spoken the words. While in his cabin, listening to his humming lullabies, feeling the warmth of his gaze upon her, she was encompassed by rich sentiment, surrounded by deep, quiet currents of passion. Again, she wondered how she'd been so afraid of this man. Her first thoughts upon waking to find herself in the hands of the huge stranger were wrapped up in the desperation of flight and fear. Frantic possibilities teasing her tired brain kept her from feeling secure. What if he was no better than those beasts on the trail? What if he decided to return her to Far Winds's people to earn favor or reward? So she'd held the truth inside her and looked for an escape. Only as the days passed, she found she no longer wanted to leave. Even when she knew there was no other choice, she resisted the inevitable. And so, she spoke her arguments aloud, hoping that would make her believe them.

"I couldn't lead them to your door, Ethan. After all your kindness, I couldn't repay you with the threat of danger or death. Scotty and I have to go. We've stayed too long already." So long, it felt as though, once again, she was being torn from her home by the cruelty of fate. Fanciful thoughts of keeping house for Ethan Prescott while Scotty gurgled at his hearth were all too tempting. The memory of his deep, drugging kiss foretold the ecstasy she might find within these now familiar walls. Far better she go, quickly, before those things became a bond impossible to break.

"I'll take you out of the hills at daybreak."

There was no enthusiasm in his offer, nor did she receive it with a sense of gladness. He didn't want her to leave. She didn't want to go. He was making it easier but no less painful for her to do what she must. And while she lay in the strong circle of his arms, death seemed preferable to losing their enticing promise.

How was she ever going to leave him? How was she ever going to get Ethan Prescott out of her heart and mind? All she'd have was the memory of his kiss to sustain her, and suddenly, that was far from enough. There were too many things she had to know. How would it feel to have his large hands upon her body, not to coax the birth of a child but to tempt her passions? What would it be like to have him make love to her? Different than with Far Winds? Yes, oh yes, she knew instinctively.

She had to know. The need for discovery had her body thrumming with impatience, with anticipation. She'd known possession for the basic purpose of procreation. She'd been used as an empty vessel to be filled. Now she longed to be shaped and crafted by a loving touch. Now she ached to experience the pleasures his kisses promised. Now — for there might never be another time.

Aurora lifted her head from the hollow of his throat to meet his dark, penetrating gaze. Did he know? Did he understand the desperate need these waning minutes provoked?

"Ethan . . ." Her voice faltered and failed. She tried again. "Ethan, Scotty and I — Scotty and I will

102

always love you."

He had no response. His throat seemed swollen shut. His heart tightened around those words like a fist, crushing them, cherishing them. He'd never wanted to hear those words again, yet when she spoke them, he realized he'd been craving the sound of them from her sweet lips.

Made uncertain by his silence, Aurora touched his cheek with tentative fingers. His beard was thick and soft, like one of his precious pelts. Her palm stroked it. Her fingertips grazed the warm, bronzed skin over his cheekbone, then trailed down to sample the pulse in his corded neck. The pattern of his breathing had altered against her, coming fast and hard where his chest pressed to the yielding softness of hers. She eased back slightly, giving her fingers room to travel nimbly down his shirt front, freeing its buttons for her further exploration. Firm musculature was covered with more crisp fur, coaxing her to thread through the dark mat as a deep vibration rumbled beneath her hand. The tremor quickened an answer within her, glorious in its ferocity. His strength excited. Though he could no doubt snap her in two with the power at his command, she felt no trace of fear, no intimidation. Only the tantalizing knowledge that all his massive swells and corded sinews were tethered by his care for her into an aching gentleness. His body shook with the effort of restraint, yet he waited, coiled and controlled, for her to satisfy her need to know each rise and hollow of his chest, his ribs and taut belly where the springy curls of hair tapered and trailed irresistibly beneath the band of his trousers. Her fingertips paused there and his breath suspended, sucking his middle inward to create a tempting gap between the enticing trickle of hair and guarding fabric should she choose to continue. Nervously, she

103

moved her hand back to safer terrain near his shoulder and his lungs expelled in a heavy mixture of relief and regret.

Aurora's chin lifted and Ethan responded to that wordless invitation. His mouth sought the beckoning pleasures of her lips, tasting with the scrub of his tongue across them, tempting with little nibbles along their pouted fullness and finally taking deeply, possessively, from their willing part. From that exacting plunder, his kisses moved with a maddening leisure along the gentle slope of her cheeks, to the frantic pulse-point on her arched neck. Her fingers clenched in the curls of his unevenly cut auburn hair, twining, twisting, a mimicry of the sensations he woke within her.

He'd undone her coarse wool shirt and pushed it away. Exposure brought a sudden chill, puckering her coral-tipped breasts into tight, firm buds. Far Winds had touched them once, not in passion but in curiosity of their milky whiteness. It had been nothing like the way Ethan's rough palms skimmed up from her jerking ribcage to slowly fill to overflowing. His thumbs moved in lazy, arousing arcs, encouraging an expectant stiffening in each taut peak. The teasing stimulation sent shocks of icy hot tingles coursing through her until they had her whole body trembling in breathless anticipation.

"Ethan," she whimpered, pleading for relief from his exquisite torture and, at the same time, begging him to continue. She gave a ragged moan as his head lowered, his beard rasping over delicate and deliciously sensitive skin, to where his big hands surrounded their tender prey. He nuzzled between the warm, swollen mounds while her fingers spread wide and clutched to hold him closer. Susceptible flesh sizzled beneath the trailing tongues of fire spiralling upward toward one throbbing tip. She gasped at the first taunting flicker then sighed when it became a hot laving. An answering heat pulsed below her belly, beating hard with longing, crying out for his attention. Her legs shifted restlessly. Her hips rubbed against the mighty evidence of his desire, begging him to tend the fires he'd stoked and let blaze out of control.

He tugged at one turgid nipple, mouth hungry for the taste of her, then drew back in surprise. Moaning in protest that he should stop while passion yet pounded unrelieved, Aurora forced her eyes to open and stared up at him in dazed inquiry. His eyes gleamed dark and hot, contrasting with the sudden flash of his white grin.

"I'd best be careful or I'll end up stealing Scotty's breakfast."

The husky sensuality in his drawling tone heightened the power and awareness of her femininity. His look intoxicated her. His eyes, nearly black with desire, caressed her, and his smile faded. She could feel herself melting from the searing heat of his expression as it intensified into sharp angles of male longing. A shiver shook through her, prompting her to reply with the same suggestive humor, "I have a spare, Ethan, if you haven't noticed."

His big hands squeezed lightly. "Oh, I most certainly have."

Then, he came up to capture her softly smiling lips, finding that enticing curve too provoking to ignore. She gave herself fully to that kiss, meeting his tongue half way and engaging it in a sensuous duel. His hand slipped lower, down across her fluttering middle to where his oversized shirt grazed her thighs. Aurora shifted her hips, making it easier for him to seek out that which she longed for him to find. And as his fingertips stroked up to claim her, she uttered a rapturous cry against his lips. And similarly, across the room, Scotty began to wail.

"Damn," Ethan murmured upon her eager mouth. His hands ceased their exquisite fondling and he sat back. Aurora could only stare up at him, apology and unanswered need glazing her golden eyes. "I'll fetch him."

She watched him cross the room. There was little else she could do with her senses spinning and her limbs as wobbly as a drunk after a bout with the bottle. So she watched, vowing to etch everything about Ethan Prescott upon her wildly churning heart. He'd left his shirt in a tangle next to her. In the firelight, his every movement brought a series of muscle into play, rippling beneath his bared skin like eddies across bronze satin. The evidence of his strength was delineated in the swells and ebbs of his arms as he reached down into the cradle.

For a moment he stood there before the hearth with Scotty wiggling expectantly against his chest. He smiled down at the infant, heroically showing no aggravation at his untimely interruption. The baby looked so small, so soft and helpless where he lay along the length of one brawny forearm. That contrasting of a man's virile power and a child's vulnerable sweetness lodged a poignant lump of emotion within Aurora's breast. Never had she beheld any sight quite so stirring or so beautiful as Ethan Prescott cooing over her son. Moved to the point of tears as that tenderness swelled inside, she blinked quickly lest he see how affected she was when he brought Scotty to her side.

And as Scotty suckled noisily and Ethan busied himself at the fire, Aurora wondered in a daze of devastation how she was ever going to leave.

Chapter Seven

How was he ever going to let her go?

There was no end to the torment of that question. By the time Scotty took his fill and they sat down silently to the breakfast he'd prepared, silvery threads of daylight spread out along the floor in a damning reminder of his promise to set her free.

Logically, Ethan could consider every angle and agree there was no other way. But those answers didn't satisfy a heart torn asunder. It was as impossible for her to stay as for him to go. Their worlds and the unfair rules that guided them allowed for no middle ground where love and happiness might grow or flourish from the roots set down within his single room. Both would wither away in time. Until then, he would get used to the pain all over again.

He'd thought he would go mad after losing Olivia and the baby. A slow, seeping chill of grief had stolen his link to life, leaving him in a cold, lonely limbo. He'd been unable to think or feel, so instead he acted on some basic instinct that dragged him through the days. He moved through the hours like a sleepwalker, not wanting to wake to find everything gone. On that numb plane, he'd existed, a shell moving through the motions. He never thought to question why he continued with a life that had no meaning. Out of habit, he supposed, and through the propelling force of a regimented background where a breath could be drawn only if it was carefully scheduled. He was slowly, silently suffocating in Texas.

If his days passed in an empty blur, there was nothing peaceful about his nights. He awoke drowning in his own sweat, strangling on his ragged cries, head filled with the thunder of cannon fire and the creak of a fine Manila rope that was somehow the louder of the two. It was then he began to fear he was going quietly crazy. Finally, the somnolent spell was broken and he got the hell out of Texas before he ended up as insane as his poor departed wife.

The Dakota Territory was a land of shining gold, as vast as his beloved home state, with a touch of wildness that let his spirit soar unfettered. There the sun shone golden nearly every single day of every season, bright and clear in the freshness of spring, baking the soul in July, melting into the warmth of Indian summer and sparkling off the January snows. It glazed the tops of the hills like honey and shimmered on the surface of its waters. At night, an endless tapestry of stars vied with the dazzle of the northern lights as they flashed a cold green-gold across the sky. There was gold in the plant life; a profusion blooming softly in the early crocus, dancing boldly in the waving sunflowers, delicately decorating the cacti. Gold shimmered on the wings of its soaring eagles and thrummed at the throat of the meadowlark. All its wildlife took on those tints of bronze; the coyote, the antelope, the deer, the prairie dog, even the rattlesnake. The nourishing corn, wheat, oats and barley crops became a golden stubble along the landscape after harvest time. Prairie grasses continued that color, waving tall on the east river hillsides and curing golden on its short western stems. And it was the golden dreams of greed that filled its hills with miners tending dented pans and rocking sluices and caused town to spring up overnight with its tough inhabitants. And now, the most precious gold of all reflected in the gaze of the woman he loved and was about to lose.

Love was the last thing he'd been looking for when he settled in the Black Hills. He'd come in search of inner peace and settled for plain hard work. Those long, back-breaking months it took to erect his home and outbuildings, to lay fences, to cultivate the land, to purchase stock in Spearfish Valley and goods in Deadwood left no time for sleepless nights. It was toil from dawn to dusk then drop, exhausted into a dreamless slumber. In a way, that merciless drive to create his Lone Star Ranch restored his soul. As he watched his cattle grazing, he could almost dare to dream, until the past returned to haunt him.

And then this second dream was snatched away as cruelly and unfairly as the first.

After that, there was no self-pitying languor, no time to mope and bemoan his loss. He began to carve out a new world for himself, a world in which he would live alone, where no one could intrude upon the small, bitter dregs of dreams he allowed himself to keep. Happiness wasn't one of them, nor was love, yet when his mysterious flame-haired guest had fallen asleep at his hearth with his knife clenched in the folds of his baggy shirt, he suspected she might bring him both. And it scared the hell out of him. For he knew it would end just as it was now ending; him with nothing but broken dreams.

Aurora looked up in wonder as Ethan swore fiercely under his breath and muttered something that sounded like, "Damn that horse for stumbling." He shoved away from the table with an angry scrape of chair-legs, frowning as he gulped the last of coffee that was so weak it had the consistency of pale tea.

"We're losing daylight," he growled, smacking the empty tin back onto the table.

Aurora was perplexed by his surly humor. She wanted their last moments together to be . . . beautiful. Since Scotty's cries had pulled Ethan from her arms, he'd been increasingly moody and distant, making no attempt at conversation and no overtures to support the intimacies shared a scant hour ago. Now, he seemed anxious to be rid of her and her son, to wash his hands of the burden they'd forced upon him. Or was he angry because he'd have no chance to finish what they'd started upon the creaking rope bed?

Well, she was angry too, angry at the circumstances and disappointed that such a splendid beginning would have no glorious end. She felt as though she'd been coaxed up to an incredible height on faith alone and then left to dangle at a precipice, breathless and unsure. How she'd wanted Ethan to carry her over that edge, how she'd needed his tender passion to restore her joy of life! For so long she'd lived in the shadow of her fears, not daring to express them, having no choice but to submerge all that hinted at hope and happiness. His kisses had renewed her spirit as his care had her strength. And now it seemed he was eager to withdraw both and get on with his solitary existence.

Somberly, Aurora gathered up the dishes and carried them to the washbasin. When she picked up a rag, Ethan spoke out sharply.

"Don't bother with that. I'll do them later." He'd need something to do when he returned to the dismal emptiness of this room.

But Aurora saw only his haste in hurrying them on

their way. God forbid that she should force him to suffer an extra minute of her company. She jerked the privacy curtain closed. It bobbed on the line for a goodly while, in evidence of her pique, as she pulled on a pair of faded long johns, her moccasins, and the heavy shirt Ethan had once been so anxious to take off her. Finally, she brought her ruined society dress out from under the bed where he'd stored it, and she rolled it carefully into an easily totable size. That was all she owned, save Scotty. She was leaving nothing behind, no sign she'd ever been a disturbance upon the cold still waters of his life. And that knowledge hurt, for she was taking with her memories more precious than any memento.

She drew the blanket back slowly, chagrined by her earlier loss of temper. Ethan Prescott had done not the slightest thing to incur her wrath. Instead, he'd given a wealth of new feelings on which she could exist forever if she had to. No, she couldn't fault him. He hadn't asked for a pregnant, runaway, white squaw to shatter the sameness of his days or for the wails of a newborn to interrupt his nights. He didn't deserve the danger she was bringing to his very door. he'd done nothing but care for her and treat her with the respect due a lady. It wasn't his fault she'd tumbled in love with him. Nor could she expect him to act upon her feelings. She'd wanted to believe he cared because she needed to. Perhaps all those small gestures showing affection were merely her interpretations of the truth. Perhaps he was, after all, just a kind man who'd allowed them to overstay their welcome. Perhaps it had been the lust of an isolated trapper and a trace of nostalgia she'd seen coloring his expression. He'd come after her because he couldn't bear the thought of their violent deaths upon his conscience. And now, he was willing to let her go—to *take* her, even, when she wished he would come up with some way for her to stay. She couldn't—wouldn't—beg him to come down from the hills to be with her. No. She had her pride and she had Scotty. And she had the most wonderful memories. It would have to do. She was used to making the most of what little she was allowed. She couldn't blame him for not wanting them to stay in his life.

Then she was treated to the sight of Ethan preparing Scotty for the long, cold journey, and she knew how foolish all her summations had been. He cared. Oh, how deeply he cared. Large hands carefully swaddled the baby in expensive pelts. Gently, he caught one tiny fist as it waved contentedly in the air and placing a quick kiss upon it before tucking it inside the warm wrap of furs. Dark eyes brimmed in a face screwed tight so as not to lose his tenuous control of his emotions. That sorrowful gaze betrayed everything he tried to hide behind brusque words and deceiving scowls.

"Ethan?"

His head jerked around and he glowered to cover any vestiges of a vulnerable heart. Aurora saw right through him. So this was how he hid away pain and loneliness. That *I don't need anyone* glare would never fool her again. If she asked would he say the shininess in his eyes was caused by smoke from the fire? Probably, so she didn't ask. She didn't have to. He was as miserable inside as she was.

"He's all ready," came Ethan's rough report as he stood, towering above Aurora like one of the forest's majestic pines. He passed the baby into her hands, releasing him after the slightest hesitation. Then, he turned to snatch up his coat and his rifle. "We best get started."

When he received no response, he looked back, and

112

that was the image he would hold in his heart: of her standing before his hearth with Scotty in her arms. Wisps of fiery hair, having escaped the strict confines of her braid, flirted along cheeks that appeared wan and pinched. Lips that he'd enjoyed the hell out of kissing seemed ripe for more. Her eyes, golden Dakota eyes, demanded the very heart from him with one eloquent gaze. She didn't speak—thank God for that—nor did she reach out to him. Had she done either, he would have been lost to his convictions. Lord, he was going to miss her. How purposeless his routine would seem without them to add joy and distraction. How long the nights would be without the hope of somehow realizing the dusky daydreams he spun from his fireside bed. Mightn't the risk be worth it just to have the two of them where he could look up and see them, where he could reach out and touch them?

Aurora wanted to go. She had something waiting in the valley below, and, with a slight start, he realized he didn't know what that was. Could it be she had a husband waiting to enfold her back into his arms? A curl of cold, unreasoning jealousy tightened in his belly. Whom had she been coming home to? She had another life out there and none of it included him. In fact, he knew nothing of her beyond her amusing anecdotes of the East and the tribute of her bravery among the Sioux. Who was his flame-haired Aurora who'd come to him with a stylish gown and no last name?

"Ora, where is it I'll be taking you?"

"My father has a ranch in the valley."

Was his relief too obvious? Father not husband. But his sense of well-being was of short life.

"Perhaps you've heard of him. Garth Kincaid."

A blackness like death descended over Ethan Prescott's mind and that abysmal darkness was shot through with scarlet tongues of rage. Garth Kincaid! His daughter! The irony was too bitter to be believed.

"Ethan?"

Something terrible worked in his expression. Aurora watched in alarm as all traces of softness fled. For a moment, he looked at her through eyes so hard only hatred could whet that cutting sheen. Then the brilliance dulled, first into pain, then into a carefully crafted indifference.

"I'll see you as close as I can. I'm swinging down to do some trading for my furs and Kincaid's spread's out of my way a considerable mite. I'm almost out of supplies. It's a long ride and I want to be settled in by dark with whatever entertainments they offer."

The words were unnecessarily cruel, and Aurora received them like the ruthless back of his hand. She stood stunned for a long moment, white and motionless, until pride goaded her temper. In a tone as crisp as a blue norther, she replied, "Don't go out of your way for us. We'll manage just fine. Set us down where ever its convenient."

As he slogged out to the lean-to to saddle up his horse, Ethan felt like the lowest kind of varmit. There'd been no excuse for snapping at her the way he had, no reason execept the awful gnaw of truth upon his vitals. He'd seen her face blanch with hurt, yet he couldn't stop the lash of brutal fury that took hold of his words. He'd wounded her intentionally because she belonged to that bastard Kincaid. And he couldn't forgive her for being the spawn of Kincaid's loins and holder of his own heart.

He cursed low and frequently as he adjusted the straps and buckles of his worn tack, causing the sorrel to snort in surprise and displeasure when he gave the girth a vigorous jerk about its belly. As he assembled the makings of a travois on which to carry his pelts, his mind spewed out a slew of incoherent thoughts, all corrupted by what he saw as Aurora Kincaid's betrayal. She'd lied to him, or rather let him believe in a lie, by not telling him who she was. She'd allowed him to fall under the spell of a red-haired siren wreathed in intrigue and sensual promise. She'd lured him into thinking crazy things about a future, a family, things he knew he would never, ever have. Damn her! And worst of all, with a treachery so low it made him sick to consider it, she'd let him fall in love with the daughter and grandson of his eternal enemy.

She was waiting outside the door of the cabin with Scotty strapped to her back. Good. He didn't want to suffer the sight of her at his hearth, not after knowing the truth. He freed a stirrup and put down a gloved hand to assist her up behind him. Wordlessly, she settled in close with her long red-flannel-clad legs straddling the outside of his thighs and her arms seeking purchase about his middle.

The way she'd have wrapped herself around him while they made love.

"Hah," he called out sharply and the big sorrel leapt forward. Smaller hands clutched dearly at his coat as he felt her bump hard against his back. Quickly, she adjusted her seat to suit the harsh gait. He wished it was that easy to rearrange his emotions to cushion against the inward shocks of hurt and sorrow. Damn Kincaid for finding one more thing to strip from him.

The ride was rough and prohibited conversation. Aurora determined the big Texan intended to see that it would. He was rigid as fence post in front of her. Whatever demon chewed inside him at the mention of her father's name was still cutting away in a silent, ravenous frenzy. She'd no idea what had sparked so

115

bitterly between the two men, only that she was being burnt by it unfairly. Had she been brave enough to loose one arm and still retain her seat as the horse plunged through the remaining snows, she would have cuffed him sharply upon the head. How dare he look at her through such blameful eyes, with such venom, when she was innocent of its cause. How dare he spend their last hours together in a surly temper, refusing her the courtesy of even the meagerest explanation. Did he believe the sins of the father trickled down? Garth Kincaid was not the sort of man to encourage that degree of contempt and loathing in any other individual. In fact, Garth Kincaid was just about the best man she knew, holding an honored spot in her heart right next to the man who so obviously hated him. If only Ethan would talk to her, then perhaps she could understand the reason for his fierce withdrawal. But how could they talk here, on the jouncing back of a cantering horse, with a cradleboard slapping rhythmically against her spine and her breasts thrown into the unyielding starch of his back at every stride to drive the air from her lungs? Obviously, this was not the place. And she feared there was never going to be a right time.

How could she dismount and let him ride away, carrying with him whatever anger so contorted his soul? Shouldn't she have the chance to defend herself against whatever charge he'd leveled at her with that silent, damning stare?

As if Scotty agreed that his mother be allowed that opportunity, he set up a loud bawling beneath the muffling of furs. It was a forlorn wail that even Ethan could not harden his heart against. The big sorrel was reined in.

"What's wrong with him?" Ethan called back over his shoulder. The curt tone failed to cover his concern.

116

"Most likely he objects to having his insides beaten about like sourdough biscuit batter," she returned tartly. "I suspect the ride has knocked the better part of his breakfast out of him and he's in need of changing."

Trying not to sound chagrined, yet feeling guilty for not considering the baby's delicate constitution before pushing his mount in vent of his anger, Ethan grumbled, "Take a few minutes then. We can't afford to dally here 'bouts." He was thinking of the Sioux sign they'd passed some miles back.

He was thinking of his "entertainments," Aurora concluded sourly. She swung down from the high stallion without awaiting his assistance. Numbed legs nearly buckled beneath her weight, forcing her to cling to the readiest support or risk collapse. Her hand gripped the firm swell of Ethan's thigh. She could feel the muscles jump clean through the heavy denim covering as if she'd used the curved blade of his Green River knife to stab him there. Quickly, she released him, not unaware of the snap of sensual static that unplanned contact caused. While he dismounted, she wobbled with uncertain steps to the shelter of an outcropping of rock. Unfastening the fretful child, she settled there and began to tend to his complaints.

Entertainments. Her features pulled into a puckered frown. She was not so naive as not to know what was meant by that. Drink, cards and harlots. Those were the kind of amusements men sought from the crude camps where their kind gathered. The former two she could hardly begrudge him, but when she thought of Ethan Prescott in the bartered arms of some painted and practiced sister of sin something sharp jabbed through her. Something painful and possessing. The fact that he couldn't wait to spend his passions upon some indifferent whore cheapened the beauty of what they'd begun between them. Or was that soaring splendor imagined on her part? She was unskilled in the ways of love. She assumed it was emotion which heightened his searing caresses. Could it be sheer lust, instead? A lust which could be similarly slaked with any partner? Was that all she'd meant to him? A vessel in which to discharge his needs, to be casually replaced at his earliest convenience like a dirtied wash basin or chamber pot?

That comparison fomented her ire. Anger was better than hurt. Better she feel furious at him than devastatingly betrayed. The sweet memories she'd planned to cherish for a lifetime would be flushed from his system with the first available tart. She was so incensed she nearly skewered Scotty with the pin used to hold his diapering in place. Instead, it jabbed deep and viciously into her thumb. It was a less intense pain than the one piercing her heart but still she cried out. Tears which had gathered for some time leapt at the excuse to spring forth and cascaded hotly down her frozen cheeks.

Ethan watched her as he went through the motions of checking the travois. The efficient tenderness of her hands as she saw to her son's needs began a small crack in his frigid reserve. The longer he observed her from his uninvolved distance, the wider that fissure grew until the mounting pressure snapped with all the potent drama of a spring ice break along the river. Conflicting emotions crashed together, loosening the reserve that choked him, freeing his heart by flinging great slabs of doubts and anger high upon its banks. And when that wide channel opened, the flow was engulfing, swirling, forceful—as was his love for Aurora Kincaid and her tiny son.

"All right?"

Aurora started at the quiet inquiry spoken close enough for her to feel the warmth of it upon her damp cheek. She drew the injured digit from her mouth long enough to mumble crossly, "Just stuck myself is all." She sniffed and struck at the torrent of silly tears, afraid he would think she was trying to play on his sympathy. She didn't need or want his pity. He caught her flailing hand in his stiff glove-leather and turned it palm up to examine the oozing puncture. His expression was quiet, thoughtful. The earlier fury still toyed with the angles of his face but his eyes were pensive, dark, and deep.

"I wish things was different, Ora."

That low rumble gave her a sudden shock of hope. "What things?"

"Things that have nothing to do with you. Things that can't be changed." His thumb was rubbing the center of her palm in distracted circles. She seized it, holding tight.

"What things?" she repeated more strongly. When he was stonily silent, she prodded, "Something to do with my father?"

His jaw ground audibly. "Everything to do with your father," he gritted out.

Before she could question him further, he leaned over her to run a finger down Scotty's round little cheek. "You take care of this fella, you hear." That was scarcely a whisper.

Touched by his sadness and provoked by her own unwillingness to say good-bye, Aurora offered, "I could bring him up for visits."

Ethan straightened so quickly she didn't need to hear his answer to feel its rebuff. "Better you forget where you've been, Ora. I'd as soon be left to myself. I'd appreciate it if you'd not be leading anybody to my door."

"Why?" The warning in his words made her wonder. It made her recall the way he'd revealed his name; warily, as if he'd expected a response. Was his isolation more forced than preference?

"Ask your daddy. I'm sure he'll have plenty to say on the subject."

Things she didn't want to hear. She could tell that by looking at the tense set of his mouth and the hard glare in his eyes. His stare challenged her to believe what she would without any coaching from him. Gazing up at him where he towered with the trees, Aurora knew that no matter what her father would tell her her loyalties couldn't be swayed from what she owed this man. And in her heart she knew that no matter what he'd done, it wasn't something she could not forgive.

"I won't let on where to find you," she promised solemnly.

The toughness eased in his expression. His fingertips stroked along the heavy sag of her shoulder. "I'll pack Scotty the rest of the way."

She wouldn't tell him the slump had nothing to do with the wear of the cradleboard. Rather, it was the weight of her misery settling hard upon her.

Ethan adjusted the ties to secure the baby's carrier to his back and swung up onto his big horse. Aurora was then lifted up and settled sidesaddle in front of him. The brace of one arm brought his heavy coat about her shoulders, encouraging her to seek warmth and comfort against his broad chest. There she found both, laced with an exquisite torment of desire.

The horse's pace wasn't fast now but its path was erratic. Aurora was not so easily fooled that she couldn't guess the reason. Ethan was leading her on a wandering path down from the hills, purposefully winding so she might lose all direction. So she

120

wouldn't be able to find her way back. Contrarily, she studied every dip and draw, impressing it upon her sharp mind. Ethan Prescott wouldn't be rid of her so easily. And she knew, snuggling close to the heat of his body, that she would never be rid of him. Or want to be. She would have her son know the man who'd brought him into the world. And she was fully determined that the big Texan continue her lesson in love to its proper conclusion. The uncertainty pricking her was quite simply melted against the hot brazier of his hard form. The steady pulse of his heart battered down all barriers of doubt. Aurora Kincaid was a woman of incredible patience and focus. She'd learned that beneath Uncheedah switch each day, as she looked for a means of escape while pretending submission. Once she's set herself upon a goal, like a dog with a juicy bone, she wasn't easily persuaded to let go.

Like her father.

As soon as she and Scotty had settled in below, she meant to launch her campaign on Ethan Prescott's secrets. And then, she would return to him in the woods or find a way to coax him down from the hills. He would be a part of her life, one way or the other, because she loved him too much to say good-bye.

The sun was high overhead, sending down a welcoming heat to warm their faces. It began a steady drip that would increase to a trickle, then grow to a steady, thawing flow. Soon the prairie grasses would send forth new shoots to probe upward through the remaining snow. The frozen ground would relax into spongy turf. The valley below would be abloom with signs of life renewed, but for now it was still blanketed thinly beneath a pristine white. A plume of smoke rose from the two-story frame house set in the midst of prosperous outbuildings. Looking down upon it,

Aurora felt a swell of pride. And behind her, Ethan knew a cold stiffening.

"This is as far as I can take you."

"It'll be fine. It's not far to walk." Suddenly the anticipation of what lay below was tempered by what she would leave above, and Aurora was torn with dreadful indecision. Her fingers clutched Ethan's heavy coat, as if she had the power to hold to him forever. That was, of course, impossible. "Thank you for seeing me safely almost to the door." She tried to smile and failed miserably.

"I wish I could, Ora. I wish I could." His fingers stroked along the side of her face, tipping it up so he could absorb the sight of her beauty all golden in the late March sunshine. His arms had tightened about her slender figure, as reluctant as she to part.

"Ethan—"

He didn't know if she meant to begin a question or a plea, but he couldn't bear to hear either. His mouth came down upon hers, sealing her lips into a blissful silence.

She kissed him back, fiercely, holding to her tears, holding to her promise that this would not be goodbye. This was only a brief farewell and that was nothing to cry about. They had their separate ways to go, but those trails would lead back together and she countersigned that intent with all the passion throbbing through her yearning form. She would know his kiss again. She would experience the thrill of his touch. They would come together to consummate all the longings begging to burst forth like the splendor of spring. And it was just as inevitable.

"Thank you, Ethan," she whispered against the soft bristle of his cheek, letting those three simple words take on the rich meaning of everything flowing from her heart to his. *I love you, Ethan,* was what she meant, *and I have no intention of letting you go.*

Ignorant of her silent vow and thinking that perhaps he would never see his flame-haired beauty again, Ethan crushed her close to the hard thunder of his chest, willing her not to forget him, wishing he could carry her boldly right up to Kincaid's door. Living without Aurora and Scott would be like losing an arm and leg; even after they were severed, the ache of their being there would linger.

Brusquely but with the utmost care, he dropped her down from the saddle; then, with greater reluctance yet, he shrugged out of the precious pack, and passed it into her uplifted arms.

And because he couldn't frame the words to express the agony branding through him, Ethan wheeled his horse about and headed east, away from the sight of her and her child standing ankle-deep in the snow. Away and out of her life for good, he thought.

But he hadn't reckoned with the Kincaid determination.

Chapter Eight

A low snuffling wail from Scotty forced Aurora to turn her attention from the trees into which Ethan Prescott had disappeared. She took a deep, uneven breath to push back her own desire to wail, and she regarded the fussing child with a resolute smile.

"We'll see him again, Scotty," she assured the babe, and at the same time, herself. "I know we will." As if he understood and was comforted by the certainty in her voice, the baby quieted.

Looking upward into the hills, Aurora found some of the heaviness gone from her heart. Yes, they would see Ethan Prescott again. Count on it. Exhaling a bracing sigh, she maneuvered the cradleboard onto her back.

"Come on now, *cinksi*. Time for you to meet your grandfather."

The awareness of what she'd called her child, the Sioux name for "son," struck her with a sudden and mighty significance. In the months she'd carried him and during the time they'd spent with Ethan, Scotty was simply her child, loved and accepted for his sweet innocence and precocious nature. When she came down out of the hills, he would become something else, an *iyeska*, mixed blood. She'd come to take for granted Ethan's indifference to the child's heritage, not realizing how truly special such an open attitude was in this day, when the massacre of the Seventh Cavalry was still remarked-on in fear and fury. Aurora was convinced that her deep, maternal love for her son could ward off most of life's cruelties, at least during his early years. For no other opinion mattered or would be counted. None but that held by the man in the ranch house below.

In all the emotional upheaval over her parting with Ethan, Aurora had scant time to consider her first meeting with her father. Now, as she trudged down the slope, she was beset by a nervous quaking of doubt. What a surprise she was bringing to Garth Kincaid's door: a daughter he'd thought dead and a half- cast grandson as well. How was she going to fit into the life he'd carved within this lush Dakota valley? She wasn't the same dewy-eyed girl coming home from the East in her fancy silk dress. So much had changed since then. Too much? she wondered anxiously.

As she walked down the gently rolling hillside, Aurora had ample opportunity to take in the panorama below. The Bar K, her father's dream. She'd been there only once, having come home for the holidays to beg him to let her stay. Life there was too rough, he'd told her. Then, it had been little more than a frontier soddy and a few earthen outbuildings, with land, miles and miles of lush, cow-growing, rancher's dream land. And he'd shipped her back East at the end of her vacation in spite of her tears. In the last treasured letter she'd received from him just before leaving Boston, he'd boasted in his matter-of-fact way of wintering 8,000 head of Texas cattle trailed up from Ogallala, Nebraska, a work force of 35 men and a ramuda of 200 horses, and she'd nearly burst with pride for him and his accomplishment. It was then, she knew, the time was right for her to come home. She'd wired him of her arrival and had boarded a train on the same day, before he had the opportunity to order her not to come—as if he could, once her mind was made up.

From as early as she could remember, Garth Kincaid had dreamed of cattle. He'd been a freighter in Minnesota. He'd seen western cattle-raisers grow rich buying up the fractious longhorns in Texas at $4 a head, then selling them in Minnesota for $40. With his eyes on the fertile land west toward the Missouri, only his deep devotion for his wife, Julia kept him from pulling up stakes. Her frail health kept them tied to city life. Her doctors concurred that so great a move would be the death of the delicate Julia Kincaid. Garth locked away his dream but continued to feed his bank account. Just in case.

Then, while Aurora was little more than a child, tragedy rocked the Kincaid family. In '62, Julia and her sister took a coach ride to a neighboring settlement to visit their ailing aunt. They never returned. Starving Santee Sioux went on a bloody rampage, killing some three hundred and sixty settlers. The thirty-eight Indian ringleaders were hanged in a mass execution in Mankato. Garth Kincaid had attended to see those who murdered his wife pay for snatching the light from his life. It hadn't been enough for him. Pursuing the Santee who fled into the Dakota Territory to join Sioux relatives, and to place each one of them personally in hell—that might have been enough, had it been possible, but his responsibility to his three remaining children checked his lust for vengeance.

On the heels of their mourning came a telegram.

126

Twenty-year-old Jed Kincaid, who'd rushed to enlist and fight the damned slave-mongers of the South, had been killed. His company had been wiped out to a man at some obscure creek in Virginia. Eight months later came word that red-headed Sergeant Seth Kincaid had been wounded in a battle at Chancellorsville. His destination was a death knell—the Southern prison, Andersonville. He never returned.

And so it was just Garth and his young daughter, Aurora. And nothing to keep them from heading west. Selling everything not essential to survival except for the one hundred-piece set of Haviland china and the parlor organ that had been her mother's favorite belongings, the two of them, father and daughter, joined in the land-seekers pouring into the rich bottomlands along the Missouri. The roads were lined with immigrant teams. The green hills were covered with droves of cattle. And on every gurgling brookside, in every cottonwood grove, rose smoke from a new claim-cabin.

After paying his $18.00 filing fee, Garth Kincaid plotted out his one hundred and sixty acres west of Yankton, granted free under the Homestead Act of '62, and turned his cows loose to graze on the natural hay of the prairies, the bluestem and buffalo grass. For an expenditure of $2.80, a sod house went up, and it was there Aurora grew into young womanhood, helping to break the required acres to plant and tending cattle with the skill of a slender cowboy. She never complained about the lack of female companionship or guidance as she strode about in her Levi Strauss's. Garth called their effort a partnership and made a big show of letting Aurora have a voice in all decisions. Consequently, she felt betrayed when he called her in off the range with the announcement that she was going East to his family to acquire polish and schooling.

It was no greater surprise then his own had been when he'd looked out the door to watch her cut out a calf and had seen the ranch hands studying the snug stretch of her shirt over her budding breasts. His daughter was a young woman, and he wanted to do what was best for her, the way Julia would have wished, regardless of whether it was what Aurora wished for herself. He was prepared to pay the price of loneliness to see to that obligation. And he wasn't idle in her absence.

While she was in Boston learning to pour tea and share the spread of civilized gossip, Garth outgrew his one hundred and sixty acres the same way she'd outgrown the right to ride and play in britches. Hemmed in on all four sides by fellow homesteaders, he began to look, again, to the west, as the Black Hills were opened between the forks of the Belle Fourche and Cheyenne Rivers, south of Cheyenne to Fall River and a strip along the North Dakota line. Everything else was still Indian land. It was the last great natural pasture of the high plains, and Kincaid wanted his piece of it; a cattleman's paradise, which included some of the finest grazing land on earth and came with built-in markets, from miners to the military and Indian annuities. Between the Centennial prairie and Spearfish Valley he put down roots as deep as the native grasses, and like them began to spread.

Though she'd absorbed the polite amenities with a natural aptitude, Aurora's dream was to return to her father's side, to resume her share of the partnership and to stand him proud. She thrived on his sparse accounts of progress, filling in the spaces between the lines with vivid images of what the Bar K must look like. And once she'd seen it, she couldn't wait to sink her roots there as well. She could no longer be a wrangler, but she could serve as his hostess and in that way contribute to the future of the Bar K. With the encroachment of the railroad and the growth of boom towns, they wouldn't be isolated for long. Already Deadwood boasted gaslight and as fine a theater entertainment as one could find in the east playing at the Gem and the Bella Union, even though the audience settled for boxes made of rough log and seats made from wooden slabs laid atop stakes. Progress followed prosperity, and with it would come the need for the skills Aurora learned in the east. Until then, she was looking forward to a pair of britches and a good Manila rope in her hands.

And now, after being routed from those dreams for nearly a year, she found them again within her reach, and they had lost none of their appeal. Her weary steps quickened, carrying her toward home. Though her chest ached with fatigue, joy leapt in hurried beats. Home!

One of the cowhands tending stock at the corral paused to take in the odd figure approaching afoot, clad in what appeared to be — red long johns? He shaded his eyes with the brim of his Stetson. Would you get a look at that red hair! He hadn't seen hair of that peculiar shade since . . . With a pang of sadness, he remembered the slip of a girl who'd outridden the best of them in Yankton. Hell, they'd all been half in love with her. But it couldn't be. . . .

"Why Johnny Taylor, if you're not a sight for these sore eyes."

He stared like a poleaxed steer, eyes going glazed and round, jaw dropping before the pull of gravity. No . . .

"Well, what are you looking at? Not like you've never seen my legs before."

"Orrie?" By God, it sure as hell sounded like her. "I'll be damned!"

"I'll see to it personal if you don't quit scraping snow with your chin and get up to the house to tell the Major I'm home."

Johnny Taylor backed slowly, unwilling to avert his bugged eyes lest the vision desert him. He didn't want to be the one to rake up the coals of Garth Kincaid's grief over some snow-blind specter. He respected the old man's pain too much for that. Not to mention his job and his very hide.

"I swear, Johnny, you haven't got one lick quicker since Yankton. Get the lead outta your boots."

He jumped as if she'd touched an iron to him and fled toward the house, screaming as he did, "Major! Major, come quick!"

Aurora had intentionally sent another to announce her arrival. She hadn't wanted to just appear at the table and assume her place as if she'd never been gone. This way, he'd have time to compose himself before confronting the child he'd thought dead and crudely buried, without her glorious red hair, at the site of a stage coach massacre. And she would have another moment to steady her own erratic emotions. As cold and wet and weary as she was, she didn't go into the house. Not until invited. Instead, she stood at the porch steps, anxiously watching the door, waiting for it to fill with a familiar frame.

The commotion reached her even where she waited. The sound of her father's deep voice bawling through the halls quickened a tightness around her heart. No sweet symphony could move to tears with greater ease. Dear God, it was him. How many times had she heard that beloved bellow shake the eaves? But never had it sounded so wonderful.

The door flew open, banging against the wall with the strength to start a slide of snow down the porch roof. It filtered in a glittering diamond-bright curtain

130

between them, momentarily obscuring the features each longed to see.

"Orrie?"

"Yes, Major." She'd always called him by that endearment, that rank he'd proudly earned fighting in Mexico. Spoken in a quavering voice, it was no less reverent than "daddy" or "poppa" or "my dear father." And if that choice of title had not convinced him, she concluded frailly, "It's me. I'm finally home."

With a roar only slightly softer than that of a charging buffalo, Garth Kincaid lurched down the steps. He drew up when they stood face to exuberant face then gently reached out to grasp each forearm in his huge gnarled hands. The gaze that devoured each remembered line of her countenance was unashamedly damp. His booming voice was hushed.

"God in his heaven, I never thought to see you again, girl." Her shivering and flushed features impressed him then, for he was quick to shout, "Well, let's not stand out here with icicles freezing on our faces. Come in, girl. Come in and get yourself warmed."

With one arm still firmly in his possession, as if he dare not let go for fear of losing her again, father led daughter up the steps into the house he'd expected to never share with another. Kincaid steered her into the formal parlor room; a somewhat odd use of space for an isolated ranch. It was a day's ride to their nearest neighbor. But, it was in this elegant room he sat each evening to imagine the lovely Julia at the keyboard of the organ, Seth and Jed arguing over a game of chess and a young Aurora pretending to stitch while her eyes were full of faraway dreams. Now, he would have at least one of those long ago ghosts, returned miraculously from the dead, to share his long prairie twilights. His big hands shook as they poured two glasses of hearty brandy.

Nothing had changed. Aurora realized that in some surprise as she peered about through the shimmer of her welcoming tears. The interior of this new log house was reconstructed right down to the velvet and lace at the windows and parlor organ as a replica of the Minnesota home where the five of them had lived so happily together. He'd pieced it together, she recognized with a bittersweet pain, so he might live among memories if not among his loved ones. A great ache thickened in her throat, and she swallowed it down resolutely. He had her now and she vowed to fill these shrinelike rooms with love and laughter. She and Scotty.

Time and repeated losses hadn't changed Garth Kincaid. He was still the big bear of a man she remembered as a child. Though he was not a tall man, his sheer bulk gave an impression of size. His shoulders looked like a miniature mountain range stretched beneath his broadcloth shirt. Fondly, Aurora was reminded of a shaggy buffalo with his great mane of dulled titian hair and thick neck set atop a deep, barrel chest. She knew he would be pleased by the comparison to that two thousand pounds of ill-tempered, bellowing, dim-sighted fury of the plains that could turn in an instant to disembowel horse and rider with a single toss of its foot-long horns. Only, where his daughter was concerned, Garth Kincaid was about as fierce as a domestic milk cow. He'd always spoiled her shamelessly, giving before her every whim. Except in the issue of schooling. Then, he'd been as stubborn as that disappearing beast of the prairie, and Aurora had been sorely tempered to see his great shaggy head mounted over the fireplace.

She was smiling when he turned, and she saw him

132

hesitate, struggling to control his emotions. Then, he shoved the glass toward her with a gruff, "You've got some explaining to do, young lady. Like how is it that you're standing here bold as brass with all your hair when you're supposed to be in some shallow grave? Explain that to me, missy."

"You sound disappointed." That coaxed a wavery smile and a stern snort. Taking the glass, she offered softly, because the pain was still so fresh for both of them, "I was taken off the stage by the Sioux unharmed."

"But the body of a woman was found murdered and—and scalped." His voice was raw with the remembered agony of that picture, of his beloved daughter stretched out stiff in her final death throes on some lonely road, her beautiful red hair cruelly peeled from her skull.

Her tone gentled to soothe that hurt. "A saloon girl boarded at the last minute. She must have bartered for the passage if there was no record. She was killed. They must have assumed she was me when they notified you."

"And so you've lived all this time among the savages?" Horror tinged his words, horror and a trace of disgust for a way of life he abhorred and a people he hated. His eyes made a quick scan of her oddly clad figure. "You look well enough, girl. You were not treated harshly?" He sounded disbelieving. He, like she, herself, had heard so many tales of white slaves forced to endure terrible ordeals at the hands of their red captors. And that was not all he'd heard and now feared. She could see the question building in his stare, too horrible to voice aloud. *Had she been raped by the savages?* Had they abused his darling daughter?

There was no easy way to tell him and no purpose

for delay. More frightened then she'd ever been of anything in her whole life, yet braced with a steely pride, Aurora shrugged out of the crude cradleboard. Scotty, who'd been soundly sleeping, awoke at the movement and began calling for dinner with impatient gurgles.

Garth Kincaid froze at the sound. He didn't need to look into the face of the babe Aurora uncovered to know what he would see. An Indian child. Conceived upon his innocent daughter by some lusting savage. Spawned by one of the red devils who butchered his wife. It was some sort of sick revenge. They had slain his beloved Julia, spoiled his precious girl and left him with a taunting reminder of their brutal misdeeds. No, he wouldn't look. He wouldn't not dishonor his sweet child by acknowledging her disgrace.

"I'll kill the bastard who did this to you!" he pledged through gritted teeth. "Or were there more than one?"

Aurora stiffened, hurt etched in her fine features. It must have been the shock. Why else would he be speaking to her so horridly. With a quiet dignity, she said, "The man who fathered Scotty is already dead."

Hardly placated, Kincaid moved back to the sidetable and poured himself a huge tumbler of brandy. He gulped it down like a man thirsting. His thoughts were reeling through a sluggish agony, as a drunk would stagger in search of solid purchase. Without turning, for he couldn't look upon her while she yet held that copper-skinned whelp in her arms, he spoke slowly, firmly.

"No one needs know of this. It's not too late to salvage your reputation. While you were in Boston, one of your beaux, a Judson Pierpont, petitioned me more than once for the right to pay you court. I said no, thinking you too young. We'll wire him, telling

134

him I've changed my mind. Your Aunt Bess can concoct a satisfactory story. You'll go to Boston and marry this Pierpont fellow. It's not what I would have chosen for you, nor you for yourself perhaps, but it's a way to escape the ruination of your name and future. You can live well without the stain of what has happened here. We won't ever speak of it again."

Aurora stood in disbelieving silence as her father spoke his cold calculations. Of course he meant only the best for her, but how could he think she'd jump into such a lie? Judson Pierpont? She retained an image of faded blue eyes and faded blue blood. Objectingly, the memory of Ethan Prescott's hot dark gaze and hot, virile blood pushed it away.

"I couldn't marry Judson," she said softly. "I don't love him."

Her father's voice was impatient. "And I'm sorry for that. I would have wanted you to have what your mother and I shared, but that is impossible now. I'll send the wire in the morning and—"

"No."

"Orrie, you must be practical about this. Who in these parts would wed a woman known to have lived amongst the Sioux?"

She flinched at that harsh truth. She couldn't dispute it. Having met her distant neighbors during her holiday visit, she knew their sentiments. They would shun her. Regardless of her innocence in the tragedy, they would fault her none the less.

But one man hadn't cast blame. The future wasn't without promise.

She clung to that just as she clung to the cradleboard. Scotty wiggled in the tight embrace, reminding her of the biggest objection to her father's scheme.

"And just how do I explain away a child to Mister Pierpont?"

Kincaid turned then, and for the first time he glanced briefly at the infant in her arms. He took in the shock of black hair and the swarthy skin. There was no way the child could be taken for anything other than what it was. A half-breed. His gaze was hard and angry. It cut through her heart like the slash of a knife. "One more red brat at the agency will never be noticed. Not with those savages breeding like mongrel dogs. I could arrange it immediately."

No!

Aurora's arms clenched about the baby. Within her breast, a terrible pain awakened. What in God's name was he suggesting?

"Red, black, purple or green, this child is your grandson!"

"I'll claim no heathen's bastard seed."

"I was married to Scotty's father," she told him quietly.

Garth Kincaid's features swelled like a red blister. "Do not blaspheme the Lord's sacraments in this house, girl. Such things are not recognized amongst the Godly, not when they're products of abduction and brutal rape. I'd think you'd want to tear that ugly reminder from your heart and mind."

The only ugliness was in what she was now hearing. Her stomach rolled with it. Sickness gathered in her throat. "He's a baby," she cried out. "He's not to blame for the circumstances of his conception."

And then he said it, the unforgivable thing that poisoned his mind.

"How could you."

Aurora blinked, sure she hadn't heard right.

"How could you lay with a savage and beget his brat?"

Blinded by her sudden tears, Aurora swayed and finally dared to ask, "Would you rather I had died?"

The words hung between them, awful words that ought never to have been conceived, let along spoken, and Garth Kincaid said nothing.

Aurora's heart broke.

With Scotty hugged protectively to her breast, she lifted her head in defiance of the numbing pain. "Well, I didn't die and what happened, happened. This is my child and no one is going to take him from me or make me ashamed that I bore him."

Silence.

Her father's look hadn't softened, nor, apparently, had his heart. She suffered his rejection without an outward sign, while inside she withered and wailed in torment. How could he turn from the flesh of his flesh? The blood of his blood? She could imagine no greater cruelty than the condemnation of his stare.

"I can see I have no home here," she choked out at last.

Unsure of where she would go or what she would do, Aurora began to turn. She couldn't endure another second of his unreasoning scorn.

"Orrie . . ."

It was a tentative offer, edged with the fear of her leaving, hardened by the circumstances. She paused.

"This is your home. I am your father and I love you. That hasn't and will never change."

She gave a soft sob but kept her back to him.

"Don't go. You're all I have."

Then, she did look around. Her chin quivered with the emotions shaking through her, but her golden eyes were steady and determined. "You have Scotty, too."

The fury settling over his face was frightening to behold. "That misbegotten babe is no kin of mine. He'll not have my name nor will he have my heart."

Her chin firmed and went up a stubborn notch. "Whether you choose to claim him or not, Scotty is

137

my son and I'll not be parted from him."

Aurora waited. Silence thickened. She stared up into the face which had never to this moment ever looked upon her with any emotion other than love. Even when he was his angriest at her in the past, that warmth had remained to temper his wrath. She'd always been able to use his fatherly affection to turn the tide in her favor. In the end, she'd always gotten what she wanted. Now she saw anger, disgust. Disappointment. And she wanted to writhe beneath that stern, dispassionate glare. She could see it all churning there in that beloved facade: his fury at the fates, his anticipation of their neighbor's scorn, the memory of her mother's murder, the image of a red man sowing his heathen seed within his daughter's pure white body.

Dear God, he was going to cast her out!

Numbing terror cinched inside her. With it, came an agonized longing for the relationship they'd once shared—and never would again . . . because of the child she held between them. If not for Scotty, he might have pushed the past away and taken her back into the fold of his devotion. But the baby's tiny form put a gulf—perhaps an impassable one—between what was and what would be.

Within this house, surrounded by tender mementos of the past, she wanted desperately to go back to those days when she was the pampered daughter of Garth Kincaid. Because of the harshness she'd suffered over the past months, more than ever she yearned for the simplicity of that life. She craved the security of her father's love, the protection of his name. She needed him to regard her proudly, with love. Their hearts ached to be filled with what the other could give.

But Scotty was between them.

The little figure squirmed against her, and Aurora

knew, with a sad certainty, that she could not go back. This was her future, this beautiful child placed so trustingly in her care by a God who seemed both benevolent and cruel. The price of returning to the past was too great. She would not allow her child to be taken from her arms and secreted away like some embarrassment.

The impulse to plead for her father's sympathy fled. Instead, Aurora stood firm, Scotty cradled in her arms with a defiant care. If Garth Kincaid wanted her to stay, he would have to accept her baby. She waiting, watching his rigid features, willing to abide by whatever they foretold.

It was an incredible struggle. Kincaid seethed with indecision. His precious daughter for a bastard child. *Think of the shame.* There would be no keeping this vile secret. His beautiful daughter would be ruined. She would never find a fine husband once the stain of her circumstances was known. Disgrace would settle over their house. *Breed-lover.* He could hear the taunts and recoiled inside. No one had reason to hate the Sioux as much as he did. Every time he was forced to acknowledge the child's existence, his wife's cherished memory would suffer. Yes. Yes, it would have been better had his daughter died. He admitted it to himself and was tortured by guilt and grief. Better she'd left him to his pristine memories.

But she was here. And she held a savage's baby in her arms. *Think of the loneliness.* Lord, these rooms echoed with it. He remembered her laughter, the musical peels of it delighting, lifting his spirits. He recalled how she had determinedly filled the void of three lost loved ones, easing his pain by suppressing her own. He remembered the slender tomboy clad in britches clinging to the back of a mustang, her exuberant joy like a second sun in the sky. Dear God, he could have that back again.

She had always been a stubborn little thing, digging in her heels like an ungrateful mule once her mind was set on something. This was no belligerent stand over the right to wear britches or to learn horse handling from their nighthawk. There was a strength of purpose in her golden stare, and by God if he didn't admire her for it, even though he detested its cause. His mild, sweet Julia would look that way when protecting her brood with a mother's fierceness.

There was no having one without the other. His jaw worked spasmodically.

He was going to let them stay.

She knew it the moment his eyes softened with remembering. She vowed he would never regret it. Somehow, she would help him to love the baby in her arms.

"This is your home, Aurora. If you must keep the child, keep it out of my sight."

With that, he stalked from the room.

It was not the homecoming she'd longed for. But she was home.

Chapter Nine

"Miss?"

Aurora turned at the quiet voice, a female voice, surprised until she remembered Ruth. She was her father's housekeeper, and Aurora had met her during the holiday visit. Women were scarce in the Territory. Most weren't fit to invite inside the house. But Ruth was a treasure. She was a silent shadow instinctively seeing to the needs of those in her care. Her manners were as refined as any Eastern lady's maid. She saw to an excellent meal and a tidy house. Just the thing for a rambling old widower. And she insisted upon respect from the men who worked the ranch. No hanky panky in the kitchen with the hired help. Ruth managed an off-limits attitude that yet exuded an approachable warmth. Aurora couldn't understand why such a gem would be willing to stay out in the desolate prairie without the whisper of female companionship, when she could have garnered a prime post in any larger settlement. Or why she hadn't married. That was the primary reason for the lack of female servants; as quick as they were settled into a position, they plumped with child and rushed to the altar. But Ruth didn't seem that frivolous sort. She appeared content with her life on the Bar K. At that time, the young woman had been impressed by the older's quiet efficiency in caring for her father's home. Now, after spending months among the Lakota people, she was struck by a new and startling insight.

Ruth was part Sioux.

She was a handsome woman. Her features were too broad to be considered beautiful, yet they were chiseled in a striking manner. Her hair was a rich sable color worn in the tidy plait down her back, and her eyes were of warm hazel. Had Aurora given it any degree of thought before, she would have assumed with her light bronze complexion, Ruth was Mexican. Now, she knew better.

Did her father know?

"Miss Aurora?"

The woman was waiting, her gaze impassive, and Aurora was staring pointedly. She gave herself a mental shake. "Hello, Ruth."

"I have readied your room if you would come with me please."

Aurora followed the housekeeper's gently rustling skirts up the flight of stairs. A soft floral scent drifted back, making her aware for the first time of how she must look in her men's long red underwear, Indian moccasins and bulky hide coat. She felt decidedly unattractive compared to Ruth's crisply feminine appearance. It had been a long time since she'd considered how she looked, or, for that matter, since she had cared. But now she was painfully conscious of her weather-chapped skin and work-worn hands. She looked more squaw than lady of this fine house, and that she meant to change as soon as possible.

It was the same room she'd used on her prior visit, occupied with furnishings from Yankton and her own personal belongings. Seeing them, those small private touches of the girl she'd been, brought a poignant ache to her soul. Could she be that pampered, carefree person again? Or had she lost that along with her virtue? There was no going back. That was a cruel truth of life. What frightened her now was the uncertainty of finding a place here among these familiar yet curiously detached surroundings. A place for her and Scotty.

"You will want to bathe and rest," Ruth was saying in an inflectionless tone as she parted the draperies at both windows so a weak March sun could filter through the foggy panes. "I will have water carried up. Will you be wanting something to eat? Supper's not for another four hours."

"If it's no trouble."

She remembered saying those words before and the curt rejoinder that followed. A sudden fullness crowded her chest when she thought of Ethan Prescott. And she felt a keening loneliness within the comforts of her own home. It wasn't supposed to be that way. Something was wrong. She felt a stranger among her own things. And all she could think of was how desperately she wished for that isolated cabin in the woods—and the strong arms which had come to mean security. Give it time, she cautioned. It would require some transition to move from one world to another. Now it felt as though she was hovering precariously between them.

Ruth withdrew soundlessly. Aurora put the cradleboard down atop the quilt her mother had handstitched in the evening lamp-glow long ago in Minnesota. It was made out of squares cut from her own childhood dresses. They had laughed and smiled together over the memories each patch held. The green taffeta was from her fifth Christmas. The cream-colored satin from a church social. She'd worn the beige moire to see Seth and Jed off on the train. It was the last time she'd ever seen them; they hadn't been able to return for their mothers' funeral. Her fingers lingered over the squares, her mind over the images. Each piece was representative of her past. Her mother had died only months after completing it, making it that much more valuable. The memories had faded with time, just like the once brilliant colors of the quilt, but they were bound together with unbreakable threads of love.

Scotty's fussing jarred her from her melancholy musings. With an apologetic smile, she lifted him from the bed of furs and swaddled him in his last clean square of cloth. As he gobbled hungrily at her breast, she made note of the things she would have to have to accommodate her new child. Diapering, clothes, a bed. She thought of the maple cradle, lovingly crafted for her son just as the quilt had been pieced together for her. She'd hated to leave it behind, and she made a vow to herself that soon she would fetch it from the hills — as good a reason as any to warrant a visit. Wistfully, her mind returned the picture of those big hands shaping the wood — stroking, rubbing, caressing — until it gleamed. And she found herself breathless, her eyes half closed, her flesh impatient with the memory of his touch.

"Soon," she whispered raggedly, gazing down at the downy dark head pressed into her bosom. "We'll see him again, soon."

Aurora was buttoning the rough shirt together when a soft knock sounded at the door. Ruth appeared with a tray, followed by a corps of cowboys toting a big metal tub and buckets of steaming water. Each was careful not to ogle her directly as they tromped across her floor in their Cuban heels and jangling spurs, but she was very aware of their curious glances. Already, she'd caused a stir on the Bar K. That was natural, she supposed—not often did one come back from the dead. It was the way they canted stares at Scotty that wrought a stiffening inside her. Those glimpses were cold, hate-filled. It took all of her will not to snatch the child up from the quilt where he was sleeping and hug him fiercely to her breast. Damn them, all of them, for their narrow bigotry! She remained seated, tall and proud, the daughter of Garth Kincaid, pretending to ignore those jabbing looks as if such things were beneath her. But each glare marred her with its ugliness and woke a deeper fear. These were her father's men, men who loved the man they worked for and who were well aware that her child shared that same blood. If they were so unbendingly hostile, how would others react? Neighbors? Townspeople? If they would cast such malevolent looks at an innocent sleeping child, what did the future hold for Scotty as a boy? As a man? This was only the beginning.

By the time they filed out, tipping their Stetsons to her one by one in a respectful manner, it was all she could do to smile graciously. Her heart was cold and heavy with this glimpse into the future. Had she really thought it would be any different?

She wasn't aware of Ruth, that the other woman had been stoically watching her face and the slight shades of expression it revealed, until the housekeeper spoke.

"If you would like, Miss, I will tend the baby while you bathe and rest."

Aurora's gaze flew up to her, instantly suspicious

and filled with the protectiveness of motherhood. Then, she saw the way Ruth was regarding the baby. Her eyes were soft, her small smile warm with maternal emotion. It was the way an infant should be regarded; with wonder, not animosity. And Aurora knew at once that this part Indian woman could be trusted with her precious child. She nodded.

Quickly, eagerly, but with infinite care, Ruth lifted the sleeping child. Her brow puckered as she examined the creative diapering.

"I will see if I can find something a little more . . . practical," she announced.

Aurora said nothing. She was thinking of Ethan Prescott swaddling the tiny hips in pieces cut from his long johns.

How empty the room seemed when Scotty was taken from it. How alone she felt. She was amazed how attached she'd become in such a short time to that little baby. She determined then that her mother's love would make up for any hardships her son might suffer. He would never doubt its strength and loyalty.

The food was good, but the thought of a hot bath made her gulp it down in anticipation of those steaming waters. The heavy shirt and baggy long underwear skimmed from her body, and, with a sigh, Aurora settled in the tub. Heaven! For a long while, she just lounged and soaked, letting the water lick between her breasts and around her bent knees. Her muscles uncoiled and relaxed one by one until she was luxuriously limp. She refused to think, selfishly wanting this moment for herself, to recoup her spirits. For she would need them when she dined with her father.

The second that crossed her mind, rest was impos-

146

sible. She sat up and began to work a lather from the fine milled soap between the friction of her palms. Garth Kincaid would not be easy. The knowledge that he did not love her child simply because it was a part of her and therefore, of him, cut bitterly. She could forgive him that reaction now that she had time to reflect upon it. It had been a tremendous surprise, finding her alive and then discovering she'd borne a child. A child fathered out of recognized wedlock, a child whose blood contained the taint of his hatred toward the Sioux. Hating the Indians was an acceptable part of the white culture. It made the stealing of their lands more palatable. She'd been raised on stories of their savagery, of their heathen inhumanity. The very cry of "Indians" was enough to freeze any white man, woman, or child's blood in their veins. It was a constant terror they lived with the moment they stepped west of civilization. She'd adopted that belief unquestioningly.

But now she had questions, plenty of them. She'd lived among the Lakotas. Yes, they were cruel. It was because their existence was cruel. Yet even while she schemed to escape them, even while she rejected integration into their clan, she could not prevent a respect from budding. They were a proud people, a noble, honest people, not the mindless animals of the settler's frightened whispers. And she was moved to sympathy for her captors. They were starving, driven like dangerous beasts from their land and into the less generous hills. No wonder they were angry. Anyone watching their child shrink in hunger would be angry and desperate. She could understand that now. She didn't hate the Lakota people blindly, the way those on the Bar K and the surrounding ranches did. Not the way her father did.

He looked at Scotty and saw the people who murdered his wife.

He will look beyond, Aurora vowed. *He will look upon Scotty and see his grandson instead of split heritage. And he will accept him and love him.*

I pray to God he will.

The water had cooled and Aurora no longer cared to linger. After toweling herself dry, she opened the large wardrobe, hoping she could find something feminine to wear. Or at least something that fit. She stared. There, in the cupboard, hung all her gowns, neatly arranged with their dyed shoes lined up like soldiers beneath each hem. For a moment, she didn't understand, then she realized these were the dresses she'd shipped from the East. They would have arrived after she did. Or rather, after she didn't.

And her father had kept them.

Emotion tightened in her chest. He'd kept them. As if she'd be returning at any minute to dress and join him for dinner. The sadness of it nearly choked her. How he must have been tortured to cling so desperately to these fabric and lace substitutes for the daughter he had loved. Fighting back her poignant tears, she selected from the lacy underthings and began to dress. They were tight. In fact, she could hardly force the dainty fastenings of her chemise to meet. For one who had never needed the artificial shaping of a corset, Aurora was stunned. But then, she realized with some chagrin, she'd never borne a child before. Her breasts were heavy and full. Her naturally slender hips were rounded and her middle still soft. She was no longer a slim girl who could wear britches and be mistaken for a cowhand. That notion pleased more than it provoked.

Molding her figure with the only corset she

148

owned — a lightly boned affair that compressed her ribs like an overabundant meal — she chose carefully from the gowns her father had treasured. She selected a peacock-blue silk, detailed with swags of black lace and black embroidery. He'd always loved the color on her. After months of wearing loose Indian garb, the endless yards of fabric seemed engulfing as it billowed over her head to settle snugly about her hips. The dress was awkward and heavy, with its piles of bouffant drapery loaded in the back and Aurora smiled wryly. It was like carrying a child in the rear instead of up front.

With the gown in place and black kid slippers on her stockinged feet, Aurora moved to stand before her cheval glass and looked upon a near-stranger, a stranger whose skin was dark, almost as coppery as Scotty's. Older eyes glowed golden from that face, lacking the deviltry of youth. She saw a woman there, one of ripe, maternal curves, one who displayed a matured wisdom with her half-smiling lips. Calloused hands, squaw's hands, rose to twine heavy red hair into a fiery coronet. Her hands were shaking, and she realized it was because she was unnerved by the woman she observed, the woman weighted by so much grim responsibility. No longer Garth Kincaid's protected little girl, she was a woman, a mother, a stranger now. And she was unsettled by the role she had assumed almost without being aware of the changes.

What would Ethan think if he could see her? Confident in her surrounding comforts, elegant in her imported Parisian finery. She had exchanged the pinched look of a terrified runaway squaw for the sleek sophistication of a woman educated in the east and come home to act her father's hostess. As her hand fingered the heavy black lace of her gown's shawl collar, Aurora wondered and frowned— frowned because she didn't think he would like it at all. Because looking upon her here, like this, he would only see her father's daughter, not the woman whom he'd helped through childbirth upon his bed, or the frightened female he'd pursued through the snow and cradled in his arms. She frowned because she hated to lose even a fraction of his regard. But she couldn't change who and what she was. Not for Ethan Prescott. Nor for Garth Kincaid. She was Aurora Kincaid, woman of Far Winds, mother of a mixed breed babe. And not at all ashamed.

It was easy to feel brave and certain when facing one's own reflection. However, when the time grew near to face her father, Aurora knew an increasing dread. Always before, she'd been the doting and, for the most part, obedient daughter. Now, she was meeting him on a different level, a tentative level. She was an independent mother, yet still his child, dependent upon his support. It was going to be a fine line to draw, one which wouldn't endanger her position beneath his wing, while allowing her the freedom she would need to act on her child's behalf. Submissive and assertive. Opposites she would have to mend together if she was to stay beneath her father's roof. And she wanted to. Her memories were here. Her sense of security lay within these rooms, with that booming, burly man below. She wanted desperately for it to work between them and said a quiet little prayer that she would not be forced to choose between father and child—because there, she had no choice.

The gentle tap sounded again upon her door, and she called for Ruth to enter.

150

"The boy is sleeping," the housekeeper told her. "I thought I would keep him in the kitchen with me while you and the Major have your meal. That way, you would have time to get — reacquainted." And that would be easier to accomplish in the absence of her child; Aurora understood and was grateful for the older woman's sensitivity.

"If he wakes and demands to be fed, come for me immediately."

Ruth smiled and promised she would. Then, she concluded, "Your father is waiting."

How ominous that sounded. How nervous she felt, her stomach all aflutter with jiggly doubts and fears. Drawing a deep, composing breath, she descended the stairs. The dining room was to the right. Already she could hear the sound of glass clinking as he poured. Was he just as anxious about facing her? She couldn't remember him needing a before-dinner drink in the past.

He turned at the sight of her — silk and lace, glass in hand, features still. She paused just inside of the door, uncertain of what she saw in his assessing gaze. Then, there was no doubt. His eyes clouded.

"My God, you remind me of your mother standing there like that. So beautiful," he murmured thickly. His arms opened and Aurora rushed to fill them without reservation. His embrace was all-encompassing, making her feel again like a little girl. She was aware of the same scents: tobacco, bay rum, and — always — cattle. She breathed them in deeply, letting them tease back memories from the warm recesses of the past, a past they had lovingly shared through good times and bad. It was that shared fondness she would have to tap if she was to win her father over.

151

She stepped out of his arms and looked about with a wistful smile. "How can things be different yet still the same? I can feel Mama and Seth and Jed just like they were here with us. It must be the way you've kept them alive through their belongings."

"No," he disagreed softly. "It's the way I've kept them alive in my heart. The way I kept you alive in my heart. If you can still feel them, it's because I've never let them go. They're as much a part of my life now as ever, as you will always be."

Hope welled up in Aurora only to be tempered by his next words.

"I'll let nothing tamper with those memories. They are the most precious thing I possess."

A warning? She wondered. Was his pure and untainted image of her more important than the woman she'd become? If that was so, there was little hope for acceptance. There was little chance of building upon that pristine memory or of returning to the innocent enjoyment of their former relationship. Just what did that leave her? Troubled by that indefiniteness, Aurora assumed her seat at her father's table.

They were served quickly and in silent efficiency by Ruth—a teaming feast spread before the young woman who had learned to live for days on a strip of dried pemmican. There were juicy slabs of fresh beef, fluffy potatoes, syrupy canned peaches and raisin pie. And strong, dark coffee, the kind that would draw Ethan Prescott down from the hills. After nearly a year among the Lakota's, she had to consciously remind herself of table manners ingrained from birth, as if learning all over again what it meant to be white. To please her father, she made the effort to appear unchanged by her absence from civilization. She wanted nothing to distract them from a father-daughter evening together, in which memories could swell and bind past to present.

It was going well. She could see her father relaxing by increments. It was almost as if she'd never left his table.

Then, Scotty set up a howl from the kitchen.

Garth Kincaid stiffened.

Aurora sat in frozen indecision. Her son was hungry, but was her father any less needy of her attention? She looked at the older man's fixed expression and knew if she stood, abandoning him to tend her child, there would be a wider gap to span.

The wails continued.

Aurora began to refold her linen napkin. A light hand touched her shoulder and Ruth leaned close to whisper.

"Finish your meal, miss. I will quiet him with a sugar teet."

The golden eyes lifted gratefully. "Thank you, Ruth."

Garth's gaze was still wary when his daughter picked up her tableware and resumed her carving. The distressed sounds ceased. An uncomfortable silence swelled across the tabletop.

"How did the herd winter, Major?"

That casual question took the surly gentleman by surprise, then warmed him cleverly to his favorite topic of discourse. He took up his knife and fork, looking smugly pleased with his accomplishments. "Well. Very well. We'll be fixing to round 'em up in the next few weeks. Can't wait too long after the first thaw or those damn sooners will jump the branding date. Mavericking, they call it. Rustling is more like it. I don't aim to lose any of my un-

153

branded stock to those lazy thieves. It's been pretty quiet with just the eight men I kept on over the winter. Hired thirty more and mean to work 'em hard. You, too, if you've a mind to help out."

Aurora brightened and Kincaid shook a finger at her.

"Mind you, Miss, not on horseback. There's plenty that needs doing right here on the ranch. There's records to keep, clothes to patch for the cowhands, business correspondence — you know how much I hate that scribbling work. I'd be grateful to turn it over to you."

He would be grateful! Aurora almost wept with relief. His offer was like a great big warm embrace, drawing her back into the fold. She fought to keep the quavering emotion from her voice as she told him, "My penmanship was always better than yours."

"Your math, too," he begrudged fondly. "I'll get the books out for you in the morning. I need to write out a draft for supplies in town, anyway. Now that we got four times the mouths to feed, we don't have nearly enough in the larder. Them bunkhouse boys go through flour, meal, bacon, coffee and peaches like a range steer in sweet grass."

"Riders are going into town tomorrow?"

"Right after daybreak. Don't like 'em traveling on the road after dark when they're loaded down. An easy target for them savages." He said that without a blink or the slightest softening to his gruff growl, so Aurora broached him cautiously with her request.

"I'd like to ride in with them, if I might. There are some things I need — for me and the baby."

The goodwill left Garth's face. His jaw tightened into a square of formidable granite. He had hoped,

154

somewhat naively, that his daughter's presence and that of her bastard child could be kept secret. Of course, that was a ridiculous hope. It would be the first topic to spring from the lips of his men upon ordering up a dust cutter in the closest beer hall they encountered. Then, the rumors would fly. Garth Kincaid's daughter, captured by the Sioux, their prisoner for nearly a year, home now with one of their half-breed brats strapped to her back. His teeth ground in silent misery and shame. Not for Aurora but for his own reputation. How would it look, one of the valley's most prosperous ranchers raising a red-skinned devil under his own roof?

He saw her waiting, her face pale as the table linen, her eyes glinting like newly minted gold eagles. And he wished at that moment, though it might cost him an eternity of hell fire, that she'd never returned to his door.

"You got a trust set up at the bank. Use it for whatever you will. Just don't expect me to support your bastard."

"I didn't expect you to," she answered. Her words were softly spoken, yet threaded with steel. He'd hurt her with his bluntness, but she'd be damned if she'd show it. She cut another piece of tender beef, keeping her gaze on her plate so the dampness gathering in her eyes would not betray her.

How quickly things shifted. The mention of Scotty threw all the tentative overtures aside. Once again she could see the torment in her father's eyes. The picture of her writhing beneath a wild savage on the dirt floor of a mountain tipi. Conceiving the spawn of a red Satan. And in that look, something deeper, darker. Anger. An anger directed at her. Because she had allowed it. Because she had survived it. Decent women didn't but Aurora Kincaid had. That's what she saw in her father's gaze.

Conversation was impossible after that. At the next chorus of hungry wails, Aurora quietly excused herself to fetch her son from the kitchen. It wasn't until his little figure was stretched out next to hers, atop her downy quilt, contentedly suckling, that she gave way to her discouragement and silently wept.

Ethan awoke with a jerk, wrapped in a sheet of sweat. The harsh rasp of his own breathing replaced the sounds of cannon fire and the creaking of rope. He lay still, those hard gulps for air exploding from his tight chest, his heart thrusting against his ribs with the force of a fist.

Just a dream.

He stared into the darkness, refusing to think of it as more than just that, a dream. But it was more, so much more, and he knew it and was tortured by it. Because every tentacle of fear and horror escalating from the time he'd closed his eyes was true. He'd escaped it for nearly four years, yet it was still vivid in every terrifying detail. The nightmare of his past.

Would it never leave him in peace?

Slowly, the fierce grip of recurring dream released him. It was the liquor, he decided. Never much for spirits, the shots of gut-twister aptly named Tarantula Juice scrambled his senses like a load of .00 buckshot to the brain. But it wasn't the cannons and the noose he was trying to forget. It was the feel of silken flames scorching through his fingers. It was the haunting vision of a tender golden gaze.

It hadn't worked.

He raked the fingers of both hands through ragged hair and pressed his palms over hot, aching eyes. God, another memory to torment him. As if he hadn't demons enough.

Ethan came suddenly aware of the saggy mattress beneath him and the pungent odor of cheaply distilled perfume. Where the hell was he? And with whom? He forced himself up on his elbows and lit the lamp on the crude bedside table. The light flickered and flared. One glance around and he knew the darkness was better. What a sty. Not fit for pigs, let alone a man. Closing his eyes, he fell back with a groan. Now he remembered. The squalid saloon with its overflowing spittoons and the rough sign over the bar snarling "No Injuns Served." The painted hurdy gal cajoling him with crimson lips, her thin hip intentionally rubbing, encouraging a long-denied thickening in his trousers. Kate? Kathy? She'd told him but he couldn't remember. Couldn't remember because it didn't matter. Gals like her weren't supposed to. The flesh had been more than willing to surrender to her practiced care. She hadn't been pretty but she was passably clean. She'd used his coin to purchase a room behind the saloon. Her embrace had been impatient, scented with the reek of flowers now permeating his head. She'd kissed him, and he recalled she'd tasted of whiskey and tobacco—hers or someone else's. The swelling in his loins throbbed to match an anguished heart and someone like Kate or Kathy was what he needed to give both ease. Wasn't she? So why hadn't she? Why was he lying alone in her dirty crib suffering both aches?

Because she wasn't Ora.

Damn.

He remembered her puzzled look when he pressed

the coins into her hand — not for her company but for her absence from this filthy room. He'd collapsed upon the bed while she philosophically shrugged and went to find another customer. And the dream had come. Not sweet images of Ora's tempting flesh but ones of death and dread.

Ethan struggled off the soft mattress. He was surprised and grateful to find the coin still in his coat pocket. How easy it would have been for the tart to pick the profits from such a foolish mark. She must have felt sorry for him. Not as sorry as he'd been feeling for himself. His boots were at the bedside. He thrust his feet into them. And though the sky showed only the first dingy grey threads of dawn, he went to claim his horse. His trading was done, his supplies garnered. Enough to last a man alone an entire season. Time to head back into the hills. There was nothing for him here. He would head up into the soaring timbers because he could not go where his heart would lead.

To a woman and her half-breed child.

Chapter Ten

Scotty had been nursed and Aurora had Ruth's promise to supplement his noon feeding with cow's milk. It wouldn't be the boy's preferred meal, but, as she wouldn't return in time to see to it herself, he would just have to adapt. And he would, Ruth assured with a comforting smile. The older woman's arms made a natural cradle for the child, and Aurora was a bit surprised that she should feel only the slightest reluctance in leaving him in her care. She could have taken him with her, of course, but the ride to Deadwood was a long one for so small an infant.

And she wasn't ready to cope with the stares of the townspeople.

Coward!

She was. This one time, she was. She wanted to go into town and mill about with others of her race, not to be stared at and pointed to. Selfishly, she wanted to spend a day as Garth Kincaid's daughter before she became *that woman with the half-breed child*. Her wish came at the cost of terrible guilt; not for what the townspeople would say or think, but because of her betrayal of her son, and she lost some of her enthusiasm.

It was a beautiful day. The sun shone golden and warm, hurrying the spring thaw. The girl she had been would have embraced such a day as this by racing across the muddy yard to throw a saddle on her favorite horse. The woman she was moved slower, heavily weighted by the abandonment of her child and by the absence of her father. Out on the south range, she'd been told at the empty breakfast table — avoiding her after their words of last night, she knew. And so the glorious day became just another day in her battle to be accepted at the Bar K. Another day to get through as best she could.

The wagon was hitched and ready. The cowhand who'd been lounging against it sprang upright at the sight of her and ground his cigarette beneath his boot. When he grinned, his teeth gleamed like a row of keys from her parlor organ.

" 'Morning, Orrie. Mighty good to see you again, if you don't mind me saying so."

Jack Lawson. Aurora remembered him from Yankton. And she did mind the familiarity of his tone and the roving path of his dark eyes. Most women would consider him handsome, she supposed, and she knew he thought of himself that way. His features were even, his blond hair worn long in a boyish tousle and his smile was quick to charm. Aurora wasn't sure what triggered her aversion to him. He'd always gone out of his way to impress and be polite. Too far out of his way, perhaps. From the moment he'd signed on with her father, he'd followed her with his eyes. Though he'd never made an improper move, she was certain he had many an improper thought behind his caressing gaze.

To her thinking, Jack Lawson was like a range slough. Water might stand on the surface and glimmer prettily, but beneath there was deep, treacherous mud waiting to coax the unwise into a cold, final embrace.

He stood there at the wagon, posing for her appreciation, so she obliged him with a glance. Dressed in typical range fashion, he wore Levi Strauss britches with suspenders buttoned on the durable tan fabric, a stripped pullover shirt with mule-eared collar, a big kerchief draped around his neck, and high, tailor-made boots that probably cost a month's wages. His canvas duster was fleece lined and tucked back to display a brace of blued Colts. That was where typical ended and Jack Lawson's cocky arrogance began. Cowboys were discouraged from carrying firearms. Cale Marks, her father's foreman, had a hard and fast rule against it, saying to tote a six-shooter was an unnecessary provocation. Guns were carried rolled up in saddle blankets not boasted on hips. So why was Lawson decked out like a gun-slick on the prod? And why wasn't Cale on hand to slap some sense into his inflated head?

Aurora's gaze lingered disparagingly on the flashy sidearms. So pointed was her stare, the swaggering cowboy had the sense to look a mite chagrined and to flip the ends of his coat down over the offensive hardware.

"All set to go?" He was grinning, obviously pleased with the duty of escorting her to town. His smile was intimate, causing her to freeze on the spot as if the temperature had plunged a quick twenty degrees.

"Where's Cale? I thought he always drove into town himself when supplies were needed?" Her gaze flickered about the yard, hoping for a glimpse of the big man whose company was preferable to this bantam rooster's.

"It's the foreman's job and you're looking at him."

Aurora couldn't help but stare, surprised and slightly aghast. Jack Lawson was the Bar K foreman? How on earth had that happened? She couldn't see this sneaky, self-serving sidewinder in such a position of power. To replace the stalwart Cale Marks with this grinning, strutting fool—had her father lost his mind?

"Get your skirts atwitching there, honey. We gots to be going."

With that, he took hold of her elbow to assist her up into the buckboard. Aurora had been climbing in and out of wagons all her life, and the new foreman's generous boost by way of a hand on her fanny was hardly necessary. As she swept her skirts out of the way, her foot kicked back with apparent lack of intent and caught the smirking cowboy a direct hit on the chin. She had the satisfaction of hearing his teeth click together like the snap of a sprung trap. Demurely, she arranged her petticoats and perched guilelessly upon the seat.

Rubbing his jaw, Jack Lawson circled the wagon and climbed up on the other side. He gave her a suspicious scowl, then shook his head. Naw. She couldn't have meant it. Not a purty little thing like her. He gathered up the reins and gave a slightly painful smile, thinking of the ride to town and back with the most beautiful creation in the valley all to himself. Then, his smugness soured as two outriders fell in behind them. Kincaid's orders. No wagon was allowed to leave the ranch without armed escort. Oh well, at least they could talk without being overheard. It was high time he started some serious spooning with the desirable Miss Kincaid. And with that red brat of hers and her maidenhead busted in some dirty Sioux camp, she might be right grateful for his attentions.

Aurora did her best to ignore Lawson's scheming smile. It was easier than ignoring his presence. He'd settled himself in the center of the seat, giving her precious little room or privacy as the slightest bump caused them to collide. She gripped the edge of the seat with whitened fingers, determined not to end up on Jack Lawson's lap as he steered for every dip in the road. They didn't speak on the long ride, Jack grinning, Aurora grimacing.

There was always the return trip, Lawson told himself.

Deadwood was a raw frontier town built on gold and run on vice. It had the distinction of surviving the erratic waves of miners, unlike some of its predecessors. When gold was found in Deadwood Gulch, the thriving town of Custer City had gone from a community of six thousand one day to fourteen the next; a ghost town of fourteen hundred empty buildings, abandoned diggings and broken sluice boxes. The Gulch proved a rich strike and from one end to the other, the long, narrow canyon became a makeshift city; one hell-raising, gun-fighting, whiskey-guzzling, gold-digging mass of twenty-five thousand.

Deadwood was thrown up almost overnight, boasting a reputation as raucous as Dodge City, and its saloons were more populous and profitable than any other business. At first, these dugouts and lean-tos of canvas were the only buildings of substance, serving rotgut to miners. But like a new wine, with age came respectability. In 1877, Deadwood was an exciting but mostly a peaceful place and Aurora was amused by its impertinent claims to culture. Along its muddy streets was the wealth to supply the best money could buy but not the good taste to appreciate it. Miners poured in each evening to soak up fine entertainment from one or both of its theaters, buying an admission ticket with a coupon tacked on the back to be redeemed at the bar. Who was to say if they really enjoyed the high-brow classics as much as the baser pleasures to be found in the rowdy "badlands," where seventy-six saloons catered to every whim. Ticket prices rose from fifty cents to five dollars and the "Mikada" ran for one hundred and thirty nights to meet the demand of the rough-edged miners and cowboys. As Aurora predicted, with prosperity came the want for finer things — whether one liked them or not.

The town was full of those who didn't work their claims in the winter and with area farmers and ranchers taking advantage of the open roads to replenish their supplies. Jack Lawson sent their wagon hurtling down the wide, marshy road, scattering pedestrians before it like settler's panicked hens. When Aurora called for him to slow the pace, he grinned and said the anklers were in need of a little excitement after hibernating on the prairie. Fuming, she clung to the wagon seat, knowing he did it for show and to draw attention. That he achieved, as many a mud-splattered citizen rose a fist and a curse at his passing.

Their reckless race to the general store brought notice from every man and woman on the uneven sidewalks. That annoyance quickly became curiosity, then speculation. For with Garth Kincaid's foreman rode a beautiful woman with hair as red as mail-order long johns. Only once before had they seen her like. But that wasn't possible. Aurora Kincaid had been slain by savages . . . hadn't she?

Jack vaulted lightly to the street, tethered the team then hurried around to help his passenger down. His brawny hands spanned her waist before she had a chance to protest and he swung her easily to the relatively mud-free boardwalk. He grinned at her high color, mistaking it for a flustered blush when in truth it was from the effort not to deal him out a smart slap for his familiar manhandling upon the public street. Aurora straightened her jacket and strode by the smirking cowboy into the warm mustiness of the mercantile.

Lem Keane was proud of his store, feeling it the bastion of civilization in the wilderness. He'd owned a fine establishment in the East and was determined to improve the livelihood of those poor souls starved for the niceties he had shipped in by the boxcar. He was looking to the future, when the sea of mud would become even cobbles and the chaw-spitting miners would hanker for the plug hats, garters, arm bands, bow ties and stiff collars he stocked along the south wall. Along the north wall, he kept women's merchandise, everything as current to the fashion as he could come; drawers, kid gloves, jewelry and bolts of silks, velvets, crepe de chines, serges, linens, and calico, each bolt wrapped in paper to keep the dust off. Beneath his thick glass-topped counter were the fancy buttons, laces, and braids, with stools lined before it where one could look and dream while waiting for an order. Groceries were along the west wall, canned goods that came by freight in wooden boxes — he sold the boxes to newcomers who couldn't afford real furniture. Atop his main counter was the coffee mill and everything else in bulk; cheese, flour, sugar, candy and cookies by the box that fit into slotted racks. Eggs and butter brought in by area farmers were kept in his basement, and the kerosene and vinegar pumps were in back where their disagreeable scents wouldn't clash with more palatable ones. He also carried crockery, fancy dishes, drawers of every size chimney imaginable, lamps and tobacco but no ready-made cigarettes.

And when the bell hung over his front door tinkled merrily, the retailer glanced up to give a hopeful smile. Now there was the kind of customer he envisioned; stylish, discriminating and wealthy.

" 'Morning, folks. Be of any help today?"

Jack swaggered to the counter and drew a sheet of folded paper from his pocket. "Got this here list to be filled. No hurry, though. And the lady's got some shopping to do. You treat her real nice, you hear."

Assessing the value of the young woman's silk travel gown, Keane was only too happy to nod.

Aurora was already scanning the store for the necessities she had in mind when Lawson sidled up to her. She glanced up in irritation and stepped back to prevent an intimate closeness in front of the shopkeeper's attentive gaze. Jack wasn't discouraged. He gifted her with his most endearing smile.

"You take all the time you want, Orrie honey. The boys and me'll be right across the street wetting our whistles. When the order's ready just have ole Lem send someone to fetch us."

Her stare could have frozen milk on the teat. "I won't be long, *Mister* Lawson so I suggest you keep your whistle wetting to a minimum."

Jack Lawson blinked and flushed a ruddy color. "Yes, ma'am," he muttered in a surly undervoice. *Uppity bitch,* he growled to himself. *Needs taking down a few pegs.* He wheeled about with a flip of his duster and clatter of spur rowels and stalked from the store.

Impressed by the sharp comeuppance, the pretty lady dealt the smart-alecky cowboy, Lem Keane adopted a servile manner while questions percolated behind his meek smile. Who was this woman who booted the Bar K foreman from his establishment as

166

if he'd been a cur dog that had soiled his braided rug? He glanced at the supply list. It was long and spoke of a good return, yet curiosity held him at the counter when he should have hurried to fill it.

"Be of any assistance, ma'am? Don't believe I've had the pleasure afore."

"I believe I'll just have a look around for a moment, if you don't mind. Please go ahead and see to your order. I'll let you know if I need help."

It was a gracious refusal but a dismissal nonetheless, saying mind your own business. Bound by the code of the West, that wouldn't permit badgering a stranger with questions, he reluctantly began to assemble supplies for the Bar K behind the counter.

Aware of the storekeeper's gaze, Aurora moved about the room leisurely, fingering different items and generally enjoying each one as evidence of civilization. She lingered wistfully over a selection of flosses and finespun yarns. How beautiful they'd look made up for Scotty. She thought of the fawnskin clothes and moccasins she'd painstakingly decorated with porcupine quills and the sets of fawnskin diapers lined with the hairy fruit of the cattail. White Cloud, Far Winds's mother, had shown her how to fashion the tiny garments from the soft hide he provided. She'd left them behind when she fled the camp, in a wish to divorce her child from his Indian heritage—foolishly, she realized now, for his coloring would mark him more clearly than the little robes stitched with a bone awl and sinew. There would be no hiding what Scotty was with fancy embroidery and laces.

Made somewhat melancholy by her thoughts, Aurora picked threads and yarn, in shades of blue and gold, along with several bolts of soft fabric. She would use her evenings to cut, sew and adorn gowns for her son, no longer clinging to the hope that those hours would be filled with laughter, music from the parlor organ, and affectionate talks between father and daughter. She would be just as alone as she had been alone in the Miniconjou camp. And she would fill the emptiness in her heart with her love for Scotty.

As she laid her purchases down on the glass counter, Lem Keane scurried over. His trained eye assessed the collection of goods then canted discreetly at her flat midsection.

"These here yarns make up into right fine baby blankets," he commented conversationally as he tallied the amount.

"I'm sure they do," Aurora answered simply.

Keane sighed, his curiosity whetted by her refusal to be drawn out. Knowing women loved to talk about their little ones, he pulled a box from beneath the counter and opened it for her inspection.

"Just came in, if you're interested."

Aurora glanced inside the box and an unbidden smile warmed her features. She lifted out the tiny white cambric cap and knitted-wool cloth barrowcoat. The deep fold at the bottom would keep even the wiggliest infant's feet covered and warm. She turned it lovingly in her hands to admire the stitching, imagining, as she did, tying the ribbons over Scotty's stout little chest. It would be a day or two before she could assemble some proper chemises, and she longed to see him swaddled as befitting the grandson of Garth Kincaid.

Perhaps if he looked more like a white baby . . .

The thought slipped in and just as quickly, Aurora chastised herself for considering it. She refolded the small garment and replaced it in the box.

"It's lovely and I will take it."

Unmindful of the lady's somber tone, Keane eagerly tacked the cost onto her total. "And how would you like to pay for these?"

"I've an account at the bank," she mentioned distractedly. "Aurora Kincaid. You can forward the total and they'll see you're issued a draft."

Lem Keane's hands paused in their wrapping. His gaze flashed up, undisguised shock rounding them. "Aurora Kincaid! I heard—"

"You obviously heard wrong," she snapped more harshly than intended. Of course the man would be surprised. She was supposedly dead. Killed by rampaging Sioux. She could see the startled shopkeeper return to his wrapping but his movements were slow, his thoughts, contrarily, racing. She could imagine the direction in which they spun. Not killed by the savages, captured and returned nearly a year later. And in his store buying infantwear.

Frustrated by the unworthy flush of color that was breaking her vow not to appear ashamed, Aurora hoisted her chin a notch and looked about the counter—anywhere but at the speculative merchant. Her gaze touched on the coffee mill. She was unprepared for the wave of longing, for the scent of roasted beans, for the weak taste of them in a battered tin cup at Ethan Prescott's table. Then, she smiled, remembering, too, an arrogant promise to see his supplies replenished.

"I'd also like five pounds of coffee and a tin of Bull Durham." She couldn't think about Ethan without the wreathing aroma of coffee and good tobacco. Her smile grew positively mischievous. "Do you by any chance have tea cakes? A package of those, as well."

"You want me to add those on to the Bar K account, Miz Kincaid?"

"No, on my own, please."

"You and your baby living with its father?"

It was blurted out innocently but she could feel the heat flame in her face. With all the dignity she could muster, she said, "My husband was killed not long ago. My son and I are living at the Bar K. If you've no more questions, you can ready the order while I go down to the bank to insure you receive payment."

"Begging your pardon, Miz—Miss—" When she offered no solution, he ended lamely with, "ma'am."

"Then, if it's no trouble, could you have someone inform Mister Lawson that we are ready to leave."

"Yessum."

Aurora stepped out into the brisk spring air and drew it in deeply to cool her. She'd handled it badly. She'd pounced upon the man for expressing his natural curiosity and by her own reaction, had intensified it. She had behaved as if she had something unsavory to hide. Was this what it was going to be like every time she had to explain who she was? Would she have to face those blank, disbelieving looks and fend the inevitable question. *If the Indians didn't kill her, did they do worse?*

As she walked along the boards, she approached several women. From their withered appearance and faded calicos, she assumed they were wives of local farmers. She smiled and nodded, slowing her pace. It would be wonderful to speak to women again about things like church and socials and even the weather. Hopefully, she waited as they drew abreast. Instead of the expected polite return of greeting, the women huddled to one side of the walk and quickly skirted passed her as if she was contaminated by some vile disease. Aurora paused in a curious hurt. What. . . ?

Then she understood. There was no mistaking the hostility in their blatant stares. *Indian lover.* It was so plain, they might well have slapped her with their censure. No decent woman would dare show her face after whoring for savages.

Aurora stood for a moment, going white with shock. The women hurried on, casting glances back at her, whispering. She could well imagine the words. They spun within her head, reeling about in dizzying condemnation until she felt ill. For a brief instant she feared she might swoon dead away on the dirty boardwalk. Wouldn't that give them something to gossip about. That thought giving her strength, she was able to cling to her precarious composure long enough to hurry inside the bank. She was breathing hard, trembling slightly. How dare they glare at her as if she'd done something horrid. All she'd done was survive.

Adjusting her shoulders into a proud line, she went up to the manager's window. There, she was met with an icy gaze no less condemning than the farm women's on the street. Dear God, did everyone in Deadwood know already? How? Then, she remembered Jack Lawson's mulish petulance when she'd chastised his impertinence. He'd spilled the story in the saloon. She just knew it. There was no telling how many sordid embellishments he'd added to her already stained reputation.

As briefly as she could, she explained to the man behind the wire mesh what she needed. Though he wouldn't jeopardize her father's hefty account by snubbing her directly, the manager was cool in his attitude and more chilly in his words. It was a thankfully short interview. By then, the bank was filled with more than she would assume the normal amount of customers. They were the curious, gawk-

171

ing, pointing, whispering amongst themselves. While she pretended not to notice their rudeness, Aurora was sick with despair. She mumbled a quick "good day" to the bank representative and fled without so much as a nod of acknowledgment toward those who followed her with their postulating stares.

She marched down the walk, a quivering mixture of rage and woe. They had ogled her like a freak-show attraction, the women with disgust, the men with unflattering supposition. *Had she been raped by her captors? Was it true she had a half-breed child?* It was as if she were villain instead of victim. Was it her fault the Sioux attacked their coach? Was it her fault she alone survived? Was it her fault she chose a life of shame over a quick martyrdom?

Yes. Yes, those hard looks told her.

Well, she would not meekly submit to their jaundiced views. The unfairness of it chafed her tender sensibilities. The horror of it rubbed her moral fiber raw. The angrier and more upset she became, the faster she walked until she fairly barreled into a tall man who stepped out of bat-winged doors.

The collision sent her reeling. Strong hands gripped her forearms, holding her erect. Before she could utter a word of apology and thanks, she was aware of the reek of liquor and a twisted grinning face pressed close to her own.

"Well how do, Miz Kincaid," the fellow gushed in a flow of whiskey fumes. "Fancy running into you like this. You look a mite peaked. Like to step in for a bracer? I own the Tangle Foot and if I do say so myself, it's the finest thirst parlor this side of Abilene. Be my pleasure to stand you for a drink."

A drink? In a saloon? Aurora gaped at him. Her heart beat furiously against her stays. Color flooded her sculpted cheeks, giving them a brighter hue than

172

the painted doxies winding around the tables inside. What kind of man would suggest such a thing to a lady?

But his lewd grin said it all. He didn't consider her a lady.

His hands were still on her arms, pinning her almost against his stained satin vest. She tried to pull free, but his fingers tightened to the point of pain. Fear rose to battle with her outrage. How dare the man accost her right on the sidewalk, in the middle of the day! Why wasn't any one coming to her aid?

Because they didn't think her worth assisting.

Managing a modicum of control and a voice that didn't shake too badly, Aurora said, "Please, unhand me, sir. I do not wish to drink with you. If you'll excuse me—"

The saloon owner laughed, issuing a strong blast of fermented spirits. "Don't go getting all het up, purty lady. I don't mean no disrespect. Not like you're bound to come across if yous planning to stay in town."

"I don't know what you mean," she blustered, but she was afraid she did.

Again, he laughed, a cruel sound at her expense. "There ain't a man, woman or child that don't know who and what you are, Miz Kincaid. I just wanted to let on that I don't hold it agin' you. And there's plenty who wouldn't consider you unfit for a white man after spreading 'neath an Injun. At least, not inside the Tangle Foot. 'Course no sane man'd take you for a wife, being spoilt and all. Purty thing like you could do all right for herself and it'd be a sight better under a white man and more profitable, too."

Aurora couldn't breathe. The things he was suggesting—no, saying flat out to her face—strangled the air from her until she felt close to collapse. She

173

made another feeble attempt to pull free but the man was drawing her with him, toward the slatted doors of sin. Heaven help her! If he got her inside, she would be forever ruined. She began to twist and struggle ineffectively. He just kept grinning, panting the effusive odor of decadence into her chalk-colored face.

When his buttocks began to part the saloon door, Aurora senses returned with a vehement rush. She dug in the heels of her fancy half-boots and wrenched backwards, earning her freedom and nearly landing on her bustle in the process.

"You sotted swine," she spat out at him as she recovered her balance and her temper. "My father will shoot you down for your vile tongue."

Or would he?

She refused to let her inward doubts register on her fiercely arranged features. When the presumptuous lout had the audacity to strain his dirty waistcoat with a full-bodied belly laugh, she clutched the strings of her bag, readying to let it fly at his whiskey-soaked head.

"And iffen he don't, I will."

The cold tone and even colder nudge of the humorless barrel of a Colt .45 choked the man's mirth off into an near-apoplectic gag.

Aurora looked gratefully to Jack Lawson then scowled at the coarse roughneck who'd abused her name. "Just be glad I'm not packing a piece or I'd have blown off your claim to being a gentleman. You, sir, are not one."

"Skeedaddle on inside, now, afore I gets to thinking that'd be a right fine idea," Lawson drawled menacingly.

"Just funning the lady, friend," the pasty saloon man stammered.

174

"I ain't your friend. And you remember what I said afore you goes aflapping those loose lips about Miz Kincaid." He jabbed the business end of his revolver into the man's ribs to emphasize his point. With a jerking nod, the fellow fairly fell over himself in his scramble back into the saloon.

Aurora released a tremulous breath. Her gaze canted up gaugingly toward the young cowboy. Could she have been wrong in her dislike of him?

"I appreciate your intervention, Mister Lawson."

"It's Jack, Miz Orrie and don't go on about it. It was my pleasure."

He took her elbow with surprising gentility and offered escort back to the loaded buckboard. In her gratitude, Aurora forgot that he more than likely started all her troubles by spreading gossip in the Tangle Foot. All she knew was he had taken a stand for her honor and that went a long way toward erasing the bad feelings she held toward him.

As he settled himself on the wagon seat beside the comely Miss Kincaid, Jack Lawson thought it had indeed been his pleasure. He enjoyed the chance to display his fearless gun-handiness, especially before the admiring eyes of his boss's daughter. He would have plugged the man without compunction, just as he would any varmint that got between him and what he wanted. Riding the range gave too little opportunity for him to show his makings. And after all, he reasoned, as he slapped down the reins, a man couldn't have any one calling his future wife a whore. Even if it was the truth.

The first time he'd seen Aurora Kincaid as a spindly, flame-haired thirteen-year-old, he formed his destiny in his clever mind. Lawson wanted to bc a rich man. Lacking the ambition to work for it, he had no qualms about marrying into wealth. And

175

that's just what he planned to do. Fate dealt him a cruel slap when he'd thought her dead but now that she was back, everything was on track again. He didn't care if she'd lain with one red man or twenty or even if she'd banged beneath old Red Cloud himself. The color of her kid wasn't half as important as the color of her old man's money. The fact that just looking at Orrie Kincaid made his loins stand up and take notice didn't hurt. He'd dreamed of laying her down in a big feather bed up in the master house for a lot of years and the idea that she'd been fornicating with a bunch of heathen devils didn't lessen his lust one jot. In fact, knowing that she was experienced flavored the fantasy. She'd know just what to do when he parted those pearly thighs.

"I'da taught that skunk some manners if you'd said the word, Miss Orrie."

Aurora glanced at the handsome cowboy and actually blushed with satisfaction. "There was no need but I do thank you."

The duster shrugged on broad shoulders. "I jus' didn't want you to think that every man looked at you thata way."

Her gaze lowered as quickly as her spirits. That was what they'd thought, all of them in Deadwood. That she was a whore because she hadn't let them kill her.

It was what her father thought, as well.

And while she could endure the contempt of strangers, realizing her only family held her similarly, crushed her will.

Taking her silence for an opportunity to promote himself, Lawson jiggled the reins and smiled. "No, ma'am. I'd never think less of you because of what happened. It took a lot a gumption, I reckon, to take what you did. A lot of us on the Bar K feels

176

thata way. And if they didn't, I'd change their minds right quick."

She said nothing and he grew bolder in his designs.

"Some of what that critter said is true, though. Finding a husband who'll over look your past and a mix-breed babe won't be easy. You might never have considered it before but I'd be right pleased to look out for you. Looky here what I got."

Aurora accepted the small silverplated rattle with a sound of genuine pleasure. "Why, Jack, it must have cost dearly. I couldn't possibly—"

He waved a hand to shush her protest. "I'm making $125 a month as foreman of the Bar K. I know it ain't a lot to folks like you but I've been putting aside a nest egg hoping—well, I was kinda hoping . . ."

He trailed off and abruptly, Aurora recognized exactly where he was going. She was off balanced by his sudden chivalry and his thoughtfulness where Scotty was concerned, but in no way was she ready to hear his words of courtship. As quickly as she could, she seized upon a change of topic.

"Jack, what happened to Cale Marks?"

If he was annoyed by her change of subject, he didn't express it.

"Ole Cale up and got hisself kilt by a nester 'bout a year ago it was. Took over for him 'cause your daddy thought I was the man for the job." He glanced at her to see if she looked impressed. Tears welled in her golden eyes, and he realized with some chagrin that they were for the crusty former foreman. He continued rather gruffly. "The Major's been right pleased with my work. Ask him yourself. He'll tell you. I got me some big plans, Orrie honey, and now that I'm foreman, I means to see to them."

Again, Aurora grew uncomfortably aware of him giving the conversation a personal turn. And although she didn't feel the repugnance she had once felt for him there was only one man she wanted to consider with any degree of intimacy.

Thinking of Ethan brought up a whole slew of questions she'd forgotten to ask of her father—forgotten or purposefully delayed. Perhaps it would be wiser to find out the truth from an uninvolved third party. And here sat Jack Lawson all eager to talk.

"Jack, what do you know about a man named Ethan Prescott?"

The cowboy regarded her with a stunned expression. "Where'd you hear that name?" he demanded curtly.

She lied quickly. "In town."

Jack Lawson scowled over the backs of the team, and for a moment his jaw worked in silent fury.

And then, her world collapsed at his blunt answer.

"Prescott was the nester who shot Cale down in cold blood."

Chapter Eleven

"Oww! Damn!"

Aurora set aside the tiny white garment she was stitching so it wouldn't be stained by her wounded finger. As she put the throbbing digit to her mouth, tears swam in her eyes. Not because the jab of the needle hurt her. But because the truth was a pulsing ache within her heart.

There had to be some mistake.

She told herself over again for the hundredth time. And still, she was tortured by doubt.

Try as she would, Aurora had been able to wring no more details from the suddenly close-lipped foreman. She understood his fury. Cale Marks had gotten him the job with her father over the Major's reservations. Lawson was wild, Cale agreed, but he just needed a place to belong. And the boy hadn't disappointed him. He'd stayed on and learned. Marks had been the boy's mentor. The foreman's death must have devastated him. His words yet rang in her head as she sat before the parlor fire determinedly sewing a chemise.

She'd returned from town to find that her father had already taken his meal without waiting, so she had Ruth bring a tray to her room. After relieving her burdened breasts and settling a sated Scotty in his makeshift packing-crate bed, she'd drifted downstairs in a daze, thinking to discover the facts from her father. But Garth Kincaid had closeted himself in his study, asking not to be disturbed, so she was resigned to an evening of tortuous doubts alone before the fire.

How could it be true?

How could the man who delivered her son and coaxed her guarded heart into embracing love be guilty of murder?

But how could she close her mind to the possibility?

Again, she began the quick flurry of stitches in Scotty's bed gown. They were uneven at best, and peripherally she knew she would have to rip out each hasty seam, but it occupied her hands while her thoughts flew ahead.

What did she know about Ethan Prescott? He was a Texan. He had an expectant wife at some point in his past. He'd been a surgeon but now chose a life of isolation (or had killing Cale Marks forced him to hide in the hills?) He hated her father. And she loved him. Sketchy facts upon which to base such an enormous leap of faith. She would trust him with her life and Scotty's, but she could not in good conscience absolve him of all wrongdoing.

What in God's name had triggered an explosion of violence in a man who expressed so much tenderness with his hands, with his words, with his kisses? If he had done the terrible deed, there was some reason for it. There had to be. Ethan Prescott was no stone-cold killer. She knew it in her heart, but her head needed convincing.

The memory of Cale Marks increased her agonizing. He'd taught her how to sit on a horse, how to fire a gun, and how to gut her first hunting kill, and he hadn't laughed when she'd promptly tossed up her breakfast. He'd been her father's foreman in Yankton, his right hand man, like an uncle to her. No man was fairer, wiser, kinder. And Ethan had killed him. Try as she would to excuse the act, she couldn't think of a single thing Cale Marks might have done to provoke his death. He was not a man of quick temper. He valued talk over truculence. True to his own edict, he never even wore a gun.

And Ethan had shot him down.

It was late. Her eyes were tired. Her sewing was a disaster. And she was no closer to the truth. Only two men knew it; Ethan and her father. It was a truth she had to discover if sleep was to come.

Resolutely, she set aside her stitchery and went to her father's study. The door was open upon an empty room. He'd retired for the night without so much as a word. An added ache weighted the burden in her chest. How far apart they'd grown. Irreversibly it would seem. She swallowed down the salty taste of her tears and began to climb the stairs.

A light shown beneath her father's door. Would he resent her disturbing him? Would questions about Ethan Prescott widen the gap of their alienation? She hesitated, torn. It would be easier to seek solace in her own room. And more cowardly. Furthermore, she could envision the night stretching out into timeless seconds of turmoiled thoughts.

Aurora raised her hand, readying a knock. The gesture was stilled by the sound of voices within. She didn't want to eavesdrop, but she was so surprised that one of the voices was female, she inadvertently leaned closer to the wood panel. She couldn't distinguish words but tone was clear. Lovers' murmurings. Her father's. And Ruth's.

She took a step back, so startled she stood for several minutes as still as a one of the stuffed trophies

Kincaid displayed in his study. Her father. And Ruth. Her father and Ruth. She expected a rush of hurt feelings, a sense that he betrayed her mother's memory, but neither came. She couldn't doubt he yet held Julia Kincaid in his heart. The fact that he sought a man's comfort in another woman's arms in no way tarnished the love her parents created between them. Julia had been gone for fifteen years and her father still lived. He hadn't died with her and she couldn't demand he act as though he had. She didn't begrudge him happiness with the handsome housekeeper. But inside, she felt a deeper pain.

How could her father invite Ruth to share the most intimate aspect of his life, not caring that she bore the blood of the Lakota and then, in spite of it, deny her son the slightest affection for that same reason? He had no trouble embracing the half-cast housekeeper and yet could not bear to recognize Scotty within his heart. His selfish selectivity woke her resentment. How self-serving were his opinions. No, she didn't begrudge Ruth her father's interest. The woman had gone out of her way to make her feel at home. She just couldn't understand the workings of her father's fickle heart. It brought a pang of bittersweet awareness, emphasizing how alone she truly was. Garth Kincaid had taken another into his life. Who did she have?

She had only to look into the serene face of her sleeping child to know that answer. She had Scotty. She wasn't alone. After tucking his blanket in about his feet, she went to her window and looked out upon the night. There would be no answers from her father on this evening. And after what she'd discovered, she couldn't go to Ruth. That left one avenue open and once she'd decided, a restlessness shivered through her.

Ethan. She would go to Ethan for the answers.

They looked blue at first then, at a distance of twenty miles, the island of mountains rising out of the rolling sea of the Great Northern Plains appeared black as coal. Aurora rode hard, sending her mount galloping across her father's pasture land, pushing until the hills became a deep changeless dark green, until she could identify the straight red pillars of ponderosa pine. Only then did she loose an exultant smile.

They climbed, horse and rider, up through dense thickets of saplings, over meadows just beginning to green, in a weaving dance between spruce and birch and quaking aspen, duplicating the erratic trail Aurora kept faithfully engraved upon her heart. Occasionally, she reined in the horse and paused, letting it blow while she surveyed the way they'd come, watching for signs that she'd been followed. She didn't expect company. She'd been careful, waiting until the last possible moment to tell Ruth her plans to go into town for a dress-fitting as she handed the baby into her arms. Then, she'd run to the barn, saddling her own mount and riding out with the suddenness of a winter storm before anyone could question or follow. She'd ridden toward town for the first few miles; then, when she came to a copse of trees that would conceal her change of route, she had veered abruptly from the road, toward the hills. Toward Ethan.

She didn't notice the chill. Her blood was hot and thick in her veins, pounding an excited rhythm that had nothing to do with the perils of her journey. Her breasts jounced within the flannel shirt she wore. Like the trousers and flat hat clapped over her fiery braid, it had been her brother's. She'd adopted them to make the trip easier, not suspecting the mannish garb would heighten her anticipation. Her nipples swelled and tingled against the friction of cloth. The chafe of the saddle between her thighs spread a pulsing urgency upward to throb at a precarious pitch. Her breath came loud and harsh in the cold morning air, sending out plumes like a locomotive gathering steam, gathering momentum, as every hitch and lunge of her stallion upward brought her nearer to the man she loved. It wasn't about questions, this ever sharpening tension. It was about the answers to things left unresolved between them. How it would feel to taste his welcoming kiss, to lie gloriously naked in his arms while they explored passion's promise? How she wanted the fulfillment of that promise.

What if it wasn't what he wanted?

That seditious doubt almost knocked the wind from her. A tight constriction seized her chest. Her knees gripped the stallion's sides to halt their sudden trembling. What if he didn't want her to come back to him? He'd blocked her suggestion of a return in both word and deed. Hadn't he led her in circles so she wouldn't be able to find her way? He hadn't counted on her gifted memory, just as she now counted upon the last long, hot look he'd given her. The look saying even if he didn't ask, he wanted her to come back to him.

Jaw squared and grimly set, she urged her horse onward. Of course he'd want to see her. After experiencing the plunging heat of his kisses, after feeling the impatient thickness in his groin, she knew—of course, he would be glad.

But there was so much about him she didn't know. Like the dark past he hid behind his silences and impassive stare. Could she be rushing into the arms of a cold-hearted killer?

No! No, he wasn't and he would prove it to her satisfaction once they were together. He would take away her doubts the same way thoughts of him took away her breath. He would heal them with his gentle surgeon's hands. And she would not regret this impulsive return.

He wanted her.

She would make sure of it.

And his loving would reassure her that all was right and well. That all was yet possible.

Damn you, Ethan Prescott. Don't you dare disappoint me!

Aurora was upon the secluded cabin almost before she realized it. She drew in the horse at the edge of the clearing to drink in the sight — and to give herself the chance to collect her courage. She was too anxious to feast her eyes upon the tall Texan to linger for long. Nudging the stallion ahead, she was aware of a frantic flurry of emotion. It was like coming home, only this time she hoped the feeling would sustain itself, as it hadn't when she returned to her father's ranch. Her fragile expectations had been cruelly crushed. Could her needy heart stand another rejection?

He wouldn't turn her away.

Dear God, don't let him turn me away!

After tethering her horse next to Ethan's big sorrel in the crude lean-to, and seeing it rubbed, watered and fed, she couldn't delay any longer. Sucking in a bolstering breath, Aurora marched toward the cabin door. She thought about knocking but that seemed so — impersonal, as if she was a passing visitor. That wasn't what she intended to be. So she pushed the door open.

The room was smaller than she remembered and more primitive after the comforts of her father's ranch house. But the warm memories swelling inside

185

more than compensated for the lack. Scotty's cradle stood empty before a cold hearth. He hadn't put it away. That touched her heart strangely. The cord was still strung across the room, the blanket still draped over it. He hadn't wanted to push them out of his life. Everything was as she'd last seen it. He'd moved nothing.

Then the truth of it settled.

Because Ethan wasn't there.

He'd run out of excuses to stay away.

The traps were set and baited and two fat jackrabbits strung over his shoulder. Game was slim. He'd had to track the rabbits half the morning. Once they'd been so thick they lay on scoria buttes like droves of sheep in their winter white coats. Civilization was crowding this land of plenty, and he felt its squeeze.

So did the small band of Lakotas he'd seen that morning. They, too, had been hunting, with no success. Their faces looked pinched. They were hungry. It made him think of Aurora when she'd first come to his cabin. She hadn't been able to get enough to eat. Perhaps these braves were of the same camp. Perhaps their women and children had that same hollow, ravenous look about them. Compassion clenched in his gut. He'd made an offer of the rabbits, but they'd proudly declined. They would starve in their woodlands before accepting white man's charity. He respected them for it but he didn't have to like it. Soon, there would be no room for the Lakotas or for Ethan Prescott. In a way, they were allies against a common enemy; time and the tide of greed from the valley below.

He trudged onward, lost to glum thought. He would skin the rabbits, spit one for his dinner, and save the other for the next day's stew. He would eat his fill and try not to think about those who went without. He would stare into the fire, rocking the empty cradle with the toe of his boot while his mind took him to forbidden places. And he would spend another sleepless night. Danged little to look forward to. On this night or the next or the next or the one after. There was nothing to fill his empty hours, to change the monotonous pace he'd once enjoyed. No one to distract him from his loneliness or his shattered dreams.

Damn her! She'd given him a taste of heaven and made his life pure hell! Solitude no longer satisfied, not when the silence was mocked by the memory of her laughter and the sound of Scotty's coos. No longer did he feel in control of his destiny. He was a miserable man in hiding, denied the chance to seek out happiness. Holed up like the Sioux to live half an existence with only the vestiges of pride and the illusion of freedom.

He approached his clearing without enthusiasm. Nothing waited but nagging memories, there to torture him with what he could not have, an isolated prison to contain his passionate nature until years and empty yearning withered it like a winter apple on the limb.

Smoke wreathed up from the chimney.

He hadn't left a flame kindled on the hearth.

Ethan swung the Henry up, resting its sights in his left palm. He neared the cabin with cautious, Indian-light steps. The whinny of a strange horse distracted him for a fleeting second. With the sound of his heartbeats hammering in his ears, he reached out with the muzzle of the rifle to prod the door open.

It was the last thing he expected, but everything he could wish for: Aurora Kincaid standing before his hearth looking so beautiful his heart jerked up into his throat; she'd come back.

They regarded one another in breathless silence; he with the Henry cocked and ready, she with the bulky old Sharps hauled up to her shoulder, each expecting to defend against an intruder. One long second passed, then another. Finally, both barrels lowered simultaneously.

"What are you doing here, Ora?" His voice was taut, strained.

Aurora clenched her teeth to keep her jaw from trembling. She was scared. His stalking approach had taken her unaware, making her think of the Miniconjou and their slippered cat feet. And now he stood staring at her with that hard, impassive look, displaying no emotion, no welcome. Dear God, had she made a terrible mistake?

When she didn't speak—she couldn't speak—Ethan glanced toward the empty cradle and lines of consternation creased his features. "Where's Scotty? Has something happened?

She shook her head in answer to his curt question and forced a smile to move the tense muscles of her face. He looked so good. The sight of him affected her with heart-wrenching gladness. Only his guarded expression held her from throwing herself upon his broad chest and burrowing close into the outdoorsy scent of his coat. Why hadn't he opened his arms to her? Instead, he stood braced and wary like big bear run to ground in his lair, as if she posed a threat. This was not going the way she would wish. Had she been wrong?

"Scotty's fine. Growing so fast you'd hardly know him."

"It's only been a couple of days, Ora," he chided gruffly.

No. A lifetime, she argued silently in her soul.

"I owed you some supplies." She gestured toward the pack of goods she'd carried up with her. Her voice had that same hollow distance that echoed in his words.

He moved then, nudging the door closed behind him with his heel, slinging the rabbit carcasses down upon the table and shrugging out of his coat. All the while, his dark, shuttered gaze never left her. She could smell the crisp traces of pine and cold and gunpowder that clung to him like an exclusive cologne. Her delicate nostrils flared as she breathed it in, savoring it until she felt lightheaded watching him examine the sack of coffee beans.

"You didn't have to do that."

"I wanted to."

Again the stilted silence settled. Aurora's blood was pounding. She felt faint, uncertain. Yet the desire held her. Even if he didn't want her, it was where she wanted to be. And if he wouldn't take her in his arms, she would take her fill of him with her eyes, with her quivering senses.

"I've some coffee ready. And some tea cakes. I remembered you saying you didn't have any." Her attempt at humor went achingly flat. Still, the corners of his grimly-set lips twitched and turned up into a ghost of a smile, telling her he remembered, too.

He remembered too damned much.

Ethan reached up to retrieve two cups and poured from the steaming pot. Metal clattered on tin. *She was here.* As stunning as the first spring sunrise. His mind was dazed, his heart cartwheeled crazily. Finding her in his cabin had stopped him as cold as a .45 caliber bullet. It took an eternity to recover. Now, he fought against the gnawing need to jerk her up and fall with her upon his rumpled bed, ripping loose her

189

clothes to get at the creamy sweet skin that tormented his memory. The imaginings filled his groin with fiery demands. His hands shook. His flesh felt cold and damp while blood surged hot beneath it. Tea cakes! Laughter burbled up inside him like a fresh well spring. God, the woman was exasperating. Amusement choked off into an intolerable ache. Why the hell did she have to come back? He would have gotten over her—in a hundred years or so.

Ethan schooled his features to betray none of his tumbling emotions, then turned with a brimming cup in either hand. She'd come up behind him, so close she was nearly brushing his shirt front with the tempting roundness of her bosom. Startled, the breath crushed from him by the abrupt constriction of his chest, he reacted by taking a quick step back. His hand jerked just as she took hold of the tin cup. Scalding coffee sloshed over the brim.

Even before the cry of hurt died on her lips, Ethan had plunged Aurora's hand into the bucket of cool drinking water. The searing pain instantly abated. Yet when he drew it out, to cradle in the palm of his own while he examined the tender skin for signs of redness, tears shimmered in her eyes. That glittering brightness wasn't caused by pain of the flesh but from a rending of the heart. How gentle his healing touch. How warm and firm his clasp.

"Nothing serious," he said with pronounced relief. "Just a little singed, is all. Shouldn't blistered up but if it does . . ."

His gaze rose from the small hand to lock into hers. Longing pooled in her eyes. The golden depths glowed, pulling him in. He didn't resist. Slowly, he brought her injured hand up to his lips, grazing the sensitized skin with his moustache, laving it with the wet rasp of his tongue, deliciously heating rather

190

than soothing. Her body flamed in response.

"Ethan—"

It was a fractured plea, and he'd taken an oath to ease all forms of suffering.

He lifted the hand he held, settling it over his shoulder while his other opened wide to span the curve of her back. Both tightened their holds into greedy clutches, pulling them inexorably together until lips met and breaths mingled and tongues tangled in a greeting long delayed. It was an intense reunion, fueled by the short but interminable separation—and by the knowledge that soon they would have to part again.

Ethan said her name in a raw sort of whisper and pulled away. He was breathing too hard. Too fast. Things were spiraling rapidly out of his control. He wasn't the sort of man to take advantage of a woman—and God knew Aurora Kincaid was lost to the worst sort of vulnerability. She was fragile now, clinging to him as some kind of salvation from the brutal captivity she'd endured. He wouldn't use her, as Far Winds had used her, satisfying his needs and giving nothing to her in turn. And there was nothing he could give this lovely rancher's daughter who had the comfort of a good home and fine name. Nothing. He stepped back even farther, until distance cooled the combustion of their closeness.

"Danged fool female," he scolded, trying to sound angry or even annoyed. The words came out like a sultry caress. His stern look was spoiled by the dark smolder in his eyes. "What do you mean by coming way up here all on your lonesome? Didn't you give a thought to the danger? How'd you find your way?"

She smiled, a slow, satisfied woman's smile. "Did you think to put me off with a few wrong turns? I'm a determined woman, Ethan Prescott. You should know that by now."

"I surely do. A crazy one, too. But you didn't answer me." His fingertips sketched the finely shaped bones of her face. His voice lowered to a hoarse rumble. "Why'd you come?"

"To see you." It was that simple. What other reason could she give. Truly, none other existed as she melted beneath his simmering stare.

He tried to smile, to lighten the moment before it sank into an irreversible whirlpool of passion. "You mean it wasn't to share tea cakes and coffee?"

Her small hand settled upon his shirt front, feeling the hard pumping of his heart beneath it. Her own was working in a similar runaway rhythm.

"That's not what I want to share with you."

"Oh?"

His fingers slipped back behind her head, spearing into her tidy braid, opening wide, then clenching to ruin the woven tendrils of flame. Such a sensuous feel, rippling like raw silk.

"I want us to make love."

Had she actually said that out loud? Aurora bit her lip in regretful horror. Did decent women make such wanton proclamations, demanding pleasure from a man who was not her husband? Probably not. Was she, then, everything the whisperers in town believed? She didn't care what they thought, only what figured behind the suddenly still expression on the tall Texan's face. Had she shocked him? Had she disgusted him with her forthright request? She couldn't tell. Why hadn't she waited for him to say the words? Was it because she feared he wouldn't? Dear God, she'd made such a muddle of it all.

In a very small voice, she ventured to speak of what writhed painfully in her heart.

"Don't you want to?"

The breath exploded from him in a tortured moan. He snatched her up, kissing her breathless, senseless, until there was no room in her ecstasy-flooded mind to hold to any doubts. He groaned her name, taking her bold little mouth with deep thrusts of his tongue while she strained up against him on tiptoe. Had he ever wanted a woman this much? Never! Not any woman.

Her hands worked in the fabric of his shirt, impatient with the impersonal cloth. She murmured her complaint into the cavern of his mouth as his lips grew more demanding. She dissolved against him as hands now hard with urgency stroked down her back and buttocks, stopping there to cup that insolent trouser-clad bottom in his palms, to press her into the thick evidence of his need. She was lost, undone. Hands that once kneaded now clung as excitement weakened her knees. His mouth touched her temple, her cheek then lingered on the fluttering pulse point at the silken junction of neck and shoulders. Pleasure was a living thing, squirming inside her, eager for release. Desperate to communicate that need, she rubbed her hips over the rigid length of his arousal and thrilled at his answering growl.

"I want you, Ora," came his rumbling oath. "God, I want you."

One big hand captured her face, holding it poised as he kissed each perfect feature. Her lips parted, hungry for the hot, heady taste of his passion, but he bypassed them in favor of her arched throat. There, he nipped and nibbled while his other hand rose to claim the heavy globe of one breast. Small circles of his thumb brought an aching hardness to throb against the fabric. He nuzzled his face into her hair. It had worked loose to form a fiery spill about her shoulders. Deft fingers manipulated buttons through buttonholes, and soon she sighed as his rough palm moved over bared flesh. Then she cried out as he caught the taut tip between his teeth. Her hands twisted in his hair. Her knees shook. A flood of hot need pooled between her thighs.

"Ethan," she begged.

He lifted her easily and carried her to the bed. He'd done it in his imagination a thousand times. One, two, three, four steps, then the heavenly descent into her arms. Impatiently, he hooked his fingers at the waistband and shucked the indigo denim from her slender hips. Her shirt had fallen open. Her skin glowed with a lush pearlescence. She lie still, letting him look his fill with a dark, desire-drenched stare. Then quietly, she coaxed him from his reverie.

"Love me, Ethan."

He couldn't tear out of his clothes fast enough to join her on the pungent pine-filled mattress. She reached for him, urging his mouth over her eager lips, teasing his tongue into mating with her own with quick, taunting flickers. Her arms wound about him, possessively stroking the cording of his neck, the swelling fan of shoulders, the sleek tapering length of his back down to his taut buttocks. She could feel his manhood beating hot and hard against her thigh. The anticipation grew unbearable.

He had buried his face between her full white breasts, abrading the soft flesh with his beard, kneading them roughly with his lips. Briefly, he tasted their sweetness, then moved on, for that realm belonged to Scotty and he felt a guilty trespasser.

Thinking of Scotty woke another concern. Ethan's hand rested on the slight mound of Aurora's belly, dragging her from her daze of delight with his sudden stillness.

"Ethan?" she queried softly. "What is it?"

"I don't want to hurt you, Ora. It hasn't been that long since you gave birth."

She could hear the seething effort of restraint in his voice, the way it labored his breathing. And she smiled. "I'm fine. But examine me to make sure if you like, Dr. Prescott."

Her husky suggestion woke a craving so voracious it curled his toes. He stared down deeply into her molten gaze and unfurled a lustily wolfish grin. "Be my pleasure, ma'am," came his lazy Texas drawl.

He eased down on the bed, lifting one long bared leg to rest atop his shoulder. An exquisite tension coiled in her middle as his burning gaze assessed her.

"Everything looks fine but I best be certain." The words rasped out dryly as the smile stiffened on his lips. His palm rubbed over red-gold curls; fingers parted the damp folds below. Then he ducked his head, and she felt the exploring probe of his tongue.

Lightning struck. Aurora gasped as a sizzle and snap of raw sensation ran the length of her limbs, causing them to quiver and quake and finally to jerk. A stunning jolt scorched through her insides, wringing a cry from her as it burst with thunderous force. She was twitching nervelessly as the crackling static flickered out when he rose up over her. She stared up through round, awed eyes, wondering blankly what he'd done to wreak such havoc through her system.

"Fit as a fiddle," he pronounced with a rumble of satisfaction and his mouth dropped down upon hers. She could taste the saltiness of her body on him and it was wildly exhilarating. Incredibly, the throb of desire intensified.

"Ethan, I love you."

Aurora pressed her face into the crook of his neck as he sank himself inside her. She arched up in welcome, sheathing him tightly, as greedy to hold him as he was to claim her. With each driving thrust, he told her of his need of her, of the longing, of the loneliness. And she gave back with equal fervor. She couldn't believe such sensations existed, that each stroke of him could arouse her to a frenzied response. Though her body had been conquered by another, not so her heart and soul. What they had between them was no impersonal mating, but a meeting and melding of one into the other. And though she could feel his climax imminent in the strong tremors seizing his powerful form, he held back, waiting, urging her onward, upward, to join him at that breathless pinnacle where no other had ever taken her.

It was upon her like a Dakota blizzard; sudden in its approach, frightening in its fury, surrounding her in a swirling vortex of pleasure. She clung to Ethan's slick shoulders, desperate for solid purchase, but was swept up by the sensual storm. She moaned and twisted away from his plundering kisses to gasp for air, for sanity. It was then Ethan saw her lovely face, taut and passion-glazed as the throes of her release surged over her. He could feel her body shuddering beneath him, around him, and he surged deeper, harder, wildly, until taken violently by like tremors.

And when the fierce buffeting pleasures ebbed, he eased down over her slender form the way the snows covered the lush valley below. He felt her stir languidly, heard her low, sated murmur as her lips moved against the hollow of his throat. A great tide of emotion rose to lodge beneath those nibbling lips, shutting off his air, draining his senses to the point of dizziness. And because it was the only way he could think of to relieve that collecting ache, he spoke the words she'd inscribed with her soft little cries of fulfillment upon his soul.

"I love you, Ora."

Her eyes squeezed shut as she savored those precious words. But before she could echo them back, he concluded harshly, almost angrily . . .

"Damn you."

Chapter Twelve

Aurora lay silent and stunned as Ethan rolled onto his back to glare up at the rough cut ceiling. She could see emotion working along his jaw beneath the heavy beard and was suddenly afraid to question its source. All the wonderful honey-warm delights he'd showered upon her were abruptly lessened by doubt, by undeserved pain. He'd cursed her as if the beauty spawned between them was more plague then pleasure, as if he regretted the magic woven from one soul to another. She bit her tender lip to still its weak trembling, while she listened to the savage sawing of his breath beside her.

"I'm not sorry," she said at last, stubbornly, pridefully because she wasn't even if he was. Then she waited, hoping he would say something sweet, something kind to deny it. Tears began to build with a fiery brilliance as the silence continued. Why did he cruelly allow her misery to mount?

"Why did you have to come back?" he said at last. It was more accusation than question. He wouldn't look at her. "I swore I'd never twist in that kind of trap again."

They stung, those quiet, angry words. They reached straight into her heart and strangled every ounce of bliss until only an aching resentment remained. First, he cursed her, now he blamed her — as though all were her fault. As if she were guilty of leading him into bed against his will. As if he hadn't been just as impatient as she to strip off clothing and objections. As if he hadn't encouraged her return with the sultry temptation of his mouth. Damn *him!*

"It wasn't my intention to *trap* you. Have your precious freedom if it means so much to you."

With that, Aurora rolled away and swung her slender legs off the bed. The room wavered through the sheen of her tears, but before she could stand, Ethan's hand caught her arm. Angrily, she resisted, jerking hard to pull away. She was blinking fiercely and choking down sobs by the time he sat up. Her struggles were futile as he drew her back against his bared chest. Strong arms surrounded her quaking shoulders. Her hot, damp face sought shelter in the warm hollow of his throat. There, he held her for a long moment, offering the comfort of his big body and gentle hands, but when he spoke, it was not with consoling tenderness. It was with bitter truth.

"It's no good, Ora. Don't you see? It doesn't matter what either of us wants."

She wrenched back to stare up into the harshly drawn angles of his face. His dark eyes burnt down into hers like coals from the fire, smoldering with feelings he would deny by the taut set of his mouth. That intense look begged her understanding and refused explanation. She didn't want to be calmed by the unspoken sentiments in his gaze. She needed to hear them upon his lips. She'd come too far to be discouraged by silence.

"Why? Because you killed my father's foreman?"

His recoil was so controlled that only the convulsive tightening of his arms betrayed him. Wariness skirted the taut edges of his closed expression, that and something even deeper. Disappointment?

"Is that what you believe?" he questioned softly.

"That's what I've heard," she countered. Her golden eyes grew pleading. "Ethan, I came to you to hear the truth."

His stare grew even more distant. His breathing was as jagged as the peaks above them but his words were smooth and still. "Find it in your heart, Ora," was his quiet challenge.

"I've searched there and—"

"And?"

"And I can't believe it."

"Can't or don't want to?"

Her reply was a whisper. "Both."

Ethan released her and she felt adrift. He lay back on the rumpled bedcovers, head pillowed on one forearm, the other braced across his eyes. She waited for him to say more, desperate for assurance, needing reason to back her faith. But he offered none. She put out a hand, letting her fingertips ride the movement of his chest. The hard pulse beneath them contrasted with the veneer of his calm.

"Ethan, talk to me."

His arm dropped, unveiling a somber stare. "You won't like what you hear."

"I haven't liked anything I've heard so far," she argued. His hand passed over hers and her fingers twisted tight between his. "Trust me."

He observed her steadily for a moment, dark eyes penetrating, probing as they weighed the risk. Under that cautious scrutiny, her anxiety mounted.

"Please trust me."

Ethan took a deep gulping breath. "Guess I'll have to."

A smile trembled upon her lips. It wasn't happiness she felt. It was a grim satisfaction. She started to prepare for the worst. Whatever he had to say was not going to be easy to listen to. She was further alarmed when he encircled her with one arm and coaxed her down into the snug security of his side. It was a protective gesture, meant to guard her against what? The truth? Could it be that awful?

Then, he began the telling.

"The first time I saw it was in '74. I'd come up on the Texas Trail. It was ninety days of eating dust, wrangling horses, cussing the cook and collecting calluses from the Rio Grande all the way north across the Red, Cimarron, Republic and Platte. When we forded the Belle Fourche to push into Montana, I got my first eyeful of God's country. And I knew here was where I was going to end up for the rest of my days. The hills were all Indian territory then, but Custer was heading up his gold-finding expedition and I knew it would be only a matter of time before greed and demand made the government forget their promise that the Sioux could roam the land as long as grass grew and water ran. And I knew I'd be back to set in roots. Thinking about the ranch I'd have in the valley was all that kept me going for the next two years.

"When the hills opened in '76, I staked out my one hundred and sixty acres of prime valley grassland. I built me a cabin out of cottonwood logs and fenced my stock in pole corrals. For the first year, I lived off my own beef, sowbelly, beans and coffee until I could make my first sale. Holding the profits in my hands, I thought I had it all. I thought my future would be as sure and set as a Dakota sunrise. That is until my new neighbor turned loose his herd and his men to overrun my land. Public domain, he called it. Never mind that I had clear title. So I put up fences and he tore 'em down. I went to the law but they wouldn't do nothing for a Johnny Reb trying to hold his own against a hero for

201

the Union. Hell, the war'd been over for ten years and here I was fighting it again." His words grew harsh and angry but with a breath he controlled them enough to go on. "I was a Southerner and a homesteader and a piece of paper saying the land was mine didn't stack up to a hill of beans."

Aurora could picture him fighting to keep his claim, frustrated by the failure of the law to guarantee his due. How that would rile a man like Ethan Prescott. A man of honor and principle. A man who went by what was right and honest and expected it in return. How disillusioned he must have been. And angry. She'd seen hints of temper simmering inside him. Had it made him angry enough to kill? With cause or at the slightest provocation?

"So I went to my neighbor," he continued, and Aurora caught a softening to his tone. Oh, the anger still throbbed in them, but they were tempered with a quiet regret. He had tucked her head down beneath his chin so it was impossible to see his expression. She could imagine it; all sharp lines and shadowed valleys. As unyielding and rawly beautiful as the hills. "This ambitious man determined to gobble up the grasslands to feed his own cows. I tried to make peace with him. There was plenty of grazing land. All I wanted was the right to tend what was mine and to be left alone. And you know what he did? He laughed at me, he laughed because his dream was bigger than mine. Said he was of a mind to go over me rather than around less I wanted to sell out. Told me I could name my price but what I had in that valley couldn't be bought. It was my home, my right to peace of mind and self-respect. I told him he could try to swallow me up with the Bar K but I planned to stick in his craw till he choked on me."

Her father.

Of course.

Now she understood the nuances in his voice. He was trying to spare her without keeping her innocent. Why? She knew the kind of man her father was. He was ambitious, yes but hardly unreasonable. She could fathom why the two men would collide over territory like bull buffalos. She could almost hear her father's bellowing and Ethan's cold, stubborn drawl. And she could guess what passed between them. The Major would take an instant dislike to Ethan Prescott, the Southerner who had had the temerity to stand in his way. She imagined an explosion of temper. But could that clash have led to Cale Marks's death? Over a piece of land legally owned by the Texan? She didn't want to believe it. So she lay still and listened and tried not to judge.

Ethan felt Aurora's resistance to the truth. She was the man's daughter after all. But he couldn't sugarcoat it for her. Garth Kincaid fully meant to chew him up. Days and nights had been filled with an anxious terror. Ethan's hand began a slow stroking along Aurora's fiery hair as those remembered feelings twisted in his gut. Wells were poisoned, stock run off, crops trampled, but it was the threat of fire that kept him sleepless. Afraid to leave his ranch to purchase supplies, he was held hostage to fear upon his isolated island in the vast unfriendly sea of Kincaid grasslands. There seemed no way to win against the greater power, but the Texan was too stubborn to give in. He refused to be bought or bullied, and he lay each night in his darkened room, expecting to hear the hungry crackle of flames eat through the beams overhead. His dream became a waking nightmare.

Aurora listened with a mounting sense of helplessness. Her emotions were stretched taut and pulled apart like taffy. Her father. She couldn't believe it of him. He'd always been strong and aggressive but fair. The man who'd held her on his knee and talked of the endless acres they'd someday own was not the land-grubbing tyrant Ethan described. Her father was no monster, void of conscience and mercy. He wasn't! He'd had to struggle too hard to know his own dreams to deny them to another man. She tried to picture him callously giving orders to plow under another's hopes — and couldn't. Not her father. Not Garth Kincaid.

But Ethan's words shook with the passion of truth. She could feel his frustrated rage, his pain, his fear vibrating in every corded sinew, in every bitter beat of his blood. And she ached for what he'd suffered. A vengeful fury would have consumed all else in her mind and heart — had the villain been other than her father.

It couldn't be true.

She couldn't imagine Cale Marks sneaking up with torch in hand to burn out her father's troublesome neighbor. She couldn't envision the gruff, honorable foreman taking orders so heinous even from his boss and friend. He just wouldn't. She knew it as surely as she knew Ethan believed his misfortune was dealt by Garth Kincaid. And just as certainly, she knew Ethan wouldn't have killed without reasonable cause. Had his life been in danger, she could forgive him. If it was self-defense. Couldn't she? The sound of Cale Marks's good-spirited laugh echoed through her memory, and her heart clutched tight.

Swallowing down the great lump of distress that had risen in her throat, Aurora asked, "Why did you kill Cale? I can't believe he meant you harm. He wasn't the sort to threaten violence, much less carry it out. What did he do to make you draw on him?"

Ethan heard the anguish in her question and the frailty of her belief. Could he expect any different? He'd known it wouldn't be easy. Had he thought she'd let the word of a man who was little more than her lover overturn a lifetime of loyalty to his enemy? But with her lying next to him, naked in his arms, he couldn't help being wounded and angered by her doubt. It made his explanation short and harsh.

"Oh, I had me plenty of reasons. Defending my home. Defending my life. Those good enough reasons for you, Miz Kincaid? They sure didn't mean squat to your father."

Prodded by his sneering tone into taking an uncomfortable stand, Aurora's temper rebelled. "Of course they did and do," she snapped. "You don't know my father. He wouldn't do the things you accuse him of. He's an honorable and law-abiding man. He would never send his men to terrorize the helpless."

But then, Ethan Prescott hadn't been helpless. He'd shot down Cale Marks.

And she had bedded down with the man who killed her friend.

Abruptly, she felt a constricting panic. How was she to go home with the knowledge that she'd come to her father's enemy and known bliss in his embrace? How could her father forgive that, on top of all else? She shivered beneath the shadow of disgrace.

Seeking a way to rally her pride and her faith in all she knew and believed in, Aurora claimed, "Perhaps you're blaming my father for your own bad luck."

Ethan went cold inside. Could he expect any different from a Kincaid? A haughty, self-serving Kincaid? Just like her father.

Just like a woman.

"My bad luck? Oh, yes. You could say that. My bad luck started with the war and has been following me ever since." Right up until the day his horse shied in the middle of a blizzard. Or had that been the worst stroke of them all? His sigh couldn't budge the heaviness that settled inside.

205

"You'd better go, Aurora."

The quiet words held the strength of a roar. Horribly, unhappily, Aurora realized the presence of her father made a wide, unspannable gulf between them now. Suspicion and uncertainty threatened the crossing, and trust was too frail to encourage it. Held close to his chest, still secure in his arms, she felt, nonetheless, a barren distance forcing them apart. Reluctantly, she drew away.

"Yes," she murmured softly, her heart beating in that single syllable. She sat up and reached for her discarded shirt. Ethan made no attempt to stop her. She knew it was for the best. But she wished he would. In her soul, she prayed that he would seize her and plead with her not to go. What would she answer, she wondered wildly. What could she say when love and logic pulled two ways?

But Ethan said nothing.

Taking a resolute breath that trembled despite her determination, Aurora slid her arms through the sleeves of her brother's shirt. Seth had been a Kincaid and proud of it. If he'd heard someone so defame his sire, he'd have made them eat their words with a liberal dose of lead as a chaser. So would Jed. She and her brothers were raised to believe no finer man walked the earth than Garth Kincaid. Could she allow her confused emotions to betray the memory of a bold father and his brave sons? Hadn't she done enough to stain the name already? Guilt enveloped her along with the coarse folds of the shirt, wrapping her in misery. She owed it to them to take a stand against all she wanted, against all she loved beyond the reach of family. And she would try. For them, she would try. She stiffened her spine and with it, her pride. Ethan Prescott was wrong. As stubborn in his beliefs as her father, he wouldn't listen, he wouldn't be swayed from his own version of the truth.

So what good would staying do? It would only confuse the issue. Only confuse her heart. She couldn't change what had gone on before her arrival in the hills. She couldn't take back the fact that she'd lain with her father's enemy. But she could walk away with some of her dignity intact. She could. She had to. Because she was a Kincaid. She was her father's daughter.

She was leaving.

He'd told her to with words and brusque actions. And he'd told himself it was what he wanted. To be shed of another deceitful female. To be free of that tempting and fatal trap. He watched her slip her silken arms into the ridiculously long shirtsleeves and tried to conjure up the strongarm tactics of her father. He followed the movement of her lithe fingers down the row of buttons and thought of them straying down the length of his long, hard form. To where desire began to build and throb. How he wanted her. How he wanted to believe she could give him all the things a cruel fate denied. He wanted to forget who she was, what she was linked to by blood. But he couldn't, and it made him as angry as it did frustrated. And it didn't do one damned thing to discourage his need of her. Now.

He never should have reached out to stay her. He never should have touched her. He should have been honorable enough to let her leave with yet a scrap of self-respect. But as soon as he felt the sweetly curved satin sleekness of her thigh beneath his palm, reason fled. Only desire remained. Blind, desperate desire.

"Ora," he called thickly. Enticingly.

Her breath caught and expelled unsteadily. Shoulders tried to square within the loose wool flannel but shook instead. Slowly, she looked down at him. The eyes that met his were round with upset and dismay, and they hit him like a ten-pound sledge. Guilt wreathed his longing. He couldn't face his responsibility for bringing that daze of doubt and dread to her beautiful features, so he blotted them out with the intensity of his need. His hand cupped her head, pulling her down to him, blurring that blaming gaze as her face grew closer to his own. She resisted. He could feel her tension as she pressed back against his palm. But it wasn't difficult to overcome her struggle. He did it with a greater strength. He did it with the hungry persuasion of his mouth upon hers and the combination melted her objection. She was no fool. She knew how to give in to a mightier force. The role of captive was a familiar one. He felt her warm, willing flesh go stiff and cool as he tried to stir passion with the rough eagerness of his hands. It was like molding cold clay. She didn't resist. Nor did she surrender.

Her passivity was an attack he hadn't expected and knew not how to conquer. It made him feel weak. It made him no better than Far Winds who had used her, not brutally in body, but ruthlessly in spirit. Nevertheless, he couldn't stop. When she rode away, it would be never to return, and he couldn't release her until he'd made more memories to sustain him.

She was panting. The rapid jerks of breath caused her breasts to graze his chest in a hurried dance of agitation. She didn't fight his kiss but neither did she respond to it as he would wish. He allowed her to pull away, slightly, far enough to observe her flushed expression. There was no fear in it. Had there been, he would have let her go. Or he hoped to God he would have. She stared down at him through golden eyes all hot and bright with mixed emotion. She wanted him. But she didn't want to want him. He could see doubt war with desire. It wasn't fair, the advantage he took with the soft brush of his thumb along her cheek. It made her eyelids flicker and her breathing falter. Still, she wouldn't come to him.

"Ora," he coaxed quietly. Then, he waited.

A low sound rumbled from her, not quite a moan, nor a growl. Weakness of flesh overcame fortitude of mind. With that primitive noise rising in her throat, her protest fled. Her mouth came down upon his, seeking, demanding all he could give her. Her kisses were urgent, wild, hurting in their desperate inexperience. She straddled him, a long, well-developed leg hugging either side as though he was something untamed she meant to ride and break. Red hair, the color of a Dakota dawn, cloaked her shoulders and spun down in tendrils of fire. His hands caught at the collar of her oversized shirt and impatiently pulled. Buttons gave before the wrench of fabric and the bounty of her full white breasts spilled out to taunt his avid stare. He could feel her moist woman's flesh hot against his belly. It was too much.

Groaning her name, he heaved up on one side, toppling her, rolling her beneath him upon the rumpled bedding. His mouth ground over hers and she opened for him. The stab of his tongue was met with the aggressive tangle of her own. Ethan wrapped his hands in her fiery hair until they became silken bonds from which she had no will to escape. Her long legs laced with his, urging him with the arch of her body into the cradle of her hips. And there he sought and discovered paradise.

She took him in with a soft cry of renewed wonder. Her slender figure shuddered as she conformed tightly about him. Ethan paused. Blood beat in his head, robbing him of his senses. Desire pounded in his loins, a hard, savage rhythm echoed by the throbbing warmth encasing him. Breath tore from his lungs, from a chest aching with raw, completing passion. And when he looked upon her and saw the answering glaze of satisfaction etched in each perfect line he lost all control.

The bedframe banged against the wall with every demanding thrust. Aurora's moans of pleasure were driven from her in a matching tempo. Her fingers clenched his thick beard, compelling him back to the hot luxury of her lips. Almost too soon, he felt tremors quicken beneath and around him into sharp spasms of helpless ecstasy. They shook through her and he knew a wholly indulgent, totally male gratification, for he was the first to take her there. And with one last poise and plunge, he joined her.

He lay for a long moment atop the hills and valleys of her form, feeling them quiver beneath him. The shivery motion didn't ease even after his own breath was recovered. Then, with some distress, he felt the wetness of her tears where their cheeks were pressed together. He lifted up reluctantly to meet the evidence of his selfish shame. Her gaze was molten with pain and hope. And he, bastard that he was, had no cure for either. Wordlessly, he withdrew and watched her struggle to clothe herself in self-respect. Tears glittered. For a moment, strength nearly failed her. Her breasts jiggled poignantly as she fought to fend off the mounting pain. A pain of separation. Of mistrust.

Then, just as he was about to reach for her, the vulnerability was gone. He forced himself to refrain from the offer of sympathy, to watch with bittersweet admiration as she gathered her scattered clothing and dressed. Dampness tracked her face but a fierce pride in her expression denied them reign. What incredible courage she displayed in that refusal. How small he felt in comparison. Her sobs might have gained her anything from him at this point but she would not lower her stubborn dignity to plead. To her credit, she was every inch a Kincaid.

Aurora Kincaid. His insides tightened. His jaw tensed. Daughter of the man who destroyed the last of his dreams.

Don't go. Don't go.

He clamped his teeth and bit down hard on the sour truth. He was better off without her.

Without her. God!

He watched as shaky hands divided her hair into three long tails of fire then wove them into one heavy braid. She worked his emotions just as neatly, but the design was not as uniform. Logic twisted about truth. Love bent around betrayal. Faith intertwined with fear. It made an ugly, ragged pattern.

Kincaid.

How could he trust her? How could he ask her to have faith? How could he expect her love to last? He couldn't. In answer to all of them. He couldn't.

And it was killing him. Choking him the way her father would—with a rope around his neck, until no flicker of life remained. The way Olivia had. The creak of the rope. His blood froze.

Aurora stood then and hesitated. He knew she was waiting for him to say something but he couldn't. He was strangling on his panic. In that silence, she found her strength. Her backbone went straight as a Ponderosa pine, and she stepped away from him.

As if in the slow-motion throes of a bad dream, he rose to pull on his long johns, buttoning them only as far as the waist. By then she was fastening her heavy coat before the fire. Her gaze never once strayed to the bed where she'd lusted for him and with him. Nor did she look at him again until she'd opened the door. Then, she looked long, through somber eyes. There was no blame held in that last lingering stare, but that didn't stop him from heaping it upon himself. Finally, she turned and strode out into the wash of weak afternoon sunshine, to where her horse was tethered.

Ethan stood in the doorway. A network of fine shadows played upon his broad expanse of chest and shoulders. He didn't feel the cool brush of air over bared skin. There was no room within the crowded wellspring of remorse.

Why had he touched her? Why had he lured her back with passion's promise? Why hadn't he let her go earlier, when there was a chance she'd escape with heart bruised but spirit not yet broken? Then she might have ridden away and not looked back. Then she might have been able to forget him.

But that wasn't what he wanted.

No matter what he might tell himself to appease his doubts, to soothe his fears, he wanted Aurora Kincaid's interference in his life. For without it, what good was living?

She didn't look back, not then. She pointed her mount toward the valley and rendered a swift jab of her heels. He remained in the door until the flame of her hair flickered and faded and was gone. Just as certainly, the heat was gone from his existence.

Chapter Thirteen

"Where have you been?"

The question, fired with the stopping power of a .44-.40, brought Aurora up short in the hall. Slowly, she turned to face her father where he stood in the door to his study. Some of her inner turmoil must have been mirrored in her expression, for his brow puckered and his already thinned lips took a downward plunge.

"Riding," she answered simply, knowing immediately that would not satisfy him. She'd hoped to slip in unnoticed, to collect her thoughts and emotions before confronting her father. But there was no chance for that now. Here he was, his face florid with fury, his hands balled into fists at his hips; not the picture of a man willing to listen to his daughter's woes. Aurora felt a moment of cowardly faintness.

"Don't try spinning a tale about going to town, because I know you didn't."

He *had* sent men to follow her. The realization gave her a moment's distress. No, she calmed herself with logic. If he knew her destination, he would have met her on the doorstep with her belongings packed. And Ethan Prescott would be dancing from a tree branch.

That image frightened her to the marrow and was a restorative to her will. The desire to protect him clashed with her desire to once again be enfolded in her father's care. All she had to do was say nothing and put the memory of her Texas lover behind her. With diligence, in time, she knew she could regain her father's love. She could become, again, his cherished, pampered child, his helpmate, his companion—if she surrendered her quest for the truth, and at the sacrifice of her love.

In those few seconds as she faced Garth Kincaid, her thoughts flew ahead to what the future would contain for her if she chose the easy way, the coward's way, and said nothing. She would exist under her father's roof like those treasured mementos of the past. He would expect her to keep the memories alive and pure. Scotty would be tolerated, perhaps someday even accepted. She would have her security, her childhood dreams, but at the cost of her woman's wants.

A staunch rebellion quickened in her soul. Hadn't she already given enough? She'd had her innocence torn from her. Must she surrender all hope to happiness, too? She thought of Ethan Prescott, of the desire and longing smoldering in his dark eyes, of the searing promise of his touch and the tormented claim that cut straight to her heart. *I love you, Ora.* Those words, those beautiful words sang in her soul.

Then she was cruelly recalled to his rejection; because of her father, because of her mistrust. He hadn't asked her to believe him. He'd asked her to look to her own heart. And that heart was torn between contrary pulls of affection: for the father who deserved her loyalty; for the man who had earned her love. Only the truth would free her: without it, she could not look upon her father without the stain of

214

doubt. Without it, she could not go into Ethan's arms without a snag of suspicion. Somewhere between the two dynamic men in her life stood a truth that would answer all. And one would fall for the sake of the other. That was the price of her happiness.

"I didn't go to town," she said softly. The words were so difficult. Once spoken, she would be forever different in her father's eyes. And he, in her own. She could well be about to shatter the mythic place he held within her heart. She might well be pushing him from his exalted pedestal. Did she have the strength — or the right — to make him fall? Or to help pick up the pieces?

"Well?" He waited, a scowl darkening his features like a thundercloud over some craggy Black Hills peak.

She drew a deep breath and forced her answer out with a tenacious will.

"I was with Ethan Prescott."

"Prescott." He mouthed the name as his mind refused to take it in. Slowly, his color faded, going pale, then abruptly purple. "Prescott!" The rafters shook with his incredulous roar. "Where the hell did you fall in with the likes of him?"

The suffering Aurora had felt over his failure to ask for the details of her ordeal lent a tartness to her reply. Never once had he thought to question beyond the obvious. She'd been taken captive. She'd been raped. She was back at home with a bastard baby. All harshly black and white — and all he needed or wanted to know of the last year of her existence. He didn't want to hear how she'd managed to survive, of how she'd spent her days, of how she'd held to her hopes. He hadn't asked how she escaped. Well, she wasn't about to volunteer any more than she had to until he showed some interest — some caring concern. "He saved my life and that of your grandson."

It was too much. He turned away from the bewildering creature who had once been his darling and strode for the whiskey on his sideboard. After a few quick gulps to cut the haze of disbelief, he was ready to face his contrary child. She stood in the hall, hands demurely folded before her, but her expression betrayed a mulish capacity, a trait he rightly recognized as his own, though at the moment he took no pride in claiming it. What had happened to the pleasing child she'd once been? The girl who would endure a stampede of longhorns before causing him a moment's grief? And grief was all he'd known since she'd returned to him, sullied beyond redemption. She'd brought a half-breed babe beneath his roof . . . and now this.

"Talk fast, girl. What do you know of Prescott?"

"Only what he's told me."

"And what lies were those?"

"Are they lies?"

Kincaid's jaw whitened with the pressure of his grinding teeth. "You have to ask?"

"I have to know." Her truculent tone softened with a note of pleading. "Did you run him off his land?" Deny it, her gaze begged of him. Please don't tarnish all I've ever believed in. Her chest filled with anguish as she watched his expression harden. Her heart thrust against her ribs like a trapped animal frantically seeking its freedom. And through tear-glazed, wide-open eyes, she saw her idol fall.

"Of course I wanted his land," the Major growled. He spoke with an arrogance, as if he had every right to covet what his neighbor owned. "That damned Southerner squatted himself down plum in the middle of the best grazing acres in the valley. I needed his water."

"So you took it." Her stomach roiled. Her senses reeled. She continued to stare at this man, this *stranger,* with complete incomprehension. "How could you?"

Garth Kincaid gave her a tight smile. "Don't look so surprised, Orrie. That's the way things are done out here. It's the only way a man can survive betwixt the bloodthirsty Indians and the cruelty of the land. You take what you can hold onto. Prescott couldn't hold on. Is that my fault?"

Aurora couldn't believe what she was hearing. "Yes! Yes, it is! Just because you're stronger, that gives you the right to steal from others?"

"It's not stealing, Orrie. It's public domain."

"But he owned his property."

"Says him. I never saw no paper."

Aurora shook her head. "That's no excuse. Or did you need an excuse? He was in your way so you ran right over him."

The depth of her contempt finally touched him. His voice gentled persuasively. "Now, Orrie, don't you know me better than that?"

Her eyes were wide, glittery. "I thought I did."

"Prescott bit off more than he could chew. He didn't have the acres or the manpower to run a spread. He would have gone under on his own. I offered to buy him out. Offered good money, too. Tried to explain to him that he had no future in this valley but he wouldn't listen, he couldn't get it through his thick Panhandle head. I tried to be a good neighbor."

"So you poisoned his water and tore down his fences." She gave a hysterical little laugh. "Is that what you call neighborly?"

217

Her father's features darkened into a storm cloud of outrage. "I did no such thing."

And she almost believed him.

He saw her doubt and it nearly killed him. Something precious shattered within him, something he'd always handled with fragile care and reverence. In spite of all his efforts to preserve it, that cherished memory held in his heart, fractured, leaving sharp, painful pieces to tear at him. And it was that Texan's fault. His fury brought a numbing cold to the raw fissures.

"Grow up, Orrie," he bit out fiercely and she recoiled with a satisfactory shock of response. "You had no objections to what I was doing when it kept you all fine and cozy in the East. I was making a home for us the only way I could. If that meant stepping on a few bullheaded nesters, I did what it took. But I never broke any laws."

"Whose laws?" she cried out in torment. "God's, man's or your own?"

"Out here, they're one in the same."

She turned from him, from his failure to hold true to her image of him, shaken to the soul. She gave a tiny start as big hands settled on her shoulders. Hands that had soothed her fears and hurts as a child. It would have been so easy to lose herself in his engulfing embrace, to tell herself it didn't matter, to forget all but the strength of their bond as father and daughter. Aurora knew if she turned back, she could seek that same comfort upon his broad chest. But there was no going back. And a tremendous sadness seized her.

Her rejection wounded a man who prided himself on his tough hide. The slight stiffening of her shoulders pierced straight through those carefully erected

218

walls to the tender center of him. It hurt and he reacted instinctively to ease the pain.

"I did it for you."

Aurora rounded on him. Her lovely face was awash with tears. "You did it for yourself!"

"For us," he protested. "For the dreams we used to talk of. They're not dreams any more. I've made them come true."

"At the cost of someone else's."

Her scorn wrought indescribable agony. To fend it off, he chose to attack rather than defend a weakening position. He'd learned that trick in Mexico. It had won him a battle and a medal. Now, he sought only to win his daughter's respect.

"Aren't you forgetting one thing in your crusade for Prescott? Aren't you forgetting Cale?" When she paled, he knew she hadn't. He pressed on mercilessly. "I sent Cale out to talk to him one last time to offer him cash money to move on. I was trying to be reasonable—neighborly! Cale went without a passel of strong-arms so Prescott wouldn't feel intimidated. He wasn't even armed." The Major's voice snagged emotionally and Aurora felt her heart twist in response. It had to be the truth. Such agony couldn't be summoned falsely. "My men found him dead, shot down on the doorstep with my money thrown down over him. And Prescott was gone."

The picture was horrible. Aurora squeezed her eyes closed but could not shut it out—Cale Marks sprawled in a pool of blood, hands spread and empty of the means of defense. Hot thickness rose in her throat. The view expanded to include Ethan Prescott at the door, smoking gun in hand.

"No."

She shook her head to scatter the image.

"No?" her father roared. He gripped her chin in his hand, forcing her gaze to meet his. "No? You think Cale went there to threaten him? You think Cale Marks did something to deserve what he got? Do you, Orrie?"

"No," she whispered faintly.

"Prescott killed him and ran," he said with cruel deliberation. He watched dispassionately as confusion distorted her features. Then he restated it for lasting emphasis. "Prescott killed him in cold blood."

Aurora wept soundlessly.

"Where is he, Orrie?"

The cold chill of his words woke her like a slap.

"Where is he?"

She stared at him, seeing blood-lust in his eyes. Seeing Ethan's dangling reflection there. And she rebelled. "I can't."

"You'd defend him, the man who murdered Cale?" He looked at her as though he saw something too loathsome to believe.

"He rescued me from a blizzard. He delivered Scotty. I owe him." And she loved him, but that, she would not speak aloud.

"His kind killed your brothers. He killed Cale. And you owe him for birthing your half-breed brat?"

Nothing he could have said would have turned her more quickly from his cause. Aurora went rigid. Pridefully, she angled up her chin. Staunchly, she declared, "Yes."

Rage quivered through Garth Kincaid. An Indian's whore and now the protector of his greatest enemy. "What's become of you?" he wanted to know. He couldn't understand this vile transition from beloved child to defiant adult. "I thought there was a special love between us. I thought the honor of our family

220

name meant something to you. Yet you'd betray both to save a murderer from justice. I'm ashamed to claim you as my daughter."

With a desolate sob, Aurora tore from his grasp and fled the room. He could hear her footsteps pound up the stairs and the slam of her door overhead. Then, there was silence.

"I've lost her, Ruth," he said quietly, aware of his housekeeper's presence even before she spoke.

"No." She moved gracefully into the room and went to knead the hard knots of tension from her employer's shoulders. "She is confused. So much has happened. Give her time. She will return to you as before."

"No," he disagreed sadly, thinking of the black-haired baby. "Not like before." He sighed as the strong fingers worked their magic. If only she could manipulate the anguish in his heart as easily.

"This has been such a lonely house. Let her fill it with her love."

"I don't know if that's possible any more." He stepped away from the woman's healing touch and poured himself another whiskey. He needed its bitter scorch to purge the last vestiges of hurt. "I buried her once, Ruth. I can do it again if I have to."

Sensing her upset, Scotty fussed angrily at his mother's breast. Hi's pint-sized tantrum forced Aurora to get control of her emotions. She sat by the window, calm of body if not spirit, while the babe suckled greedily, and she looked out over her father's domain. Such beautiful land, newly greening and spreading out so far it seemed to reach into tomorrow. A hard mistress to hold, won with the blood of innocents. Earned through treachery. That was how the white man stole it from the Indian. And how her father had taken it from Ethan Prescott. It seemed so unfair but that was the way of life, she was rapidly learning.

How naive she'd been a year ago on that coach ride to her personal paradise. Then, she'd thought men deserved their dreams, that they earned them honorably through hard work and perseverance. She'd been all too eager to further the myth with her expensive bustled gowns and society manners, standing proudly at her father's side to give acceptability to his sly doings. Had that been his purpose all along? To get her out of the way so she wouldn't be witness to his shady dealings? Had he thought she wouldn't understand the measures necessary to conquer their dream? He was right. She wouldn't have and she still didn't. She didn't understand this hard man's world where might and gunpowder granted right of way. Laws couldn't be bent to serve one master, even if that master was Garth Kincaid.

And conversely, if she would hold her father to the law, what of Ethan Prescott? He'd killed a man. Could she hold her father responsible for his deeds and excuse her lover of doing worse? Could she go to Ethan with the body of Cale Marks between them any more easily than she could step into her father's arms without remarking on his viciousness? No. She couldn't. And it was agony to accept.

If she was to wave her flag of righteousness, she should be first in line to see justice prevailed. She should be willing to lead the law to Ethan's door.

But she wasn't.

And it wasn't just because she owed him her and Scotty's lives. She owed him her very existence, her self-respect, her chance to hold to hope. His love warmed a soul she'd thought chilled beyond redemption. His regard affirmed her decision to endure at the hands of the Sioux while others—even her own father—would make her question what she had done. She owed him and would not repay that debt with betrayal. No matter what he'd done.

The Major would never accept her choice. He'd made that painfully clear in their confrontation below. His cold stare spoke volumes. In his eyes, she'd done the two worst things imaginable. She'd succumbed to the savages who killed his wife and defended the Southerner who took his sons and friend. She dared step into the path of his ambition, just as the Sioux and a Texas nester had done. And in time, she believed, he would hate her just as completely. It was a knowledge that ripped through her heart with ruthless clarity. Her defiance placed her against him, regardless of her reasons. To Garth Kincaid, there were no shades of gray, only the pure white of his cause and the depthless black of those who opposed him. What would he say if he knew she'd been rolling in blissful abandon with Ethan Prescott just hours before? She'd slept with one of his enemies, why not all? She was just as guilty in his narrow gaze.

Garth Kincaid didn't want the woman who'd borne a half-Lakota child. He wanted no part of the survivor of a Sioux captivity. Not once had he asked the particulars, not of her life with them, not of her escape. Not of Ethan's role in her rescue. It was as if he chose to believe the year between her abduction and her arrival on his front porch had never happened. Only her insistence upon keeping Scotty forced him to acknowledge it. And he resented the child even more so for that fact.

Unhappily, Aurora placed the sleeping child in his bed. What did the future hold for them? She was not such a fool as to believe the people in town would forget her ordeal or that they would take Scotty to their bosom. Nor, she realized miserably, would her father. To stay at the Bar K would be to live under a shadow and it was not her way to meekly hide and accept censure. Had she her father's support, she could have withstood the rest, but to be so alone within one's home . . .

She could go East, she reasoned, as she tucked the soft blanket about her child. She could lose herself in the city and claim herself widowed. There she could eke out a living in anonymity among strangers who didn't know or care about her past. And she would still be alone. Her love for Scotty could not fill the tremendous void in her soul that loving Ethan Prescott had created. The only time she'd felt complete was at his table, before his fire and within his arms. She'd found a rapturous haven in his woodland cabin — a haven that, woefully, couldn't last. He'd chased her from that Eden because of her father's taint. Or had it been because Ethan refused to force her to join him in hiding? He was a fugitive from a frontier law that ended in a noose. There was no future there and he knew it. And she hated him for making her see it too. What happiness they might find would be fleeting at best. Her silence could only earn him a brief respite. Eventually, he would be discovered and lynched for the killing of Cale Marks. Because his dream hadn't measured up beside Garth Kincaid's.

Had she only herself to think of, she might have disregarded the risk. She might have returned to the snug cabin to take greedily of all she could before consequence caught them. But there was Scotty to consider. It was no life for a child, the fear and con-

MORE PASSION AND ADVENTURE AWAIT... YOUR TRIP TO A BIG ADVENTUROUS WORLD BEGINS WHEN YOU ACCEPT YOUR FIRST 4 NOVELS ABSOLUTELY *FREE* (AN $18.00 VALUE)

Accept your Free gift and start to experience more of the passion and adventure you like in a historical romance novel. Each Zebra novel is filled with proud men, spirited women and tempestuous love that you'll remember long after you turn the last page.

Zebra Historical Romances are the finest novels of their kind. They are written by authors who really know how to weave tales of romance and adventure in the historical settings you love. You'll feel like you've actually gone back in time with the thrilling stories that each Zebra novel offers.

GET YOUR FREE GIFT WITH THE START OF YOUR HOME SUBSCRIPTION

Our readers tell us that these books sell out very fast in book stores and often they miss the newest titles. So Zebra has made arrangements for you to receive the four newest novels published each month.

You'll be guaranteed that you'll never miss a title, and home delivery is so convenient. And to show you just how easy it is to get Zebra Historical Romances, we'll send you your first 4 books absolutely FREE! Our gift to you just for trying our home subscription service.

BIG SAVINGS AND FREE HOME DELIVERY

Each month, you'll receive the four newest titles as soon as they are published. You'll probably receive them even before the bookstores do. What's more, you may preview these exciting novels free for 10 days. If you like them as much as we think you will, just pay the low preferred subscriber's price of just $3.75 each. *You'll save $3.00 each month off the publisher's price.* AND, your savings are even greater because there are never any shipping, handling or other hidden charges—FREE Home Delivery. Of course you can return any shipment within 10 days for full credit, no questions asked. There is no minimum number of books you must buy.

stant hiding. And the danger. She couldn't overlook the danger of being so close to the people of her child's father. The safest place for Scotty was on the Bar K and the best thing she could do for Ethan was stay silent and stay away. It was a harsh path to follow but she could honestly see no other choice.

"Miss Kincaid, I brought you something from the kitchen."

Aurora lifted a tired gaze to Ruth's kind features and managed a smile.

The handsome woman set the tray upon the night table, then lingered. She was troubled by the other's distress and the ripples it caused throughout the household. If only there was something she could do to calm the choppy waters.

"He loves you, you know."

Aurora received that with an expression of doubt. "I don't think so, Ruth. He loved a frivolous young woman who no longer exists."

"She still exists, inside, and he loves you because he knows that."

"Perhaps." That was said noncommittally. Without hope.

"It was quite a shock having you come home. Give him time to get used to the idea."

"I fear he never will. He would rather I died than to face what I lived through."

"Never say that!" The housekeeper was truly appalled.

"Saying it or thinking it, what's the difference. I'm not the girl he sent East to get an enviable polish. I'm a woman with a stained past and a bastard child. How foolish I was to think he'd welcome me with open arms."

"This is your home, Aurora. The home he built for

you. Don't you dare deny him the pleasure of giving it to you."

As if she suddenly realized how outspoken her words appeared, Ruth ducked her head but not before Aurora saw the anger burning in her eyes. The woman loved her father. That startled but did not dismay her.

"I appreciate your honesty, Ruth. I would like to consider you my friend. I have no one else to confide in."

The strong registers of her voice quavered and that was enough to bring Ruth to embrace her.

"Do not blame him, child. He holds so much hurt in his heart. He is a good man, a courageous man but that does not mean he does not need love."

"He's my father, Ruth. How can I not love him? It's just — it's just that —"

"What, my child?" she urged gently, holding Aurora to her shoulder as if she was her own daughter.

"He's changed so much. His eyes are so hard, so unfeeling. I don't remember that about him. I remember a kindness, a caring for others."

"You saw him through the eyes of a child and you are a child no longer. He is your father but he is also a man."

And no less a man for his weaknesses. It was no easy task to recognize humanity in one she revered. But if she was asking him to accept her, blameless sins and all, could she do any less for him?

"Thank you, Ruth," she said at last and straightened from the other's arms. "I'm glad you're here."

"And I am glad you are home, both you and the child."

They were the most welcome words she'd heard since coming to the Bar K. Aurora felt a mist of gratitude cloud her vision. Perhaps, Ruth was right. Perhaps time would heal all things. Perhaps now was when she needed to cling to hope with the greatest strength.

"May I join you?"

Garth Kincaid looked up from his solitary plate in some surprise. His daughter stood behind one of the chairs, an expectant expression softening her features. Not repentant, he noted, but when had his headstrong child ever come begging forgiveness? Even when she'd been at fault as a girl, she sought other means to apologize, indirect avenues that would cause no loss of face. It had amused him then and caused him to react to that remembrance now.

"It's your table, too."

Accepting the tentative truce for what it was, Aurora slid into her chair. The Major regarded her with a moody frown, probably wondering with what wiles she meant to win him over to her way. It was a game they'd played in happier years. This was no game and she didn't take it lightly. Nothing had ever been so serious. She was bargaining for her and her son's future. And she needed a place at the Bar K and a space in her father's heart.

As they dined on a thick stock of beef and winter vegetables, Kincaid observed his daughter. She looked lovely, gracing his table. The fiery hair was tamed back into a sedate coronet, and apparently her temper was in equal check. In the green plaid taffeta gown with its black fringes and lace, she looked nothing like the hoyden who'd confronted him in his study. This was the young woman he'd dreamed of having at his side. For a moment, he indulged himself in that illusion. Would that it were true. Looking at her, garbed like a vision, her face as sweet as any angel's, one would hardly guess at the trials she'd suffered. How he loved her! His world had ended at her apparent demise.

Here she was, at his table, a second chance few would ever have. Had he completely overlooked that blessing in his anguish of shame and pride? She was his daughter, his little Orrie, the impish child who lightened his grief and gave him reason to live. Didn't he owe her a little understanding now? She would come to see his side of it over Prescott's. She was, after all, a Kincaid.

"Jack told me what happened in town."

Huge golden eyes lifted. It was a guarded stare. "Oh?"

"It won't happen again. I've had the matter taken care of."

How sure he sounded, as if there was nothing he couldn't change with the wave of his hand and the mention of his name. Perhaps there wasn't. The notion frightened her. How easy power corrupted, and here was Major Kincaid, a despot in his grassland kingdom.

"Do you plan on having Jack follow me in every time to shoot anyone who looks crosseyed at me?"

The Major snorted but his gaze dropped just enough to hint that he'd considered it. "Don't be ridiculous."

"I refuse to hide out here behind the Bar K name," she challenged. It was a bold noise but she was in no hurry to brave those blaming stares in Deadwood. They made her feel dirty and angry at herself for allowing them to.

"You have the name Kincaid already and that's always been enough. Let them stare, but if one of them dares approach you again, they know what to expect."

What had he done? An unpleasant chill took her.

228

Something horrible and graphic. Had he ordered the man at the saloon beaten up? Had he put the fear of the prairie God into the women on the sidewalk? Where would it end? That wasn't what she wanted. Acceptance out of necessity for life and limb. How could he think it was? What was he protecting? Her honor or his good name? She didn't really want to know that answer either.

"I've been thinking, Orrie," he began mildly and she was instantly alert. "There wouldn't be so much reason for talk if you were to—"

"I'm not giving up my son!"

He lifted his hand to still her protest and managed to look hurt. As if he'd never asked her to do that exact thing. "Let me finish. I only meant to say, there wouldn't be so much talk if you were properly wed."

Aurora was so stunned for a moment she could only gape at him. He had the audacity to look pleased with his solution.

"That way the—the child would have a legal white father and you, a Christian marriage. That would still the loose lips and idle talk."

Aurora smiled grimly. "And whom did you plan for this supreme sacrifice?"

"It wouldn't be, believe me. In fact, it was his idea."

She could scarcely form the question. "Whose?"

"Jack Lawson's."

Chapter Fourteen

"Jack Lawson?"

"Now, Orrie, don't go getting all het up," Kincaid interjected, seeing protest all over her unbelieving face. "I want you to think on it a minute. Just listen to me."

Aurora sputtered like a candle flame guttering in hot wax. *Jack Lawson!* The very idea! Why it was—it was outrageous. Ridiculous.

Frightening.

"I know you haven't had much use for Jack but he's not that same cross-grained, gun-handy pup you remember. He's done a lot of curing since Cale died. They were mighty big shoes to fill and he's been doing his darnedest."

True, his intervention in town did take the edge off her dislike of the cocky foreman, but it hadn't altered her opinion. Jack Lawson was a showy braggart with a powder-keg temper. He lusted after the Bar K money, and it was plain in his hungry stare that he— Aurora blushed hot to think it. Suffice it to say, he wanted all that he saw at the Bar K.

"Orrie, you think about it. What you need is a husband and, face facts, there aren't going to be a lot of comers for that job. Considering." Not for a used woman with a half-breed son, was his unspoken summation. Aurora stiffened. "Jack's willing to overlook what's happened. He'll give the boy his name and raise it as his own. Good God, girl, what more could you want? You aught to be damned grateful, and there you sit looking like you swallowed a peach pit."

Yes, she thought in a bitter daze. From the Major's viewpoint it would seem like providence. A lusty cowhand willing to take on his stained and temperamental daughter. He would consider Lawson the perfect mate. A man under his thumb. A man steeped in his interests. A fellow would think twice before insulting the wife of the trigger-happy foreman. He was hard riding and straight shooting, and he coveted the Bar K. What more could a man want for his daughter? She felt ill.

When she had nothing to say, Kincaid assumed she was being sensible for once and was seriously considering his words. His mood mellowed. Generously, he stated, "You don't have to give an answer right now. I know you'll want to mull it over. Marriage isn't a sudden step. Just remember, Orrie, you'll not have another opportunity to find an honorable name for your child. What other chance will he have?" Self-serving as it was, it was the closest Garth Kincaid had ever come to acknowledging the existence of his grandson. And it sat about as well with him as a big dose of castor oil.

Wisely, Aurora gave vent to none of the turbulent feelings bursting inside. She maintained an outward composure while her mind worked furiously behind it. Dear God! Tied to Jack Lawson. What could be worse? In her father's eyes, a lot of things. Such as harboring a disgraced daughter and her Sioux spawn. She smothered the impulse to decry the whole situation as intolerable. She did have to think. If her father wanted to believe she was weighing the advantages of being Lawson's wife, she wouldn't enlighten him. It would give her the desperately needed time to think of an alternative. What argument could she give him, after all? That she wouldn't consider marrying any man other than Ethan Prescott? Oh, how he would love to hear that!

The Major's guarded gaze followed her as she stood. He wasn't completely lulled by her silence. He knew his daughter. She wasn't one to capitulate so easily. He studied her serene expression for a clue to her thoughts but found none.

"It's been a tiring day. I'm going to bed. Good night, Major."

She came to brush a soft kiss against his weathered cheek. While she bent near, his hands captured her forearms and squeezed hard. When she straightened, his eyes had a moist sheen.

"Good night, daughter," he murmured huskily, then finished, "You think about it, now, you hear."

"I will," she promised.

How could she not?

Hours crept by as Aurora paced her room and thought long and hard and frantically. What was she to do? Her father considered the matter settled and was smug about the solution.

Jack Lawson.

She hugged her arms about herself to hold in a shiver of revulsion. Once before she'd been forced to endure the caresses of a man she did not love. Her survival had depended upon it then. Would her father make the circumstances just as unbending this time? She was isolated on his ranch, a veritable prisoner to his will as long as she remained. Her father loved her, yes, but he would, in the name of that love, force her into doing what he thought best. She remembered his staunch refusal to heed her wishes when it came to schooling in the East. She might well have tried to move a mountain with her tears. She hadn't needed those years of pampered restriction beneath her Aunt Bess's fussing and fretting. She hadn't wanted to stroll in gardens with strangers and to struggle with polite conversation in stuffy, overheated parlors. She wanted to be where the wind blew clean and wild. She'd needed to be with the only family she had left. She'd wanted to be at her father's side. And he'd sent her away. The years in the East were best for whom?

He would be just as unswerving in seeing this edict served. She wasn't fooled. He was giving her no choice in the matter. He'd posed it as an option to mollify her, but in his mind, the situation was decided. He would marry her to Lawson for her own good—and for the good of the Bar K.

She thought of Lawson's slick grin and his dark, greedy gaze. She could imagine it hotly devouring her. She could almost feel his rough, hurried hands upon her skin, pulling at her clothes, squeezing her breasts. She could imagine his mouth, wet and demanding over her own. And the feel of him, hard and heavy, covering her on the bed they would share.

No! Never!

Her steps quickened in agitation. Never would she allow another man to paw at her to serve his own lusts. She was not her father's chattel to be given for the best bargain. His word would not bend her will. She would sooner be banished from his grassland kingdom. She would sooner forfeit her Dakota dream.

The Major was right. She had Scotty to consider. What kind of father would Jack Lawson be? She couldn't picture him cooing over her child or boasting his achievements with any degree of pride. Lawson wanted her and he wanted the Bar K. Scotty was but a bit of unpleasant baggage that went along with the deal. And she would not allow her son be treated as such. A difficult life lay ahead for her half-caste son, and he would need a strong man to guide him. A man who would not consider him an embarrassing nuisance. A man who would care for him. Love him. And one man was already all those things.

Aurora leaned against the window frame and expressed a futile sigh. The solution was so simple. And so impossible.

What was she going to do?

Morning brought no ready answers, and Aurora was a tense coil of distress. After tending Scotty, she pulled on her brother's britches and strode down to the barn. Her father's men were instantly alert, but she paid them no mind as she saddled a horse. Nor did she acknowledge the two of them who rode out with her.

The moment she cleared the ranch compound, Aurora's heels smacked backward, startling her mount into a gallop. Cool wind burned her cheeks and whipped her hair from its braid into a fiery stream behind her. Heavier men laden with hardware struggled to keep up. Let them try, she thought with an arrogant pleasure. She wanted the freedom the morning could bring. She needed the clarity that came with crisp air and unblemished hills. She needed to be out from under her father's domineering thumb. If just for a moment, she needed to be in charge of her own world. And it felt wonderful.

She had no set direction at first. It was speed she wanted, and the breathless exhilaration that came with it. Slowly, she came aware of a destination, one that had lingered in the back of her thoughts with seducing promise. She leaned the reins against her horse's lathered neck to guide their direction and urged it over the prairieland. Wandering cattle scattered at her hell-bent-for-leather approach, shaking their six-foot spread of horns menacingly and bawling in annoyance. The melt-softened ground flew up in clumps beneath the horse's tearing hooves. She paid scant attention to the beauty of the surrounding buttes and dwarfing hills. Another time she would have paused to admire their glorious palette of colors; olive and lavender, buff, brown and brilliant white, interspersed with splashes of emerald and scarlet flame. She sought more than the dazzling lushness of the land, and as she crested a rise, all her dreams spread before her.

From the top of that long hill, she had a far-reaching vista into the valley below. Nestled half way between the low-lying hills was Ethan Prescott's Lone Star Ranch. Or what was left of it.

He'd chosen a breathtaking site. Dark blue hills gave shelter from the tearing winds. Cottonwoods dotted the rolling acres of blue gamma providing shade from the merciless summer sun. There was a clear creek edged with small timber and brush; elm, ash, box elder, plum and chokecherry, an endless source of corral poles and firewood. She could well imagine how it would look in a month's time: wildflowers everywhere, massing to paint the hillsides with the color of their blooms; pink, blue, yellow, and the lavender of wild sweet peas. She breathed in deep, almost tasting the heady fragrance to come. And there were miles of Dakota short grass; blue gamma, western wheat grass, needlegrass and buffalo grass, those hearty varieties that didn't wilt on the stem in winter. The wealth that caused her father to covet that which he did not own.

From that hilltop, Aurora coveted her dream. The

house didn't look like much, neglected and alone, but in her mind she could see a different picture. A tidy yard. A line of fresh, white wash. Lace curtains. A clean-swept porch with twin maple rockers. In her imaginings, the corrals stood mended and teaming with blooded stock. The rich range hosted the truculent Texas steers bearing the Lone Star brand and carrying a prosperous future. She could conjure a young Scotty scattering seed for chickens and a red-haired baby cooing on a blanket. And to cap that perfect idyll was the image of herself and Ethan standing on that porch, surveying all before them with a tranquil satisfaction. She would be leaning back against the firm wall of his body, and his arms would be about her, protecting, cherishing, permanent in their regard. Her eyelids closed wistfully, and that sweet fantasy danced upon them. She and Ethan and the Lone Star Ranch. Raising Scotty and the children they shared between them. Sharing the work and the reward. Sharing the sun-drenched days and deep-starred nights.

The sound of blown mounts approaching jerked her from her musings. Her father's men. Her guardians. Their presence sombered her mood from wistful fantasy to hardened fact. She looked below again, and this time she saw Cale Marks laid out on the dusty ground, sightless eyes staring heavenward. Her chest constricted tightly. Her eyes squeezed shut.

Oh, Cale, you didn't deserve such a fate.

She forced her eyes to open and looked again, long and hard. She studied the yard with its open approach to the front porch. It would give no cover to a man coming up to the door. Whoever was inside would have plenty of time to carefully site and fire. Her belly clenched in objection as she pictured Cale Marks; her friend, blown off the porch with a blast to the chest.

236

Unarmed. Fury worked inside her and she could taste her tears. She studied the scene where a terrible injustice had been done a man she respected and loved.

Ethan Prescott had killed him.

He hadn't denied it.

Aurora tried to muster up a degree of the hatred consuming her father. It should be easy. But it wasn't. She was angry that it had happened. She mourned the loss of a trusted friend. And she was frustrated by the mix of feelings churning through her.

Try as she would, she couldn't place Ethan standing over him with a gun. But that was what happened. And it made no sense at all. Why would he have shot Cale? She couldn't believe it was in an irrational rage or in retribution for her father's treatment. Had he felt falsely threatened? Had he believed Cale held a weapon? Self-defense, it was the only answer. But not cold blood. Not murder.

Not Ethan.

Only he knew the truth of it, and what chance would he have to tell it in Deadwood? What chance would he have of ever reaching a court if the Major's men got hold of him first? Her father wanted Ethan out of the way and clear claim to his land more than he desired the truth. It served his purpose to call it murder, so why would he be interested in entertaining another possibility? Ethan must have seen that right off. He'd not been blinded to the Major's true character—as she had been. He'd known they'd come after him with a rope. So he'd run and hid in the hills. Trapped like the animals he hunted. And holed up with him was her only hope of happiness.

She took one last long look upon Ethan Prescott's dream. How well it would have fit her own. The house was near to falling down, and in time the prairie would reclaim it. No happy laughter would sound

237

within its carefully chinked log walls. No sighs of pleasure would echo in the night. Instead of sleek horses and rangy Lone Star stock, her father's herd would roam free over the lush acres. Fences would fall beneath the weight of snow and force of wind. There would be no sign that the tall Texan had ever dared to challenge her father's domain. How sad that was, how bitterly unfair. And she felt soiled to be a part of it because her last name was Kincaid.

Now, she understood Ethan's hatred.

Because of who she was and what she was, she was to be denied her dream. She would never live out her life in happiness with Ethan Prescott upon this snug little ranch. Not if her father had any say in it. She would be a possession of the Bar K. And she would do what was best to further the future her father planned for them. She would live in his house, a prisoner of fate. Scotty would grow without the nurturing attention of a good man to guide him. And her nights would be spent, not sharing and caring for the husband of her choice, but in the loathsome company of Jack Lawson. He would demand all the rights of a husband, as Far Winds had. And she didn't fool herself for an instant into thinking the leering cowboy would be tender in the taking. She'd not suffered beneath Far Winds, not physically. She'd endured his claim with reluctance, but he had never made her feel like a whore beneath him. It had been a nearly chaste, an almost sacred act between them. But it would be different with Lawson. It would be a wicked, rutting lust and she would not be allowed to hold to her dignity. A shiver of revulsion shook her clear to the soul. How would she ever endure that? How could she ever express a degree of self-respect if she gave in before her father's wish and became Lawson's prize for loyalty? Perhaps he could force the townspeople into keeping their dislike carefully veiled, but how was she to live with her dislike for herself should she submit with no hope of salvation? No rescue. No escape.

"Miz Orrie," called out one of the cowboys in a worried tone. "There's riders a-coming fast. We be-best be skeedaddling back to the Bar K."

Her bright head flew up in alarm. Wide, frightened eyes scanned the horizon until she made out six shapes skimming the low hills.

Indians.

Only Indians traveled single file to disguise their number. Only the Sioux were such magnificent horsemen as to appear one with their unshod mounts.

"Oh my God," she moaned as her gaze tracked them in fearful fascination. They were headed in an unerring path—straight for them.

In a wild panic, she hauled her horse's head around and applied booted heels. The animal lunged forward and exploded into a run. It darted between the cowboys, who were freeing their rifles from saddle scabbards. They were quick to follow her horse's flying flanks.

Sioux.

The name struck terror into her heart. They were too distant to determine the tribe but she would wager they were of the Miniconjou. Whether they were of Yellow Bear's clan, she didn't want to hazard a guess. Their purpose at being so close to the Bar K was another thing she didn't wish to dwell upon. Because if she did, her mind would numb with terror. She didn't want to believe they were after her. She urged her horse to greater speed, flailing at it with the ends of her reins.

Let them be a roving band of renegades made curious by their smaller number. Let them be turned away by the proximity of her father's ranch. These things she prayed over and over while her frantic thoughts echoed one thing: *Please, God, don't let them catch us.*

She couldn't go through it again. She wouldn't allow herself to be paraded back through the campsite, bound hand and foot like a prized doe fit for slaughter. She imagined Uncheedah's gloating sneer and the rage of Far Winds's family. They would put her to death. Of that, she was sure. A horrible death to avenge his supposed killing at her hands. And, like Ethan Prescott, she would find no one willing to hear her words of explanation. If they captured her, she would be dead.

The horse's sides heaved between the clench of her thighs. It still had not recovered from the earlier race across the fields of grass. That fact could well determine her chance of survival. A Lakota warrior could fell the fleetest elk with a well-placed arrow. She'd seen them do it.

Don't let them bring me down.

She had to make the ranch. She had to get back to Scotty. If anything happened to her, who would care for him? She was sobbing into the horse's slapping mane.

Only when the outline of her father's compound showed in the distance did she dare risk a backward glance. A gasp escaped her. They were so close! She could see the trail of glossy black hair and the glint of rifle barrels. Why hadn't they fired? The three of them were easily within range, ready targets. Surely they wouldn't continue the pursuit with the Bar K up ahead.

But they did.

One of the cowboys fired off a volley of shots behind them. Aurora tensed, expecting return bullets to fly their way, finding her exposed back at any minute.

No shots sounded. She hunched low over the horse's neck and continued her chanting prayers in harsh sawing breaths.

Rifle fire alerted the Bar K. A group of riders headed toward them, bristling with weapons. Aurora cried out when she recognized her father among them. The distance between them closed and soon they were safely ensconced within the crowd of Bar K riders. Shaking and weeping with relief, she looked back and knew a dazed bewilderment.

The Sioux warriors had pulled up but not retreated. They held their horses in a single line, rifles drawn but not up in an offensive pose. They appeared to be waiting. Then, she recognized among them members of Yellow Bear's elite *akicita,* the policing society who saw to the enforcement of their tribal laws. And she knew with a sickening certainty that there was no coincidence in their arrival.

One of the warriors extended his rifle in a gesture of faith and approached alone. Aurora didn't know him by name but she knew his face. She'd seen him at Far Winds's fire. As he grew nearer, there was a chorus of rifles brought to ready from her father's men. The Major calmed them with a wordless signal until the warrior drew up his fine mount scant yards before them. He glanced at her once, his black eyes glittering dispassionately. If he felt any animosity for the woman thought guilty of slaying his friend, it didn't show in his stoic gaze.

"We have come in peace to bear the words of our great chief, Matogee," he claimed in carefully phrased English.

There was a grumbling amongst the Bar K men, who didn't hanker backing down when the odds were in their favor. A severe glance from Kincaid silenced them.

"I'm listening."

"Matogee has sent his messengers to find rest for his son's spirit sent to the Other World by Wadutah, his wife." He looked briefly at Aurora so they would take his meaning.

"You red bastard," Kincaid bellowed. "You think I aim to just let you waltz in here and steal my daughter back? Your chief's son can rot in heathen hell for all I care."

A clatter of hammers pulled to full cock backed his words.

The warrior's expression never flickered but Aurora could guess at the fury stirring his heart. The dead's journey to the afterlife was a scared thing to the Sioux. To bring the name of the dead out in conversation was considered grossly impolite. To mock it was a grave insult. Sometimes a fatal one.

"We have not come for Wadutah, of the scarlet hair. She is dead to us, banished from our circle. It is the little one we seek."

Scotty!

Aurora knew a cold, consuming terror. They wanted Scotty!

"No," she cried out, forcing her winded mounted ahead so she could confront the brave with all her mother's fury. "You'll not have him. He is my son. It was my right to take him, by your own laws."

The Lakotas muttered between themselves but their spokesman didn't falter. His black stare was unwavering.

"My brother's *tun* has returned from the sky to dwell in the little one's body. The *wihmunga,* she who hums, has said it was so."

Uncheedah's mother, Aurora thought angrily, wondering what black mischief the jealous woman had set her to. She had seen the old woman on several occasions, her grey hair streaming loose in the wind, her bent body clad in nothing but a tattered buffalo robe to hide her shriveled limbs. The young white woman had been disturbed by her intense stares. The Miniconjou gave great credence to the words and visions of their witchwoman. If she claimed the soul of the departed returned within Scotty, they would believe her without question.

"And if it has?" she challenged boldly. Her knees clamped tight to the saddle to still their trembling. She would not let them see her fear.

"Uncheedah claims the child to replace the man you have stolen from her tipi. She will raise him as her own. You will give him to us in restitution for your crime."

"I didn't kill Far Winds," she cried.

"He will be raised as his father before him among the Dwellers of the Prairie," the Indian continued, as if she had never spoken. "He will not be a *wagluhe,* living without pride among the white man."

She couldn't believe it. She'd thought this kind of terror a thing of the past. She'd thought herself safe from the far-reaching hand of Sioux custom.

She'd been wrong.

Aurora sat numbed upon the back of her trembling mount. A wild panic overtook her. For a moment, it occurred to her to have her father's men open fire. They could cut down the Miniconjou warriors and no word of her would trickle back to Yellow Bear.

But even as she thought it, she knew the desperate craziness of her idea. They would come. Regardless of what happened to these men, they would come. And one more crime would be heaped upon her. She had to think. She couldn't risk giving before a dangerous impulse that might jeopardize them all.

243

"And if I will not give him to you?" A faint tremor betrayed her.

"Then when the sun follows the new moon, we will come and we will take him."

Two days. Two days before they would come with the threat of bloodshed to tear Scotty from her arms.

Chapter Fifteen

Aurora approached her father's study in a terrible panic of uncertainty. He'd spoken not a word to her since the Miniconjou braves had turned their horses and faded like shadows against the horizon. She'd fled to her room the moment they returned, escaping the accusing glances of her father's men, to hug Scotty to her and weep endless tears of fright. That had been hours ago, and now Ruth brought word that the Major wished to see her. It was an interview she dreaded to the depths of her soul.

For a long second she stood in the open doorway and regarded her father. He was seated at his desk, mulling over the Bar K ledgers. That he would involve himself with ranch matters while her whole world crumbled rasped upon a raw nerve. When hadn't he placed their future plans above her? Looking back, she could see it clear. Only his beloved Julia had commanded a greater elevation in his heart. After her death, all his energies turned to achieving his dream upon the grasslands of the Dakotas. Had he ever looked to her as a separate entity, apart from that dream? Had he ever considered her wanting anything other than what he saw ahead in his ambitious plans?

She hadn't thought it odd that he never asked, for they had always worked as one toward the same end. Until now. What would he choose now? Her or the prosperity of the Bar K? The question ate at her confidence like a half-starved wolf in winter, because in her heart she knew — and didn't want to face the truth of it.

"Father?"

He looked up and she saw he was surprised. She never called him that. She and the boys had always called him the Major, as if he was their personal hero. Or maybe he preferred it that way because the term "father" implied too personal a need, too immediate a claim upon his time and responsibilities. As the Major, he could deal with them on a different level, one removed from the workings of the heart to the works of the ranks. He delegated, but had he ever been devoted? He'd said he loved her, but did he really comprehend the consequences of the word? Did he understand it went beyond duty, beyond obligation, beyond self? Observing him now at this critical moment, Aurora wondered and was frightened by her doubt.

"Come in, Orrie. Sit down."

She continued to stand, wringing her hands until they twisted together in a tangle of trembling fingers. She looked pale and unwell. He couldn't recall ever seeing her so upset. It was her way to meet things head-on in a fiery challenge. Not to shrink like a delicately budded primrose. Confronting the savages must have scared her near to death. Anger rose in his chest. Damn redskins. He wouldn't rest until all of them were driven from the hills. Or dead for what they had dared do to his wife.

And to his daughter.

"What do you mean to do about Scotty?"

Direct. Right to the point. Even in a quiver, she had the pluck to speak her mind. She did a man proud and he knew then that she would have the courage to do what she must.

"Orrie, you're my daughter, my only living heir, and I would risk every piece of the Bar K right down to its last timber to keep you safe. There isn't a man here who'd see you turned over to those devils. They'd fight to the death, every last one of them."

A fluttery relief made her knees weaken. Unsteadily, she sought a chair before her father's desk and basked in his benign smile. Everything was going to be all right. He'd chosen her. Worries fled and she suffered from the guilt of having doubted. He was her father. He would take care of everything. He would protect her, comfort her as he had when she was a little girl. That hadn't changed. He hadn't changed. How wrong she'd been to think so.

"We have to give them the child."

Huge golden eyes flew up in shock.

"I don't see that we have any choice," he continued with a reasoning calm. He watched a cold stiffness come over her face as if each soft line was suddenly crafted from stone. He was not without sympathy. Poor girl. The sooner it was done with, the better. He was taking the decision from her hands, sparing her the last, most difficult choice. Because he loved her. "Orrie, they'd murder us to a man. You know them better than any of us. Do you think they're bluffing?"

"No," came her strained reply. No, they weren't bluffing. They'd swarm down from the hills with a blood vengeance. She could hear the remembered cries echoing through her head and her skin chilled. And if they couldn't overrun them in the first charge, they'd retreat and slowly pick them off one by one. They'd kill every man who went out to tend the stock or to fetch water or supplies. And in the end, they would all die. That was the ugly truth of it. The Lakotas never bluffed. Not when it came to the commands of their spirit world.

"Will they harm the child?"

Again, the faint, "No." Scotty was the son of chiefs. He would be revered. There would be no danger to him. Children were considered *wakan* during their first year and because of that sacred status they were treated with great respect and love lest they be taken home to the nether land. No child was ever neglected, for it was part of a greater family, claiming kinship of the entire clan. The care of children was a family obligation not to be taken lightly. He would be governed and trained with patience and tolerance. He would be a Miniconjou.

But that didn't matter. It wasn't important how Scotty would be treated in the hands of the Sioux. She was his mother. She would not allow him to be taken. Never!

"You can't give him to them. He's my son."

Kincaid brushed that fact aside with an impatient hand. His indifference was wounding. And terrifying. He was discussing his grandchild as though he was a misfit stock animal. Better to get rid of it than contaminate the purity of the herd. The Major's summation said all. "He's the son of a savage. What kind of life could he have raised among people who would scorn him?"

"The way you scorn him?"

He frowned at that thin accusation. "Orrie, be sensible. I won't ask any of my men to die for a halfbreed whelp and I'm sure none would offer."

She swayed dizzily in her chair. A cold like death seeped through her. An emptiness like the grave waited to suck her down. How could he do such a thing? To his own grandson? To her child? He might as well ask her to cut off her own arm. Or tear out her heart. For wasn't that what he was doing?

"Think, Orrie. It might sound cruel to you now, but it's for the best. The boy will be well cared for amongst his own, and you have your own life to live. You're young and handsome. You could marry well once talk dies down. Have children, fine, Christian children, with your husband."

"Another child won't replace Scotty," she cried in horror. "How could you think it would? Could anyone replace Seth or Jed when you lost them?"

"We're not talking about your brothers," he argued tightly. He flushed hot at the thought of comparing them; a breed to his treasured boys. It was a ludicrous and, furthermore, a blasphemous pairing. He would not consider it.

"We're talking about my son! Your own flesh and blood!"

"He's a damned Indian, Orrie. For God's sake—"

"No! For your own sake." She surged to her feet, causing the chair to scrape noisily across the floorboards. "What a convenient way to brush the family dirt under the rug. Gone and forgotten, is that it? You monster. You unfeeling, bigoted monster."

With that fierce utterance spat out at him, she fled the room, dashing past a stunned Ruth on her way to the stairs.

Muttering an oath to himself, Kincaid turned to the comfort of whiskey. For there was none to be found in Ruth's expression. She'd overheard, of course. Nothing went on beneath his roof without her knowing it. The housekeeper's gaze was uncharitable, to say the least. And her look bordered on betrayal.

"She'll get over it," he vowed in surly confidence.

"No," his housekeeper disagreed. "No, she won't.

You're not talking about taking away a favorite plaything. You're thinking of tearing a child from its mother."

"For damned good reason. You want to keep your scalp, woman? Or do you want to go live with the savages after they've murdered us all?"

"Sometimes I wonder who the savage really is."

He stared at her in surprise, then in outrage. Part of her carried that taint of blood. He forgot that sometimes when passion got a hold of him. When she was warm and willing in his arms and he got to thinking about other things. Impossible things. But now he saw clearly where her loyalties stood. And he didn't need her meddling in his decisions. "Hold your tongue, woman. Don't lash it out at me. You don't have the right."

"I have a right to my opinion," she countered softly. "If nothing else."

"And I don't have to hear it." He slammed the empty glass down upon the sideboard. "Get out, Ruth."

"Easier to hear than to live with, Major."

"Get out!"

Once it was over, they would both realize he'd done the right thing, he told himself as he poured another drink. Women were just too danged emotional. That's why they were entrusted to the care of level-thinking men. He was doing it for them. To save all of them. Why couldn't they understand that? How could they be so blind to the facts? No Indian was worth the life of his good men. And no amount of his daughter's tears would convince him that in time she wouldn't forget the ill-gotten babe and put the whole mistaken episode behind her. There would be other children to fill her arms and other babies for him to love as he couldn't bring himself to love this one.

Monster, she'd called him. He trembled when he recalled her voice. And her look; that horrified, inconsolate look that ripped his heart wide open. But he was strong enough to bear her blame and her misery, too. He would have to be. And in time, she would come to him with the offer of forgiveness to be his cherished daughter once again. Then, he would open his heart to her. Then they would share all the glorious dreams they'd made together. Never, he vowed, never would he look back upon her behavior this day nor would he hold it against her. She was distraught. Her attitude could be excused but it would not be catered to. In time, she would understand and thank him.

It was for the best. For all of them.

And for the Bar K.

Ruth expected to hear frantic weeping when she approached the closed door. The silence she came upon was somehow much more frightening. She knocked softly, then entered to find the despairing younger woman with child clutched defensively to her breast. Her stance was protective, as if bracing to meet an enemy.

"You've nothing to fear from me, child," Ruth said gently. "I can understand your pain."

And Aurora believed she did. Her posture eased but not the torment in her eyes. "What am I going to do, Ruth? I can't—I won't give up my child."

"You would see everyone on the ranch destroyed to save him? Even your father?"

The firm chin trembled. Golden eyes liquefied. "It's not my choice to make. It's not my fault. None of it's been my fault." The anger felt good. It dwarfed the fear and made it more manageable. The words poured out, fiercely, cauterizing raw wounds. "I won't pay and keep on paying for what I had no control over. I didn't ask to be captured by the Sioux. I didn't ask to be taken and filled with a child. I didn't kill my husband or ask his people to pursue me here. And I will not, *I will not,* be made to suffer for it now by giving up the only good thing to come of it all. Scotty is innocent of my decisions. I'll not allow him to be a pawn between my father and the Sioux."

"You must get away."

It sounded so simple. Aurora stared at her, unable to grasp an answer that was so obviously suited to settle all. If she were gone, the Sioux would have no reason to attack. Her father would be safe. Though she despised him for his lack of compassion, he was still her father. Part of what he was yet inspired love within her breast, enough to not wish him any harm.

And she would have Scotty.

"They'll be watching." She voiced her fears aloud as she crossed to the window and stared out into the night. The darkness revealed nothing but shadow, but they were there. She could feel them lingering. Watching.

"They will be watching for a woman and child, and that is not what they will see."

Aurora turned to Ruth with a questioning look. A hopeful look. It was met with an answering grin, woman to woman.

"I'll go now, while it's dark—"

"No, you must wait until morning. They would stop anyone leaving under suspicious means. You must go boldly, right under their noses."

Aurora stopped for a moment and studied the other woman in perplexity. "Why are you doing this for me, Ruth? I know—about you and my father. Why would you risk his disfavor?"

252

The handsome features took on a regal cast. "I may be your father's servant and I may be his woman, but I am no man's slave. He would treat his own daughter as one, selling off her child. I saw my grandmother's family herded like animals inside the wire of the Standing Rock Reservation. There was no dignity in it, and everyone is deserving of dignity. Even a child. He should not be bartered like something less than human because his blood is that of the People. That I cannot allow to happen." She looked away from Aurora and down upon the peaceful baby. An aching wistfulness came over her expression and her voice was thick with it when she continued. "Long ago, I bore the child of the man I loved. A beautiful baby girl. The small pox took her and I never got over the loss. Some things you never recover from. Only a mother would know. Your father is very wrong to think you could."

"And what happened to him? To the child's father? Was he your husband?" It was more than curiosity. Aurora needed to know, to understand this enigmatic woman who seemed to feel her pain so personally.

"No. We were never married. He was the son of a powerful white rancher and I was not good enough to carry his name. Before I could tell him of the child, his father sent him away to school, away from me."

"And you never saw him again?"

Tears glimmered in the soft hazel eyes, tears of remembrance that still brought pain, despite the passage of years. Ruth shook her head. "It was not to be. But I never forgot what it was to love, what it meant to hold a child in my arms. I would not have you suffer that same emptiness." Yes, she understood, and Aurora was quick to embrace her.

"In the morning," Ruth told her, getting control of her faltering voice. "In the morning you will go. Have

253

you any idea where?"

Without a second's thought, Aurora answered, "Yes, I know."

Anyone who noticed saw a raggedy cowboy leaving by the kitchen door with a swaggering gait and a jingle of roweled spurs. A cask was balanced upon one thin shoulder. Beneath the low-tipped Stetson, golden eyes surveyed the distance between house and barn. It had seemed so easy while she was squirming into the tattered clothing Ruth rescued from the wash, even while they were working out the particulars in hushed voices from the safety of her room. In theory, the plan was perfect. But it didn't seem quite so simple now, in the light of day.

Aurora forced herself to leave the porch, moving with an exaggerated roll of her weight from one side to the other. Her knees pointed outward to shape her legs to a perennial saddle-worn curve. All cowhands seemed bent to the rounding of a horse's girth, and she must appear no exception. With the long canvas duster draped to hide her soft figure, her hat shading her features, and her walk a slouching imitation of a range-ready drover, she prayed no one would give her undo heed; not those on the ranch, not those in the hills.

Half way to her goal, she was horrified to see two of her father's men approaching from the corral. Ducking her head and drawing herself up to appear taller, she continued toward them. Her heart was banging so loudly in her chest they must have heard it, but they gave no sign as the pair parted to let her pass between them. It was then Scotty decided to wake with a mewling cry.

"Whatcha got in that there barrel, boy?" one of the

men demanded.

Aurora kept walking. All her instincts prodded her to break and run, but she made herself keep to the nonchalant stride. She felt a trickle of fear run icily from hairline to collar. She fastened her eyes on the barn. So close!

"Hey, you deef? Whatcha carrying, boy? Iffen it's our breakfast, you'd best kill it first."

The other man laughed and they both turned to begin following her, eager for a little fun.

Dear God, what if they decided to look in the cask? Or under her canted hat brim?

"You boys leave him alone," came a call from the house.

The two men drew up to see their boss's good-looking housekeeper standing on the porch. In the heat of the kitchen, she'd opened several buttons on her modest dark gown. Sweat glistened and the effect was far from modest in the eyes of the two cowmen. They grinned at each other in appreciation.

"I asked him to take care of a prowling ole tom cat that's been pestering my laying hens something fierce. Go on with you, boy," she shouted, and Aurora continued toward the barn. The hat concealed her grin of relief. On the porch, Ruth gave the cowhands a particularly inviting smile. "I've some fresh sourdough bread a-cooking. If you fellers wouldn't mind giving me a hand in fetching some supplies up from the cold cellar, I'd be partial to sharing it."

"Be our pleasure, ma'am."

And the young cowboy with his whimpering parcel was forgotten.

It took Aurora no time at all to slap a blanket and saddle upon a frisky paint and shove a bit between its teeth. After securing her precious cargo, she swung up lithely and urged the horse from the barn. A quick glance told her the yard was empty. Casually, she let the animal meander toward the front gate, while her pulse moved ahead at a full-flung gallop. Her spine prickled. Damp hands worked the reins between them. Her ears strained for the sounding cry of discovery. But there was silence. Only when she'd cleared the compound did she lightly apply her heels to coax her mount into an easy canter, a ground-eating stride that would carry her into the hills.

She knew they were tracking her with their dark, shrewd stares. She could feel their eyes, and her body responded with a nerveless quivering. No longer within sight of the ranch, a single rider would be easy prey. The painted pony was all the provocation needed—that and the carbine she held in a sweaty palm. She kept the horse moving upward while below, Ruth would be concluding their plan. The housekeeper, with a red shawl draped over her own dark hair, would be pacing the front porch with a blanket bundle cradled in her arms. To the distant eye, it would look like Aurora Kincaid taking her baby out for the morning air. At least that was the distraction they were counting on. A lone rider hiding for the hills was not their target, after all. Not one of the Sioux braves would consider for a moment that the white woman and her child would run into the heart of their territory to find safety.

Which was exactly what she was doing.

Each mile took her closer to the source of the threat, but farther from the actual point of danger. How long before her father discovered her gone? Would he be saddened or relieved? With heavy heart, she assumed it would be the latter. By her leaving, the Bar K would be safe and his sterling name preserved. And didn't that mean more to him than a contrary daughter beneath his roof? She swallowed down a

256

sob. She might never again see the Bar K or Garth Kincaid, and the memories she carried away with her were far from fond.

He'd betrayed her, and how that yet stung. Her father, the man she'd worshipped through innocent eyes. Those eyes were opened now, and she didn't like what she saw. Greed, blinding ambition and hate, so much hate. Those were the things that had reshaped her father from the gruff, tender-hearted man she had held dear. They had corrupted him the way the glitter of metal in the high streams had warped those before him. It was the promise of the land, so wild and seductive, like a harlot eager to claim a man's last dollar for the offer of a moment's paradise. And she hated the Bar K, with its sprawling acres, for stealing her father away. For turning him from family into the embrace of profits and pride.

His own grandson. The infamy of it still shook her. How could he turn away a child, a helpless infant? How could he place upon an innocent head the sins of its parents? He would have sacrificed the child of her body to save himself from disgrace. Gladly. That was what hurt most of all. He would do it without remorse. What manner of man was her father? She no longer knew. Or wanted to care.

She blinked away the dampness threatening her sight and nudged her mount onward, away from the treachery below. She wouldn't think about Garth Kincaid and all she left behind. She was moving forward, not back. Never back. The future was ahead, not in musty memories that no longer held true. Someday she could cherish those remembrances again, but not now. Not when they cut so deep.

Scotty. She would think only of Scotty. Her child. Her only family now. Now that the ice-breaks had freed the Missouri she could take a riverboat downstream. She still had friends in Yankton who would help her. Perhaps she would get a job there until she had enough saved to go East. That seemed the only solution. She would think only of what was best for Scotty. Her own dreams no longer mattered. They'd proved to be without substance. All that was important was getting Scotty out of the hills to safety, away from the threat of his father's people. The thought of her child clutched in Uncheedah's vindictive arms was enough to steel her resolve to do whatever necessary.

The higher they climbed, the more the woods seemed to come alive with menace. Every sound alerted Aurora to the possibility of attack. Terror rode with her, a cold companion. The only blessing was in Scotty's silence, as he was rocked to sleep in his improbable cradle. The soft ground muffled their passing but would also disguise an unfriendly approach. Aurora knocked her hat back so she could nervously scan the trees. She'd come too far to lose Scotty now. He needed his mother, and she vowed to always be there for him. To always keep him safe. She would not fail him, as her father had failed her. She would protect him to the limit of her life. And, in these unwelcoming woods, she prayed it wouldn't come to that.

Every so often, it settled upon her, the feeling of being followed. She'd rein in her horse and wait, scarcely daring to breathe. And she listened. All she heard was forest sounds, the rustle of nature waking in the spring. Yet the disquieting sensation lingered, teasing along her back when it was turned, causing a prickling through the short hairs at her nape. It was fear she experienced. Latent fear. That would explain it. No threat crept up behind her, though she whirled often in an attempt to catch it. She was alone.

When faced with the prospect of fleeing for Scotty's sake, one destination came readily to mind. To find shelter. To seek security. The only place she could trust. It wasn't the man, himself, who lured her into the hills, it was what he offered — what he'd offered since that snow-covered day she'd awakened in his bed. A haven. Uncompromising safety. She'd found it in his arms and Scotty would find it in his care. Ethan wasn't an end to her troubles. She knew better than to expect an eager welcome. But he wouldn't turn her away. She prayed she knew him at least that well. He would aid in her escape. He wouldn't begrudge her the momentary sanctuary. That was all she could ask. Too much lay between them for her to ask for more. There she would find the help and strength to go on. She knew it in her heart. She realized it in her soul. Her eyes strained ahead for her first sight of the little cabin even as they continued to rake the surrounding brush for possible danger. And never had she been so glad to see the whisps of smoke rising from Ethan Prescott's chimney.

Her legs were weak and trembling when she slid down from the saddle. For a moment, she had to cling for support. It was then she realized just how afraid she was. While riding, the imminent danger kept her too alert for conscious thought. Now that safety was at hand, the terror of the past hours shook through her like a mighty wind. Nerveless fingers unlaced Scotty's bonds. Tottering legs carried her to the door where she waited for several breathless seconds before she knocked.

The door swung inward and Ethan Prescott's figure filled its frame.

Ethan regarded her for a long heartbeat. Sundry emotions washed across his face, not the least of them surprise. Not the least of them longing. She was like a dream standing on his doorstep, one he never wished to wake from. He was almost afraid to reach out, lest

259

she fade away, as dreams of her did every morning upon his waking. Only his dreams never looked so good. So damned desirable. A surge of desperate need rooted him to the spot. He was almost dizzy with the desire to pull her up against him, to let her feel the proof of his passion. But memory of their parting stayed him from making such a demonstration. He remembered her teary eyes, her blaming gaze, her hurt. And he was wary. What brought Aurora Kincaid to his door? It should have mattered more than the simple fact that she was here. But it didn't.

Then he took stock of her appearance. She wore men's clothes — but then, he'd never really seen her in suitable female garb. Her comely features were pinched with dread and shadowed with distress. The gold of her eyes glittered wetly in her pale uplifted face. He'd seen the same paralyzed look of terror in a young doe about to be pounced on by a crouching cougar. A thread of that fear tightened about his heart.

"Ora?"

Seeing him standing there, a bastion of broad-shouldered assurance, the last of Aurora's will collapsed. Tearing sobs escaped her tight throat as his arms went fast about her.

"Ora? What is it?" his deep voice rumbled against her hair. And it was the sweetest music she'd ever heard.

"They want to take Scotty from me," she ranted wildly. "Oh, Ethan please don't let them take him. He's all I have. He's my son. Don't let them take him."

He felt her quake against him and his embrace banded like a cooper's ring, circling her tight. One big hand lost itself in the tangle of her fiery hair and meshed to press her damp cheek to him. The feel of her in his arms brought a sense of completion to him, as if that empty space she filled was shaped to hold her.

"I won't."

Two words. She clung to them with a desperate gratitude. And she believed.

Chapter Sixteen

Ethan made a pot of strong coffee while Aurora saw to Scotty's changing. The baby nestled down to sleep the moment she placed him in the familiar cradle. It was as if he, like she herself, felt the security of home around them. The fire was warm, inviting rest. It was impossible not to succumb before its basking glow. Drained by exhaustion and fear, she was tempted to curl up on the corner bed, to sleep and let things take care of themselves while Ethan kept watch. But the questions in his dark, guarded gaze would delay her peaceful search for sleep a while longer. He deserved to hear her explanation.

And as they sipped from the dented cups and Ethan rocked the cradle with the toe of his boot, Aurora unburdened her heart by telling the events of the last two days. The big Texan listened without comment or reaction as she spoke heartbreakingly of her father's treachery. Only a ripple of cheek muscle beneath his beard betrayed the furious grinding of his teeth.

"So I came here," she concluded wearily. "I didn't know what else to do." Her gaze lifted from the empty coffee cup, a pleading gaze that cut right through to the heart of him, begging him for assurance. Not for her-

self. She hadn't asked anything of him to her own benefit. Just for Scotty's safety. "I couldn't let them take him
from me."

"No," he agreed softly. And they wouldn't. Not if he
had any say in it. That single word took the starch from
Aurora like a cool splash of water. She wilted in the
chair, her eyes pooling with grateful tears. He followed
her glance to the tiny figure curled trustingly beneath
warm furs. A small smile curved his lips, and all the
anger stockpiled inside him ebbed away. The little fellow *had* grown. In no time, he'd be running and playing
and sprouting toward manhood. Where? And with
whom to look to for manly advice?

He looked at the boy and considered what it must
feel like to regard one's own child. It was a sensation
long denied him. He thought of what he would teach
his own son, the lessons on life and love, the tutelage
that would ease his way during the awkward middle
years and shape him into a fine adult. A man could
commit himself to no worthier task. He could create no
better and longer-lasting tribute. Who would guide
Scotty Kincaid, the son of a rancher's daughter and
grandson of a great Lakota chief? He would need
someone wise, someone willing to wrestle the demons
of prejudice that would torment him for his copper-colored skin and glossy black hair. He would need someone to lend more than support. He would need the
strength of a good name.

The one thing he couldn't give.

So did Aurora. He looked up at her and his gaze detailed every delicate angle of her face, every sweet expression that molded them into a beguiling portrayal of
what resided in her heart. She was a strong, independent woman, but no one woman — or man — was meant
to bear what lay ahead of her alone. Yet she would, un-
complainingly, out of love for her child. Just as she'd

endured amongst the Sioux out of love for life. But she didn't have to struggle alone. She needed a man — not to smother her, but to share his support. A husband for herself, a father for Scotty.

His darkening gaze drifted downward from the full, inviting swell of her lower lip to the ripe rounding of wool flannel that hugged her breasts as she leaned forward. The pattern of his breathing altered slightly, growing ragged and quick. A woman like Aurora Kincaid needed a man for more than protection. He was painfully recalled to her passionate response. She would want a man for a bedmate as well as helpmate. An unwelcomed image seared through his thoughts; of another man's fingers tangled in her glorious web of red hair, of another man levering his weight between her creamy thighs, of another man relishing her keening cries of pleasure.

He wouldn't be the one to share her future. She hadn't asked him to and he couldn't if she did.

Ethan thrust back from the table. He ignored Aurora's startled glance and stalked to the simmering pot of coffee. His hands were shaking as he poured himself a second cup. Every fiber in his big body was taut and trembling in denial of the picture branded in his brain. Of Aurora Kincaid with another man. Living with him. Loving with him. The jealousy was vicious in its power, worrying his emotions with sharp, unrelenting teeth. It hadn't been like that when he thought of her with Far Winds. That was in the past, and he believed her when she said she found no satisfaction in the Lakota's claim. He knew it, in fact, for he was the one to teach her those soaring lessons in love. Teachings she would take to another. Lessons she would share willingly with another.

And he hated it.

But it didn't change anything.

Even if he wanted to, he could make no commitment

to Aurora and her son. Even if he was willing to trust another woman with his guarded cache of feelings, there was no future for them. Because of who she was. Of who her father was. Fact had nothing to do with what beat within his breast.

Then he turned and received the unexpected, both-barreled brunt of her appeal. By God, she was beautiful, sitting there before his fire. Dancing flames reflected in her molten eyes and played about the loose wisps of her hair.

He couldn't have her.

He kept telling himself that as if it would ward off the stirring effects of her charm.

It didn't work.

Firelight caressed the curve of her cheek. His fingers quivered at his side, wanting to likewise sketch that softness. He tried to tear his gaze away. He tried to shatter the smoldering tension thickening about them.

"If you're hungry, I can fix something."

The words, the thought trailed off as the tip of her tongue moistened the part of her lips. His mouth went suddenly dry as Texas Panhandle dust.

"Don't go to any bother," came her hushed reply. Her wide, uplifted eyes were deep drowning pools.

"No bother," he murmured, diving into those hot shimmering golden seas and sinking without a struggle. "I'll just put on some slabs of venison. Only take a minute."

A long minute passed. He hadn't moved. His conscious attention wasn't on the task of putting together a meal. It was fixed upon the rapid rise and fall of wool flannel.

"Sounds good," she said softly, mesmerized by the intensity of his stare. "I could eat the whole thing, antlers and all." Yet she made no move to prompt him to the chore.

265

"Only take a minute," he repeated vaguely, still rooted to the spot.

"Fine," she whispered back. The sleek muscles of her throat worked jerkily to force a dry swallow.

Then, at last, he moved. Instead of reaching behind for a skillet, he reached ahead for the tempting contour of her cheek. His fingertips grazed her jawline, stopping where a frantic pulse throbbed through her veins. He could feel her breath, warm and fluttery, against his wrist. It aroused the same disquieting sensations in his chest.

"Ora, dinner'll keep." His words rasped.

She nodded.

Ethan stepped forward and she stood at the same instant, bringing them in sinuous contact as she slid up against him, arms twining around his waist. Caught in the rough cup of his palm, her chin was tipped back at a near impossible angle, preparing her to receive the downward swoop of his mouth. His kiss was fiery and laced with longing. Both knew it would not be enough.

Ethan's free hand moved impatiently up and down the curve of Aurora's spine. Finally, he rucked her shirt tail from the trouser band and knew the satisfaction of her satiny flesh gliding smoothly beneath his palm. The feel of her ignited his senses. His mouth grew more demanding. He crushed her slender form against his own hard, unyielding body, holding her there with a force that would break bone or meld one into the other. She made a quiet whimpering sound beneath his ravaging lips, whether of pain or passion he didn't know. Abruptly, his grip eased and she clung to him in a weakened daze of desire while her limbs knew an odd liquefaction. She gazed up at him, her eyes glazed and unseeing, her lips bruised from his and wetly offering. Need growled through him, yet he hesitated.

He hadn't meant to drag her off to his bed like some

266

primitive beast. She hadn't come to him for that. She'd come for shelter, for support, not to sate his rutting appetite. She wasn't going to stay. She wasn't his for the taking. He cared too much to use her so callously, as others had used her to their purpose. He didn't want to do that to her, yet how to stop when all he desired since he'd opened his door was to lie down with her and sink inside the velvety heat of her body? To stroke them both to the edge of ecstasy and beyond. To fill her with the chance for a tomorrow. To exhaust his loneliness and lose himself within her arms for at least this one more time. As if once more would be enough.

"Ethan?" Her gaze had focused and was calling for answers.

"Ora, I —" What could he say? How could he frame his reluctance in words? How could he make her understand how loathe he was to hurt her, to give her false hopes? To take from her without the hope of a return.

To open himself up to the agonies of the past.

He couldn't.

And so, he began to push her away. Only he hadn't counted upon her unwillingness to go. Her fingers caught in the folds of his shirt. She resisted his repelling efforts.

"Ora, don't. It's no good."

She looked at him in confusion and shook her head. "Oh, I know that's not true," she argued. She leaned into him, letting him feel the tormenting fullness of her breasts.

His fingers tightened on her arms as they fought the urge to close about those glorious impertinent globes. He wracked his suddenly numbed mind for some reason to deny them both and seized upon the most obvious.

"Scotty —"

"Scotty?" Aurora looked down at the slumbering

267

child and laughed softly. "Scotty would sleep through a tornado, which is at least a little louder than what I had planned." Her gaze canted up beneath a coy fringe of lashes and gleamed with promise. He groaned as his body's response betrayed him. He was falling fast before her suggestive lure.

"How 'bout that dinner," he said abruptly and hauled himself away from the temptation of her lips. He moved with a rigid control to slap two sides of venison into a pan and mindlessly began to douse them with liberal seasoning. He could feel Aurora's puzzled stare burning into his back. Determinedly, he avoided it and went to kneel at the hearth, thrusting the skillet over the flames.

Aurora frowned. Blood beat hot and hard in her veins, too hot to be cooled by the Texan's inexplicable retreat. Too hard to be quieted by the frustration of a dismissing back. What had happened? One moment she'd been engulfed by his passion and now, this awkward chill. Had she done something wrong, something to strike down his desire? She knew so little of intimacy between a man and woman, yet recognized instinctively that he played no game. There was too much emotion in his shadowed gaze. Too much tension in him even now to convince her he was as indifferent as he would pretend. He wanted her. So why the disrupting halt?

He didn't trust her. That was it, she realized in dismay. She'd allowed her mixed feelings for her father to separate them. She'd refused stubbornly to hear the truth when he'd told her. And now she would suffer for it. For not believing in him. For not taking his side. But she was not one to suffer in silence.

"Ethan?"

He straightened slightly but didn't turn.

"You were right about my father."

"Oh?" That was noncommittal. "Right about what?"

"About the kind of man he is. I wouldn't listen to you before and had to find out the hard way. And it still hurts."

"I didn't do it, Ora."

He followed that sudden claim by revolving on his heels to face her. His features were grim, somber as he searched hers for some sign of belief. She simply stared at him, incomprehensively.

"Your father's man. I didn't murder him."

She smiled uncertainly, hoping to give him ease, hoping he'd show her some mercy and alleviate her guilt. "I know," she said finally. "I realized that the moment I left. You couldn't have shot him down in cold blood."

"I didn't shoot him at all."

She digested that slowly, like a particularly tough and stringy piece of beef. It lodged in her throat, refusing to go down. After a moment's struggle, all she could manage was a faint, "What?"

"I did not shoot him."

"But—"

"I wasn't even there when it happened."

She continued to stare, her face void of emotion. When at last some response registered, it wasn't at all what he'd expected.

"Why the hell didn't you tell me before?" she hurled at him angrily. Hot, furious color fused in her cheeks. Her breath seethed noisily. "You let me torture myself, making up all sorts of excuses for you, so I'd feel better about lo—about liking you. You black-hearted snake. How could you lead me on like that? Why didn't you tell me?"

"Would you have believed me?"

Aurora sputtered but that quiet provocation snuffed out her upset. His intense stare called her back to her feelings when they'd parted. She remembered the terrible, hurtful doubts. The hot, angry words. The empty desolation. He knew the truth but she had to speak it. In some chagrin, she had to admit, "No."

"There was an outbreak of measles in Yellow Bear's camp," he went on to tell her. "They knew I was a doctor because I'd set the arm of one of their children when he was thrown from a horse near my place. Their medicine woman had tried all the magic ceremonies and prayers she knew and couldn't appease the angry spirit she believed caused the sickness. She had called upon the men of the tribe who were afflicted to drown their wives and children and then themselves to drive out the evil. Seeing as how Yellow Bear's wife and son were sick, he was wise enough to test the white man's magic before sticking them in the river to die."

Ethan watched Aurora's features carefully as he concluded, "I was at the Sioux camp treating the sick when Marks was gunned down in my yard. I didn't even know about it until I heard the murmurings in town when I went to pick up some more vaccine. You can appreciate why I didn't go back to the Lone Star to tell my side of it. Bar K men were already stirring up an interest in a real quick necktie party. I grabbed up all the supplies I could carry and headed into the hills. I don't know who killed him. A renegade buck, maybe. It wasn't me, Ora." His dark eyes probed hers. Waiting.

An incredible relief shivered through her and with it, a wondrous hope. "So how are we going to get my father to believe you?"

"You believe me." It was a whispered affirmation not a question.

She was impatient with his reaction, with the surprise etching his expression. "It explains everything," she stated simply as if all was that simple. "You told me to look to my heart. I knew

270

it couldn't have happened the way they said it did."

He gave a wry smile as the back of his hand grazed her cheek. "I wish I could convince the law to share your faith in me."

She gripped his hand in hers to squeeze fiercely. "We will."

We. Had he ever heard a more gratifying word?

Using her hand to draw her down, Ethan leaned forward to meet Aurora's lips half way. Their kiss was long and lingering until she murmured, "Ethan, it's burning."

"Umm." Burning. Yes. His insides were all aflame. He found her mouth again and drank from its accepting sweetness, licking over each delicious curve before plunging in to explore that honeyed cavern.

"Ethan," she moaned breathlessly, "Dinner."

"What?"

"Dinner's burning."

The scorched scent of charring meat teased his nostrils and woke him fully to her meaning. With an irritated oath, he turned back to the fire, snatching at the skillet and, in the process, searing his palm. The heavy pan dropped with a clatter, flipping its contents onto the coals.

Muttering curses and doing his best to ignore Aurora's muffled chuckles, Ethan nudged the pieces of venison out of the flames and back into the pan. The meat was burned to an even blackness. Scowling dangerously, he brought the skillet to the table. When Aurora saw the crispy strips, she had to use both hands to smother her exclamations of helpless mirth.

Reluctantly, Ethan's mouth twitched. "I hope you like your meat well done."

She choked. Her eyes were tearing. "Well done is not the same as a burnt offering, Mr. Prescott."

He gave up then and laughed with her, his low rum-

271

bling chuckle twining intimately about her melodious peels of humor. Finally, sides aching and both of them grinning foolishly, a silence settled. And through it all, Scotty slept undisturbed.

"I didn't mean to laugh," Aurora said at last.

"Yes, you did," he accused, still smiling. "It felt good." Then, his smile faded and his expression intensified. "But not as good as what came before it."

"It gets better."

He believed her.

She reached out and stroked a hand down his thickly bearded cheek. All traces of amusement fled. Then, purposefully, her fingers went to the first button on her flannel shirt. And to the second. And the third. Until only a thin camisole covered her. The wispy fabric left little to the imagination. Dark crests were clearly outlined as they puckered against it. His thumb was drawn to rub one sassy peak into a hard bud of longing.

"Much nicer than the long johns," he pronounced in husky satisfaction.

And she had to agree when his head lowered and she felt the wet tug of his lips upon first one, then the other, through the damp cling of linen. Her fingers dug into his dark auburn curls as she shuddered with exquisite delight. At last he straightened, releasing her from his rapturous spell.

"Come on, sweet thing," he drawled in his husky Texas best. "Let's us two-step over yonder and commence some serious socializing."

She'd never heard it put quite that way. Or quite so enticingly. "Shore thang," she purred, mimicking his twang. "Y'all prove to me that everythang's bigger in Texas."

His grin dazzled. "Be right pleased to, ma'am."

Before she could react, he stood and swept her up easily in his arms, bearing her in three long strides to the bed. She gasped as he laid her down. The bedding was cold against her nearly bared back. But thinking how quickly it would warm, she reached up for him. Pulling him down, she poured kisses over his mouth, his furred jaw, his throat. Her hands busied themselves with the removal of his heavy shirt then luxuriated over the sleek, hard feel of him. All the while, her thoughts sang.

He was innocent.

He hadn't killed Cale Marks.

The truth was an unexpected aphrodisiac. The hope it provided lent a sharp edge of anticipation to their love making, a hunger that could be sated and renewed. Over and over. Without end. Without the need to end.

Ethan had freed her hips from the snug cling of man's britches and shimmied them down her long legs. When he reached for his trouser band her hands were already there, tugging, loosening with jerking impatience. He almost smiled, but forgot to when her first hesitant touch thrilled him. Then her hand closed about the thick, hot length of him and he groaned with an urgency of his own.

Aurora moved against him, lost in her desire. Full white breasts grazed the crisp hair on his chest, taunting them into a quivering arousal. Her knees parted so he could slide between them. The damp delta of her womanhood rubbed along one strong thigh, anxious to find ease from the binding pressure throbbing through her. She found his hips, then his hard buttocks, clutching them to pull him even closer.

"Ora," he moaned into her avid kisses. "God, how I've dreamed of you." Then, unable to restrain himself any longer, Ethan thrust inside her, filling her, completing her with the claim of his desire.

It was a wild, urgent reunion. Hands, mouths, hips; none of them were still in their need to pleasure and know pleasure in return. Labored breaths became harsh pants as they strained together for freedom from their forced separation. Finally, a hard, rhythmic pattern wrung their passions into a single explosive end, one that left them limp and trembling with a splendid relief in one another's arms.

From his fireside bed, Scotty set up a lusty wail.

Ethan expelled a breathless laugh. "Damn, that boy's got fine timing."

Aurora could only stir a small, lethargic smile.

Warmed and smug at the evidence of her exhaustion, Ethan kissed her lazy mouth. "Don't you move, sweet thing. I'll fetch him for you."

She was only too willing to obey. Languid eyes followed him across the room, charting each detail of his impressive form, from rock-hewn shoulders to the tempting flex of taut flanks. A leisurely heat flickered through her, fanned by a possessive joy. Hers. She could have him now. She and Scotty. They could live together on that little ranch, raising Texas longhorns and their own passel of Texas-bred babes.

Aurora closed her eyes and listened to the low croon of Ethan's voice as he calmed the impatient child and saw to his dry wrappings. What a good father he would make for the boy. In her heart, he already held that position, and had ever since he'd lifted the wet, wriggling infant into the world.

"Whatcha looking so cat-in-the-cream about?" Ethan demanded. He settled the baby beside its mother; then, instead of retreating, he resumed his spot next to her upon the toasty tangle of covers with Scotty between them. "Don't go getting no crazy notion that I mean to spoil you like this every time." His smile said he wouldn't object if she did.

Without hesitation, Aurora guided Scotty to her breast and let him suckle greedily. There was too much familiarity between the three of them for her to feel embarrassed. Rather, a deep, satisfying pleasure warmed through her as Ethan watched her nourish her child. It was the most natural thing in the world for them to share the intimate moment reserved for family.

Ethan's hand was so overwhelming compared to the tiny fingers clutched tight about one of his. The contrast woke a surge of such tender emotion that Aurora ached inside with the effort to contain it. Her moist gaze moved up from the two hands; one of man, one of child, to the shadowed features of the man beside her. His back was to the fire so she could have been mistaken about what she saw in his expression. But she didn't think so. She'd seen it before. A look so poignant, so sorrowful it cut upon the heart to observe it. His dark eyes seemed to swim with misery and remembrance. What did he see when he gazed upon her infant son? Suddenly, it was imperative to know the answer.

"Ethan, what happened to your wife and child?"

His very lack of reaction warned she trespassed on hallowed ground

"They're dead," he stated flatly.

He didn't look up at her. She didn't have to see his face fully to know all traces of emotion would be gone from it. It was that shuttered, cautious gaze that closed her out so completely. That he would think to withdraw from her now sparked a stubborn rebellion. It overcame her desire to protect him from pain. She was not inclined to allow the retreat. The secrets he carried held the key to their future. Instead, she prodded, not unkindly, with another question.

"When did it happen?"

He answered with the same toneless voice. "A long time ago. Back in Texas."

Instinct warned to proceed with care, but impulse overruled. "How did it happen?"

275

His gaze came up then and she was stunned by the violence seething in the dark depths. It was a fury directed, not outwardly at her for her insensitive probing, but inward with a castigating force.

"I don't see that you got call to go a-poking around in my business. It's got nothing to do with you, Ora."

But it did.

She knew it the moment he would deny it. It had everything to do with her. And with Scotty. With his reason for taking a pregnant stranger into his cabin and into his heart — but not into his confidence.

"I think it does, Ethan," she challenged softly.

"A helluva lot you know." He made an abrupt move to one side as if he meant to roll out of the bed in avoidance of her as well as her questions, but she stilled him with the touch of her hand upon his shoulder and the quiet call of his name.

"Ethan, please. It's because I don't know that I ask. Can't we have the truth between us instead of misunderstanding and secrets? If we can't be open about the past, how can we hope to share anything in the future?"

He was so still for a moment that she thought he meant to give no reply. Then he swiveled to glare at her with an expression so terrible it nearly made her gasp in alarm. His voice was raw, his words ruthlessly blunt.

"My wife killed herself and my baby along with her. Is that open enough for you?"

His gaze came up there and she was stunned by the
weary reality in the bleak depths. It was a face that
had not known laughter in some time.
He let those words settle in for the
weight of years. But then he remembered. That's when
her eyes became

Chapter Seventeen

Aurora could only stare, aghast. Finally, she stammered hoarsely, "My God, Ethan."

He spared no sympathy for her shock. She'd wanted — no, demanded the truth of it. And there it was, the ugly, bitter truth. He turned to place his bare feet on the cool floorboards and stared sightlessly across the room. He didn't see the neat, compact home he'd made for himself. He saw a prairie soddy sweltering in the Texas heat. He saw the body of his wife turning slowly in the hot, airless breeze. And heard the creak of hemp grating against the ceiling beam. The horror of it remained, shuddering through his big frame. Years hadn't dulled the force of that hideous discovery. Nor had it slaked his overwhelming guilt. For he'd killed her just as surely as if he'd kicked the stool out from under her feet. And for that, there was no forgiveness.

"I met Olivia in a military hospital in Georgia. Her father had been brought in with a mini ball through the lung. She was small and pale and about the only pretty thing I'd seen in three years of blood and pain. Her daddy lingered for almost a week before he died, and by then I'd come to know her fairly well. She'd lost everything in Sherman's sweep, and now she was burying her

277

only kin. She didn't have anyplace to go. I got her a job at the hospital so she'd have a bed, at least, but she couldn't stomach the work. The first time she was handed a young soldier's arm for burning, she dropped like a sack of meal. She felt real bad and all, but she swore she couldn't go back. Can't say I blamed her. A lady's eyes weren't meant for such sights."

He hadn't been able to stop thinking about the fragile Olivia Roth, about where she'd go, how she'd live in a world gone cruel and mad with deprivation. The thought of her wandering the streets, prey for the wicked who roamed them, tormented his mind and his well-bred Southern conscience. In the end, he set her up in his meager room at a nearby hotel and spent his nights at the hospital where he was needed around the clock. And to show her gratitude, Miss Roth brought a little light into the gloom of his days with the offer of genteel discourse and a comely smile that wasn't rigid with death's grip.

"When the hell of it all ended, I couldn't just ride back to Texas and leave her. So I took her with me, as my wife. She'd wanted to go, or at least she told me she did. She had nothing to keep her in Georgia. And by then I was so head-over-heels crazy about her, I couldn't see that she was hanging on to me for salvation, not out of any kind of love. She didn't want to be alone and didn't know how to make a living for herself. It was desperation and I saw it as devotion. A blind man could have seen it but I didn't."

His voice thickened with a bitter hindsight. Now, he could look back and see the way she'd endured, rather than responded to, his touch. She must have looked upon it as the price she paid for his protection. His gut ached with the gall of that knowledge. Then he felt Aurora's palm lightly press to the small of his back. Just that, no more. No gushing sentiments, no clinging empathy. Just a simple, quiet support. That was caring. What Olivia had shown him was self-interest. How clear that was now.

"She talked me into settling in town and setting up practice there. It was a tolerable living and we had a fine house and Livie had a passel of pretty clothes. She got so excited about new things, I was all the time buying gifts for her. And while I was working all hours to establish myself, she was out in them pretty things I bought her, having herself a grand old time at the theater and at parties. And never at a want for company. It went on for nigh on a year before I heard the gossip. Maybe I knew and just didn't want to hear. Rumor had it that my wife was right free with her favor when I wasn't at home. She was receiving gentlemen callers at my house, serving them my brandy. I don't know if she was serving 'em any more than that but what I knew was plenty. I knew I didn't want to watch some other man's seed grow inside her after she'd played the whore at my expense. I wasn't about to deliver my wife of a child that wasn't mine. I knew I couldn't bear to look upon the face of her deceit every day and be expected to claim it as my son or daughter."

Aurora flinched at his harsh words. She could feel Scotty at her breast and thought of the way his tiny hand had looked curled about Ethan's finger. Was he telling her he could never love her son because Scotty was another's? She kept that pain of doubt private as Ethan continued his increasingly grim recital.

"When I confronted her with it, she was all tears and pleading for forgiveness. She blamed me for being away and for leaving her to temptation. Fool that I was, I felt guilty. I wanted to take her away. I wanted to get away. I couldn't stand doctoring anymore. I just couldn't shake the sounds of the screams. What I'd done during the War wasn't healing. I hacked off bits of soldiers and sent them back out to lose another piece. Some of them crossed my table two, three times. I couldn't come clean from their blood on my hands. It tainted everything else I tried to do. Them poor boys a-looking up at me thinking I was going to save them. I killed more than I spared. I had no equipment, no quinine, no morphine, no sleep for days on end. It was like cutting away at a Chicago packing house. And I saw it again every time I closed my eyes.

"Livie didn't understand. All she knew was that I was dragging her from civilization, away from the comforts of my profession to punish her for her failings. And I guess in a way I was punishing us both. The minute she saw the prairie she hated it, the emptiness of it, the sameness of it. And she hated our soddy even more. It was warm and dry with plenty of the necessary comforts, but all she could see was the newspapers pasted on the walls for insulation, the buffalo chips and twisted hay for burning, the crates for cupboards and the dust. There were no lectures, concerts or theaters, no calling, no gossiping, no parties, no daily mail and no neighbors for thirty miles."

Aurora could feel for the other woman's panic, for the incredible isolation she must have suffered. It was easier to be weaned from civilization slowly, going west increments at time so the shock wasn't so sudden and complete. But she could understand Ethan's reasoning, too. And she felt an aching sorrow for them both. How awful it must have been for them, trapped in their unhappy existence, forced to live the other's expectations. And how much worse for a gently-bred female used to companionship and gaiety and family ties. She couldn't fault Ethan for not understanding his young wife's anxiety. Men were raised with the taste of freedom in their lungs and taught to look for adventure where women were reared to a complacency out of step with the independence of the frontier. How dismayed Olivia Prescott must have been, how homesick and insecure. And it would have been worse for her not recognizing the love of a good man for the treasure it was.

"I was working for a nearby rancher, trying to scrape up enough to run my own herd. I was gone a lot and was glad to find Livie was expecting. The child would be company for her and would give her something to occupy her time. And it was my child, I had no doubt about it. My child. I was so full of — of hope."

Aurora heard in his voice that aching emotion. She could feel for his longing. She could imagine him making plans in his mind and in his heart. Sympathy thickened in her throat. It was agony for her, listening, knowing there was nothing she could do to change the tragic course his life had taken. Wishing, when she heard him speak so poignantly, that Scotty could be his son. Silent tears filled her eyes for Ethan Prescott's pain.

"I got the chance to make a drive up to Abilene. The money was good and I wouldn't be away for long. It was the money I'd need to get us our start, to build for the baby. I left Livie with plenty of supplies and she promised me she'd take care of herself. Before I rode out, she smiled and told me she'd make things work out, that she'd try real hard to make a home for us when I got back. I remember feeling better about things than I had in a long time.

"When I rode in, the door was standing open. I recall thinking how odd that was because Livie hated the thought of dust and critters getting inside. I hollered to her but no one answered. Then, I went inside." His voice fractured. "And found her where she'd hanged herself in the middle of the room." He was seeing all over again the stool he'd made for her, tipped onto its side. Then, the tips of her buttoned shoes suspended in the air. They'd been coated with Texas grit. Above them, her petticoat belled and swayed. And for a long time, he hadn't been able to look higher.

"She'd been gone for less than a day. If she'd just waited, if she'd talked to me, if she'd told me how she was feeling inside. Instead, she just went quietly, politely crazy from the lonelies. I didn't see it coming. I thought she'd adjust. She told me she was and I wanted to believe her. Dammit, I wanted to believe everything was going to be fine." He took a deep, shuddering breath and was silent.

Scotty had finished his meal and was dozing contentedly at her breast. Careful not to wake him, she gathered him up and slipped by Ethan to place the baby in his hand-crafted cradle. Then, she looked back to where Ethan sat, dazed and devastated. Tears quickened more fiercely but she blinked them away. He didn't want her pity. She wasn't sure what he needed from her. Perhaps just being with him was enough. No words, no reprimands would remove the sting of his self-blame. He would have to live with it, the way she had to live with her time amongst the Sioux. Surviving wasn't easy. Olivia Prescott had chosen the easier route. It was the living that was tough, not the dying. It took no courage at all to give up. And Aurora had an abundance of courage.

It faltered when she considered the slumped figure of the big Texan. For all his strength, there was a certain fragility too. A sensitivity of spirit both bane and blessing. It made him a man of compassion and caring, of conviction and control. And it also left him wide open to the agony of feeling too much, too deeply. With a personal torment that sank clear to the soul. Her heart broke for him. She longed for the power to heal him, for the magic to restore his faith in himself and in those around him. But she had no such magic. All she could do was love him.

The feel of her palm against his cheek brought focus to Ethan's gaze. Aurora came down on one knee before him, commanding him with her presence to come away from the past. But it wasn't easy to escape.

"I ran, Ora. I ran as far and fast as I could. And I thought I could forget. Guess I'm still running."

Her hand stroked along his jaw. "No, Ethan. Today you stopped."

And she kissed him.

Her mouth moved slow and sweet upon his, making no demands other than he accept what she would give. His lips parted at the subtle persuasion of her tongue, letting her slip inside to taste and tempt. He moaned softly and lifted one big, calloused hand to rub from elbow to shoulder and back. She was all supple strength and silken steel. Like the bright Dakota dawn that issued forth each day, she was his light, his hope, and as he gathered her into his enfolding embrace he realized the truth of what she'd said. She had run him to the ground and neatly trapped him. And he didn't mind it one damn bit.

Darkness was complete outside. The cabin's interior was washed with a warm haze of firelight. It cast a hot, molten contour and secret shadow over the figures intertwined upon the soft, pine-filled mattress. The hiss and pop of sapwood melded with quiet, breathless sounds of discovery and delight. Upon the chinked log wall, twin silhouettes portrayed a slow, sensual dance of desire; merging, moving, mingling in an age-old rhythm until finally all was still. From the hearth, an ash-whitened log toppled with a sigh. In his cradle, Scotty murmured in his sleep. And upon the table top, two charred slabs of venison remained untouched.

He couldn't let her go. As he held Aurora's slumbering form close against his chest, Ethan admitted it to himself. Solitude had no further lure for him. It was emptiness, not independence. He had been running, hiding from the past, from commitment — and thereby disappointment — and from himself. Aurora Kincaid had ferreted him out and dragged him back amongst the living. And it was good to feel again. He was like a great brown bear prodded from hibernation, grumbling and roaring his displeasure, even snapping sullenly at whoever dared disturb him. But once up and out, the pleasures of a solitary slumber were forgotten. He was sniffing a new, fresh breeze. He was stirred by the springtime mating urge. He wanted to strike his claws against the nearest tree to stake his claim in defiance of trespassers. He wanted to hold to what was his.

And Aurora and Scotty were his.

She'd come to him still weighted with doubts about his innocence. When danger threatened, she brought her child to him for safety. As passion sparked, she'd become a mountain cat within his arms. Lord, how the very vibrance of Aurora Kincaid cast the past into dim shadow. How had he ever believed love touched his life before she horned into it? Her possessive passion, her unswerving faith caused the foundations of his cynicism to shudder and fall. Here in his arms was not a fragile flower in need of constant nurturing. Here in his bed was not a fickle female clutching in self-interest. Here he had a helpmate, a strong, dauntless supporter, a uniquely separate being who sought to share with him, not smother him. She'd chosen to bestow her

284

cherished affection against the odds, not because of them.

No, he no longer wanted to hole up in the woods, licking festered wounds and snarling in surly temper. He wanted what he'd always wanted but felt he could never have again. A woman to love, who would love him. A family bonded close in devotion. A dream, a hope, a future. Aurora Kincaid thrust those possibilities back into his life and made him face his desire for them.

He looked down upon her sleep-softened features, which were glazed to a golden beauty in the tender hearth-light. Her long hair spun about her like a lake of fire, and his emotions burned hot and quick and simmered warm and lingering. He remembered the first time he'd laid her out on this bed, all frozen and huge with child. He'd thought her a threat then. And how right he was. She'd challenged his sanctuary, she'd ripped away his cloaking wall of remoteness. She'd forced him to reenter a world of the living; a realm that plainly scared the hell out of him. Once he'd felt the crushing agony of a trap snapping shut and shattering bone, he wasn't so quick to test unfamiliar ground or taste from tantalizing offerings. The unknown was a baited risk. But Aurora had taught him that some risks were worth the taking. How many had she dared by coming back to him? She was defying her father, defying the law, defying the security of a set future. And yet she'd come. Because of trust. Because of love. And damn if he hadn't felt inspired by her bravery. And double damned if he would fail before it.

She made a contented sound in the throes of some sweet dream and rolled toward him. Her nose pressed into his shoulder. One slender arm snaked possessively about his middle. Even in slumber, she was sure of what she wanted. He'd been less sure until this minute but now, he knew. He wanted this intriguing woman and her child. Tomorrow and always. And he would find a way to make it so.

Scotty's soft fretting woke Aurora to a cold, clear dawn. The fire had burned low, and the promise of chill floorboards had none of the lure of Ethan Prescott's long, warm body stretched out beside her. She lingered for an indulgent moment against the unyielding curve of his side, molding her figure to its contours. It would be heaven to remain, but the fussing calls grew louder, drawing her from desire to duty.

Not wishing to wake Ethan, she slipped carefully from the bed, then bit her lip as bare feet touched freezing floor. No traces of lethargy tarried. They were brutally shocked from her system. Quickly she squirmed into the men's britches and the rough folds of wool flannel, chafing the coarse shirt fabric up and down along her arms as she padded to the hearth. After adding several small logs to the fire and establishing a satisfactory flame, she looked to the cradle and smiled. Scotty was wide awake, peering up at her through somber eyes — golden eyes, like his mother. Realizing his demands were about to be met, he raised his arms and waved them about in welcome, giving her a gummy grin. Then Aurora no longer needed the fire to warm her. Love for her son fanned an emotional fire within. She lifted him from his bed and held him close, turning her face into his soft wisps of black hair. For a moment, he gurgled happily, then wriggled in impatience to remind her of his need for dry wrappings and a warm breakfast at her breast.

After complying with the first request, Aurora settled into a hearthside chair to see to the second. As Scotty clutched her bosom with tiny, anxious fists and nursed voraciously, she let her gaze wander back to the corner bed. This was the view Ethan had of her every one of those first nights. She could see his shape sculpting the covers, but the details of his face lay in provoking shadow. The buffalo robe shifted with the movement of one long leg. Her breath caught in her throat. She imagined the feel of that muscled thigh rubbing against her and the thought quickly spiraled into others more explicit in nature. Then she winced at the sudden pinch of Scotty's hard gums. It was as if he was jealous of her distracted attention.

For a moment, she cooed to the child and quieted her lustings. Presently, when both were settled, she began to think of all the things said between them. Two very disturbing questions wavered the calm surface of her complaisance. She mulled them over in her mind, hoping their worrisome eddies had stilled during the night. But they hadn't and they needed to be faced before she could make any other plans.

Ethan said he wanted no part of a child that wasn't his. Would that be true with Scotty? Would he be able to look upon the boy as his own or would his copper skin and raven hair be an ever-present reminder of her past? That she had lain and conceived with another. It seemed not to be an issue now. The tall Texan appeared to dote upon her son. The bonding of birth had touched him as well. Could time's passage sustain that closeness? Lord knew Scotty would find enough alienation as he approached manhood. She could not — would not allow that isolation to extend to the man in her life. Her happiness was secondary to Scotty's well-being. She'd made her child that promise and would adhere to it even at the cost of her misery. If Ethan wanted her, he would have to take Scotty. Not as unavoidable excess baggage but because he wanted him, sincerely, from the heart and would willingly place himself in the role of father. Was that too much to ask of a man? To take on another's child and love it as his own? Could Ethan promise that Scotty would not lose his affection if and when they shared other children between them? Or when the questions began of Scotty's parentage? Pride was a holy issue to the male. Was Ethan's secure enough to weather what was bound to come?

Yes. Looking at him, weighing what she knew of him, yes. And she felt a partial relief before turning to the next issue. One far more discomforting.

Was Ethan Prescott's interest in her wrapped up in Scotty and the past? Would he have been so willing to take her in and let her stay if not for her child reminding him of his own loss? Were she and Scotty mere replacements to conveniently fill the empty pockets in his heart? The thought chilled her. Still, she pursued it. She didn't think it a conscious thing. He wasn't purposefully, cold-heartedly using them to fill that void. But how easy for him to seize upon them to assuage his guilt. And she couldn't blame him if that's all there was to it. He'd been hurt, crushed in heart and spirit by his wife's unfair and final act. He'd never had the chance to make amends or to know the child he'd fostered in her womb. Did he see her and Scotty as that chance? And if he did, how much did she mind it? Was her love such that she would willingly walk in another woman's shoes? Would she allow his wife's unsettled ghost to haunt her security and bedevil her mind? Or should she force the issue now and risk losing . . . everything?

The massive shape turned upon the bed and her thoughts turned just as restlessly. She could well lose him by pushing for the truth of it. Then where would she go, what kind of life could she lead? All seemed so irrevocably entwined with the man tangled in warmed bed covers. He had given so much. He promised so much more. Was it selfish of her not to grant him this one thing? Would it be cruel of her to wrest away his last illusions to calm her own insecurities? Asking would hurt him either way, whether he loved her for herself or for the sake of his dead wife's soul. Would that pain atop all the others he'd been forced to suffer be enough to drive him back into hiding? Excluding her, shutting out the chance of a future together? How was she to know what to do? What was the right thing for both of them? Or was there a right or wrong in this perplexing twist of passions?

" 'Morning."

The gruff, sleep-tousled word accelerated her pulse like a sudden, brisk wind. She answered him with the same, only softer, so as not to awaken the sated child.

Ethan gave a long, limbering stretch that popped bare toes from the end of the blanket. Aurora's hungry stare charted the unintentionally sensual motion as he raised his arms overhead with fingers laced, pushing upward until the muscles corded. He was a sleek as a big cat and as powerful as a brown bear. A strong, vital male animal. And she was excited by the display. "You shouldn't have let me sleep." That was husky with suggestion and she simmered in response.

"I had to tend Scotty," was her verbal reply. Carefully, she twisted and settled the baby in his bed. He didn't stir. Dark lashes fanned his golden cheeks, and his little chest moved in a gentle rhythm. Aurora's tender smile was automatic as she tucked in his covers.

Seeing that smile, Ethan knew a perfect contentment. She was so Madonnalike when she performed those maternal tasks and yet so provokingly female when those golden eyes met his and gleamed with sultry hints of pleasure. It created a churning sensation in his belly. And a burning tension, lower.

"Well he's been tended. Now come see to me." He flipped back the buffalo robe to expose more than just a warm, waiting spot beside him. Her stare darkened as it took in his magnificence. It was not an offer she could — or would refuse.

She peeled out of the denim britches and left them where they dropped. The shirt was similarly discarded. Then there was only the delicious feel of hot flesh on flesh when she climbed in the bed and was pulled close by the impatient loop of his arm. The robe was tugged over them, though no longer necessary for heat — they created enough of that between them.

"Good morning," he intoned.

"I believe you said that already."

"But I don't think I mentioned what was so good about it, now did I?"

"No, I don't believe you did. And?"

"Umm?"

"What's so good about it?"

"You're what's good about it, sweet thing. You being here like this." His arm squashed her to the hard wall of his chest for a wonderful mashing.

"In your bed, you mean?"

He caught the prickly overtone and chuckled. Her cheek rode the vibration as it rumbled through him. "Oh, yes indeed, there's that all right." Before she could become as rigid and cold as last night's venison steaks, he gave her another rib-bruising squeeze. "That and the way you looked a-sitting there with Scotty. A man'd give an — um — arm for a sight like that every morning."

"Arm?" she teased with a provoking lift of one fair brow.

He grinned down at her. "It's easier to live with than the lack of the other."

"You're certainly a lusty old bear in the mornings, Mister Prescott."

"You complaining, Miz Ora?"

His big hand rode from smooth shoulder to sleek curving buttocks, and her answer sounded very much like a purr.

"Not at all, Mister Prescott. Not at all."

His palm cupped one firm globe and pressed her groin into the fullness of his own. "Glad to hear it, ma'am." Then, his mood sobered. "Danged if you don't make me crazier than a steer on loco weed."

She was all too glad to welcome the seeking insistence of his mouth upon hers followed by the branding claim of his tongue. She opened for him; her lips, her thighs, her heart, and he was quick to thrust inside to possess all three.

Afterwards, he held her in the bow of one strong arm while his other hand caressed her with slow, leisurely strokes. Stoking the fires, keeping them burning. He kissed her lips, her cheeks, her chin, and her throat, while she lay luxuriating in his attention. Passion throbbed heavily, lazily, with an indolent satisfaction, as if they had all the time in the world to enjoy one another.

And they would. If Ethan had anything to say about it, they would.

"We'll go to Texas," he announced suddenly against the fluttering pulse at her neck. Its pace took wing in surprise, and he nipped the tender skin lightly. "No one will look for us there. You'd like it, Ora. It's not as green as you're used to, but its wide open. Plenty of room for Scotty to grow."

Aurora held her joy in check. We, he'd said. What a

wonderful word! But then, he was taking her and her son back to the homeland he'd shared with another. Was it coincidence or subtle planning? Did he think he could make her into Olivia, and Scotty into the child he'd lost? And suddenly, she knew. She didn't want to live in the shadow of another woman. She wanted to be the only one Ethan Prescott saw when he looked at her with those piercing dark eyes.

"And what of the memories you have there?" she asked softly.

He didn't hesitate. "The ache I carried over Livie is gone. You and Scotty have filled that emptiness inside me. He's the son I never had the chance to know. You're the woman I was never able to reach with my love."

"Or with your apology?"

She moved so quickly she was up and off the bed before Ethan could anticipate it. Denim was jerked up over the silky seduction of her female curves and the bulky shirt pulled together almost like a defensive shield. He was lost in her tempest of emotion. Why was she so upset? A moment ago she'd been rubbing up to him as friendly as a she-cat, and now she was all bared claws.

"Ora?"

She didn't respond but rather went to put coffee water to boil. Her movements spoke her tension clearly; all short and swift and slamming.

Ethan sat up to watch her move about his makeshift kitchen, preparing breakfast the way some men readied to go to war; all stern and fierce and frightened. What the hell was eating her?

"Don't you want to go?"

She froze for a moment, her back to him, tears bright on her cheeks. Her voice was low and gruff. "I'll have to think on it, Ethan." Then the skillet banged down on the tabletop and shards of potato flung inside from the flashing blade in her hand. Did she want to be with him. Yes, God yes! Did she want to play the guilt offering to his wife? No. Never! He was saying none of the things she wanted to hear, none of the things that would calm the gnawing demon in her breast. Did he care for her, for Aurora Kincaid? Or was she a comfortable filling for the lonely misery in his heart?

Ethan frowned and puzzled over her odd shift of mood. Was it the mention of Texas? Didn't she want to leave her father? Didn't she want to be with him? Or had he totally misread her passion? Could it be she was using him to bait her father, to earn his attention and his good graces? How could that be? What purpose would coming here to him serve in that battle of Kincaid wills?

And then came his answer.

From the dawn-washed woods outside his front door, there came a bellowing shout.

"Ethan Prescott, we got you surrounded. Come on out with your hands high."

Chapter Eighteen

There was a moment's silence within the cabin. Hearts forgot to beat for that long second.

Then, Ethan was off the bed, jerking up long johns and wrestling with his Levis as he ran to the front window. Through the shutter chinks, he got the unmistakable flash of sunlight off a rifle barrel, a wink of destiny that spelled his end.

Aurora pulled herself out of the fireside chair. Her legs had undergone a rubbery transformation and nearly refused to hold her. Through a wide, horror-filled gaze she watched Ethan spin around to lean his back against the wall. He stood that way for a timeless minute, panting to force down panic, his eyes squeezed shut as he tried to think of some way out.

"Ethan?" she asked in a small voice. The sound of it woke him from his inactivity. She was standing stiff as a pole pine, eyes huge in an ashen face. There was an odd glaze to her expression that gave him a moment's pause. Regret. Agonizing regret. But he had no time to puzzle over it. He bolted across the room, snatching up his gunbelt and whipping it about his hips in a defiant statement that paralyzed Aurora with terror. Speechless, she followed his quick movements as he fed cartridges into his Colt. Reality hit hard and sank deep. "You're going to fight it out with them?" Her words quavered.

"Well I surely ain't going to let them waltz in here and string me up." He took a moment to meet her petrified stare then canted a glance toward the cradle. He felt sick. They would be trapped inside with him and he had no magic to protect them should the men outside be ruthless killers after a quarry on leg-bail. Would they be safe in such indifferent hands even if he surrendered to them? He looked at Aurora's beautiful face and at the way her hurried breaths etched the outline of her generous breasts beneath the heavy shirt. The feeling of nausea thickened. The thought of their leers and dirty touch upon her was far worse than that of his own fate in their captivity. He'd no idea what his dodger read, whether it was *Dead or Alive* or just plain *Dead*. Knowing Garth Kincaid, it would be the latter.

"Can you shoot?" His question was rough, and it hit her like a slap. Glazed golden eyes blinked once, twice, and life flooded back into them. Grimly, she nodded. "Grab the Henry. If they're bounty men, you'll be in as much danger as I am."

Aurora paled slightly in understanding, then went to fetch the repeater where it leaned against the hearth. She brought it up to her shoulder to expertly test its balance. Ethan noted the move with a wry smile. Hell of a woman. She was right beside him when he moved to the window. At that moment, he wanted nothing more than to grab her up against him, to tell her how he loved her for her courage, how he— how he just plain loved her! But there was no time for he saw movement in the trees. At least three, possibly four men. He tried not to consider the odds of Ora being hurt. Or Scotty. It would only make him crazy.

"Prescott, we know yer in there."

Aurora trembled at his side, then stiffened with determination.

"Come on out and there'll be no bloodshed."

She straightened as if struck by lightning and leaned toward the window, trying to peer outside. The voice, even roughened as it was, sounded so familiar.

"I'm sorry, Ora," Ethan told her softly without risking another glance at her lovely profile. Had he, he would have been alerted by her oddness. The gun in his hand felt out of place. His heart was hammering so hard, the beat echoed in his temples. It made him think of cannon fire. He could almost scent the acrid powder in his nose, feel the vibrations roar through his chest, hear the screams in his ears. And then there was silence and the rhythmic creak of the rope rubbing on rafters. He forced a swallow to keep himself from strangling on his memories. This was real. This was now. And there seemed no way out.

"Send the girl out, Prescott and it'll go easier on you."

That was followed by a more concerned call of, "Miz Orrie, you all right in there?"

Johnny Taylor. Aurora's knees almost melted in relief. They were her father's men, not the savage scum that were every bit as bad as the men they hunted. They could be reasoned with. She could talk them into taking Ethan alive. There was no need for gunplay.

Her relief was short-lived. Ethan apparently had come to the same conclusion. Before she could turn to him, she felt the cold bore of his Colt jammed against her cheekbone and heard his words, whispered low and raw.

"You brought them."

She was so stunned, she couldn't say a word and her silence damned her in his mind.

Of course. The logic of it was so clear. Ethan's thoughts scourged savagely. Betrayal was a bitter bile rising hot to choke him, nearly as hot as the fury trembling on the edge of control. Why hadn't he seen it? A Kincaid. A damned Kincaid. As treacherous as her father. Had she used him for her pleasure and would she now turn on him to earn her daddy's approval? A game. Was that all it was? A game of power between two greedy, amoral souls — souls he hoped to see in hell. It explained everything. Her sudden arrival. The way she'd shied from the mention of a future together. Her strangeness this morning. She knew her father's men were outside, rallying for an attack. He could see it in her lovely face. She'd led them right to his door. Had she been nervous about being caught in the middle? Had she felt the tiniest regret about spending the night in his arms? Was she having second thoughts, or did she fear being found out before the major's men could free her? Was she afraid he would forget she was a woman and blow a hole clean through her? He hoped so. He hoped she drown in a sweat of terror. What poetic justice to become exactly what Garth Kincaid was trying to make others believe he was. And to do so by sending him home his whoring daughter's body.

In his white-hot rage, his finger actually tightened on the trigger as the revolver was fully cocked. The sound had Aurora as straight and rigid as a hangman's pole. Her huge eyes canted toward him wildly.

"Ethan—"

"Shut up!"

She gasped as the muzzle pressed to her throat. Deadly steel rode the movement of her frantic swallowing. Desperately, she made another attempt to reach the dangerously remote stranger at her side.

"I didn't know," she told him hoarsely. "Please believe me, Ethan. I—"

"Shut—up!"

He could hear that same breathy voice ringing through his head, only this time, calling to him in straining passion, begging him for release. And now she was begging again, for quite a different reason. To manipulate his conscience as she'd deliberately played earlier upon his desire.

His free hand grabbed a hank of her hair and made a sudden twist, looping the fiery tress about his wrist. With a quick, painful tug, her head was snapped back, leaving the slender length of her neck exposed. She could feel the lethal tension coiled inside his big body, the scorch of his murderous hate, as he beheld what he saw as his betrayer. The violent instability of his mood caused her to cry out in fear and pain but he showed her no sympathy. Not until Scotty's mewling wail sounded behind them.

Tears brilliant upon her pale cheeks, Aurora tried to twist toward her child.

"Scotty."

The way she said her son's name was a plaintive moan. Her composure dissolved into a series of jerky tremors. Breath came in tortured sobs, as if fearing each would be her last. The infant's wails grew louder.

Abruptly, the cruel grip on her hair loosened. The Henry was snatched from her hand and she was pushed away with a careless force that sent her stumbling. She scrambled to the cradle and clutched the upset babe to her breast. That she would use a child to shield herself from his retribution disgusted Ethan to the core but it was an effective measure. The boy played no part in his mother's villainy and he would never, ever knowingly harm an innocent. And of course, she knew it and used it to her advantage. He wouldn't harm her as long as she held the baby between them.

"Damn you," he hissed and turned back to the window.

And damn his own decency.

He was still for a moment. Aurora had silenced Scotty's cries. He had to think. He had to get past the horrendous pain in his heart that made clear thought so cloudy. Finally, he turned back to the traitorous woman crouched by the hearth.

"Call them in," he urged in a low, sinister tone.

Aurora's gaze went from the handgun, to the rifle and then up to the dark void of Ethan Prescott's eyes. She fought not to cringe beneath the cold contempt of his stare. Behind that frigid glare she saw a man wounded beyond recovery and driven into a corner. There was no telling what he might do. But she had an unpleasant suspicion. She knew at least one of the men outside and knew him to be a good man. Her father's men were acting on orders, believing themselves within the law. They thought she was in the clutches of a heartless bushwhacker. She had to make them hear the truth. There had to be a way to defuse the confrontation before anyone got hurt.

"No."

Thinking she didn't understand the perilousness of her situation, he repeated the request, only to have her impertinent chin angle up and her sweet lying lips thin into a stubborn line.

"I won't," she said more forcefully. "I won't lure them in so you can kill them."

"Of course not," he sneered at her. "That's what you had planned for me." He lifted the Henry, sighting it in on the bridge of her nose. "You sing out real loud and tell them you have me."

With a studied care, Aurora bent to place Scotty in the cradle, out of the line of possible harm. Then she straightened and stared directly down the metal bore. "And how do you plan to make me? Are you going to shoot me, Ethan? Do it, then. Go on," she goaded harshly.

For a long moment, the barrel remained leveled with Ethan's black stare on the other end. There was a sharp click and Aurora jerked. It was the hammer disengaging. Her tension spilled out in a shaky breath.

The Henry slanted down.

"Get the hell out of here, Ora. Take Scotty and go."

She stood for a second, considering his offer. More than anything, she wanted Scotty safely away. The thought of him exposed to gunfire was a horrifying one. All she had to do was carry him out the door. She would be safe among her father's men. Then she could talk sense to them and get them to take Ethan alive. She wanted Ethan to come through the ordeal in one piece.

But no. Logic, cold, cruel logic told her that wasn't how it would happen. She knew the minute she stepped out of the cabin, her father's men would converge upon it, regardless of what she told them, and the killing wouldn't end until Ethan was dead. They fully believed Ethan had murdered their friend and they wouldn't feel beholden to show him any mercy. She was the only thing keeping Ethan alive.

"No, we're staying. Scotty and I are staying with you."

There was something in her eyes, something he hadn't expected — or wanted to see. A liquid softening. Of pity? He wouldn't allow that. He couldn't believe it could be anything else. Fury froze him up inside.

"Pick up the baby and walk on out of here before I throw you out to them," he snarled.

"Ethan," she began but his unyielding anger stilled her. He would do it. He would see her and Scotty clear, then fight to his own death. And probably welcome it if she was any judge of the anguished madness in his gaze. She knew just as clearly that she could not stand by and let the guns of her father's hired men tear the life from him. Not for something he didn't do. Not before she could make him believe in her innocence. She remembered Far Winds dying in her arms, his dark eyes filled with the belief that she'd betrayed him. She couldn't let the same happen to Ethan.

His back was to her as he peered through the shutter slats. Steeling her heart for what she planned, Aurora reached down into the pocket of the duster she'd left draped over a chair back. Slowly, she advanced on the big figure braced at the window. His breath sucked in with surprise at the sudden dig of her pistol barrel in the small of his back.

"Give me the rifle," she instructed. Her voice was strained with a shaky bravado. She took the Henry from one slack hand and tossed it aside. "Now the Colt."

301

He made no move to release it.

She prodded him.

Still, he wouldn't give up the revolver.

"Please, Ethan."

Tension rolled through the muscles of his shoulders. She could see it plainly in the ripple beneath his snug long johns. He was readying for some foolish move. Her breath came in quick, anxious pants.

"Don't." Then, smaller still, "Please, don't."

"You won't shoot me in the back, Ora." He sounded more confident than she felt.

Roughly, she jammed the barrel into denim just above the back of his right knee. "Not to kill but I'll do what I have to to see no one dies. Please don't make me hurt you, Ethan. I don't want to hurt you."

"You can tell me that again right before your father hangs me."

His right hand moved slowly out to the side. His handgun did a spin to dangle by the trigger guard off his forefinger. Aurora reached cautiously to claim it, and only then did she expel a shuddering breath. Even unarmed, she wasn't lulled into believing him harmless. Or out of danger from the men outside.

"Ethan, I'm so sorry."

She brought the barrel of the Colt down against the back of his head with a swift angled chop, felling him like an oak.

The constant swaying motion brought up waves of sickness with the ebb and flow of consciousness. He was on horseback. Moving downhill, to judge by the angle of his seat in the saddle. He didn't open his eyes, afraid of what the piercing daylight would do to the already merciless pounding inside his head. His awareness wasn't necessary. He was bound like a trophy buck to the saddle horn. And his hunters weren't about to let their prize escape them.

Ora had struck him down. Why did that knowledge atop all else surprise him so? She was taking him to her father as a peace offering. Probably as a bargaining chip to assure Scotty's place on the Bar K. If it had ever been in any danger. Had she made it all up? The threat to Scotty? Her quarrel with the major? Had it all been a part of the plan to fool him into lowering his guard? He'd sure lowered everything else quick enough.

A fool. Oh, yes, she'd made him into her fool. Shouldn't he have learned after the first time that he was no judge of womankind? Or was it because he'd wanted to believe in her so very, very much? He'd wanted to believe that the name Kincaid was nothing more than a word. And he'd seriously underestimated the thickness of blood. She was her father's daughter, without a shred of honor in her. Without a trace of caring in her cold, cold heart. He'd woken her to lust, but lust and love were worlds apart, and he'd gambled all on the wrong emotion.

Bitterness rose to rival dizziness and gave him the courage to slit a glance toward his lovely captor. She rode beside him with Scotty tucked beneath her duster in a makeshift front pack. Her flame-colored hair was braided into a long trail of fire. Long enough to loop around her treacherous neck and strangle her. But he'd have no opportunity to do it. He'd be testing the breeze at the end of a length of Bar K hemp by morning. And he didn't care. It didn't matter. Nothing did. He closed his eyes again and let his forehead rest atop his bound hands, while pain and shattered promises beat angrily behind them.

Aurora bit her lip as she watched him weave in the saddle. She knew he was awake. She'd felt the scorn of his glance cutting through her like a knife. It would take two more hours, at least, to reach the Bar K, hours that could be filled with a damning silence or used for another desperate purpose. She had that long to convince him of the truth of her motives. If he would listen.

"Abe," she called ahead to the wrangler in charge of the expedition. "Can we stop for a minute? I need to tend my son."

Horses were drawn up in a sheltered copse. Ethan's bonds were loosened, and he was allowed to fall heavily to the ground. Aurora lurched forward, then forced herself to hold her ground. There was nothing she could do to ease what he'd already suffered. She watched with a stoic expression as the hog-tied Texan struggled to a sitting position; then she winced at the stab of hate he hurled her way with one brief glance. She carried Scotty to a spot not far from where he sat with head on bent knees and settled there, despite the disapproving looks of the Bar K hands. She reached for her shirt buttons and paused with a meaningful stare at the cowboys.

"Could you fellows give me a little privacy? Mister Prescott isn't going anywhere."

They blushed and muttered but moved far enough away so as not to intrude upon her nursing. Or, as she'd planned, her conversation with their prisoner.

"Are you all right?"

He wouldn't answer. Nor would he favor her with a look. Which was just as well. She could imagine what worked within his dark gaze.

"Ethan, I want you to hear me out. I had nothing to do with those men coming after you. Had I any idea I was being followed, I never would have come to the cabin. I guess it is my fault for not giving my father credit enough to figure where I would run."

He gave a low, derisive laugh. "Never underestimate a Kincaid."

"I'll do everything I can to see you're not harmed."

Again, the bitter chuckle. "That why you came near to bashing in my skull?"

Her breath snagged on a sob. The way his head was bent, she could see the discolorations of blood mingled in the dark auburn curls. She hadn't meant to hit him so hard, but she'd no way of knowing what it would take to render him helpless. Luckily, she hadn't killed him with her good intentions.

"I had to, Ethan. Don't you see?"

"Pardon me for saying I'm not seeing much of anything too clear right now."

"I couldn't risk you trying something or one of them shooting you when they came in. Knocking you out was the only way I could think to save your life. It was the only way I could be sure they'd take you alive."

She made it sound so plausible. Her voice snagged with just the right amount of anguish. Maybe if his head wasn't clamoring like a Sunday church bell, he would have considered what she said with some degree of fairness. But as it was, he ached. His mind was stunned by the pain that roared with every beat of his blood. His thoughts were numbed by the knowledge of the woman he loved clubbing him down to his knees. In an effort to save his life? Or her own?

He lifted his head then. It was an effort. The twist of his smile was cruel. "Should I thank you then for saving me for your father's rope? You figure that's a more humane way to meet your maker? There ain't no good way, Ora. Dead's dead."

She stiffened inside. "I won't let them hang you for something you didn't do."

"Why thank you, Miz Kincaid. I'll sure rest better knowing that. I'll carry your assurances right to the very end of the noose."

With that, he dismissed her, resting his forehead on his hands to block out the sight of her anguished face.

"I'll talk to my father," she persisted. "I'll make him listen. I'll make him hear the truth."

"Why would he want to, Ora? You forget, I know all about talking to a Kincaid. See what it's gotten me so far?"

"We'd best be moving, Miz Orrie," Abe Carter interrupted uneasily. He didn't like the idea of the boss's daughter talking with the likes of Prescott. No more than he liked the task of telling the major they'd lost his only child's trail and she'd spent the night alone with him. Doing what, he wondered, leaning in for a quick glimpse of curved white bosom as she buttoned her shirt together. He knew what he'd be doing. Orrie Kincaid was one ripe and ready female. He'd have never thought that way about the major's proper eastern-schooled daughter. It would have been too disrespectful to conceive of her as an earthy female, rather than as one of his boss's fine possessions. But her a-coming back suckling an Injun babe and cavorting with the likes of Prescott, why that spoke of a totally different kind of female; one a man could lust after fairly, one who'd tasted life and enjoyed its wanton flavor. Miz Kincaid a man could only dream about. This woman was not near as unobtainable. After all, look what she'd taken up with.

He let his gaze linger over her lush form — even the mannish garb couldn't contain her tempting assets. Jack Lawson had taken to bragging about how the major's daughter was going to be his. Well, he didn't know about that, but maybe there was more than enough of her to go around. He began to smile hopefully. Then, he looked up from the ogling of her bosom and caught the full bore of Ethan Prescott's glare. It fairly split him in two with the intense thrust of its fury. Abe flushed and turned awkwardly away before puzzling over why the outlaw she'd turned in cared how she was perused by others.

Ethan managed to mount his sorrel and sit straight in the saddle. When one of the cowhands came to truss him up, Aurora said curtly, "There's no need for that." With the length of rope dangling from his hands, the flustered man looked to Abe Carter for direction. Abe shrugged in deference to Aurora's will. What did it matter? Prescott wasn't going to be running off with two guns itching for his back. All of them had liked Cale Marks. Each of them would be more than happy to claim the bullet that sent his killer to the hereafter. Sensing that, Prescott wasn't likely to do anything stupid.

However, as they began to move down from the hills, Ethan wasn't thinking about escape. He was stewing over the straw-haired cowboy's grin. The man had all but drooled down Ora's cleavage. He'd wanted to strike that smug supposing right off the other's face. If Garth Kincaid had no more control over his men then to allow them to rape his daughter with

307

their eyes, he hated to think what she had in store as the only available female — and a danged fine-looking one at that — for miles around, smack in the middle of a herd of rut-crazed cowboys. They had no call to view her so cheaply, like one of the painted harlots strutting in Deadwood. Ora was a lady and deserving of their respect. If she were his woman, he'd . . .

Ethan caught that turn of thought and crushed it fiercely. Aurora Kincaid was not his woman. What did he care how the men of the Bar K looked upon her? Maybe they were right. To get him into her father's hands, she'd played whore's tricks with a natural talent. For all he knew, she might have encouraged those ravening looks, even enjoyed them. What did it matter if she chose to spread for every bunkhouse ramrod on the Bar K? It shouldn't have, but bringing even the image to mind made him grind his teeth like a grist wheel.

Frowning, he regarded her where she rode abreast of him. She was careful not to look at him, pretending an indifference, but he knew she felt his gaze. A particular tension came over her, lining her shoulders, stiffening her spine. Lordy, she was an eyeful, a fiery beauty with a spirit to match. Brave and beautiful. And Ethan hated himself for so admiring her.

For still loving her.

Better he hang onto his hate for the symbol of Kincaid. Better he not think too long or too deeply on her pleading words, lest he begin to believe them. The last thing he wanted was to go to the grave twice the fool. He'd never understood his own wife, and they'd lived together under one roof for almost two years. How could he claim insight into a woman he'd known for less than a month? One named Kincaid.

Aurora was painfully aware of his stare. What was he thinking, she wondered miserably. The worst, no doubt. How quick he'd been to judge her even after all they'd shared. His conclusions stirred an ache in her breast. She'd been wrong to assume that intimacy implied closeness. He didn't trust her, no more than he had on first meeting her. He'd wanted her. That was all. Just as all men wanted desirable women. She'd been aware of that fact of nature the first time she put her hair up in Boston. But she wanted more than lusting looks or a pleasurable dalliance beneath the sheets. And she wanted it from Ethan Prescott. What more could she do? What would prove to him the depth of her love? What would make him look upon her, not as a woman made in the mold of Olivia Prescott, but as a woman he could trust enough to love? Maybe nothing. Maybe Olivia had hurt him so deeply, so fatally, he would never recover from it. Maybe all her hopes were based on something she could never change. Perhaps the heart of Ethan Prescott was too badly scarred to ever heal, and her own would only break in the trying.

But try, she would. He was worth it. Oh Lord, he was worth it. He was everything she wanted in a man, in a father for her child. If only she had known him before he'd been so bent by treachery. If she had Olivia Prescott before her now, she would kick the stool out from under the destructive weakling herself. How could she have done such a thing? To herself. To her husband. To the child within her womb. Aurora couldn't understand it. But she wished with all her heart that she could help Ethan come to terms with it. If there was time.

Knowing she could well be leading him to his own

death made for no easy ride. Her father wouldn't want to hear of his innocence, not when guilt was more convenient. Her belief in the tall Texan was not going to sway him. He'd simply say she was being led by her desires. There had to be a means to prove what she knew to be the truth. There had to be some way to give Ethan back his dream of the Lone Star Ranch. And in doing so, restore her own dream.

She never heard a warning. Not a rustle in the brush. Not a whisper in the wind. It was a feeling that seeped through her marrow and left her cold. What was it? Her father's men continued unaware. Perhaps, it was nothing. She'd just begun to turn to Ethan to see if he'd noticed anything out of the ordinary. He met her gaze with dark, distrustful eyes. Eyes that suddenly widened as if with an amazed discovery. He opened his mouth and she waited for his words. Words he never spoke. For abruptly, he was falling, pitching headlong from the saddle. As he slid toward the ground, her stare was arrested by a long, thin shaft protruding from his back. Quivering on the end of it were bright horizontal feathers, designed to guide a killing arrow between a man's ribs. A Sioux war arrow.

And she screamed.

Chapter Nineteen

The attack was swift and silent. The Bar K riders had no chance to prepare. They were intent upon their prisoner, not upon the threat of the woods around them. In the seconds after Ethan's fall, there was confusion. Rifles were raised and riders twisted, searching for a target amongst the shadows flitting through the dense trees. Before one shot was fired, all four men had toppled from their saddles in a barrage of deadly arrows. Until only Aurora remained.

It was a nightmare returned. Aurora saw the men atop the coach falling through her memory. She heard the undulating wail of a Miniconjou war cry, echoing loud and bold in victory, and her blood chilled. Panic surged. Her first instinct was to run, to apply heels to horse and pray to outdistance them. But the sight of Ethan Prescott sprawled facedown on the pine-covered ground froze thoughts of flight for that first crucial minute. And then, by the time the Lakota braves separated from the cloaking trees, it was too late. Seeing them snapped her paralysis. It was happening all over again. Even her shock-numbed mind couldn't accept that. She couldn't surrender into their hands without a fight. Not this time. She had Scotty to think of.

With a wild cry, she slapped the rein tails against her horse's flanks. The animal lunged forward, half-rearing, half-plunging. Holding Scotty tight with one arm left her with little control over her panicked mount. A warrior angled his horse to block her escape, and she sawed frantically on the reins to swerve around him. Her horse wheeled in a close, rump-scraping circle and leaped in the direction from which they'd come. From the corner of her eye, she saw a bronzed hand reaching for the bridle. With a savage shriek of denial, she lashed at it with the leather reins and hauled the horse in another semicircle. There were at least a half dozen of them. She saw that and knew the hopelessness of what she attempted, but still she had to try. For Scotty, she had to try.

Aurora seized upon a break in the dense trees and aimed her mount's head for it. At a full, breakneck gallop, horse and rider rushed for that spot. And, abruptly, the hole was closed. One of the Miniconjou rider's stopped it with his paint stallion. Too late, Aurora tried to gather the reins. Her horse had the bit in its teeth and paid no mind to her desperate signals. The animals collided with a thud of hide and muscle as shoulder struck haunch. Her free hand flailed out for the saddle horn and felt the smooth knob slide across her palm. The horse's head flung back, hitting her full in the face, knocking her from her seat in a daze of pain. She was falling. She saw sky. She caught the movement of crazed hooves dangerously near her head. Then impact. Stunning, forcing air and sensibility from her. She'd managed to twist her body to land on the flat of her back, protecting the child in her arms.

It took a minute for the Lakotas to get the horses

under control. They had no desire to lose any of the Bar K's fine stock. By the time Aurora was able to suck sweet air into her burning lungs, they had formed a solid ring about her. Still disoriented and breathless, she staggered to her feet and revolved in a tight, defensive circle with Scotty clutched to her chest. Blood was wet and warm on her forehead from a split above her left eye. She was panting and hurt but apparently fierce enough in her expression for the warriors to be cautious. They respected bravery, and in a woman were awed by it.

One of the warriors she recognized. He was Black Moon, a familiar visitor to Far Winds's tipi. She focused her attention on him, knowing he spoke English tolerably well and was probably in command of the small band of renegade raiders.

"I will not go with you," she declared with all the strength she could muster.

"It is not you we seek, Wadutah. You are cursed with a bad spirit. Our medicine woman has seen its shadow upon you. To strike you down would free it to seek another host. You may go unharmed, but the child will come with us."

Terror clasped about her heart at the uttering of that single phrase. Her own safety meant nothing to her. It was an empty exchange. With Ethan lying dead on the ground, Scotty was all she had in the world. Without him, her life had no purpose. They didn't understand. Just like her father, these arrogant Miniconjou braves couldn't fathom the link between mother and child or the desperate lengths to which she would go to protect him.

"No," she snarled, her arms tightening possessively about the now squalling baby. "He is my child. I will

313

not give him up because of Uncheedah's lies. You will not steal him from me or I will curse you all through him."

That created a superstitious stir among the braves. Black Moon waved them off and he studied the fiery *wasichu* woman narrowly. "You will give me the child or we will ride upon your father's walls until no one is left alive."

She couldn't show them that their threat had her trembling inside with dread and horror. "Do what you must."

Black Moon smiled. It was a cruel twist upon his harshly handsome face. "You are of a strong heart, Wadutah. I can see how my brother was so taken by you. Were things different, I might be tempted to take you for my own second wife."

She received his compliment without reaction.

Pride affronted by her indifference, Black Moon frowned. His words were delivered with a cold certainty. "We shall see how strong you remain when we bring the men from your father's house so you can watch them die for your stubbornness. Soon you will be glad to give up the child to us. We are his people. We will embrace him into our hearts. He will live well among us."

"You would raise him to hate the part I gave to him. No. There is no future for him with the Sioux. Even the great Yellow Bear will be caught and made to live upon the reservation lands like his brethren. There will be no hills, no freedom for any of you. That is not what I want for my son."

Anger clouded the proud features. "You speak a lie, woman. No pale eyes will tie the mighty Matogee to their tipis of wood like a miserable camp cur. No more talk. You will give us what we want or we will do what I have said."

Aurora stood firm. Inside her mind, the horrible images of death at the merciless hands of the Sioux had already begun a subtle torture. How long could she remain resolute? While they tormented men she'd grown up alongside? While she watched them writhe and scream and ultimately die? Until they brought her father. She knew enough of the Lakota fears to keep herself safe and Scotty out of their hands, but could she hold out against their means of persuasion? Scotty was all she had. Did she owe her father loyalty to that extent? Could she sacrifice the only thing of value that remained within her heart to save him who'd betrayed her and those who would scorn her? She was no longer so certain. How could she endure the memory of her father's death atop the horror of seeing Ethan fall? A fierce tremor of doubt shook through her. She was strong but inevitably she would break before the untold tribulations to come. At what cost? And how would she live with the nightmare of memory afterwards?

Scotty wiggled in her arms. She looked down at him through a glaze of panicked tears and saw the trust in his sweet expression. Her child. Anguish wrenched her heart. She'd carried him safe within her for nine long months and had brought him joyously into the world with a vow that she'd protect him. And already she was about to fail in that promise. No longer would she feel him kneading her breast with tiny hands as he suckled. She wouldn't wake to the sound of his impatient cries, nor would she see his toothless grin of greeting. She wouldn't see him grow from child to man under her direction. They wanted

315

to take more than her baby. They wanted to rip away part of her very being.

No.

Never.

Not as long as she yet breathed.

Black Moon must have seen the answer forming in her pale face for he made a few quick motions to his warriors. They slid gracefully from their powerful ponies, knives drawn.

"We will start by lifting the hair of these who have fallen and by tonight the ground will run red with blood."

In an agony of loss, her gaze was drawn to the body of Ethan Prescott. Darkness pooled about the shaft jutting obscenely from between his shoulders. Ethan. Her eyes squeezed shut and her soul shuddered with the want to wail. How could life be so cruel? To slay her love and threaten to tear her child from her arms. She began to sway as silent sobs forced their way upward to clog hotly in her throat. Oh God, how she'd loved him! How could he be dead? Grief-stricken eyes filled with one last look.

And saw with disbelieving clarity his boot jerk.

Dear God!

She watched and waited, breath suspended in tight anxiety, tears rolling in anguished hope. Could he be alive? She needed some sign, some movement to prove it was so.

His fingers opened and closed upon the ground.

A Lakota brave knelt down at the Texan's side. His wicked blade gleamed wetly. Just as he seized a handful of auburn hair and jerked up to make a taut white bow of his victim's throat, Aurora screamed.

"No! No more. Please!" Her frantic gaze swung to

316

Black Moon in desperate supplication then returned to the knife edge poised at Ethan's hairline. "Stop. Stop it!"

Black Moon made a staying motion with his hand and the white man's head thudded heavily to the ground. He looked at the distraught *wasichu* woman with a puzzled frown. He'd expected much more resistance. She'd quelled over the mutilation of a few dead men. White weakness, he attributed with a snort of disgust.

"Take him," Aurora said in a fractured voice. She was sobbing freely now, great waves of sorrow wracking her body. There was no reason to pretend strength when they were carving the very heart from her breast. "Take him and let me bury the dead with honor."

Black Moon gestured toward her and one of the braves approached. When his copper-colored hands extended, she clutched her child with instinctive reluctance, and then, without daring a last look into the bundle of blankets, placed her baby in his care.

Scotty.

She gripped the Indian's arms just as he was about to turn away. He gave her a long look. It was not without compassion. He had sons.

Hands unsteady, Aurora touched her baby's face, his small fists. Her splash of tears discolored his soft white linen chemise. It could well be the last time she ever saw him, this beautiful child of her body. Her words were raw with emotion.

"I'm sorry, Scotty. Some day I may be able to explain."

She couldn't let Ethan die for the sweet luxury of keeping him with her.

"Be careful of him," she cautioned the now stoic brave.

He put his back to her and carried her child away.

"He will be raised to be a great warrior, Wadutah."

She looked up at Black Moon, her features etched with a deeply female suffering and said simply, "See that he becomes a good man."

He gave a brisk nod then jerked his mount around. The others followed, disappearing into the woods as silently as they had come.

Taking Scotty with them.

Spiritlessly, Aurora sank to the ground. Face covered with trembling hands, she wept long and hard for the emptiness of her arms, for the emptiness in her heart. Nothing could ever heal that fresh, tearing wound. She wailed and keened her misery until no further sound could pass the aching constriction in her throat. And then, she rocked in silence, hugging herself as she swayed. Hugging arms that would no longer be filled with the joy of life. Moving methodically in a gesture that gave no comfort. She was far from dead inside. There was too much pain. And she mourned endlessly.

It was a low groan from Ethan that finally pierced her despair.

Ethan.

Too weak to stand, Aurora crawled to where he lay, impaled and bleeding upon the ground. She crouched beside him for a long fearful moment, chewing her lip, terrified by the gravity of his wound.

But he was alive.

And she would see he stayed that way.

"Ethan," she called softly as he emitted another moan. She bent close, placing a hand on his cheek when his head turned toward her. The warmth of him flowed through her fingertips, restoring some of the vitality in her own cold body. "Ethan?"

Lashes fluttered like dark raven's wings against the pallor of his skin. Then he looked at her. "Livie?" It was a hoarse, croaking sound. He wet his lips with the tip of his tongue and looked again, eyes focusing upon the lovely face sketched in taut relief by her terror. His voiced warmed. "Ora."

"Hush now," she murmured, rubbing fingers over his mouth. "Don't talk. Save your strength."

But his questions wouldn't keep. There was the devastation in her gaze and the white-hot agony in his back. "What—?"

"The Sioux attacked us. The rest are dead. You've got an arrow in your back. Tell me what to do."

"Scotty?"

Tears trembling in her reply. "Scotty's safe."

That satisfied him for the moment. His eyes closed as he garnered strength. He didn't recognize her distress. All he knew was the incredible comfort of her touch. It soothed him even though deep in his conscious there was a whisper that he should protest. He ignored it and let her presence ease him into velvety black oblivion.

Darkness was gathering into long thin shadows when Aurora finally collapsed, numbed by exhaustion. She'd buried the Bar K dead. It had taken hours to scrape out a hollow in a shallow ravine and nearly all of her strength to roll the stiffening corpses into it. Then, she'd collected limbs and rocks and leaves to scatter over them to disguise the scent and keep predators from getting at them, at least until her father could send someone for them. It was draining work,

319

but she took a sad sort of satisfaction in seeing it done. Weariness blunted her misery and gave the hope she might find sleep.

Ethan was still. Soon she would have to decide what to do about him. It seemed such an impossible task, one beyond the limited reach of her own flagging resources. She'd stripped off her duster to provide a cover for him and was now enjoying the heat from her fire. She didn't care if it's light was seen. Protection against the night and the danger's it offered was far more important. She was hungry and thirsty and unarmed but too tired to be afraid. Even when a rustling in the underbrush grew ever closer. Blankly, she found herself staring up at Ethan's horse where it stood at the edge of the fire's light, reins trailing.

With a soft laugh of relief, she moved toward it, murmuring low until she grasped the reins and had it firmly tethered to a nearby tree. Then she loosened the saddle and found, to her thanksgiving, a canteen of water and a blanket roll. She took a shallow drink, savoring the tepid liquid, then went to kneel beside Ethan.

The wet cloth upon his brow stirred him to a reluctant consciousness. Aurora waited until reason sparked in his wandering gaze. She bestowed a wavering smile upon him and caressed his bearded cheek.

"Hello again. Think you can stay with me awhile this time?"

He managed a nod and she was heartened.

"Ethan, I'm no doctor but I know it's bad. What can I do for you?"

"Help me sit up."

It was no easy task. The evidence of his agony

made it harder work than moving the four cold corpses. Finally, she had him propped sideways against the base of a pine where he leaned, noisily sucking air and shivering.

"What now?" She was afraid of what was yet to come but determined to be strong for him.

"Where's the arrow? Show me here in front."

She pointed to a spot between collarbone and left breast, and he rubbed the area thoughtfully with his fingertips.

"How deep is it?"

"I don't know, Ethan." She was trying very hard for him not to see her panic. Eyes she'd thought could never shed another tear began to grow moist in a swimming dismay.

"See if you can pull it out."

The casual request made her gasp in shock. "I can't!"

"You'll have to if I'm going to travel or I'd bleed to death in less than a mile. Get a good hold and pull. Tell me when."

Shaking with anticipation of his pain, Aurora grasped the arrow shaft where it entered his back. "Ready?" At his nod, she tugged.

"Ahhh! God! Ora, stop!" He sagged against the tree trunk, cheek pressed into its scaly bark. For several long minutes, he gulped great swallows of air while Aurora silently wept. At last, his breathing quieted as did her horror. Until he told her somberly, "You'll have to push it through."

Push it through.

She couldn't have understood him. That would mean tearing through healthy flesh and muscle. Her silence prompted his response. He could feel her dismay without having to see it etched in her face.

"It's that or cut it out. It's too deep for anything else."

"I don't have a knife—" She clamped her lips together, fearing she'd committed herself to the other choice. To a choice too terrible to consider.

Her silence dragged on. Ethan recalled a very pale Olivia with the severed soldier's arm in her hands. He'd said it was too much to expect of a lady. What then was he asking of Aurora? How could he expect her to rally enough to do what was necessary? He damned his lack of strength. He was helpless to heal himself. Unless she was willing. Unless he hadn't underestimated her courage. Black waves of sickening pain swelled up in a threat to his consciousness, warning him not to dally. If he passed out before it was done, he knew he would never awaken. He spoke slowly, firmly. "It can't wait, Ora. It'll have to be now so I'll be fit enough to travel in the morning. Or else you'll be a-burying me too. You'll be hurting me a hell of a lot less by doing what I tell you."

She forced down her misgivings and studied the arrow. Her insides roiled. "What do I do first?"

He smiled grimly. What a woman. "Good girl." He panted quietly for a time then instructed, "I want you to break the arrow off half way down. Get a good two-handed hold on it and when I tell you, you shove it through. Don't go a-worrying about being too rough on me. Just make sure it goes clean through the first time, you here?"

If it didn't, she knew she wouldn't have the courage to attempt it a second time. She took the shaft between her hands and snapped it. Ethan jerked but made no sound. Carefully, she checked for signs of splintered wood, then braced herself.

"All set." Those two words echoed hollowly. How could she possibly be ready for such a horrendous task? One that could kill him. But he was a doctor. He would know if what she was about to do would place his life in greater jeopardy. He seemed confident. All she could see was his body spread-eagled on the ground, supposedly lifeless. All she could think of was having to roll him in on top of the others. The hands gripping the arrow shaft began a fitful shaking.

"Do it now, Ora."

Aurora pulled in a deep breath and shut her eyes. Then, she thrust forward with all her weight and strength behind it. There was a brief, dreadful resistance. Then it was done. Her head rang with the sound of a hoarse, tearing scream. His? Or hers? Then, there was silence except for their labored breathing.

"Ethan?"

Very slowly, he raised his right hand to grip the arrow where it protruded from his chest in a circle of fresh blood and in one quick move, jerked it free. With a feeble gesture, he flung it toward the fire. Aurora began to sob quietly. She needed comforting. He could feel the tremors of her body against him. Not yet. She had to be strong.

"Ora, there's—one more—thing."

His words were broken by the harsh pattern of his breathing but something in the way he tried to soften them alerted her. What could be worse than what she'd already done? Something so awful that he hated to speak of it. In fact, for a long moment, he didn't. With his right hand, he opened his coat and tried to shrug out of it. His groan prompted Aurora to assist him. She managed to ease it off without causing him too much distress, then peeled down his long johns at his direction. His skin gleamed golden in the firelight, all but the twin holes, front and back. Aurora wet her bandana and lightly bathed the wounds. She tried to blank her mind to what she was doing, but her hands shook traitorously. Then, she felt his fingertips touch to her cheek and she looked up. His eyes were dark and intense. Pain cut deep lines at their corners.

For a moment, they shared a wordless communion. Either Ethan had put their misunderstandings behind him as unimportant, or they had escaped his pain-ravaged mind. Whichever, she found in his deep, provoking gaze a wealth of rich emotion. Her fragile, frayed spirit knew a burst of renewing hope, and with it came the courage for her to ask, "What now?"

Ethan reached past her, groaning direly as he leaned forward to grasp a slender branch from the fire. Its tip glowed white against the near-darkness surrounding them. She took it from him gingerly and prompted him with an incomprehensible look.

Watching her face, Ethan said evenly, "I'm bleeding inside, Ora. If I'm going to see morning, its got to be stopped. I need you to see to it for me."

Her features puckered in concern but her head shook in confusion. "I don't—"

And he was afraid when she did, she would balk at the idea of performing the grisly deed. He'd seen seasoned doctors falter before duty not near as grim. With his free hand, he touched her pale, pale face. Her skin was cold. Her brave jaw trembled. And her eyes reflected a fear she wouldn't voice. His fate was in her hands, in her strength. And he would never trust another with its care the way he did this one seemingly fragile female.

"Ora, the tip of that there stick is hot enough to seal everything up tight. The bleeding will stop when you run it on through."

Run it on through.

A giddy lightness filled Aurora's head as the blood drained from it. A buzzing like a million crickets sounded in her ears. She'd never fainted in her entire life, so this sudden disorienting vagueness was a frightening unknown. A black curtain began to interrupt her vision, the way tears had earlier. She put out her hands, pressing them to the ground to steady herself against the abrupt whirling of her world.

"Ora." His voice sounded muffled, miles away. "Ora, if you care whether I live or die, you'll do it. You'll just do it."

I care. Dear God, how I care.

She clung to that powerful surge of sentiment, using it to pull out of the sucking dizziness. Slowly, the sickness passed and with it, her weakening. She stared at the white tip, fascinated. How could something so pure and cool sear so hot?

"When it's done," Ethan was saying, "bind me up good and keep me warm. If fever sets in, hurry like hell to the closest doctor."

She nodded stiffly. She didn't try to speak, fearing that if she did, all her anxieties would come spilling out on a wave of uncontrolled hysteria. Ethan needed her to be calm. His life was depending upon it. And she couldn't lose him. Not after the sacrifice she'd already made to save him. The thought of being all alone scared her into courage.

Never, as long as she lived, would she forget the nauseatingly sweet scent of scorched flesh. Nor would the horrible, rasping cries of agony leave her even after Ethan lapsed into blissful unconsciousness. But she did the terrible thing he asked of her. With mind numbed beyond further comprehension or thoughts of consequence, she ripped her own shirt up into long binding strips. She then used them to keep her bandana wadding snug over the ugly wounds. It was a poor job of bandaging, but the best she could manage working with the heaviness of Ethan's uncooperative form. It would serve to keep the ragged holes clean and dry, and that mattered more than efficient neatness. She redressed him in the blood-stained long johns like a rag doll and draped his coat about him. It was getting cold, and would be colder toward dawn. She scrambled to stack more wood on the fire to encourage a healthy blaze. That done, she eased the senseless Texan down upon the blanket she'd spread upon the ground.

Only then was she aware of how chilled her bared limbs had become. Her thin chemise offered little protection. Shivering, she gave thought to the coats of the dead men she'd buried, but nothing, not even frostbite, could coax her into digging them up to steal the clothing from their rigid bodies. Wrapped up in the scant warmth of her canvas duster, she huddled near the fire. Before she was aware of it, her face was wet with tears.

Don't think. Don't feel.

She dashed a hand across her eyes. Weeping would gain her nothing. She had Ethan to think of, and how she was going to get him out of the hills. Exhaustion was no longer something to battle, but something to be welcomed for its blanking relief. She would sleep. And in the morning she would get Ethan to safety. To the only aid she could think of.

In the morning, she would take him to the Bar K.

Nearly weaving with fatigue and the dragging effects of shock, Aurora laid down upon the blanket and curled close against Ethan's side. There, she found an indescribable comfort in the slow, even movement of his chest and the quiet sameness of his breathing. She closed her eyes, expecting to endure a replay of the day's horrors. Instead, there came a deep, dark sleep bereft of dreams.

Chapter Twenty

Her first waking thoughts were of Scotty. And it was more a physical pain than one of mind. Her breasts hurt. They were heavy and full of milk without the relief of regular feedings to ease them. Recognizing the cause of her distress renewed the great tearing emptiness within her heart.

Scotty was gone.

Sorrow crippled. For a moment, all she could do was curl into a tight knot of despair and moan. There was no reason to move, no reason to go on. Not without her child. She wanted to tuck into a defensive ball that would guard against the incredible pain she was feeling. She wanted the numbness back. She wanted to retreat to where there was no memory, no emotion. But she couldn't find such a place. Her world was alive with the raw, writhing knowledge that never again would she hold her child, hear him laugh or see him cry. And she didn't want to continue in that world.

"Ora?"

It took a while for the soft call of her name to penetrate her self-imposed daze. Slowly, it came back to her, the reason she wanted to go on living.

"Ethan?"

She sat up quickly and turned toward him. His eyes were open. In the pastels of morning, they shone black and hot. Despite the cold breeze, his skin was dappled with sweat. Fearfully, she put her palm to his forehead. He was burning with the fever that consumed his strength. His gaze wandered about in a sightless daze.

"No, God, no," she murmured in a sudden blank of terror. He was going to die. After all the torture, after all the horror of the night before—he was still going to die. And she would be alone. A swamping despair rose up inside her, a helplessness that rendered her immobile. Ethan was going to die.

"No." It was a stronger claim, an angry one. No, she wasn't about to lose him now. Determination cleared her mind of the fogging panic. Then, she remembered his words and clung to them for hope. A doctor. He would need a doctor. And he'd said he could travel. She observed him critically, gauging his strength, his endurance. It wasn't a heartening picture. But then, it wasn't going to get any better. She bent close, speaking calmly, factually. Perhaps he would understand.

"Ethan, you're on fire. I'm taking you down to the Bar K."

A sharp focus came into his eyes, lending them an unnatural brilliance. He understood, all right. All too well. "No. No, not there."

"It's the closest and I've got to get you some help. I can't leave you and I don't think you could make it all the way to Deadwood."

He continued to shake his head until the movement grew jerky and his chest heaved with agitation. "No. To the Sioux. Yellow Bear."

She felt his head a second time. The fever must have addled him. Why else would he suggest going to the same savages who'd nearly killed him? That was madness. She could understand his reluctance to go to her father's ranch but what choice was there? None, to her thinking. None at all. And she would save him, no matter what it took.

She gave a sudden start as Ethan's hot fingers closed about her wrist. There was nothing weak in that desperate grasp. She could almost feel bones grind together.

"I won't go," he told her in a completely lucid voice. "Not to my own hanging. Ugly way to die." His intense gaze flickered and drifted. She knew he was thinking of his wife. Gently, she covered his hand with her free one, massaging it until the crushing pressure lessened.

"I'll keep you safe. I won't let them hang you. You've my word on it, Ethan. My word."

He stared up at her then, his expression troubled as if searching for a reason not to believe her. The wariness she saw there made her want to weep. So much distrust, even now, after she'd saved his life.

And had nearly caused him to lose it.

Finally, his fingers fell open and his eyes lost their keen edge. It was then Aurora hurried to do what she needed.

After cinching the saddle on Ethan's tall sorrel, she knew she would never get him up into it nor would she had the strength to hold him there. Frantically reaching for another solution, she found it in her time amongst the Sioux. She'd seen them fashion travois to aid in their nomadic lifestyle. It would be just the thing to get Ethan out of the hills. She found two straight saplings and worked them arduously back and forth until the supple trunks gave way. Then she removed her duster, ignoring the cold as best she could, and buttoned it, slipping the limbs within to stretch it wide. The inside cavity she stuffed with pine boughs to cushion the ride. The sorrel snorted and shied when approached with the unwieldy contraption but finally stood and allowed her to weave the branches through the girth straps. She regarded her handiwork with an optimistic smile. It wouldn't get him to Deadwood but it just might make it the distance to the Bar K. If the saplings held. If the coat's seams didn't give way. If the big horse would pull it at all. No use dwelling on 'ifs,' she decided. Time to see if it would hold Ethan's weight.

With a good deal of pulling and prodding, she was able to move him to the travois. There, she took off his coat and urged him onto to canvas sled. It bowed beneath his big frame but it held. She flung the blanket over him and tucked it tight, then used the duster's sleeves to tie him securely down. No Lakota squaw could have done better, she thought with a grim satisfaction.

With Ethan's coat swaddling her chilled form, Aurora climbed up atop the sorrel and began the long trek to the valley. In a way, she was thankful for the hardship. Preoccupied by the task of winding around gullies, boulders and downed trees to give Ethan the smoothest ride, she had no time to dwell upon her own misery. It kept her from worrying over their reception at the Bar K. She had to get them there first. Then she would deal with her promise to the big Texan. She had no intention of surrendering him into her father's noose! She kept going, holding to the steady pace. There was no need to stop. Ethan was unconscious. She could tell it when she looked anxiously behind her to the long, still form. There was nothing she could do for him on the trail. All hope lay ahead.

The Bar K. Aurora drew up the sorrel and looked down into the valley below. There it spread, smug and secure in the greening grasslands, providing a cold welcome. There was no feeling of coming home. No lightening within her heart. Her father's ranch held none of the answers she sought. In fact, therein lay most of her problems. Necessity directed her back to the valley, not any degree of familial fondness. In her mind, her father had torn the last of that from her when he'd sent his men on their skulking mission. And here she was, delivering what he'd wanted right to his door.

Setting her jaw into a determined line and pushing berating thoughts behind her, Aurora nudged the sorrel forward. She had no choice. She wasn't betraying Ethan. She was trying to save him. For what? His objecting words came back to torment. Was she bringing him to suffer her father's judgement? Would it have been kinder to let him die in the hills he loved, where at least he would have known some dignity in death? Selfishly, she rebelled against that idea. She wouldn't surrender up Ethan Prescott to the hereafter one second sooner than she had to. He was all she had left. She had made the supreme sacrifice for him, and, dammit, she wasn't about to lose him now!

Girded by that single-minded fury, Aurora guided the sorrel into her father's compound. There was an immediate furor as she was recognized—Garth Kincaid's daughter, riding in all ragged and weary drag-

332

ging a litter behind her. She noticed one of the men running for the house and redoubled her purpose, steering the horse right up to the front steps.

"Ride for the nearest doctor," she called down to one of the men. A murmur rose betwixt those who gathered around the travois. She heard Ethan's name muttered fiercely. When there was no immediate response to her request, she shouted, "Do it now and ride like the very devil was at your butt. Because if you don't come back with that doctor by nightfall, believe me, you'll think he was."

The cowboy broke from the group and ran toward the ramuda. Dismissing him from mind, Aurora slid down from the tall sorrel and pushed her way through the crowd of disgruntled ranch hands. She could feel their curiosity and contempt as she bent down beside the travois and she didn't care a whit what they thought. Her hand went to Ethan's flushed face. Hot. So hot. She bit her lip in frustration. But he'd made it alive.

"Two of you men carry him into the house," she instructed as she straightened. No one moved. Either they were waiting for the major to supply the order or they had no intention of aiding the man who murdered the beloved Cale Marks. To a man, their expressions were truculent. Rage trembled through Aurora, but she held to her temper with an effort. "I am cold, tired and at the end of my patience. If I have to drag him up those stairs by myself, I guarantee that I'll see everyone of you regrets it later."

"Orrie?"

She turned. The sound of his voice still held the power to make her heart constrict with fondness. Foolish heart. She regarded her father like a bull brac-

333

ing for battle. She made herself look past the concern that softened his gaze, beyond the worry lining his craggy face and the relief that shook the rumbling timbre of his tone. She would make herself see, instead, his motives, so fouled with self-interest and greed that he would allow her to suffer to further his ambitions. Anger glittered in her glare and he recoiled from it, surprised. After all he'd done, he could still look surprised. Then, her wariness was justified when he saw the still figure in the litter.

"Prescott."

The emotions that crossed his face were distilled from pure hatred. It was as if Ethan Prescott represented every ill in Garth Kincaid's life, as if the frustrated fury he felt in losing his wife, his sons and his foremen all channeled into that one throbbing rage, focusing on the helpless Texan. Then, that trembling anger became a frightening calm and the major's thunderclap voice took on the chill quiet of a winter freeze.

"Get a rope."

No one had to spell out his intention to Aurora and she reacted swiftly to keep bloodlust from flaring in the group of surly cowboys. "No. There'll be no hanging here. He's hurt. I brought him here for medical attention not a lynching. He didn't kill Cale and he has the right to prove that to a jury."

"The hell you say," someone muttered.

"Why go a-bothering the doc with a man whose dead already. We'd be doing him a favor to take care of it now," grumbled another.

Aurora didn't waste her efforts on the crowd of disgruntled men. It was her father she had to convince. They would abide by his rule whether they agreed or not. She directed her words to the scowling man on the porch.

"I gave him my promise that he'd be treated fairly. The word of a Kincaid used to stand for something. It used to be stronger than any handshake, more unbreakable than the written bond." She remembered the major instructing her brothers on the finer points of honor. From the flush in his face, he was recollecting, too. She added firmly, "Ethan didn't kill Seth or Jed in the War. And he didn't kill Cale Marks. But he did save my life and that of my child." Her voice faltered then and it took her a moment to get it under control. "I gave him my word and I will not let you make me out to be a liar. I won't have him believing treachery runs in this family. It already cost me my baby. I won't let it strip me of my pride."

Kincaid stood immobile. For the first time, he noted the absence of the child. He saw how tenuous his daughter's hold was on her strength. She stood guard over the man on the travois, not caring that he was their enemy, refusing the facts of Cale Marks's death in favor of whatever charm the Texan had managed to weave about her senses. Though her long hair whipped about her like a vibrant flame, he could see the cold ashes of despair within her golden eyes. He knew that pain well and he knew better than to argue against it. Whatever her reasons, she would support them stubbornly, unswervingly in the name of Kincaid pride. And it was the one stand he couldn't battle against.

"Take him inside," she snapped to the idle cowboys, taking advantage of her father's silence and hoping his men would see it as agreement. "Upstairs to my room. And make it an easy ride."

335

There was no movement until Garth Kincaid very gradually inclined his head. She wasn't sure what made her father acquiesce. It wasn't due the moral rightness of her cause. Of that, she was certain. More like the stab at his honor. Nonexistent honor, she'd discovered of late. Whatever it was, she was grateful but not in the least trusting. The rivers of hate ran too deep and strong to dam up with the merest twig of her objection. For Ethan's sake, she wouldn't question it for now.

Several brawny cowhands gathered up the unconscious form of Ethan Prescott and toted him into the ranch house. As Aurora began to follow, she was stayed by her father's strong hand upon her arm. Reluctantly, she let them continue on without her and looked askance at the major.

"Where are Abe and the others?"

"I buried them."

Kincaid received the news with a jerk of shock. "Prescott?"

Her features congealed with disgust. "The Sioux," she answered searingly. "After your little planned ambush, the Lakota set one of their own."

"And the baby?"

Aurora clenched her jaw to keep it from trembling. Her gaze narrowed to contain the aching dampness burning behind it. "I gave them my son so they would spare Ethan's life."

Kincaid digested this slowly and arrived at his own twisted conclusion. His expression was cold. "So you would surrender up the whelp to save a killer but not your own father. What is he to you, Orrie? What did he do to you to turn you against me?"

She wrenched out of his grasp and in doing so,

Ethan's bulky coat came loose. For a minute, the major stared at the thin chemise that was all she wore beneath it and she rebelled against the ugliness of his deduction.

"It isn't what you think." She jerked the coat closed and hugged it about her. "Ethan Prescott is the only man I know who hasn't tried to use me for his own purpose."

"Are you bedding him, girl?"

"As if that would make any difference in how the world already sees me. The Sioux whore. Isn't that the way you think of me, too?" His silence was her heart-breaking answer. Pridefully, though her soul was torn asunder, Aurora lifted her head and looked him square in the eye. "Excuse me. I've a promise to keep. I gave Ethan my word I'd keep him alive."

"You do that, Orrie," Kincaid said with a quiet malevolence. "Keep him alive long cnough to hang in Deadwood."

Ethan shifted restlessly on the high post bed as Aurora blotted his fever-flushed face with a damp cloth. He looked huge and massively masculine in the room her father had decorated with an adolescent girl in mind. His sweat-crisped hair curled against the lacy tatting that edged her pillows in a potent suggestion of the thick mat upon his chest. His broad shoulders and muscular thighs were like oak-hewn beams in comparison to the delicate spooling of the canopy posts. To see such a strong, vital man struck so low by an injury was disturbing. The wound was hot and fever consumed him from within, draining him of his virile power. She continued to sponge his forehead while an anxious panic threatened. It seemed so little to do for him, but it was all she could think of. All she could do was to make him as comfortable as possible and keep him alive until the doctor arrived. It was a mindless, rote chore, and she fought to keep her thoughts from straying to other things—like how long she could keep him from the end of a rope. Like life without her precious child.

Resentment simmered for the man below, the man she pegged for all her troubles. True, he hadn't caused her to be abducted by the Sioux, but he hadn't made it easy for her to put that fact behind her. Garth Kincaid was not the man she thought she knew, and she didn't much care for what she was discovering with every passing day. He was a wealthy bully preying upon honest men like Ethan Prescott to further his own ambition. Unchecked, he would crowd all who opposed him from the rich grasslands he so greedily thought to hoard. And where would that leave her? If she remained, she was silently accepting what he'd become. And if she stood against him, what would become of her? How could she compare comfort and security to the righteousness of truth? It would be easy if not for the man she tended with such diligent passion. If she had never met Ethan Prescott, perhaps she wouldn't have cared how her father acquired his fortune. And that notion upset her no little bit.

Was she, as Ethan had so cruelly stated, her father's daughter?

"How is he?"

Aurora turned anguished eyes up to Ruth and the woman knew at once of her love for the Texan. And that knowledge gave her pause. Things automatically became twice as complicated between father and

338

daughter, as if not already difficult enough.

"I don't know. He warned me that fever was his greatest danger. I can't bring it down. I hope the doctor hurries."

The housekeeper had moved to the bed side and placed a comforting hand atop one slumped shoulder. "I will sit with him if you would like to sleep. You look all in, child."

She wasn't surprised by the stubborn shake of fiery tresses.

"Thank you, Ruth but I want to stay."

"The major has given his word. He'll come to no harm here."

Those gently spoken truths touched upon the crux of Aurora's misery. "And I believe him. For now. But I'd still rather stay."

The woman nodded wisely. "I'll bring up a tray then. Some dinner for you and some beef stock for him, should he awake. He will need his strength for what's to come." They both would, she thought sadly. How well she knew the perils of an inappropriate love.

"Thank you."

Ruth started to go then hesitated. She wasn't sure how to ask. Then, she just did, straight from the heart. "The little one, will he be all right?"

Aurora's shoulders jerked once with grief then sagged. Her voice was a whisper. "They will treat him like one of their own. He'll come to no harm." She swiveled abruptly to face the other woman. Her features held a terrible agony. "I had no choice, Ruth. It was the only thing I could do. They would have killed Ethan. And everyone here. There was nothing else I could have done." Her expression begged for agreement, for understanding, for relief from the crushing weight of guilt that tortured her so mercilessly with every passing minute her arms were empty. Ruth's answer was to embrace her, offering the shoulder she so needed and the wisdom sorrow denied her.

"No decision could be harder. But you made it and now you must learn to live with it." Her embrace tightened at the feel of an objecting sob. "You chose life over death, just as before. In my heart, as in yours, I feel it was the right thing, the brave thing. I know the pain of losing a child, but you must not think of it that way. He is not lost. He lives. He will grow and prosper. And in his soul, he will always hold the memory of your love for him. That is what you must remember. And you must be strong, stronger now than before. You are not alone, Aurora. There are those who love you, who share in your pain. Do not let grief cloud that truth."

That was the balm Aurora applied to her ravaged conscience over the next long hours until the doctor arrived. It was after midnight. She was limp with fatigue with only worry to sustain her. Ethan's condition had not changed.

When the doctor, a former Federal surgeon from Michigan, tried to dismiss her from the room, Aurora stood as firm as General Stonewall Jackson. While he didn't approve of vaporish females cluttering his work space, the doctor conceded to the unexpected steel in Miss Kincaid's refusal. If she swooned, he could step over her.

The wound was unwrapped and laid bare to the doctor's probings. Ethan moaned in his stupor and the doctor muttered to himself as he examined entrance and exit.

340

"How is he, doctor? Will he be all right? Can you bring the fever down?"

Pale eyes squinted up at her in annoyance. "Miss Kincaid, you will be the first to know. Now get out of my light."

Duly chastened, she obeyed.

"Who cauterized this wound?"

"I did." It was said small and anxiously.

The doctor peered at her with renewed interest. "Nice work, young lady."

Aurora gave a weak smile.

"Most likely saved his bacon."

"Then, he'll—"

"Be fine from the looks of it. The fever's the body's way of caring for its own. Doesn't look like infection has set in. Wound's clean, should repair itself with little more than rest."

Aurora nearly swooned then, from sheer relief. "Thank you, Doctor—?"

"Andrew Endicott. From the looks of it, you did all the hard work. Who pushed the arrow through?"

She paled with remembrance. "I did."

"Good thinking. If I'd had to go in after it, he might not have made it."

Her limbs knew a fierce trembling. "He's a doctor. He told me what to do."

"Then I suppose I can only charge you for a consultation." He applied some powder and ointment to the ugly wound openings and began to bind them. "If I leave the dressings, I don't wonder that you'll be able to change them."

Aurora nodded and watched Endicott wrap and tuck the linen windings until Ethan was done up as tidily as a birthday gift. A gift she would gratefully receive. She continued with the occasional nod as Endicott went on about feeding and care, but her gaze was absorbed by the contours of Ethan's face and by the strong mold of his neck and shoulders. He was going to live.

Long enough to hang.

Not if she could help it.

Endicott was putting his instruments back in his bag. "Is there anything else, Miss Kincaid? Any other questions?"

Aurora hesitated, feeling both awkward and heartsick. She studied Andrew Endicott's plain, honest features and wondered how he'd react. The same way the townspeople did? The way her father did? Could she bear up under his censure atop all else?

Sensing the silence was unnatural, Endicott prompted, "There is something?"

"Not concerning your patient. It's me."

"Yes?"

"I am—I was nursing a child." Embarrassment and anguish prevented her from elaborating. She felt her eyes fill until they ached nearly as much as her engorged breasts.

"I see."

She couldn't look up at him. She couldn't endure what she might see there, the conclusions drawn out upon his face—unwed mother, harlot. And the questions—about Scotty's parentage, about his fate. Had he heard of Garth Kincaid's captive daughter from the people in Deadwood? If so, where was the selfsame condemnation in his gaze? Then, Endicott surprised her with his calm, professional manner.

"Limit your fluids. Binding and alternate hot and cold compresses will help with the discomfort until nature catches on."

She risked a glance and found an endearing kindness in his eyes. Infant death was no oddity so far from civilization and he would naturally assume that was the cause of her distressful condition. He asked for no specifics and she had no want to supply them. There was no judgement attached when he told her, "Feel free to send for me should there be any problems — with either situation."

"Thank you, Doc."

"Take care, Miss Kincaid."

Minutes after his departure, Ruth arrived toting the first of many pails of steaming water.

"The doc told me you'd been needed some compresses. I figured a long soak would do the trick and you look as though you sure could use one."

"That I could, Ruth." She plucked at her filthy denims. They were stained with earth and Ethan Prescott's blood. Above them she wore a clean wool shirt but the skin beneath it crawled with the reminders of a sweat of fear and effort. She thought of the hot water and the cool of a soft silk robe. It was a delicious image. The bath would relax and revive her. And then she could continue her vigil.

Vapor rose from the metal tub as the pail was upended. "The major was talking of running water inside the house," Ruth said to make harmless conversation. "Imagine that. Sure will save a few steps."

"It'll be half the steps if I help you." And before the housekeeper could protest, Aurora was taking the bucket and starting for the stairs. In four tandem trips, the tub was filled and luxuriously scented with an oil Ruth distilled from crushed lavender. As the weary young woman began to ply the buttons of her shirt, the housekeeper angled a dressing screen to shield the bathing area from the bed and wished Aurora a quiet good evening.

As she closed the door, Ruth was confronted by a sullen Garth Kincaid. She made herself into an immobile barricade and raised a questioning brow.

"Does she plan to spend the night in there with him?" he growled in his displeasure. "Right under my roof."

"Worse things than your daughter tending a wounded man have happened beneath your roof."

Kincaid didn't care for the unsympathetic reply or for the closed door. He contemplated the challenge of both for a long minute but backed down before the relentless stare of his housekeeper. He would as soon face the whole Sioux nation as Ruth in what she considered a justified temper. And for some reason, the woman thought it her duty to take his wayward daughter under her wing. Females, he thought disgruntledly. There was no rhyme or reason to them. Give them the shelter of a good home and all the comforts they could want and still they'd bristle up and snap at the first hint of dissension. He had a good mind to toss the uppity house servant out on her rump, nicely shaped rump though it was. But where could he find anyone to replace what she did for his household, above and beyond her domestic tasks? Knowing he couldn't find anyone willing to put up with the isolation or the arrogance of the boss gave her the confidence to chew at him like a bothersome tick.

"Let her alone, Major. She's enough worries on her mind tonight without you adding to them."

344

"Treating a danged killer like he was some honored guest," he grumbled in a simmering fury. "She doesn't deserve the roof I give her."

"What she deserves is a little more support and a lot less suspicion. If you can't feel any sympathy for her grief at least let her work through it in peace. Your outlaw isn't going anywhere tonight and I don't think you could drag your daughter away from him with a team of mules."

A cold conclusion knotted his insides. "Are you saying she's in love with him?" Impossible! Not with a lowly murderer. A Southerner. An Indian-lover. And a damned nester, to boot. She couldn't have chosen anyone more offensive to him if she'd tried. He couldn't believe it. She wouldn't do such a thing to him. Not after all they'd been to one another. They were the last of the Kincaids. Was she doing it just to spite him? His jaw clenched. Prescott couldn't swing too soon to suit him.

"That's something you should ask her. In the morning."

Ruth gave him a push. Carrying buckets and toiling vigorously all her life lent her a strength that wasn't easily denied. With a mutter of something that sounded like, "danged females," he gave in and stomped to his room, to the preferable company of a whiskey bottle.

Feeling very much as if she'd survived the first minor volley of a lengthy battle to come, Ruth sighed. Her foolish heart may have belonged to the gruff Major Kincaid, but his daughter held all her sympathies. Had things been different, had her blood been pure and unquestionable, she might have been mother to the girl. She might have been sharing the name Kincaid with the man who boasted it so proudly. But she was what she was. She would never have more of Garth Kincaid than the darkness of night and the dictates of conscience could conceal. She knew it and she accepted it without complaint. Supporting Aurora's cause could jeopardize her own but there were some things worth standing up for. And love was one them. Right or wrong, the girl loved her father's enemy. It wasn't up to Ruth to judge, so she would aid the ill-fated romance in what ever way she could. No sense both females beneath Garth Kincaid's roof knowing love without fruition.

So, slowly and quietly, Ruth made her way down the hall and followed to where she knew she would not be turned away on this or any other night.

Chapter Twenty-one

Flowers. Like springtime.

The delicate scent teased his nostrils, inviting him to taste the fragrance with a deeper breath. The aromatic smell of it kindled not the name of a particular blossom, but of a woman. It stirred images of silken flame and soft, white flesh. Of lips, softer still. It coaxed back the memory of a figure nestled close against his side beneath a pallet of furs. Sighs of passion and satisfaction. Ora Kincaid.

But that was impossible.

She'd betrayed him.

Hadn't she?

Kincaid's men at his door. The pain in his back and chest. Aurora's tear-streaked face as she crouched down beside him. In the woods. But he wasn't there now. Besides the floral scent, there was the odor of civilization: beeswax, lamp oil, the down of a feather bed. Clean, prairie smells. He was no longer in the hills. Where then?

The Bar K.

Curiosity over how he could be at Kincaid's ranch and yet be breathing encouraged him to open his eyes. To confusion. Over his head was a white canopy, as airy as any Dakota cloud. No guarded bunkhouse or cold barn stall. He was in a woman's room. Ora's? It made no sense. He tried to move, expecting the limitation of ropes, but was checked, instead, by a sharp stab of discomfort. Not tied. He moved a cautious hand to feel the professional wrappings that bound his wound. He'd been tended by a doctor.

It had to be delirium. He anticipated the short jerk of the rope about his neck at any second. Instead, he heard a soft feminine sigh of weariness and the rustle of material. By turning his head slightly, he could see in the dimly lit room a vision of unequaled beauty, of Aurora Kincaid with her glorious hair unbound, swathed in a shimmer of ice-blue silk. Now he knew he was dreaming. Or already dead.

The vision paused. He heard the rush of quickly drawn breath and the rattle of it being hastily expelled.

"You're awake." Then softer, almost as whisper-light as a breeze, "Thank God."

She crossed to the bed and the smell of flowers grew stronger, more tantalizing. As did her loveliness. It was one vivid dream! He could actually feel his body stir in response. It must have been a dream because he couldn't imagine such carnal pleasures warming him in Heaven. Then, she sat on the edge of the bed and her fingertips touched to his bearded cheek . . . and he got the shock of his life.

It was no dream.

He was alive. In Ora Kincaid's room and she was sitting with him in a damned bewitching dressing gown, a fragile smile shaping her sweet lips.

"I'm—lost," he managed in magnificent understatement.

"I'm not surprised. Doctor Endicott gave you a

348

touch of laudanum to help you rest. He said you'd be fine. Just fine.

Did he imagine the glittery sheen in her eyes?

"Where am I?"

"The Bar K. I brought you here on a litter. You were burning with fever and I didn't know where else to take you."

"And your father let me inside with his blessing?"

"Not — exactly." She fussed about the pillows, plumping them, arranging them until the agitated movement made him groan softly. "You should be resting, not talking."

And she was being evasive. Determined not to let her slip around him that easily, Ethan gathered his strength and tried to flush the fuzziness from his thinking. The wooly lethargy wouldn't budge. It spun about his senses like sugar candy, soft, blanketing, dulling his mind, cushioning the abuses to his body. He should have welcomed the respite from what was to come but he didn't. He chafed at his situation and would have welcomed the misery if it brought him some control of his mental faculties. Some rationale for Aurora's actions. It was simply beyond his hazy grasp.

"Ora, what the hell's going on? I can't believe your father wouldn't let me bleed to death on his front steps before opening the door or actually making me comfortable."

"Let's say I convinced him to see you got a fair trial."

"Followed by a fair hanging." That bitter truth restored some of his sharpness, some of his antagonizing pain. He looked up at her sweet features and he saw Olivia bidding him good-bye with a mild, secret smile on her face. Plotting. Plotting even as she sent him off with promises. And that was one agony the laudanum couldn't dull. And instead of thanking Aurora for saving his life, he turned his frustrations upon her. "Is that how you got around your conscience, Ora? By making it all nice and legal-like? Will that take the stain of my blood off your hands? Knowing that Garth Kincaid's justice was done?"

Her features went as rigid as cold stone. In a voice just a crisply chiseled, she told him, "You rest and get your strength back."

"Why bother? So I can stand on the gallows on my own two feet? Your father draw the line at lynching a man from his sick bed?"

"Stop it, Ethan." There was a thread of anger in those anguished words. "Don't you dare speak to me like that after I—

"After you what? Went through all the trouble to get me here alive?" The bitterness of her remembered betrayal rose up to choke him. Distress made his head whirl and roar like a Texas tornado. He was thankful, then, for the dulling affects of the drug, for he didn't think he could stand the full brunt of her treachery. The best he could manage was a weak defiance. She'd hurt him far more than the Sioux's arrow. Her aim had been true, piercing his heart with savage intent.

Her gaze was pleading with him. To what? To assuage her conscience? The hell he would. He wanted to see she suffered right along with him. His words were deliberately cruel. "Why did you bother? Did you figure I'd be worth more to your father at the end of his rope rather than cold on the trail?

Aurora rallied despite her tattered emotions. She'd been trod upon too regularly to like the imprints of scorn upon her feelings. In desperate, angry defense, she reared back and struck.

"You cussed, stubborn man. Can't you trust me, not even one little bit? Can't you find a reason to have a scrap of faith in me? I wasn't the one who betrayed you. I wasn't the one who left you to drown in your guilt all these years. I'm not weak like Olivia. I don't grab for the easiest way out. I'm a fighter, Ethan Prescott and I deserve better from you. And right now, I'll be danged if I know why I bothered!"

She started up, seething and sobbing in frustration. His hand flew out to stay her. It slid off her shoulder and glanced across her chest. And Ethan went stunningly still. For he hadn't encountered the soft swell of ripe bosom. He'd struck granite, hard and bound. And he could think of only one reason for a nursing mother to be in such a state.

"Ora, where's Scotty?"

She made a small moaning sound like something injured and in need of being put out of its misery. For a second, she regarded him through eyes rich in molten pain then, she began to rise and turn away. This time his aim was better. Fingers fastened about her wrist holding her in place. He winced as she struggled then was still. He could feel the spasms of anguish along that single slender limb.

"Ora?"

"He's with the Sioux."

The truth was torn from her. She sat silent and trembling, her face averted.

With knowledge came an incredible dismay. Ethan gasped at the intensity of it, boiling up inside him. Maybe it was the drug dimming his reasonings, but something made no sense.

"They took him?"

Aurora shook her head. Brilliant, silken fire danced about her shoulders. Her tone was as dead as cold

351

ash. "I gave him up to them."

No. She wouldn't. It was crazy. After all she'd endured to protect her son, she wouldn't have just given him into their arms. He remembered her fierce love for the half-caste child, her determination to make a better world for him in defiance of his questionable heritage. He recalled her frantic tears as she begged him to save the boy. And he hadn't been able to. Despite his promise. What had happened in the hills to make her surrender up a part of herself without a fight? What could have overcome her maternal possessiveness to leave this broken shell before him?

"Why, Ora?"

She seemed to crumble at that question. Trembling became hard tremors. Still, she wouldn't turn to him. He was tortured by what he imagined in her face.

"Because they were going to kill you, Ethan. And I just couldn't let that happen. God forgive me. I couldn't let it happen." Her free hand rose to stifle the sobs shaking through her.

"Because of me," he echoed disbelievingly. *"Because of me?"*

He saw it all clearly then and it was like a mini-ball to the gut. She surrendered her son for him. Because she loved him. Loved him with a depth that would demand such a sacrifice. Horrendous shame swelled in him, for having goaded her, for having doubted her, and with it came a damning guilt. She had come to him for help and he had failed her. She had begged him, pleaded with him, and he hadn't taken the danger seriously. And she had given up everything she held dear and precious. For him. In spite of his stubborn suspicions, in spite of his foolish pride. Never had he felt so humbled by a single act of bravery. Never had he been so moved by the selfless power of emotion.

For him.

And deep within the scarred recesses of his soul blossomed a seed of indescribable joy. And pride. And possessiveness.

A firm tug of the wrist commanded attention. Wearily, Aurora obliged by facing him with her cheeks tearstained and her eyes swimming with muted grief. She looked numb, totally drained of hope.

"Ora, I'll bring him back to you."

For a moment, Ethan feared she might scoff at his bold claim. After all, here he was crippled up and virtually helpless and she had no reason to trust him. Yet, a faint warming began in the liquid gold of her gaze. Whether she actually believed he was capable of delivering upon the impossible or not, gratitude glittered in her eyes. And relief sighed out as she sank down into his awkward embrace.

"I'm sorry, Ora," he muttered into the soft mass of her hair.

"It's not important. Not now," she argued quietly. She curled against him, her head pillowing on his good shoulder, an arm sliding across furred middle and a silk clad leg riding over his to twine them tight and intimately together. And the rightness of it was felt immediately by both.

"As soon as I'm stronger, I'll go after him."

Would she believe this promise after the failure of the first? He waited, breath suspended, heart upended.

"We," she corrected softly. "We'll go after him. But first things first. Right now, we have to concentrate on getting your neck out of a noose." Mistakenly, she placed no significance on his silence. "Now, quit your yammering and let me get some sleep."

353

"Here?" He had visions of Garth Kincaid breaking down the door, hemp in hand.

"It's as good a place as any. And it is my bed. You were good enough to share yours. Let me return the favor."

And as she snuggled to fit the long hard line of his body, her lithe figure wiggling with maddening promise — one they knew couldn't be met this night — he answered a bit hoarsely, "No argument there."

Garth Kincaid looked up from his morning platter of flapjacks to scowl at his daughter. There was no meekness or apology in the way she returned his stare. It was a head-on challenge. Nor did her voice give one inch of quarter.

"Would you rather I ate in the kitchen?"

Kincaid's frown deepened and he growled, "Don't be ridiculous. Sit."

Aurora swept aside her long skirts, cumbersome female trappings she'd taken considerable dislike to, and assumed an opposite chair. In silence, she waited until Ruth supplied an extra table setting as well as a covert smile of encouragement. Then she helped herself from the center serving tray. For long minutes, father and daughter concentrated on tableware instead of table talk. The quiet thickened into a palpable tension, until Aurora was certain she couldn't force another bite past the lump of anxiety in her throat. She was about to speak when the major spoke up gruffly.

"Doc says he'll be fit to travel in a couple of days. Until then, I want him moved down into the storeroom next to the kitchen."

Aurora didn't need the significance spelled out. There was a lock on that door. Ethan Prescott was prisoner, not guest. She was about to protest then gave it a second thought. What was the use? Her father considered him a dangerous killer. How else would he think to treat him? With the courtesy of a future son-in-law? Should she push the issue, he might well lose his momentary willingness to let the law decide the Texan's fate. She had only his tenuous agreement to see Ethan safe to Deadwood. And that concession would end if her father felt Ethan was becoming a serious threat to his hearth and home. He was already wondering at their relationship. She needn't fan the fires.

Then, there was the possibility that if Ethan continued to bed down in her room, the speculation amongst the hands could well lead to violence. His very presence at the ranch created enough friction to kindle tempers to a full blaze. And the lock would keep others out as well as Ethan in.

"I'll see the room is made suitable if you'll supply the men to assist him down the stairs."

Kincaid nodded. His narrowed gaze assessed his daughter. She gave in too easily, and he questioned her motives. Surely, she hadn't suddenly decided to become an obedient child. He watched her in silence, admiring the beauty he and his wife had created between them. Too bad she had inherited his stubbornness instead of Julia's more appropriate demeanor. Once he'd considered that streak of vinegar a plus to life upon the frontier grasslands; a female needed pluck to sustain her so far from civilization. But his little Orrie had stiffened that bit of backbone into ramrod-straight independence that was not at all becoming in a member of the gentler sex. She'd tried to fill the shoes of her departed brothers in his eyes and in his heart, for so long that she finally believed they'd come to fit. He was proud of her determination but despairing of her belligerence. She needed a strong man with a firm hand to tame her. She'd run free for far too long. For her own sake, it was time for her soft willful mouth to accept the bit of restriction. It was his fatherly duty to see to it whether she approved or not. She needed a husband and babies so she would no longer dwell in the past. And the sooner, the better.

That settled, he turned his attention back to his plate, not seeing how his daughter puzzled over his small, conclusive smile.

A persistent prodding at his shoulder woke Ethan from satisfying slumber. He groaned in irritation and lifted a hand to push away the offender. It was then the dull poking became fierce undeniable pounding, not from an outside source as he'd first assumed but from a deep internal cavity of pain. It was the throbbing of his wound and the incautious movement made it roar to life.

His moan of complaint brought a cool palm to feel his forehead and cheeks. The scent of lavender embraced him sweetly, and he managed a smile as he forced his eyes to open. Bright sunlight spilled into the room, creating a glowing intensity about the slender figure bending over him. For a moment, his sight was too dazzled by it to focus on features or form. It seared through his head like a fireside poker, stabbing pain through his temples. He blinked hard and squinted against the glare until Aurora, understanding the problem, moved to close the drapes. Cool shade eased the torment in his head, and by the timed Aurora turned back to him, his vision had cleared.

And he stared.

This was not the tousled she-cat clad in the swimming folds of his shirt. Nor was it the denim-and-flannel-garbed hoyden riding clothespin with the agility of a boy. This was the Aurora Kincaid he feared to find: the one of undeniable poise and sophistication, the one of genteel manner and cool beauty, the one belonging to a life of pampered luxury and plenty. The one he could never claim.

She was stunningly lovely, a picture right out of the Paris fashion books Olivia used to pour over in envying reverie. Her attire was meant to be casual—within the circle of the cosetted elite but there was nothing plain or simple in the styling of her cloth jacket and skirt. The jacket was cut long to flare over the fullness of a bustle yet it hugged to a small waist and curving bosom and parted coyly to display the bounty of a ruffled blouse. The fabric was a finely woven beige shadow stripe enhanced by broad bands of dark blue embroidered trim and fringe—definitely not meant to endure any activity more vigorous than pouring tea. The elegant impression was furthered by a neatly arranged coif that tamed the wild flaming tendrils of hair into a docile low chignon. All that was lacking was a parasol and a passel of lounging beaux.

He was being unfair in his judgement, and he knew it, but Ethan was overwhelmed by the significance of what he saw. This was Aurora Kincaid as she was meant to be. Glamorous. Glossy. Gorgeous. Without a hair out of place. With soft white hands and perfect nails. With the scent of lavender wafting about her in a delicate cloud. Attending parties and plays. Singing and playing silly songs at the piano before a group of languid sophisticates. Ensconced in the arm of some dandy who could give her every little thing her heart desired on a whim. And nowhere in that fashionable portrait was there room for the likes of Ethan Prescott. He'd uprooted one frail flower from a zealously tended hothouse only to have it wither slowly in the harshness of the life he led. He'd not make the same mistake again.

He couldn't give her what she needed, what she deserved. And the truth of it hurt. Even if she pretended not to mind the primitive manner of his existence, he would, now that he'd seen what she was surrendering. A life of wealth. A future of prosperity. With no struggles, no sacrifices. Hadn't she already done enough of both to earn a pampered respite? How could he ask her to endure more hardships, more deprivation, then have her end up hating him and searching for an escape with another man — or through more desperate means? His conscience ached with the sound of a rope creaking.

No. This was the life Garth Kincaid intended for his only daughter, the life she'd planned to lead when the Lakotas snatched it away from her. How could he demand she surrender it again to settle for what he could supply? Even at their grandest, his plans were modest compared to what she already had at the Bar K. She would be stepping backward, down onto his level, and his pride would not allow her to make the move. Not if it meant she'd regret it. Not if it meant losing her respect. Her father would resist the match, and she would end up losing more than her life of luxury. She would be sacrificing her father's love, and he knew how close they had been — and could be again if not for his interference. How long would that cherished "we" last once he'd asked her to leave everything she cared about behind?

"The fever's gone," Aurora announced, smiling.

Then, her gladness knew a curious pause. It was the way Ethan looked at her, as though he was seeing a stranger. Through wary, tragic eyes. She'd thought they'd put that distancing chill behind them but there it was again, building a wall of uncertainty between them. A gulf of distance. And the harder she tried to tear it down, to span it, the more disheartening it was to see him retreat. Olivia. It was always Olivia. The shadow of her belled skirts swinging gracefully in midair. The scars of her betrayal etched in agony upon his soul. Would he never let her close to him? Would he never learn to open himself to the risk of love?

Was it more than the past? The threat of the noose that waved between them? Perhaps he refused to believe in a future until the troubles of the present were resolved. Perhaps he didn't want her to attach so much to a man whose prospects could end up dangling from a gallow's crossbar. Was he trying to protect her from the agony of losing him by keeping her at bay? Her heart swelled with the evidence of his affection, and her determination clenched tight.

"You're not going to hang, Ethan. I won't let it happen."

"And just what do you figure on doing? Sweet-talking your daddy into changing his mind? Sorry, I can't hold much stock in that."

His subtle sarcasm twisted the anxiety already squirming where she'd tried to repress it. She had no solid answer, so she snatched at the first solution to come to a frantic mind.

"You're stronger now. I could help you get away—"

"No."

"I could go with you. We could get Scotty and—"

"And what? Live on the run? Think, Ora. Do you

really believe your father would just let you go off with me? Do you think he'd ever—ever rest until I was at the end of a rope and you were back under his thumb? What kind of a life would that be? For either of us? For Scotty? It's no good. I told you that before and you wouldn't listen. Listen to me now, Ora. You're not going to be able to stop this. Your father is going to see me hang."

Her stubborn chin trembled and a wavering wetness shimmered in her eyes. He wasn't going to give up hope. She wouldn't let him. There had to be a way to make a man willing to fight. If her love wasn't a strong enough reason, there had to be something else . . .

"What about Scotty? What about your promise to help me get him back? Was that just talk?"

Ethan flushed hotly at her agile attack. His pride rumbled, his conscience quaked. "You were upset, Ora—"

"And so you thought you'd make me feel better by lying to me? Of all the lowdown, underhanded, sniveling tricks. You never meant any of that for a minute, did you?"

"I did. But I—"

"Don't make me any excuses, Ethan Prescott. They don't add up to a hill of soggy Texas beans and I refuse to swallow them."

He sat up. It was an arduous task but his anger with the situation made the pain easier to ignore. He grabbed her forearm and used it to pull her close. The fragrance of lavender intoxicated.

"I meant it, Ora. If there was any way on God's green earth that I can keep from kicking in the breeze, I'd ride into hell to get that boy for you."

Tears, furious and glittering with golden fire,

threatened to spill. "Don't say it. Do it! Do it, Ethan. There has to be a way."

"Only if I could prove I didn't kill Cale Marks. Or they could find who really did. And they ain't looking any farther than this here Texas boy."

Aurora's hand had come up to cover the one encasing her arm. Her fingers kneaded reflexively while her thoughts spun in desperate circles. "The Sioux. You were there in Yellow Bear's camp. If they were to come forward to testify—"

"And risk being hogtied and shipped off to the Cheyenne reservation? I don't think so. Even if they did, who'd believe them? A bunch of redskins sticking up for an Indian-loving nester?"

"I'll make them listen. I'll make them believe."

"How?"

That single word silenced her. How, indeed? He was looking at her through somber dark eyes, with a gaze not unsympathetic, but fatalistic and cynical.

How, indeed?

There was a brusque knock. Aurora had enough time to come up off the bed before the door swung open to several of the major's recalcitrant men.

"Your father said we was to carry him downstairs," grumbled one of them, obviously disgruntled by the order. He glared at Ethan, measuring his necksize for a noose.

Aurora nodded and stood away. When they stomped over in a clatter of roweled displeasure and reached down to jerk Ethan to his feet, she yelled, "Carefully! Like you were moving my mother's good china."

Handling their friend's killer with kid gloves didn't improve the atmosphere in the room. Nor did Ethan's surly claim that he could walk on his own two feet

361

without their charitable assistance. In the end, he hobbled between two of the sullen cowboys, his lips thinned in discomfort, theirs tight with disgust. But they got him down the stairs with a minimum of jostling and safely installed in the room Aurora and Ruth had fixed to house him. He sagged to the bunk they'd dragged in, sucking air and pressing his palm to his bandaged chest. When Aurora made to look at the wound, he drove her back with the growl that it was fine.

As the door closed between them, she met his gaze for just a moment then, the lock was shot home. And for the rest of the day, she was plagued by what his look conveyed.

How, indeed?

That question still troubled her when she stood out on the back porch, looking up into the fathomless evening sky. The night was surprisingly warm, so much so she hadn't brought out even a light wrap. The air was balmy for early spring and felt good whispering past her neck, teasing through the stray wisps of hair that had escaped the confines of her chignon. She would have liked to pull out all the pins and give her head a shake, but she no longer had that kind of freedom in her father's house. It was as much a prison to her as it was to the man lying on the other side of the wall with only a small window to separate them, a window too small for him to wriggle through. How utterly cautious of the major, she thought wryly. He had no intention of letting Ethan Prescott slip away — as if he had the strength. Physically, Ethan was much improved. His fever hadn't returned and when she'd changed the dressing she'd found no traces of infection. But what good was improving health when there was no prospect of a future?

Aurora sighed and looked up toward the stars as if to read an answer in their timeless pattern. *Maka kin ecela tehan yunke.* Only the earth lives forever. The Miniconjou believed that, but at the moment she was having a hard time accepting the fact that she couldn't give Ethan Prescott a little more of that precious time.

Then it came to her, not in the stars but rather slowly, stealthily through her unconscious mind. For a moment, she frowned, refusing to believe she'd found the answer. For it was an answer that frightened her to the very soul. To save Ethan, members of Yellow Bear's camp would have to be persuaded to come forth with the truth.

And someone would have to do the persuading.

Aurora clasped her arms about herself and shivered. When she'd fled the Lakota camp, she'd thought herself free of it forever. But now, she was faced with the need to return. Voluntarily. And alone. For who would go with her on such a dangerous and impossible task? She would ride amongst the people who had once stripped her of her identity and demanded her innocence, the people who had stolen her child from her arms. Her fingers made hurtful dents where they pressed into flesh but she didn't feel the pain. She was too consumed with terror.

If she was to escape from her father's fortress and find Yellow Bear's encampment, what guarantee did she have that they would ever let her leave. Or even live? They held her accountable for Far Winds's death. Confronted by her rival, would Uncheedah have her mother authorize her death? Or would Far Winds's first wife be satisfied by taunting her with her child? How could she ever leave their camp without

Scotty? And she knew they wouldn't let her take him.

Even if she survived Uncheedah's jealousy and overcame her unwillingness to be again parted from her son, what were her chances of actually talking one of the Miniconjou braves into risking his freedom by traveling to a *Washachu* village?

She had only one way of knowing.

She had to go there and find out.

Chapter Twenty-two

"There you are, Miz Orrie. The major said I'd find you out here."

Jack Lawson's voice slid down her spine like a handful of cold winter slush. Aurora couldn't repress a shiver as she turned to face him. He lounged in the light of the open door, posing so she could get a good long look at him in his fine new duds. Shiny stump-toed boots affixed with wicked-looking silver spurs were arrogantly angled from beneath fringed, yet-to-be-broken-in buckskin leggings. A huge silk kerchief was knotted over the seven-button bib front of his spanking new and stiff-as-buckram white shirt. His six-shooters jutted from either hip. Beneath the inevitable Stetson, his long hair was oiled and pushed back behind his ears. She wasn't sure if she wanted to laugh at his cocky posture or run for cover like a jackrabbit. He might have looked the posing dandy, but there was a flatness to his dark gaze marking him as a ruthless predator. And Aurora had no intention of letting him swoop down on her.

"Did he? How good of him," she drawled. Noting the direction of his stare, she folded her arms across the hard shelf of her bosom and glared until he lifted his gaze. No wonder her father looked so pleased with himself over their silent supper. He was planning to sic his foreman on her. He certainly wasted no time when it came to getting his own way. *Not this time, Major.*

Lawson grinned, unaffected by her vinegary tone. "Nice evenin'. Fine night for a long stroll." He glanced meaningfully into the heavy shadow draping the yard in intimate darkness.

"Feel free. Don't let me stop you."

"I kinda thought we might walk together."

"Did you? Sorry to disappoint you."

"That's all right. Guess we could just stand and jaw awhile."

He left the doorway and moved toward her in a purposeful swagger. The roll of his hips set his six-guns flapping. Aurora felt a sudden chill. Run, her instincts told her but she scoffed at them. It was just Jack Lawson, after all, the strutting barnyard banty with more bluff than bravado. She held her ground, having to angle up her chin when he came to rest a scant foot from her. She got an unpleasant whiff of some strong fruity cologne.

She took an unconcerned step backward and his grin widened. She was standing below the window to the storeroom. Ethan was on the other side. Knowing that comforted her. Even if he was locked in and helpless, she felt safe with him near. It gave her the starch to meet his leering stare with a cold arrogance. "I can't see that we have much to talk about, Mr. Lawson."

"No? And it's Jack, remember? Well, the way I see it, we gots plenty to say, Orrie. I've been a biding my time but a man can hold to only so much patience around a perty little heifer like you still a-running with no brand."

Heifer? Aurora bristled. "And is that what you're planning? To slap your brand on my butt?" Her eyes narrowed dangerously but he didn't take the warning.

366

"Yessiree, just as soon as the iron's ready. And that shouldn't take long. It's already hot and willing."

His meaning struck her. The blatancy of it made her flush, then pale with fury. His audacity cast her caution to the wind. "Are you thinking of inviting me to the barn for a quick have at it?"

"No, ma'am." His smile gleamed white in the darkness, a feral baring of teeth. Dark eyes did a slow sweep from the toes of her braced feet angled aggressively from beneath her gown, caressing up the shimmering folds of fabric to snug waist then on to the indignant heave of her heavy bosom. "Don't think I can wait that long."

Aurora bit back her sneering retort. He wasn't joking. She could feel it in the sudden scorch of his stare. Alarmed, she made a darting move to slip past him and into the safety of the house. He anticipated her. His agile sidestep had her colliding with his chest. Lean fingers bit into her upper arms, jerking her up closer even as she fought him.

"Take your filthy hands off me," she snarled, twisting like a saddle bronc. "My father will—"

"Whose idea you think this was?

Surprise momentarily sapped her struggles. She stared up into his flat black eyes, searching for a reason to call him liar. And to her devastation, could find none.

Lawson savored the defeat of her will and mercilessly, plunged the blade of truth more deeply into her heart. "All he said was don't go a-bruising her up and I don't plan to. Lestwise, not where it shows."

He was kissing her, his wet lips slithering over hers in an impatient foray. Shock had dulled her responses. It wasn't until his tongue stabbed thickly between them that her senses returned. She gagged at the thrusting intrusion, more sickened by the dreaded image of him

367

invading her body in the same way. It gave her the strength to resist.

"No," she cried and wrenched her head to the side.

Quickly, brutally, he whipped her around, snapping her by the arms so that the back of her head cracked against the side of the house. Lights exploded. She reeled and would have fallen if not for his painful grip. He drew close, so close that the fruity smell of his liberally doused cologne drove bile up into her throat.

"Don't go a-teasing me, girl. I won't have it, you hear."

"I'll scream." Her threat wavered pathetically. Agony beat through her skull. Along with it was the terrible knowledge that she could not escape him.

"Do that, Orrie." He was grinning meanly. "You yell your head off and see where it gets you. Not a man here wouldn't say, 'Thataboy, Jack. That's the way to show her.' A woman's got to be struck regular, like a gong, if she's to learn her place."

His cruelty and the casual acceptance of abuse against women made her want to wretch and weep. And with those weak falterings came a cold, cold truth. No, none of the men would come to her aid, not if her father approved. That Garth Kincaid would allow his daughter to suffer the hurt and humiliation of rape in an effort to control her, stunned her beyond belief. But it was true and she had to accept it. That and the fact that she had only herself to depend upon if she was to get free of Jack Lawson unscathed.

He had backed her up against the wood siding. Its rough cut abraded. His knee jammed between her thighs, forcing her to straddle his leg, pinning her in place while he leered down at her.

"Your daddy done gived you to me to do as I wanted. Believe you me, I've had me plenty of time to think on what that might be. You and me is going to marry, Orrie. And I'll have none of your smart talk. You're gonna learn, tonight, what I expect outta you. And if you mind your manners, we're gonna get along just fine."

"Pig!"

She lowered her head and butted him in the face. His blurt of pain and surprise was satisfying but he didn't loosen his hold. When she tried to wriggle away, he flung her fiercely back into the wall and held her there by roping the long strands of hair that had escaped her coif tightly about his wrist. One quick jerk brought tears and an involuntary moan. With his free hand, Lawson touched his split lip. Something dark and ugly unfurled in his expression. She tried to overcome her sudden terror by hurling insults at him.

"Animal! Do you think I'd allow your pawing? You disgust me. You always have. I'll never sit still for it. Do you hear me? I'll—"

He closed her mouth with the flat of his long, muscular hand.

On the other side of the wall, Ethan strained to hear what was happening. Helplessness seethed through him. The bastard was hitting her, hurting her, and he had no way of stopping it. The abrupt silence swept a cold fear up to freeze his mind. Then fury erupted in great scalding waves.

"Ora?" he shouted, desperately needing some assurance of her safety. His fist pounded on the wall.

Outside, Jack Lawson heard him and grinned with a monstrous pleasure. "Seems we're upsetting your loverboy with our little discussion. Best we keep it a bit more quiet." He looked down at his feet where Aurora had slumped, dazed and disoriented. A huge lump was forming along her jaw. He hadn't meant to mark her, but the major would understand. Kincaid knew how aggravating his daughter's waspish tongue could be. He'd have to be more careful. At least until they were

369

wed. Then, no man could complain if his wife sported a fat lip or a bruise or two. In fact, they would applaud him for laying down the law.

He bent down and the disheveled woman whimpered. It was a submissive sound, a gratifying sound and immediately the blackness of his mood lifted.

"I'm right sorry there, Orrie. My temper just got the better of me for a second. You best be learning not to rile me or things like this could happen again."

He hauled her up by the forearms and supported her as she wobbled on near boneless legs. When his hand stroked along her swollen face, her glazed eyes focused and grew bright with fear. That was good. Fear was good. It was right that she should fear him. He gloried in it.

"That's better. I ain't that little pup you used to sneer at. Things have changed, Orrie. I've made them change. For you. Because I've always wanted you. I've always known to have you I'd have to do some things that wouldn't set well. I've made myself into an important man so you'd be right proud to have me. And now, I'll be sleeping with you in this fine house and someday all your daddy's fortune will be mine. And I aim to keep what's mine. Ain't nobody gonna interfere in that. Nobody." His voice shook with hard passion. Then he smiled, a more frightening expression because of the vileness it concealed. "You'll be glad of this someday, Orrie. You'll see. I've taken care of everything that would stand in our way. It's gonna be just you and me. The kid's gone and I'll see to it that your Texan won't come between us. I can't have no loose ends. And I don't want you thinking on nobody else when I'm riding betwixt your legs."

It was a nightmare. Aurora moaned. Her head roared. Her insides knotted up into a hot coil of distress. There was no reaction from her battered body to

370

the frantic signals from her mind. She felt Lawson's hands upon her and was helpless to discourage them. Her jacket was pushed from her shoulders. She was nauseated and half hysterical from despair when his big hands plumped her breasts between them, pinching, plucking them into hard buds of unwilling arousal. They were unbound and she wished fervently that she worn the tight bandaging to deny him his free fondling.

"God," he groaned. "Even better than I'd imagined. I can't wait to see them. To taste them. Probably still sweet from the babe." His tone was gravelly with desire.

Aurora's stomach writhed. She shut her eyes to blot out the sight of his lust-glazed features. He was tearing at her blouse, trying to get at her flesh. There had to be something she could do, some way to stop this horror from happening.

Inside his prison, Ethan's imaginings went wild. From the small window, he could see nothing. And now he could hear nothing except the low murmur of the Bar K foreman's voice. If he hadn't been so weak and hurt, he would have picked up his cot and smashed it against the wall. It would have been a futile gesture. There was nothing he could do to alter what was happening outside the window.

What was happening?

"Ora!"

It was a wounded roar of rage.

She heard him. Somewhere in the drowning pool of her desperation, she heard Ethan's cry and she clung to the sound to pull herself up. Air was cool upon the bared globes of her bosom and quickly replaced by the hot brand of Jack Lawson's mouth. She thought of the twin six-shooters dangling with deadly promise at his sides but her hands were pinned behind her, cuffed in one of his. With complete revulsion, she realized he was suckling in a greedy fascination from first one full

371

breast then the other. He took her moan of disgust for one of desire and lifted away from his feast long enough to gloat.

"Told you you'd like it." He gave a raspy chuckle. "I don't care none that you've been passed between the knees of them savages or even if you've been pleasured by that Texan. Seems to me, I'm all the luckier for it. Got me no use for a timid female." He nuzzled back into the warm valley he'd discovered.

Aurora squeezed her eyes shut and prayed for the strength. He'd given her the answer. It was a familiar one, one she'd learned at the hands of the Sioux. Don't resist. Don't fight. She forced the tension from her body, breathing deep to flush the sickness from her throat.

"Jack," she called softly. She felt him straighten and made herself look up at him. It took every ounce of her will to mask her loathing. Her voice was breathy, as if in the throes of longing. "Not here, on the porch. Let's go inside where we can be warm and undisturbed."

She held her breath while he stared at her in suspicion. She could see him wondering over her sudden change of heart. With a gentle tug, she loosened her hands and raised them to his chest, rubbing over it with a coaxing impatience.

"I've never been with a man like you," she purred. "I want it to be—memorable."

That was all it took, that and the moistening of her lips with the pink tip of her tongue. He was much too vain not to believe he had swayed her with his prowess. His mouth came down on hers, hungry, hot, devouring. Aurora endured it for as long as she could, then twisted away, giving a husky laugh.

"Inside, Jack. I promise you'll never forget it."

He released her, his lust making him careless. Following behind, mesmerized by the bewitching twitch of her skirts, he stepped through the kitchen door. And was met by a cast iron skillet swung with desperate strength. It clanged against the side of his head, pitching him over like a poleaxed steer. As he sprawled full length onto the porch, Aurora kicked his feet clear and quickly shut and bolted the door. She leaned against it for a long moment, panting, feeling weak with fear and flushed with victory. Jack Lawson wouldn't be seeking any more favors from her on this night.

But he certainly wouldn't forget.

And she had no friends in this house. Except Ruth, who could only do so much. She was suspiciously absent from the kitchen. Her father's doing, no doubt, to give Lawson time to have his way. What would stop him when he came for her again? Her father wouldn't intercede. That was painfully clear. She began to shiver, feeling woefully alone.

"Ora?"

Expelling her breath in a sobbing sigh, Aurora went on shaky legs to the store room. Throwing the latch, she stepped into the cool dimness, expecting to find Ethan abed. She gasped when her shoulders were taken, her mind still filled with the ugly shadow of Jack Lawson. Her struggles were short-lived as she was turned into a familiar embrace. Never had the solidity of Ethan Prescott's chest been so inviting, so consoling all at once. She clung to him for a long moment, mindful of his wound and half-amazed that he was standing.

"Are you all right?" His words whispered warm and soft against her ear.

"I was going to ask you the same thing," she replied evasively. "You shouldn't be up, Ethan. You're—"

"Did he hurt you?"

He knew. She immediately quit pretending and closed her eyes as if darkness would erase the memory. She breathed deep, drawing in the scent

373

of him; the fresh linen of his bandages, the tart ointment dressing his wound, clean soap, and warm skin.

"No. Just a bit scared, is all." It was a lie but she didn't expect him to realize it. Until he led her into the light from the open door and gently turned her face toward it.

"Damn him."

She could feel the fury vibrating through his big frame even as he tenderly touched her misshapen jaw and bruised lip.

"I'll kill him."

Aurora caught his forearms in a panic. "No. You mustn't. My father's men are everywhere. They'd just shoot you down."

He thought grimly of Lawson manhandling her, of him striking her. His rage was black and without fear of consequence. That anyone would dare harm her—

"It would be worth it."

"No. Not to me, it wouldn't." She gentled his anger with a pleading look and the unsteady vow, "If anything happened to you, Ethan, I couldn't go on."

He searched her despairing gaze and ruefully relented. "What did you hit him with?"

Her smile was crooked. The side of her face throbbed. "One of Ruth's skillets."

"I hope you addled him permanently."

"Not much chance of that. He's more bone than brain. I should have aimed lower and spared myself the worry."

That she would have to worry over her situation brought back the glum helplessness of his own. His tone was intense. "There was nothing I could do, Ora. Having to stand by and let him maul you. God, it almost drove me crazy."

With his good arm, he pulled her back against him. She could feel the thunderous crash of his heart pounding into his ribs. Maybe it wasn't the best time to tell him, but the words tumbled out.

"Ethan, I'm going to Yellow Bear's camp to bring someone back to clear you."

"No." There wasn't the slightest hesitation. "I'd sooner hang than let you go there alone."

"The choice isn't yours to make." She angled out of his embrace to confront his scowling displeasure. "I can't stay here. My father gave me to Lawson." Her features twisted as if she couldn't bear to believe it, that the man she'd revered could first try to sell her son to save himself, then would callously barter her away to an animal like Lawson. Seeing her anguish, Ethan ran caressing fingertips across her cheek, brushing away the dampness he found there.

Garth Kincaid was an utter bastard.

"I can't stay here, Ethan. I thought with your name cleared, you and I and Scotty —" She broke off, uncertain of his willingness to hear her words. Had the mistrust been conquered enough to entertain such things? Would he believe she was only coming to him as an escape? She looked up at him, her heart in her eyes.

Slowly, stiffly, he bent, his mouth coming down to lightly cushion upon her. Despite the sore reminders of Lawson's abuse, Aurora's response was wild and urgent. She returned his kisses fiercely, as if she might never have another chance to know the shape and supple sensuality of his lips. As well she might not. Nothing was certain until the threat of the noose was gone.

"I have to go, Ethan."

"Not yet." His grasp tightened. His mouth traced a fiery path across her temple.

"To the Sioux," she explained and she felt the protest return to tense his body. She approached the idea in her own mind with fear and trembling. She couldn't let him know of it, of how desperately afraid she was of going

375

back amongst the Lakotas. And if she stayed, he would have the truth from her. As difficult as it was to leave the comfort and desirable strength of his arms, it was easier than pretending she was heroic.

She stepped back and he released her reluctantly.

"Don't you do anything crazy, Ora. You promise me."

She smiled and told him, "I love you, Ethan," as if that was the answer he sought. Then, quickly, before he could argue, she slipped through the door and shot the lock.

"Ora!"

She heard his palm slap against the wood. And she fled rather than betray her cowardice with tears.

It was a long, restless night. Aurora paced, knowing sleep would be denied her even if she went through the motions. Turmoil churned through her mind, gnawing sharply on the edges of her thoughts. Her torn clothing had been discarded as well as her fears over Jack Lawson. He wouldn't matter if what she planned succeeded. She trod the floor in buckskins and flannel, the garb she'd wear when she rode from the Bar K in the morning. Though her destination gave her no peace, it wasn't the source of her agitation. The Lakota weren't her most dangerous enemy.

Was she doing the right thing?

What choice did she have?

There was no guarantee that if she went to the Sioux and brought back a witness to speak in Ethan's behalf that he would be alive to benefit from it.

How could she be sure her father would let him live that long?

And how would she go on if she returned to find Ethan Prescott dead?

Her insides cramped in anxiety.

She had the Major's word. He promised Ethan would get a trial in Deadwood. But she had seen how he kept his vows and was not reassured. Had he been mouthing just what she'd wanted to hear? Would he drag the Texan to the nearest tree the moment she rode out of sight? If she did nothing, he would hang in Deadwood as a murderer. If she left to provide the truth of his innocence, she could be condemning him to die at her father's hand. There was no help from the law. The law was made up of Northerners who would have no sympathy for the Texan's cause. If he wasn't sprung from the jail and lynched by vigilantes, a man of Kincaid's power could railroad a mock trial to the desired end. Who would care? Frontier courts were a ramshackle affair. Circuit judges kept an erratic schedule. One could arrive in her absence and be persuaded to try Ethan in a rush with his pockets lined by Bar K profits. Who would know? There were no guarantees, only risks, and knowing that was eating her up alive.

Ethan.

She sighed and closed her eyes. She could almost feel the generous warmth of his mouth, the quiet strength of his hands as they shaped her body into passion's form. She saw the Lone Star Ranch as it could be; prosperous under his care, glowing with her touch, alive with the laughter of their children and Scotty growing up along side them. And she wanted all she saw in her mind's eye, wanted it with a desperation that would drive her to face her deepest fears.

Just as she would have to face her father.

Shock clouded her Garth Kincaid's features when he got his first look at Aurora's face across the length of the breakfast table. The lovely lines were misshapen

377

with a lumpy distortion on her jaw, her gently curved lips split by a dark bruise. He started to rise up, to comment on her ghastly appearance with all the outrage of a father when her cold statement drove all thoughts of it from his mind.

"I'm going to the Sioux camp. Don't try to stop me."

Kincaid blinked, dazed by the sudden announcement. Then he recovered to sneer, "After your brat? They won't give him back to you."

Aurora drew a tremulous breath and fought to retain her straight carriage as she stood in the doorway. Her father pulled no punches. He aimed right for the midsection. She, too, blinked quickly to battle the tears his callous truth forced upon her. Scotty wasn't the issue.

"No. I know that," she told him evenly. "I'm going to bring back one of the braves to prove Ethan didn't kill Cale. He was in the Sioux village that day, curing their sick. He couldn't have been in two places at once."

Kincaid dabbed at his mouth with a napkin then released a hearty laugh. "Who the hell is going to believe a whiskey-soaked Indian? They'd lie about anything for a keg of firewater."

His words stung. They echoed the sentiment she would face but she couldn't waver now. "I'll take that chance. It's the only one Ethan has. I won't let him hang for something he didn't do."

Kincaid's eyes narrowed. She was serious. He could tell by the mulish set of her mouth and by the braced defiance in her stance. She was going to do this crazy thing and possibly get herself killed. Or not come back at all. An abrupt panic settled around his heart. He might well lose her. Again. And he was angry at this damned troublesome Texan who would fill their home with strife.

"Why, Orrie? Tell me why? Who is this man that you would take his side against me? Why would you even

378

think of going back with those savages who stole your decency? You're risking more than his unworthy neck. You'll be throwing away everything you could have here."

"Like Jack Lawson?" She spat out the name as if it fouled her mouth.

"Lawson's a good man. A loyal man."

"And you'll be glad to know he was all too willing to carry out your orders." She couldn't keep the tremor of hurt and disgust from her voice. "It's no fault of his that he failed to rape me."

"Rape you?" He stared at her, seeing for the first time the dark discolorations as his foreman's handiwork. His features mottled with rage. "That son of a bitch! I told him to court you not ravage you."

"Some men think they're the same thing."

Kincaid studied the marks on her face and his temper burned. It was a genuine fury. No one was that good of an actor. "When he gets back from Deadwood, I'll have him horsewhipped. If he ever so much as looks at you again, he'll think the whole Sioux nation was lighting into him."

Aurora knew a instant of relief. Lawson was gone, at least for the moment, and her father had no hand in his rough treatment of her.

Seeing her expression, Kincaid's gut clenched tight. His words were unsteady with disbelief. "You thought I sent him to—to manhandle you? Orrie, how could you? How could you think I would allow anyone to harm you? You're my daughter. I am no monster. I only want you happy. I want you to have the chance of a good future with a hardworking, decent man, not one who'd convince you with his fists."

"Then let me go to the Sioux."

"For Prescott? Why? Why, Orrie?"

There was a moment's pause then she spoke out

clearly.

"Because I love him."

The silence brewed and built into a glorious tempest.

"Love him? Love him!" The major roared until the rafters trembled. But his daughter stood firm.

"Yes, I do. And I won't let him die just because you want his land."

"His land? His land has nothing to do with it. He killed Cale Marks. He shot him down in cold blood. And, by God, he'll hang for it. Yes, I wanted his land. I won't deny it. I pressured him to sell to me and I'll admit, I looked away from some things I shouldn't. But I didn't salt his water or poison his stock."

"Then who did?"

He recoiled beneath her scathing gaze. "You really do think I'm a monster," he said softly, and the truth of it that he saw in her hard golden glare broke his heart. His breath expelled on a lengthy, defeated sigh. "I did it for you, Orrie. Oh, I'll admit to the greed and the ambition but I wanted a place for you to live, proudly as a Kincaid, in the kind of place I wanted to give your mother and my sons. It was too late for them. Don't tell me it's too late for you, too."

The misery in his tone moved her. She couldn't help it. His features mirrored the emptiness of his existence, the loneliness he couldn't fill with his money or his might. In that moment, she saw him again as her father, as the man who spoke so passionately of his Dakota dreams and of the life they would share together. She wanted to go to him, to put her arms around the slumped shoulders, to tell him what he needed to hear. But she couldn't.

"I'm sorry."

"You're sorry," he echoed bitter. "That makes everything better. What happened to our dreams, Orrie?

380

When did you decide they weren't good enough for you? Living with those red animals? Or was it while you spread for that Texas killer?"

She winced at his brutal attack and her sympathy crumbled. Her vision cleared of its cloaking nostalgia, and she saw before her a twisted, embittered tyrant who petulantly refused to let anything foil him. She saw a tortured soul who could only deal with his pain by blaming it on others. And she would not be manipulated at his will.

"It was when you tried to tear my son out of my arms because you didn't think he was good enough to be a Kincaid. Who gave you the right to decide that?"

He wasn't listening. He'd already found his answer, one that he could live with, one that he could light into with a simple fury. One that absolved him of wrongdoing.

"It's Prescott," he declared fiercely. He glared at his daughter, daring her to deny it. Instead, she angled up her proud head, her defiant gaze clashing against his own. Bitterness welled inside him like a poison. Hate, long stoked and ever-tended, shaped his words. "He's turned you against me with his lies. An Indian-lover. A Reb. He may as well have killed your mother and your brothers. He's guilty of it by being what he is."

"He's not guilty of anything," Aurora shouted back. She felt ripped apart inside, her loyalty and love shredding her very soul. But it was Ethan who commanded her devotion, the tall Texan she would defend to her very last breath. "Ethan did not kill my mother. He didn't kill Seth or Jed. The war has been over for ten years. Why won't you let it rest? When will you stop fighting your own little war of hatred and grief? They wouldn't have wanted to be remembered that way. No one had to turn me against you. You did that by refusing to accept anything you didn't want to see. You did

381

that when you saw a Sioux whore, an embarrassment to your good name, instead of a daughter who needed you."

Fiercely, she wiped her streaming eyes on her sleeve and stood proud to declare, "I love Ethan Prescott and I don't care that that sticks in your craw. I love him and I'm going to spend the rest of my life with him. Now if you'll excuse me, I have some riding to do." She spun away.

"It's too late, Orrie. It won't make a difference now."

The quiet words brought her about. Something in them instilled a dreadful terror in her heart. She could barely whisper. "What have you done?"

"Prescott's on his way to Deadwood."

Chapter Twenty-three

"You promised."

The accusation tore raw from her throat.

"And I kept it," the major argued. "I told you I would keep hid alive to go to trial in Deadwood. It's for the best, Orrie."

"Your best," she shrilled at him. Aurora felt faint. Ethan was gone. And so was her plan to save him from a brutal execution. There was no name for the helpless pain twisting through her. "It would have been kinder for you to lynch him here. Or didn't you want to dirty your own hands with it?" She was suddenly crying and she didn't care. Ethan was gone. "How could you? He won't have a chance to prove his innocence. Is that what you call justice?"

Kincaid watched his daughter's strength dissolve on that ravaging flood of tears. It devastated him. Regardless of pride, regardless of cause, he crossed the room in long strides and pulled her to his chest. For a moment, she fought him, making muffled, angry noises into his shirt front. His arms banded her like steel, refusing to give. Finally, she succumbed to his superior might and leaned limp and shaken with weeping upon his breast. As she'd done when she was a child and he was the only person in the world who could make things better or right. And he always had. Never had he failed her.

Until now. When she needed him most.

"Orrie." His voice was a gentle rumble. "He doesn't deserve the chance. He doesn't deserve your love or your tears. He killed Cale. He is guilty. Whether you want to believe that or not, Prescott killed Cale and he is going to be rightly punished for it. I'm sorry if that hurts you. God knows you've suffered enough for a lifetime. If it was in my power, I'd give you anything to take away that hurt. But I won't turn my back on murder. I can't. Not even for you."

Stubbornly, she shook her head and then felt his large hand move upon it in a soothing rhythm, trying to still the objection. "No," she insisted doggedly. "No, he didn't. If only I had the time to prove it."

"You'd be wasting your effort, Orrie, and possibly your life. You, yourself said Prescott couldn't be in two places at once. He was at his ranch when Cale went to offer him more money. He shot Cale, who wasn't even wearing a gun. And then he lit out for the hills to hide from what he'd done. Somehow, he's tricked you into thinking he had no part in it."

"No. You're the one who's wrong."

"Orrie, I'm not just guessing. Listen to me." He pried her away and stared down, not unkindly, into her determined features. He had to shake her from her false belief but there was no gentle way to do it. "Orrie, Cale didn't go to Prescott's ranch alone. The whole thing was witnessed. Prescott was seen doing the shooting. There's no mistake."

Aurora drew a tortured breath. It strangled in her throat. For an instant, her mind went mercifully

384

blank, then flooded with horrendous doubt. Had he lied? Had Ethan held her in his arms and proclaimed an innocence that wasn't his? She could find it easier in her heart to forgive the actual act of violence than a premeditated lie spoken to allay his guilt and charm her trust. To save herself from falling headlong into a depthless well of heartbreak, she recalled the intense honesty of his dark gaze. How could it be pretended? She summoned his words, said with such convicting sincerity.

I didn't do it. I didn't shoot him.

"I don't believe you," she told her father softly in words threaded with iron. "Who said they saw him?"

"It was Lawson. He went with Cale that morning. By the time he knew what was happening, Prescott had killed Cale."

Somehow, that was wrong. She pictured the gun-handy Lawson. Ethan was no gun slick. She couldn't imagine him getting the drop on the eager cowboy. She saw those gleaming six-guns jutting arrogantly from both hips. Why hadn't Lawson gone for them. Aloud, she voiced her confusion. "And he did nothing to stop it?"

"He was wounded, too. Now do you believe me? What reason would Lawson have to lie about it?"

What reason? Something was wrong with the whole thing, terribly wrong. A piece was missing, a vital piece to prove Ethan innocent. But what?

"Jack Lawson saw Ethan kill Cale?" she repeated, trying to make sense of it. She took a step back, away from her father, her thoughts stretching, grasping for the truth. She worked through what must have happened in her mind. Cale and Jack riding up to the deserted Lone Star Ranch. Cale dismounting, walking unarmed up to the door. Finding no one there, he would have turned and . . . Then, it struck her all at once with a bolt of stunning clarity.

"My God," she murmured. "Jack killed Cale."

Kincaid stared at her as if she'd suddenly gone completely loco. "And I suppose he shot himself to cover it up."

Aurora's eyes flashed up, bright and knowing. "Yes. That's exactly what he did."

"Nonsense," her father roared. "This is craziness, Orrie. You've let your feelings for this man totally addle your thinking. Why in God's good name would Lawson want to kill Cale? They were friends. Lawson looked up to him. Cale taught him everything there was to know about running a ranch."

"Exactly."

Kincaid started to whirl away, disbelief and disgust etched upon his face. Aurora made a desperate grab for his arm and his attention.

"Please. Hear me out. You said you didn't order Ethan's wells ruined and his cattle killed. Cale never would have ordered such a thing. I say Lawson took it upon himself to do it, to earn your favor. I think he was trying to prove to you that he could get the job done through whatever means possible."

"But that's not what I wanted."

"Isn't it? You wanted Ethan gone. Jack wanted Cale's job."

"Enough to kill him?" The major shook his head. "No. There were too many other places he could have gone to become a foreman. He had the experience."

"But he wanted to be foreman of the Bar K. Don't you see?"

She did. It was incredibly, awfully clear. Why hadn't she guessed it before, last night when he had spoken of his ambition, of the unpleasant price he'd

386

had to pay to see it fulfilled. She envisioned the flat, black eyes. Soulless eyes. Killing Cale Marks, his friend and mentor had been that price.

"No, I don't see. Why the Bar K?"

"Because he wanted everything that went with it. He wanted me. He's always wanted me. And he thought by being your right-hand man, he'd get my attention and eventually he'd have everything."

Kincaid looked thoughtfully away. He spoke to himself in a soft, reflective voice. A tone colored with the fresh hues of suspicion. "And I almost gave it to him. He rode in bleeding from a wound in his arm. A graze. He said Prescott gunned down Cale and shot him before he had a chance to draw. Prescott was gone when we got there. Cale was dead. Why wouldn't we believe Lawson? There was no reason not to."

"Did anyone think to check for powder burns on Lawson's sleeve?"

She could see the answer in her father's face. No, of course they hadn't. No one would doubt for a moment that everything Lawson said was true. It was to their advantage to believe it. She could see the doubt working now, now that it was too late. Or was it?

"Jack killed Cale, not Ethan. Ethan was at the Sioux camp. If you can't believe that completely, at least give me a chance to prove it to you. At least admit there's a chance you might be wrong. A man's life is at stake. The life of the man I love. If you care anything about me at all, don't let it happen without knowing for sure. Please."

Kincaid gave her a long, somber look before speaking. "Orrie, Lawson took Prescott into Deadwood."

Her hopes went plummeting. Icy terror took their place in her heart. "He's going to kill Ethan," she said in a cold, quiet panic. "Ethan is the only one standing in his way. He'll never get to Deadwood alive."

"This is far enough."

The men riding with Jack Lawson gave him a puzzled look but obeyed him. They reined in their mounts and waited for some explanation. They were still a good hour from Deadwood. The thought of whiskey and women, both equally cheap and inviting, made them restless with the delay. The sooner they delivered Prescott, the sooner they could get to some serious socializing.

Coffin Varnish and bored harlots were not what moved Jack Lawson's mind. Nor did arriving in Deadwood enter into his plans. Here's where he would tie everything up into a nice, neat bloody bow. Then, he would return to the Bar K and commence courting Aurora again. He'd made a mistake in pushing her too fast, and how his head still ached with that lesson learned. But then, with Prescott out of the way, he would have all the time needed for some genteel spooning. It wouldn't be long before she was itching for the feel of a man and he'd be right there, ready to scratch. He'd been wrong to think the trip East had dulled her fire. She was a spark just a-waiting to take flame. The thought of her burning hotly about him was enough to make him excuse the episode with the frying pan. For now. For now, he would play the gentleman, all repentant and humbled. He would woo her proper and pressure her old man to hurry her to the altar. And when they were wed, when he had the ring on her finger and the freedom to do as he would, then, he would make her answer for the bash with a skillet. And he would take care that no bruises showed.

Lawson was smiling slyly when he looked to Ethan Prescott. The Texan should have been spent by the rigors of the ride, considering his wound and all. But he sat his big sorrel as tall as a Ponderosa pine. Soon to be cut down to size. That, Lawson would enjoy. The man had positively stabbed him with his glances all morning long. The Texan was thinking of Orrie and him, together. Let him think. Let him think himself into a real lather. There was nothing he could do about it. Jack Lawson was going to take his place on the pretty Aurora Kincaid, and his gloating smile rubbed it in thick.

He'd never liked the stubborn nester who'd clung to his little scrap of ground with the tenacity of a wood tick. He'd always been in the way. Nothing swayed him, and Lawson had grown impatient and frustrated with the big man's courage until providence provided the answer. Not one to miss the chance for an advantage, he'd had to overlook his own feelings for Cale Marks long enough to pull the trigger. It hadn't been that bad. He'd purged his guilt by sending a bullet scorching through his own flesh. No little twinge of conscience was going to keep him from what he wanted. And he'd known what that was the first time he saw Aurora Kincaid twitch her sweet little fanny. And he'd bury who ever got in his way. Even the old man.

Still grinning, he looked from the bound Texan to the three men riding with him. They weren't the men he would have chosen for the job, but they'd follow orders. Or they'd be out of work. Or out of tomorrows.

"Why don't you boys ride on into Deadwood and start your drinking. I'll take care of things here."

Their bewildered looks flashed between him and Prescott. Only the Texan immediately grasped what the Bar K foreman had in mind. And there wasn't a damned thing he could do about it. "But what about Prescott? We was supposed to turn him over to the law."

Lawson glared at the contentious cowboy and spelled out coldly, "Getting Prescott to Deadwood was never the Major's intention. There's a big bonus in it for you all if you just while the night away in town and keep your traps shut."

"And I'll be shot in the back while trying to escape."

Lawson beamed at the hard-eyed Southerner. "You catch on right quick. You should have been that smart when we asked you real nice to move on. You're the one who brought it to this."

"It's murder."

The three cowhands exchanged nervous glances at that word. To their thinking, it was. None of them much liked Jack Lawson. He was a proddy, quick-tempered son without the reverence for life that had made Marks so well-appreciated. Kincaid had given them a poor second, to their way of thinking. But wasn't that Prescott's fault? Hadn't he killed their favored foreman? Was he deserving any milk of human kindness from any of them? Still . . . murdering a man tied to his saddle.

"I don't like it, Jack," one spoke out and the others muttered in agreement.

"You don't like it," Lawson mimicked in a woman-ish tone then he snarled, "You ain't paid to like it. I'll do the honors for the major. You all just hightail it outta here like a bunch of prissy schoolgirls. Cale Marks was my friend. I thought he meant something to you, too. Guess I was wrong."

They fidgeted, looking shamefaced but still reluctant to leave their helpless prisoner's back exposed to Lawson's guns. It wasn't honorable, what he was planning. Prescott would hang in Deadwood and they'd all be there to cheer it proper. That was the right way to avenge Cale; the way he would have wanted it.

"Kincaid gave his word that I'd be tried in Deadwood," Ethan drawled softly. "Or don't a Northerner's word mean the same as where I come from?"

While the cowboys bristled and grumbled over that, Ethan met Jack Lawson's stare. He was quick to note the goose egg swelling at the other's temple and admired Aurora's aim. Thinking of the greasy foreman's hands upon Aurora had his blood boiling hot. Had he a pistol, he'd have made sure to aim more lethally. Ethan had no illusions. He'd known what was going on the moment he was railroaded from the storeroom at the break of dawn. He knew he wasn't riding toward a trial in Deadwood. He was heading for a brutal end the minute they were out of earshot of the Bar K. So Aurora would never know her father hadn't kept his word. Well, he wasn't obliged to go like a docile sheep to the slaughter.

"Or doesn't the Major think he can buy a false conviction with all his money? Me being innocent shouldn't bother y'all. After all, you weren't hired on at the Bar K for the quality of your consciences."

Lawson sensed the turmoil Prescott was brewing. And he knew his plan wasn't going to pan out the way he'd figured it. Still, he wasn't about to deliver the Texan alive. That meant he'd need a reason to draw his guns.

"Maybe the Major didn't cotton to having any more

bastards bred on his daughter."

With a roar of fury, Ethan drove his knee into his sorrel's ribs, causing the horse to wheel about, slamming into Lawson's mount. The smaller horse staggered. Too busy scrabbling for a seat to grab for his guns, Lawson floundered and cursed, then yelled at the others, "Shoot him! He's trying to escape."

While escape wasn't what Ethan had planned, it looked like his only recourse if he was to have the meagerest chance to survive Kincaid's treachery. As the cowboy's reached around for the rifles wrapped in their bedrolls, he kicked the sorrel into a plunging gallop, using his knees to direct it up the bank at the trail's edge toward the cover of a spread of trees. It was a long dash for safety. He bent low, expecting to feel the tear of bullets into his back at any moment. He heard the explosion of gunpowder charges and tensed but no pain followed.

"Ethan!"

He was so surprised, he straightened and twisted in the saddle. The sorrel responded by slowly and circling around. Aurora. The flaming hair was unmistakable — as was the joy lighting her lovely features as she rode toward him.

"Ora, go back," he shouted. His heart seized up in his chest as she rode right into the path between he and his assailants. In a paralyzing terror he sat on his horse, waiting for her to be struck by a bullet intended to bring him down. But no shots were fired from Lawson or his men and as she drew closer, he saw why.

Garth Kincaid had a pistol on his foreman and the look on his face was one that demanded a reckoning.

In her haste to reach him, Aurora had to haul up on the reins to keep from ramming Ethan's horse head-on. She was panting as if she'd run the distance from the Bar K herself.

"Oh, God, I was so afraid we'd be too late," she cried as she wrenched her horse up alongside his. Recklessly, she stood in the stirrups and leaned precariously to cast her arms about his neck. Her mouth tore at his, wildly, with a frantic, relief-driven desire. She kissed him until she realized that he hadn't — no, couldn't respond fully. Not with his hands lashed down. She surrendered her need to hold him long enough to sever those bonds with the knife she carried, the same knife with which she'd once thought to slay him.

Rubbing his wrists, Ethan looked from Garth Kincaid to the promise of the hills. He could make it. Reins quickly gathered in his hands, but one glance at Aurora held him. Her eyes were great gilded pools of emotion.

"Ethan, don't run."

"Well, I sure as hell ain't going back to the party he planned."

Aurora reached out, not for his reins but for his hand. "Please. He's come to find out the truth."

"His truth?" Ethan laughed harshly and she couldn't blame him for his cynicism.

"No. The real truth. The truth that you're innocent and that Jack Lawson killed Cale."

That got his attention. But it wasn't enough to make him trust his fate to Garth Kincaid. "You think I ought to just waltz on down there after he tried to have me shot down on the road?"

"That was Lawson. Please, Ethan. Listen to what my father has to say."

"I've heard his words and all they are is words." He looked back toward the beckoning pines. Aurora

393

could see him wavering.

"Then take mine. Ethan," she concluded softly with what would seal or sever their relationship, "trust me."

He wrested his stare from the high tree line and looked long into her beseeching gaze. He was guarded, she completely candid. He drew a deep breath, tasting freedom in that long draught. But what was freedom without the will to soar free? Without Aurora, he would be a prisoner of his own misery, suffering a loneliness worse than death. Trust her. Dang the woman. Couldn't she ever demand anything simple?

"I do," he said at last. "With my life." He canted a look toward her father and added, with a wry smile, "But I hope I don't have to put that to the test."

Returning his smile, she reined her horse around and started back to the trail where her father waited. After a moment's hesitation, Ethan followed. The two men regarded each other with a hostile silence, Aurora positioned between them.

"I don't like being wrong," Kincaid said gruffly. "It means apologizing and I'm not much good at it."

"I don't want your apology," Ethan flung back tightly.

The Major ground his teeth then cast a surreptitious look at his daughter. He snorted in displeasure when her steady gaze called him. "Guess I had that coming. Looks like this hombre here's been playing us against each other. I never ordered him to drive you out with the means he used."

"Whatcha talking about, Major?" Lawson spoke up in his defense. He felt the tide of opinion turning from him and the pattern of hemp fitting close to his throat. "I did what you wanted. You might not have

394

said it in words, but it was what you wanted done."

"You're wrong, boy," Kincaid sliced in curtly. "You read into it just what you wanted. Legal means, Lawson, that's what I told you. Cale knew that."

"Cale was a fool. If it weren't for me, you'd have never gotten the land. I arranged it for you, Major, just like you asked." His voice held an angry desperation.

"Did I ever ask you to kill my foreman? Did I ever tell you to attack my daughter?"

Lawson was sullen and wisely silent.

Kincaid turned his attention back to the wary Texan. "Looks like in my greediness for your property, I've wronged you, Prescott. But that's for a court to decide. Orrie, here, has taken to some crazy notion about riding into the Sioux camp to bring back a witness who'll say you were there when Cale was killed. If she can, I'll make sure it's believed. Only thing is, I don't want my daughter going up there alone."

"I have to," Aurora stuck in stubbornly. Her father waved her silent, his eyes never leaving the Texan's dark, steady gaze.

"You know them savages, Prescott. You been living up amongst them for years. You think you could take her in and get her out safe?"

Ethan took a minute to mull it over, ignoring Aurora's wide, imploring stare. Then he drawled easily, "Reckon I could, seeing as how I got some business with Yellow Bear."

Aurora felt a rush of emotion swirl through her. Scotty.

Kincaid sized up the tall Texan with a disfavoring glare. "I still don't like you, Prescott, and I sure as heck don't trust you, but Orrie does and I trust her. We'll be taking this here varmint into Deadwood. You take good care of my girl, you hear."

"I don't need you to tell me that, Kincaid."

They parted ways like two surly silver-tipped grizzlies dividing territory after a bloody fight, backing away, unwilling to give ground gracefully. Finally, Ethan turned his sorrel toward the hills and gave it his heels. And, with a mix of joy and anxiety, Aurora was close behind.

They rode upward, steadily upward, until barrenness was replaced by budding springtime. Tender green shoots were in evidence on every limb, on every bush, pushing up through the carpet of pine needles to stretch eagerly toward the sun. A feeling of rebirth was fresh upon the air, so clean and deliciously cool it fed the soul as if it had been hungering all winter. As if it had forgotten how sweet it was to live.

Aurora was stirred by all those things. Her senses were full of the surrounding beauty of nature and the splendor of the day. And of Ethan Prescott.

He hadn't spoken since they'd left the trail, grimly intent upon his own thoughts. She was willing to grant him his solitude. Just riding with him was enough. Knowing they were on their way to free him of the past and reclaim Scotty for their future gave her more than enough to think on herself. She was both exhilarated and afraid. They were riding straight for the Sioux.

As thoroughly as she'd prepared herself for the journey, to make it on her own if need be, she hadn't planned on the mounting degree of her nervousness. Her heart was beating fast. Fear urged its tempo. She wanted to be brave. For Ethan. For Scotty. But deep inside the long-prohibited terrors of her mind was that sound . . . the wails of the Lakotas as they swarmed the stage. Her first sight of them; their bronze bodies nearly naked, their harshly chiseled faces smeared with bright paint. And the smell and sound of death echoed with every pulse of her blood.

"Ethan, can we stop a minute." Her voice wavered like the cool mountain stream rippling hock-deep around her horse's legs.

He looked back at her. Aurora was as white as the clay of the north country table lands. She swayed in the saddle as if about to swoon. Concerned, he drew up the sorrel, but before he could dismount to aid her she swung from the saddle and knelt in the clear water. The hands bringing cups of dampness to her pale face were trembling. After a couple of splashes, the color blended back into her cheeks.

"Ora? You all right?"

She looked up to offer a strained smile. "I'm fine." It was a poor lie, so feebly given he felt bad about challenging it. Instead, he spoke out on one of the questions troubling him.

"How'd you do it, Ora? How'd you get him to listen to something other than his greed?"

"You mean my father?"

Did he imagine the slight edge of defensiveness in her tone?

"I guess he decided he loved me more."

She looked so pleased that he murmured, "I'm glad." But he wasn't. Not at all. A bad feeling stirred in his gut. Some of it he could identify as simple jealousy. Some panic. As selfish as he knew it to be, the last thing he wished for was the return of strong ties between father and daughter. "Does he know you're going to fetch the boy?" And danged if he wasn't shamefully pleased by the distress flickering in his expression.

"Scotty is a part of me. He'll accept him. In time, I

know he will."

Ethan forced a small smile to hide his doubts. There was about as much chance of that as Garth Kincaid welcoming a Texas nester to his bosom. But Aurora looked so fragile, so desperately hopeful, he couldn't shatter her illusions. Neither could he encourage them.

Aurora noted his silence and frowned to herself as she watched him kneel at the edge of the stream. His movements were slow, awkward and, for the first time in her anxious quest, she was reminded of his injury. Closer scrutiny revealed a growing pallor beneath his darkly tanned skin and a tightness about his mouth and eyes. He was in pain, but he would not speak of it aloud. And there was more, more he held silent, more that tugged his features into a taut, angular mold. He looked almost angry and that confused her. What could be testing his temper? After all, they were going to earn his freedom, his right to live back amongst his own.

And would there be a place for her? For her and Scotty?

Ethan gave a start as her cool hand fitted to his face. Dark eyes flashed up, expressing more in that instant than he would have liked. He knew the intensity of his stare alarmed her, for she went all still and speechless. Finally, she reached to open the neck of his shirt; not understanding, he jerked back.

"Your wound," she murmured and Ethan flushed, feeling foolish for his response to her touch. But he couldn't help it. Her nearness woke all manner of things inside him, not the least a desire to claim her fiercely and finally as his own, right there in the riverbed. His flesh burned for the feel of hers, all hot and silky smooth beneath him. He wanted to bury himself deep and drive her to a senseless ecstasy in which she would keen and moan his name. He needed to hold her tight and forever, to hear her say, "I love you, Ethan." To hear her vow she would never leave him.

But that wouldn't happen, because she was going back to the Bar K.

She was Garth Kincaid's daughter, and he'd always known that made the rest impossible.

He surged up and growled, "We'd best be going."

Uncertain of his mood, Aurora nodded. She was too tired, too anxious to examine the complexities of Ethan Prescott. Instead, she would look only as far as the next few hours. And what waited there filled her with dread.

"Ora?"

Her feelings must have been plain upon her face for him to sound so concerned.

Staring into the thick stand of pines, she said faintly, "Ethan, what if I can't get him back?"

He went to her then because her pain was beyond the two of them. When he put a comforting hand to her shoulder, she turned to seek the solidity of his embrace. He could feel her tremble.

"Ora, we'll get him back."

"I can't leave him there," she cried against his chest. Her fingers curled in the stiffened hide fabric of his coat. "I couldn't ride away knowing I might never see him again. Knowing I couldn't watch him grow. Knowing I'd be a stranger to him. Oh, Ethan, I'm so afraid. I want my son. I want my baby." Of all she had faced so boldly without a whimper, this was the one thing that broke her. She had no more spirit, no more strength, no more of her incredible courage. She clung to him and sobbed her sorrow until the tears would come no more. Her chest hurt. Her throat was raw and burned with anguish. But the pain wouldn't leave her. Nor would the fear.

Vaguely, she was aware of Ethan's large hand curling beneath her jaw. Gently, he lifted her away from the muffling folds of his coat. The sight of her face, all streaked with the agony in her heart, struck a cruel blow to his own. Her eyes shimmered, a rich liquid gold, rising to search his dark, fathomless stare.

"Ora, I gave you a promise and I wish to God I could tell you that I'll keep it. The truth is, I don't know. I'll try my damnedest. But I can't give you a guarantee. You may have to ride out and leave him. This time. But I don't want you giving up."

For a moment, he was lost in the glittering misery of her gaze. His fingertips brushed across one damp cheek. He moistened his lips and continued in a husky cadence.

"Ora, if for some reason we can't take him with us—if we can't get him back—I want you to know you're not alone. I know it's no substitute and I don't know if it matters but you've got me to love you. I love you, Ora. Can that be enough for now?"

Her tearing grief ebbed in that instant as she looked up at him. His expression yielded a frustrated strength, a vulnerable hope, and a need so great she stood stunned by it. He was offering all that he was, all that he had, with barriers down, with heart laid bare. Enough? A wealth of emotion swelled within her.

"Oh, Ethan—"

He'd gone suddenly too stiff and still.

"Ethan?" It was a tense whisper.

"We're not alone, Ora."

His words sunk deep, touching off waves of familiar fear. Wide eyed, frightened, she cast her gaze about them, knowing, as she did, what she would see.

From out of the thicket emerged one, two, three, a half-dozen Lakota braves.

They had found Yellow Bear.

Chapter Twenty-four

It wasn't the same campsite she'd lived within, but the similarities were enough to make Aurora's mouth dry with fear. Some fifteen tipis were standing, circles within a circle, along a timbered riverbottom where wood and shelter were plentiful. It was large for a *wicoti,* claiming closer to fifty people than the usual twenty-five. This was Yellow Bear's extended family, she could tell by the way the men had decorated the outside of the tipis; with shields and war tools and symbols of a great leader. Yellow Bear was *itancan* of the camp and one of the leaders of the *tiyospaye,* the larger band of their people which numbered in the hundreds. He was a man of respect and power. And Aurora, rightly, feared him. It was his son she had supposedly killed. And it was her son he now held captive within the circle of circles.

Riding in surrounded by the camp's *akicita* guard, they were immediately the center of attention. Women stopped in the midst of tanning hides and tending their vegetables, men went from honing their tools of war to brandishing them in a hostile welcome, and children left their games to openly stare at the two *washachu.* It was the same way she'd been greeted a year ago when brought in their midst, a stolen prize.

402

Like stepping into another world, one so foreign and frightening, she wasn't sure now how she had stood it with a degree of composure: the men with their sharply angled faces, their nut-brown skin bared and glistening with only a breechcloth and moccasins to give modesty, their black hair trailing proudly, entwined with feathers and white ermine tails; the women, so striking with their long, lithe limbs, tawny complexions and flashing eyes, clad in skins decorated with quills, shells and elk's teeth. And how equally strange she must have appeared to them in her bustled Eastern finery, her tresses tangled about her shoulders like tongues of fire. They had howled that day and the sound had startled her soul into a frantic terror. Now, they stood silent as the surrounding trees, staring. The old panic gathered, but she forced it down, forced herself to sit still and tall. Ethan was beside her. He would see her safe. And somewhere, in one of the tipis, perhaps swinging gently in a cradleboard, was Scotty.

Mama's here. I've come for you, my darling.

As much as she wanted to search him out frantically, she knew now was not the time. If threatened, Uncheedah would hide him. She couldn't bear the thought of coming so far to be denied the simple pleasure of looking upon her child. She stared straight ahead, across the circle of tipis to one that was familiar. The home of her father-in-law by Miniconjou law. Though she tried to ignore the bore of black eyes as she was recognized, she could feel them pierce her like so many cruel arrows, stabbing her with blame, with hate. Now she knew how Ethan must have felt jailed upon the Bar K. Innocent yet damned by the consensus of guilt. Her chin angled up proudly. Her hands gripped the reins to keep them from trembling. She would not let them know she was afraid. For Ethan. For Scotty.

They were met at the tipi of Yellow Bear by an unsmiling Black Moon. He gaged Aurora with cold, angry eyes, then looked to Ethan. His expression changed to one of surprising welcome.

"Ho, mita koda. What brings you to our camp with this disgraced woman?"

"I've come to speak with Yellow Bear to seek a favor owed."

Aurora looked in puzzlement between the two men. The exchange of words confused her. They spoke like friends. She remembered Ethan telling her that he'd treated the Sioux for measles but it hadn't really sunk in until now. Nor had the fact that he shared the hills with these white-wary people in apparent peace. Whereas the members of Yellow Bear's camp regarded her with hard glares, there was a respect in their study of Ethan Prescott. And with that knowledge, came a sudden burst of hope. Had he the consequence among the Miniconjou to demand the return of her child? Trust me, he'd said, but he had given no particulars. She found it hard not to turn to him in expectant question. Why hadn't he told her?

Black Moon lifted the flap of canvas and stepped inside Yellow Bear's tipi.

"Ethan?"

He spared her a quick glance and a brief warning. "Let me do the talking, Ora."

Worry and rebellion reared within her. "But —"

"Stay calm and don't open your mouth. You hear?"

Gripping her lips together into a thin line, she nodded. And silently, she fretted. Scotty was here. He was being held in another woman's arms and Ethan asked her to be calm. She was being judged by all these people as a heartless murderess, and he told her to be quiet. Protest rose in her tightened throat. The effort to obey him weighed upon her. But she did trust him.

Seeing the argument in her eyes and reading of her decision there, Ethan tendered a small, satisfied smile. He knew what it was costing her to do as asked. And he knew no other way to see his promise met.

The hide door opened and Black Moon slipped outside. He didn't look at Aurora but addressed Ethan. "Our great Matogee will hear your words now."

When Aurora began to dismount, Black Moon made as if to stop her. Ethan was quick to intercede.

"This concerns her. She has a right to sit at this council. I will vouch for her conduct."

The handsome brave turned on the Texan with an angry snarl. "This is the one who slew Far Winds. Did you not know?"

"I know no such thing," was the firm reply as Ethan eased down from the saddle. His movements were strained. For a moment, he leaned against the powerful haunch of his sorrel then stood away. "Will you stop me from going inside?" he challenged.

Black Moon glared up at Aurora then back to Ethan. Finally, he shrugged and stepped aside. His black eyes followed Aurora's figure as she climbed down from her horse, obviously searching her for some sign of danger. But he would not search her physically, for Ethan had claimed responsibility for her and he would not offend him with a display of distrust.

The scent of smoked hides and the musky odor of grease closed in about Aurora as she entered the tipi. Those smells carried her back to a time when she'd lain bound and helpless upon the ground. She'd tried to breathe deep of the familiar aroma of the earth to hold her terror at bay and to remind herself that she could endure. Then, she'd glanced up to see the hard, thick soles of Far Winds's moccasins. She could still recall the intricate pattern. They'd been quilled in long red and green triangles and beaded in white, red, blue and yellow. She'd watched them move silently around the fire to where she huddled, trying not to wail in fear.

The curl of long fingers about her forearm jerked Aurora from her remembered nightmare. Her gaze flashed up, all dark and dazed with shadows of the past, to find Ethan's upon her. In his expression, she found everything she needed. His eyes were silently supportive. The brief curve of his lips encouraged. And the iron-hard clasp of his hand spoke of strength and an angry possessiveness, promising she would come to no harm. It took all her reserve of will not to turn to him, to burrow against the secure bastion of his chest, to lose herself in the protection of his arms. Instead, she returned his smile, or at least a poor, thin imitation of it that nonetheless displayed a hint of reclaimed courage.

Three seats covered with buffalo robes made a semicircle about the fire pit. On the center one sat Yellow Bear. Smoke wafted upward toward the opening, where twenty poles, each cut from twenty-five foot lengths of stout cedar heart wood, were lashed together. The hazy cloud obscured the features of the shrewd Miniconjou chief, but Aurora recalled them well. Her *tunkasi* was a handsome man. Far Winds had inherited his father's harsh angular beauty. Black Moon gestured to the platform on Yellow Bear's left. He, himself, squatted down on his chief's right.

As she sat on the long seat of willow and hide next

to Ethan, Aurora regarded her father-in-law in trepidation. He was a splendid, haughty figure. Unlike the other braves, he was fully clothed in quilled and painted buckskins. A breastplate adorned with ermine tails and feathers spanned his broad chest. Trails of plumes and eagle feathers dressed his elbow-length black hair. Fathomless ebony eyes stared out from unseamed copper skin as he viewed the woman whom he believed had killed his only son. At first, Aurora quelled beneath that unswerving gaze, then a deep rancor grew within her heart. This was the man who'd stolen her child. This was the man who'd ordered the attack that left Ethan for dead. A man who saw fiercely to his own ambitions without a care as to who he hurt in the process. A man not unlike her own father. And suddenly, she was no longer afraid. She met his gaze with a discourteous directness. The old man frowned his displeasure and turned to her companion.

"It has been long, *Wasichu Waken*. Have you been well?" Purposefully, arrogantly, he didn't mention Aurora's presence.

Wasichu Waken. Truly, Ethan had achieved greatness in the eyes of the Miniconjou if they deemed to call him the white miracle man. Those who controlled the curing power of the spirits were held in the highest regard and awe by the superstitious Lakotas. They were a people ruled by dreams and visions and influenced by mysteries of nature. Ethan Prescott, with his healing potions, had been entrusted with the lives of Yellow Bear's people, and he hadn't failed them. Nor had he taken advantage of their regard. Until now.

"There has been food in my lodge but a great sorrow in my heart, for I, like your people, am not free."

Yellow Bear scowled. "How is that, my friend?

You have not been brought before me as a prisoner."

"No, but I am a prisoner among my own kind. At the time of the great sickness, when I was here with your people, others said I killed a white man in the valley. I've come to ask one of your braves to go with me to speak to the white man's law. I give my word that he will then be free to return to your camp."

Yellow Bear considered the request. His impassive features gave no hint of his thoughts. It was up to him to give or deny the help of his people. If he chose not to oblige the appeal, Ethan could not ask again. The matter would be at an end. Knowing this, Aurora's breath was held in anxious suspension as she looked between the two men. Neither betrayed any of the turmoil she suffered in that long moment of silence.

"I owe you much for what you did for my people, for my family. I will take your words to our council fire and see if there is one among us who will go."

Ethan nodded. He knew Yellow Bear could not command any of his band to volunteer, but a call from their chief would not go unanswered. If Garth Kincaid kept his end of the deal, the threat of the noose would soon be lifted. And that left one more matter of importance.

"There is another thing I would ask of you, Yellow Bear."

Hearing the caution in the other's tone, the Lakota chief was also wary of the request. He glanced to the red-haired woman at the white healer's side, guessing rightly that she was the crux of his friend's dilemma. He had not opposed his son's marriage to the fiery captive, though in his heart he was saddened by his choice. Their camp's *wihumnga* had warned the woman brought bad medicine, but he had attributed that to her daughter's jealousy as his son's first wife.

Had he listened and acted, his son would yet be living. And so he could not blame the white female completely for Far Winds's death. He was at fault, as well, and it was that grief and guilt that kept him from slaying her. That and the way *Wasichu Waken* looked at her.

"I listen, my brother."

"You have taken a child from the arms of my woman. My lodge rings with her sorrow. There is no room in her heart for other than her grief. I have come for the son of Far Winds. Will you return to me a life for a life?"

Aurora sat taut and still as she studied the hooded eyes of her father-in-law. They were black and expressionless, giving her no reason to hope. Within her breast, her heart lurched into a painful rhythm, beating with a constricted terror as she waited for Yellow Bear's words.

"You gave me back the life of my son during the time of the great sickness. That spirit now dwells in the body of his child. You would ask me to return that life to she who stole it?" No longer was he stoic. His ebony glare steeped with hatred as it fastened upon Aurora. And she could no longer remain silent.

"I did not kill Far Winds."

Yellow Bear's contempt curled his sharp features into a mask of disgust and disbelief."

"It is true, Matogee. Please hear my words. I did not flee from him. I did not wish him dead."

"We found the other white men," he spat out in quiet loathing. "We know it was not your hand that slew him, only your intent."

"That isn't true."

"You deny that you fled the camp with the white trappers? You deny that they lay in wait for my son to follow then killed him? Only he was a great warrior and he managed to take their souls with him." Pride and fury edged his voice; admiration for his son's final courage, anger that his life should be sacrificed in such an unworthy cause.

"He was a great warrior. It is by his bravery that I am here and that your grandson lives." She saw the chief's lips draw back to bare his teeth in a snarl of protest so she hurried on. "Far Winds followed and he saved me from the very men who slew him. It was not the white men's words that persuaded me to flee, it was Uncheedah's treachery. She forced me to go to the trappers. She sold me to them so she would not have to share Far Winds's tipi with me. I would not have endangered my son by taking such a dangerous chance so close to the time of birthing."

The thought of Scotty nestled in the Lakota woman's arms overcame any qualms she might have had in making such accusations. Aurora was fighting for her son, and her co-wife's future within the tribe was not her worry. Her mind worked frantically to form an argument Yellow Bear would heed and she used her time amongst his people for the knowledge to free her son from them.

"If you seek to place blame for Far Winds's death beyond the hands of those who wrought it, look to Uncheedah and her mother. It was her jealousy that brought disaster. She misused her mother's sacred power to cloud the truth from Far Winds. It was her ambition to become his sole wife instead of his first wife. Her greed for consequence is what caused the spirits to retaliate by taking the life of her loved one. And you have rewarded her by giving her the life force of my husband in the body of my child."

Silence. Aurora panted with emotion as she waited

410

for her words to affect the Lakota leader. She felt Ethan's fingers move across the top of her hand, and she turned it so hers could lock through his in a desperate grasp.

Yellow Bear was no fool. He knew of the jealousy between wives and he was aware of Uncheedah's possessiveness. The thought of her using the power of the *wihmunga* for her own spiteful purpose was grim indeed. It was an offense great enough to demand appeasement. Had his son been that sacrifice? He looked at the fiery Wadutah. Giving her back the child would mean severing his only link to his son's spirit. He was a wise man, a reasonable man, but he was not totally selfless.

"What you ask, *Wasichu Wakan,* is too great," he said slowly. He heard Aurora's quick draw of breath and saw, too, the way the white healer silenced her with a hard press of his hand. "You have asked for the return of the life owed you and I send one of my braves to restore your freedom. The life of my son for your own. The debt is repaid. You will go now and take your woman with you."

Aurora gripped his arm. "Ethan?" Her eyes beseeched him with a depthless maternal despair. His emotions twisted tight. Somberly, he looked to the Miniconjou chief.

"I would change my favor. The debt you owe for the life of Far Winds in exchange for his son. I ask nothing for myself."

Realizing he meant to forfeit his own freedom to return Scotty to her, Aurora cried out in objection and dismay. Seeing the conflict, Yellow Bear allowed a cunning smile.

"Wadutah, would you have your man or your child?"

411

She stared, aghast, at the clever chief and writhed in the trap he set for her. Ethan or Scotty. Her love or her child. How could she force herself through that agony again?

An image of Scotty surfaced in her tortured mind. His cherubic face, his golden eyes, his chubby arms waving happily. She could hear his gurgles of delight, his coos of pleasure, the greedy smacking of his lips as he feasted at her breast. His anguished wails as she surrendered him to the Sioux. Her arms ached to hold him close. Her heart splintered at the thought of leaving him behind.

Ethan or Scotty.

She looked up at the man beside her and saw the goodness there. He deserved his freedom. He'd earned it, by saving Far Winds's life, by saving her own and Scotty's. How could she ask him to give up his one chance, his one dream? For her child, not his.

But he'd promised, cried a selfish soul. He'd promised she would have Scotty back. She couldn't ride away with empty arms, with empty heart. She couldn't abandon the child of her body. Or the love of her life.

Ethan or Scotty.

How could life be so cruel?

"Ora, take Scotty and go," Ethan urged softly. He could read the torment in her transparent gaze; windows to her ravaged soul. He touched her cheek lightly, feeling the dampness there. "Go home. I'll be fine."

She almost stood. She almost demanded her son. Her muscles tensed, readying to rise. Then, she stared deep into the tender darkness of his eyes. And she couldn't move. Ethan. She saw beyond the generosity, beyond the willingness to forfeit all for the safe return

412

of her son. She saw the fragile heart of a man once betrayed by the selfish act of a woman and she could not make herself hurt him. She couldn't shatter his faith. Even at his command.

"You won't be fine," she argued in a fractured voice. "Without a witness, Jack Lawson will go free and you'll still be on the run for something you didn't do. It's not fair, Ethan. You could go back to the Lone Star and build it up again. I can't ask you to give that up for me."

"You don't have to ask, Ora." He shushed her protest with fingertips upon her lips. "It wouldn't work out. He'd always be between us. You couldn't look at me without seeing him and knowing what I'd cost you. I won't have you hating me, Ora. It's easier not having you at all. Go home to the Bar K and raise your son."

Hot, helpless tears rose in her throat, choking off her denial. He was right. As much as she hated it, he was right. Scotty would linger between them just as Olivia had. There could be no peace, no happiness, while those restless shadows roamed. Yet how could she allow him to surrender his liberty? And how could she live without his love? There was no answer. There was no way to decide.

"I can't." The sob ripped from her. She gripped his hand, burying her face in its roughened palm. "I can't choose. I won't choose. I couldn't live with one after giving up the other. Oh, God! Ethan, I need you both. Please. I can't make a choice."

Ethan stroked her arm with his other hand and took her gently up against him. His lips brushed her temple. The scent of lavender coaxed tormenting memory. Her weeping was muffled by the fabric of his coat as she quivered in his embrace like something frail and strained to the point of breaking. A tremendous wave of respect for her courage assailed him and the thought of her anguish was more than he could stand. He glanced across the top of her bright hair to the stoic Lakota chief who was toying with their lives. It was a heartless game, one he couldn't concede.

"Hush now, Ora," the Texan whispered firmly. "I need you to be brave. Do you want Scotty back or not?"

That challenge pierced through her misery, dulling it with a stronger purpose, just as he'd suspected. With a final shuddering sniff, Aurora straightened and looked up at him for guidance. Her fears were arrested by the assurance of his gaze.

Slowly, purposefully, Ethan brought a hand up to his wounded shoulder as if to gently ease a pain. Then, instead, he drove the heel of his palm against it with a slamming force. Aurora reached for him in stunned alarm as he gasped and went startlingly pale. For a moment, he swayed, fighting to keep a clear head as agony knifed through him. Gingerly, he put an unsteady hand inside his shirt and withdrew bloodstained fingers. These he extended to Yellow Bear. It took him a minute of heavy breathing to master sufficient speech.

"From one of your arrows. Is this how Yellow Bear sees a debt repaid a friend? It's through her courage and sacrifice that my hair doesn't decorate one of your warrior's lances."

Impressed by the white man's dramatic display of nerve, Yellow Bear appeared thoughtful. "You were not recognized by my men. It was not meant for you to die, *Wasichu Wakan.*"

"And it is not meant for a mother to be without her child. Both are mistakes that need righting. One for the other. Or is the great Matogee a leader without honor?"

Black Moon gave a growl of exception and made as if to rise to strike down he who would insult his chief. Yellow Bear lifted a hand to stay him. Ethan hadn't flinched or made a move to defend against the threat of Black Moon's bared blade. His stare was riveted to the Lakota leader's.

"You show no fear, my brother," Yellow Bear said. The words were respectful.

"I fear nothing but a life without honor. I have made a promise to Wadutah to see her child rightfully restored to her arms. Would you make me break that vow and live in shame?"

Pride, bravery, honor. Things Yellow Bear understood. Things the white man was trying to strip from his people. His admiration for Ethan Prescott was such that he would not willingly reduce him to disgrace. And he would not—had the child been other than his grandson.

"You ask me to surrender the soul of my son to live in a foreign world, to never know the pride and power of his people. That I cannot do."

Aurora made a soft distraught sound. She could see her hope of claiming her baby crumble. But she would not cry. She would not inflict Ethan with the weight of her grief after all he had done. She would not let him believe she blamed him. It wasn't his fault. She had known it was an impossible task, yet she'd taken his promise with a needy desperation. She'd wanted—oh, how she'd wanted to believe he could restore Scotty to her. But now she must accept the fact that it would never be. Scotty would be raised amongst the Sioux, and she would have to learn to live with the pain of his separation. Perhaps, she thought dismally, it could be done with Ethan beside her. Perhaps his love could fill the devastating hollowness within her heart. She owed to him to give him every chance to prove it to her.

But as she sat in the musty tipi, her eyes shimmering with withheld tears, her heart swollen with anguish, Aurora knew there was no forgetting the little one she'd brought into the world. No other child would replace him. No man's love could blot out the bond that had been formed between mother and child the instant Ethan had placed the newly born infant in her grasp. It was a pain she would suffer in silence. One she would never, ever speak to Ethan. She could never let him know that part of her died when the fleeting hope of holding her child was no more and that there was nothing he could do to make her whole again.

"Let's go, Ethan, while we still can."

He looked at her in surprise. The deadened quality of her voice shook him to the soul. Her golden eyes were dulled and lifeless. Was this what was left for him? This melancholy martyr? This forever reminder that he had failed her? No! No way was he going to leave with this spiritless shadow. He'd let enough ghosts haunt him, making his every moment a remembered hell. Not this time. What was past, was past and he'd be damned if he was going to settle for less of Aurora Kincaid than the vibrant woman who'd won his love. He was not going to live his life without her.

Ethan's scowl bewildered Aurora. His dark eyes were angry. His grip on her hand hurt. What reason could he have to regard her so furiously? Her brows lowered. Her lips turned downward in displeasure. And a spark of rebellion came into her eyes. The minute he saw it there, his fingers relaxed and his fearsome expression eased. He smiled as if they had just shared something wonderful between them. As if she'd given him some precious gift. She didn't understand but before she could question him, Ethan looked to Yellow Bear with a compelling confidence.

"Far Winds was your son. His life was in your hands. You trusted it to me when you called me to your camp to heal him and the others. Why don't you trust me now? Have I done something to earn your disrespect?"

Yellow Bear returned his stare. "No," was his even reply.

"You trusted me with your son. Trust me with his son."

The silence stretched out taut and tangible. Aurora didn't dare breathe. She didn't dare think lest her thoughts grasp at some yet insubstantial thread of hope. She closed her eyes tight, filling her mind with the image of her son, concentrating on him as if sheer power of will would grant him into her care. *Oh, please. Oh, please give me back my son.* She chanted it again and again like some witch woman's spell, one with the power to undo the *wihmunga's* meddling. So focused were her attentions on this one desperate wish, Aurora almost didn't hear the *itancan's* words.

"Bring the child."

Black Moon rose and slipped from the tipi. Aurora followed his movements in an agony of excitement. She waited, her hands gripped on Ethan's arm, her eyes glued to the flap of hide until it rolled up. It was then she heard the discontented wails.

Scotty!

The clamp of Ethan's hand upon her shoulder kept Aurora from surging to her feet, but it couldn't halt the sudden rocketing of her heart.

Scotty.

She blinked rapidly lest her first sight of her baby be blurred by tears. She wanted to see him clearly; every soft round curve, every strand of coal black hair, every wrinkle, every dimple.

He was wrapped in fawnskin. His face was an angry, mottled red from crying. But no sight had ever been sweeter. Then, Aurora's shiny gaze lifted to meet the piercing hatred in Uncheedah's glare. The two women regarded one another, the threat each one presented laid bare upon the other's face. The Sioux woman's arms tightened possessively, and Scotty screamed all the louder. Aurora fought the impulse to rise and snatch her child away; reason reminded her to be still. That and the unyielding pressure of Ethan's hand. Uncheedah skirted the fire warily, followed by her mother, the camp's witchwoman. Together, they knelt on the platform Black Moon vacated. He stood at the door watching the proceedings through impassive eyes.

Yellow Bear was far less detached. He, too, saw the look of longing spring into his son's second wife's eyes. And observed Uncheedah failure to quiet the fussing babe. It seemed to him that the boy had done nothing but air his lungs since coming into the camp. Fine now, but what would happen if they were to go on the run and depend upon stealth and silence for their safety? One wailing infant could spell death to his entire people. That knowledge sat grimly upon his heart, for he was a leader first, and only then a proud grandparent.

Uncheedah looked rather frantically between her father-in-law and the pale woman who had torn the security from her life. She had hoped never to look

418

upon the face of her rival again, not since delivering her personally into the hands of the ruthless trappers. She'd taken a smug satisfaction in stealing her husband's child for her own, but now she knew a tenuous terror. Wadutah was here with the *Wasichu Wakan,* and she could no longer be certain of her claim upon the child. If only he would be quiet! She repressed the want to pinch his buttocks sharply.

"Wadutah says you made bad magic to lure my son to his death."

Yellow Bear's words brought an immediate pallor to the native woman's face. "She lies."

"If I find my son was taken by the gods to appease your foolish vanity, I will have you and your mother banished. What say you, Uncheedah?"

Uncheedah clutched the child while her thoughts spun wildly in a tight, vicious circle. Wadutah! Hatred poisoned her. Wadutah was the reason for all her troubles—for the loss of her own child, for the estrangement of her husband's affection. And now, after bringing her life to ruin, Wadutah would have the final laugh by taking back her baby. Bitterness clogged her senses and jealousy took the fear from being cast out of her clan.

"No," Uncheedah hissed as she jerked a thin knife from her high-topped moccasin.

Aurora cried out as the blade snaked down to rest against Scotty's throat.

"She will not have the child! I would rather he be dead!"

Chapter Twenty-five

It happened so quickly and they were so far away — the few yards separating them across the campfire might as well have been a hundred. Aurora saw the glitter of the knife and knew in that instant there was nothing she could do to save her child. She clutched instinctively at Ethan, wanting to shield her eyes in the blissfully dark folds of his coat but, perversely, she was unable to look away. Ethan had her by the upper arms, his fingers gripping tight enough to bruise, nearly tight enough to snap bone.

"No! Scotty!" Her wail rose, high and thin, from her tortured soul. Aurora fought the blackness swimming up to swamp her senses in a cold, engulfing wave. She could feel the crushing strength of Ethan's hands. Scotty's cries were drowned by the roar of blood filling her ears.

Ethan watched with a mirroring horror. There was no way he could intercede in the tragedy about to happen. He held Aurora up as her body abruptly drained of consciousness. He felt an intense pain rip through him, as if Aurora's child was his own son, created of the love between them. Helplessness and horror stirred a familiar sickness inside him. It was cold and depthless, like Uncheedah's eyes. That she could slay an innocent babe right before its mother's anguished gaze, he had no doubt. He'd seen too much violence and senseless rage not to recognize its ugliness in the desperate Lakota woman. And just as with the tearing inhumanity of the war he'd witnessed, all he could do was try to piece together what was left behind in the savage wake. How was he ever going to heal Aurora?

The knife blade swept back to begin its killing stroke and was halted.

"No."

Wahchewin, the camp's witch woman spoke up with sudden authority. Her daughter's gaze flew up, wild with objection then cowed by fear at what she saw blazing in her mother's eyes.

"You will not do this thing," the *wihmunga* told her sternly. "Is not one wrongful death enough to satisfy your hate?" The knife was wrenched from her hands and passed to a tense Black Moon. "Give me the child and go. You shame me, Uncheedah. Go and pray to the gods that they be merciful. For I will not be."

A long, taut moment passed. Wills locked and struggled. And finally gave. The wailing child was passed from daughter to mother and a weeping Uncheedah fled the tipi.

The crisis past, Ethan turned his attention to the limp woman in his arms. His heart, yet churning with the terror of moments prior, quieted at the sight of her still features. Gently, tenderly, he turned her in his arms and stroked her very white face. At his coaxing touch, she moaned back to life and immediately remembrance returned. She grabbed for him. Eyes black with grief stared up in confusion as incredibly, he smiled. Dazed by her sorrow, Aurora looked at him blankly until the sounds of a child's unhappy whimpering reached her.

"Ethan—?"

"Shhh! Easy now, Ora. Scotty's all right."

Not sure she dared believe him, Aurora twisted upon his lap then gave a relieved cry when she saw the wiggling bundle in Wahchewin's arms.

Yellow Bear had watched the dramatic tableau with great interest. He didn't miss Ethan's agonizing over the fate of the child, and that started him thinking of a possible solution, one that would serve all and deny none. He looked at the child, such a small squalling pup to be causing so much difficulty. His grandson, he thought proudly, who, as a man, would straddle two worlds.

"You have a care for this child, *Wasichu Wakan?*"

Ethan regarded the elder man with complete sincerity in his dark gaze. "As if he were mine. He is the son of my woman, the son of my heart."

"And you would pledge responsibility for him?"

"With my life." That claim, he had already proven.

"And if I were to return the child to his mother, would you see he grows to know of his father's people? You will see he learns the virtues of manhood: *wacantognaka;* generosity, *cante t'inza;* bravery, *wacintanka;* patience and *ksabyahan opiic'iija;* wisdom."

Ethan hesitated only a second, realizing the magnitude of this promise should he make it. Then he spoke without reluctance. "Yes. I would see he learns the Lakota ways, from the wisest of them all."

Yellow Bear smiled faintly at the compliment.

"Far Winds was my brother of the soul if not of the blood, Ethan continued. "I held his life as I now will hold the life of his son. You have my word that he will

422

not be denied the truth of his heritage and that he will respect those who came before him and will see to those who come after."

"And I will accept your word as your bond."

Yellow Bear made a brief gesture, and the witch woman extended the screaming child. Ethan took Scotty from her. Instantly, the baby quieted. His puckered countenance relaxed into a jolly contentment as the bearded Texan smiled down at him. That more than anything that came before convinced Yellow Bear that he'd made a wise decision.

"Howdy, little feller," Ethan murmured softly and the baby chortled in response. "I got your mama right here with me and she'd just a-dying to grab onto you."

Aurora was looking up at him through wide, wet eyes. The anxiousness in them curled about his heart. Her arms stretched up eagerly, hungrily. Delivering the baby into them was the best experience Ethan could recall since helping to bring him into the world. The child was quickly enfolded where he belonged, and Ethan allowed himself a moment to watch in complete, incredibly intense satisfaction. Aurora was alternately weeping and cooing, oblivious to the others in the tipi.

"I will ride down to speak the truth to your white men of the law," Black Moon offered unexpectedly. He, too, saw the doting way the Texan handled his friend's son and knew the child would have a better life with Ethan than in the hills during the waning days of his people. A sad truth.

In the way of the Sioux, Ethan didn't offer thanks to either of the Lakota men. He nodded in simple acknowledgment and stood, assisting Aurora to her feet.

"We will go now," he announced and lifted the flap

of the tipi. His arm guided mother and child from the smoky darkness into the fading daylight.

They rode for an hour before Aurora felt secure enough to stop in a sheltering copse of pine. Only when she dismounted, with Scotty cradled in her arms, did she truly believe what had transpired. It was a wonderful elation. She was giddy with it. She smiled weakly as the baby began a noisy rooting against the front of her coat.

"Have some patience, you greedy child," she chastened fondly as she settled upon a fallen log and began to undo her shirt. Her worry that she might not be able to supply milk for his supper was ended after the first few eager tugs at her breast. With a great satisfaction, Aurora relished her role as nourishing mother. She cuddled her child, breathing deeply of the soapweed, marrow and wild bergamot the Sioux used to rub over the tender skin of their babies. She was anxious to replace that earthy scent with one of delicate talc, just as she looked forward to stripping off the fawnskin in favor of linen and soft yarns. Only then would she feel he was hers alone. Scotty was her child and he would be raised within the walls of civilization, not beneath a rafter of limbs and sky. And no one would take him from her arms again.

No one.

While she nursed Scotty, Ethan rubbed down the horses and built up a fire to warm them against the evening's chill. His movements were careful and slow. Aurora would have noticed had she not been so preoccupied with her child. There was nothing to cook over the fire. It was a good three hours to the Bar K. Darkness thickened around them so Ethan thought it best

424

to go hungry and bed down for the night. In all honesty, he wasn't sure he could make the extra miles to take Aurora and Scotty home. He was weak with pain and light-headed with fatigue. His shoulder throbbed clear down to his fingertips, making the simple task of unfurling the bedrolls into a teeth-clenching challenge.

"We'll get a fresh start out in the morning," he said at last. He could think of no other bit of busy work, and so he stood watching Aurora tend the babe. The sight worked tenderly upon him. She looked up, really seeing him for the first time since they'd left the Sioux camp, and she gave a poignant smile.

"Thank you, Ethan."

He waited for the more he longed to hear but she said nothing further, her attention returning to the child at her breast. With a sigh, he dismissed his pangs of disappointment. Of course she'd be caught up by the precious bundle in her arms. He was being foolish to expect more. There was so much he wanted to say to her, so many plans he was eager to discuss now that the future was unclouded. Anticipation crowded his heart. He and Aurora and Scotty. Together. The image was intoxicating. And he could no longer wait to embrace it. The sentiments needed expressing. He wanted to share them, he wanted to receive them in kind. From the woman he loved. If only he could think of how to begin. How to begin a life of trust, of care, of commitment. The concept had once terrified him. Now it simply scared him. But it was a pleasant kind of panic.

"Bet your father will be surprised to see you come home with the boy."

Aurora smiled optimistically. At this moment, she was unwilling to let anything interfere with the sweetness of her reunion. Not even reality. "He'll get used to the idea. In time."

"A Southerner and a half-Indian child." Ethan made a rueful face. "Maybe in a few hundred years or so."

She looked down at the baby, seeing his swarthy complexion and raven-black hair, seeing without seeing. "Scotty is my son. His grandson. Someday the Bar K will be his. He'll be a man of influence in the territory, perhaps a politician." Her smile grew dreamy, picturing him in public office, giving speeches in Washington. "My father will be so proud." She made no mention of the tall Texan in her plans.

A prickle crept along Ethan's skin. Aurora was pulling away, from the truth, from everything they'd gone through that brought them close together. He felt uncomfortable in the face of this new disconcertingly serene woman. Uncomfortable and alarmed. If he let her withdraw into a fantasy of her own making, he'd be guilty of a terrible neglect. And the consequence of that was ever present. Aurora would not become another Olivia. Yet he could sense her slipping away, closing him out. Panic stirred inside him. He felt the need to shake her, with a cold dose of fact. "If your father can see beyond the color of his skin."

Aurora's gaze flashed up in warning. "Scotty is white. He'll be raised like any other white man. He'll go to the best schools. He'll have the best circle of friends." Her words were tenacious, almost angry.

"And what about the people in town that will remember him as the son of a Lakota warrior?" he asked gently now, trying to ease her from her grand illusions. His subtly earned an abrupt and hostile rebellion.

"He'll be a Kincaid. They won't dare shun him."

"A Kincaid." Ethan echoed the name thoughtfully. The beginnings of a frown creased his face. He couldn't ignore the connotations of her claim. "Ora, he's only half Kincaid. What about the other half? The half of him that lives in the hills? The half of him they won't respect no matter how hard you try to force it on them?"

"No one needs to know." Her jaw made a belligerent angle.

"And just how do you plan to explain him? Immaculate conception? It's already common knowledge that you have a child. What are you going to tell him when he's old enough to ask questions?"

She scowled at him. Why was he being so difficult, dredging up such ugly thoughts when she wanted to cling to her joy? She didn't want to consider such complexities while yet reeling from the harshness of the past few days. Instinctively, her reaction was to defend against it. And against he who tried to force it upon her. "Nothing. What should I tell him? The truth?"

"Yes."

Aurora stared down at her child and for the first time, she felt ashamed. Bitterly, tortuously ashamed that her beautiful child should grow in the vile shadow of his past. That he should doubt who he was because of how he was conceived. That he might wonder how she could love him. So ashamed she wanted to fool herself into believing he never needed to know of his parentage. "I could tell him you were his father." She cast hopeful eyes up at Ethan to be disheartened by his grim expression.

"No you won't. Not that I wouldn't be proud to claim him."

427

"Then why not?" The illegitimate son of an expatriate Texan wasn't a completely proper lineage but it was better than a half-breed born of captivity and rape.

"Because it wouldn't be fair to Scotty."

"Oh hang your ideals, Ethan Prescott. Next you'll be telling me I have to share his upbringing with Yellow Bear." Her words were taut. Aurora clutched her baby tighter. No one was going to take her child back to his father's people. Away from her. Away from the promise of the life she could give him. What did the Sioux offer? He was white. He would never know any different.

"They're his people, Ora."

His quiet rationality woke a violent protest inside her. It was as if a wedge was being forced between her and her baby. And she wouldn't allow it to happen. "I'm his mother. I'm his family. And I'll be damned if he's going to know any other."

"I gave my word to Yellow Bear."

Aurora stared at him, agog. "You expect me to take him back to them? After what they did? To me. To you. To him. To let them teach him to kill his own kind? No. I'd die before I let him get within fifty miles of that camp. They took him once. I won't give him up again. I won't, Ethan. I would have agreed to anything to get him back. I would have lied on a stack of bibles." The pain of separation, the horror of seeing a knife blade at her baby's throat. It was too real, too close, too horribly alive in her memory. She wanted to close it out. She wanted to blot out any reminder of it, to thrust the entire business behind her. But Ethan wouldn't let her.

"I don't lie, Ora. And I'm not going to let Scotty live a lie."

428

She attacked him blindly, in a maternal frenzy, thinking only to protect the baby hugged fiercely to her bosom. Frightened and cornered by her own fear, she struck hard and unfairly. "And who gave you that right? Scotty's not yours. He's my son. My son! I won't be bound by your promise. You had no right to give it."

Had she been less distraught, Aurora would have been alarmed by the sudden shuttering of Ethan's gaze. A quiet descended over him and he backed down with a soft, "Guess not." He looked at her for a long moment, seeing how she hunched over Scotty in a defensive posture. Seeing the excluding anger in her fiery gaze. Seeing his mistake. And feeling crushed by it. "Reckon he's your boy, Ora. You do what you think best. But damned if you don't sound just like your father."

She was panting, regarding him with suspicious eyes, as if expecting him to tear Scotty from her arms. She felt a slight relief when he turned away and eased down on his bedroll. She risked a quick, cautious breath.

"I'll take you to the Bar K in the morning. You'd best turn in. G'night." With that, he put his back to her.

For a long while there were only the hurried sounds of her raw gasps for breath and control. Slowly, the awful terror subsided. No one was taking Scotty. He was safe within her arms. Where he belonged. She would watch him grow, watch him reach and stretch toward manhood. She would glory in his achievements and ache in silence over his defeats. But she would be there. No one was going to deny her that right. Not Yellow Bear. Not Garth Kincaid. Not Ethan Prescott.

How could Ethan ask such a thing of her? How could he expect her to take so great a risk with Scotty's safety after all they'd been through? After all they'd been through together. It was wrong of him to ask. It was cruel of him to make her see — to see what? The truth? She hugged Scotty, trying to flush the possibilities from her mind. Trying not to think, not to understand, not to recognize the value of Ethan's unwelcomed insights.

He was asking that she respect his word.

He was asking her to trust him.

And she hadn't.

And that truth was more horrible than any other she'd been made to hear. Against her will, she thought long and hard while rocking Scotty to sleep.

Just like her father.

Yes, she had responded just as she'd been raised, with a selfish, narrow rage toward any who would threaten. And seeing that trait in herself was another bitter truth. But she hadn't been able to help it. The thought of Scotty with the Sioux paralyzed her. It was such a foreign world compared to hers, a dying world, that could give nothing but a message of despair and defeat. The Lakota were a conquered people, being herded toward the cages of civility, entombed upon the reservations that would strip away the last of their dignity. She wanted to spare Scotty that pain. She wanted to separate him from the taint of prejudice so he might know the best life had to offer. She didn't want him to struggle as the Sioux struggled. And in wanting that, she was guilty of an equal bigotry, one more subtle but just as vile as her father's.

Aurora sat shivering and alone. She'd thought having Scotty, protecting him, was her only purpose. But she was wrong. It was Scotty and Ethan. It always had been. In her heart, she knew she'd given Ethan the right to make decisions regarding her son. He'd earned it in deed if not by document. He wasn't Scotty's father, but he was the man she'd have raise him as his own. He'd gone to Yellow Bear's camp to seek not just his freedom but their future. And she'd just cruelly denied him when he tried to claim it. What had she done? What kind of craziness had made her turn on him like an enemy, like a threat? Some inbred weakness that would cause her to fail him as he didn't deserve to be failed?

The trembling became a silent weeping. Scotty was asleep in her arms. With his golden eyes closed, he looked disturbingly like his father. Like the son of a Miniconjou warrior. It was his bronze coloring and her prejudice that threatened, not Ethan Prescott's honor. Miserably, she knew she couldn't hide from it. She couldn't let her fear cloud the promise she had made her son. Her vow that he would live with dignity—with his father's people or her own. It would have to be his choice. And she would have to trust him to make it.

Aurora made herself lay Scotty gently down upon her bedroll. It was hard' to let go, to make herself release him. The empty feeling in her arms was too reminescent of her pain. She almost reached back down for him, for the comforting softness of his little form. But she didn't. She couldn't cling forever. Her fingertips brushed his soft cheek and she straightened to look from child to man.

Trust him. It was a potent echo within her soul.

Trust him.

She straightened away from the sleeping figure of her child.

Her gaze lingered over the long, powerful contours

431

upon the other bedroll. Ethan was shifting restlessly. His shoulder was hurting him. She cringed to recall how he'd abused his wound for Scotty's sake. How much more could she demand of him? That he give up his honor to soothe her inner fears? What had he said about a man without honor having a life not worth living? When she thought of his other words to Yellow Bear, of his claim that she was his woman, Aurora felt a warmth kindle. His woman. Yes, she was. In Ethan Prescott she could find the strength to overcome her greatest doubts and fears. Together they could raise Scotty to a fine, proud manhood. How could Scotty fail with such an example to follow?

Ethan gave a start when Aurora knelt beside his bedroll. He eased over on his back and looked up at her; dazzled by the beauty of her against a backdrop of shadowed pines and heavenly brilliants. Aurora: as bewitching and unreachable as those glimmering Northern lights, always disappearing with the dawn. Had there ever been a chance to hold her? Could one man claim such a marvel of loveliness and independent glory?

Maybe yes.

He waited.

"I was worried that you might still be bleeding."

It was a hasty excuse, the best she could think of. He didn't believe it for a second. She could tell by the probing challenge of his dark stare. However lame, it was a wonderful excuse to get close to him, to touch him when words of explanation weren't yet readily at hand.

He let her open his coat and button down his shirt. Her pale skimmed over the hard, hot plane of his chest to push aside the fabric. She could feel the thunderous pulse of his blood beneath it, and inside she

432

was taken by an expectant quivering.

"It doesn't look too bad," she announced after a quick, gut-wrenching glance. "It's not bleeding any more." Her fingertips continued to graze the intriguing swells and valleys of his collarbone.

"I could have told you that."

She'd found the impatient throbbing at the base of his throat and paused to let it beat against the pads of her fingers. An excited, tempting rhythm. She couldn't look away from his penetrating stare. From eyes that questioned clear to the soul. Hurt edged that cautious gaze. He wasn't sure of her, sure of her reason for coming to him. Longing kept him from looking away without explanation. He wasn't about to let his doubts close out this chance to discover what worked inside Aurora Kincaid's heart.

"I'm sorry."

When he had no reaction, she tried again.

"I love you."

Aurora's hand slid up to capture his jaw in the vee between thumb and forefinger, angling his head to receive the lengthy luxury of her kiss. He made a low, uncertain sound of want and its husky timbre shivered through her. Nothing had ever moved her so strongly as her desire for this man. Scotty claimed all the tender protectiveness of her mother's heart. Ethan Prescott demanded all the fire of her woman's soul. She parted his lips with her own to bank that uncontrollable flame, stoking it with quick stabs of her tongue. His arms came up to clasp her, then his left one lowered and tucked tight against his side. He muttered a curse of pain and annoyance.

They shared a smoldering silence. Then, reluctant doubts intruded. Their lovemaking had never been the problem. They'd reached a searing harmony on that basic plane at the very first attempt. And it had been and still was spectacular. There were no misunderstandings or failures to communicate through touch, only through words. And simple words were what they needed to share more than the most splendid union of flesh.

She hesitated, hating to risk the intimacy of the moment. She touched his bared chest, resting her palm over the commanding thump of his heart. "I didn't mean to hurt you so," she whispered. She couldn't meet his gaze. The moment was too fragile.

"It hurt," he admitted quietly, "but I reckon I'll survive it."

Neither of them were talking about his shoulder.

"I didn't mean what I said earlier." She glanced up. Her heart clutched at the somber tensing of his expression. Would he forgive and let them both forget? Or would he retreat behind the memories of mistrust as he had in the past? She wasn't Olivia. She wasn't going to leave him because of her own insecurities or failings. She needed him to brace those areas of weakness within herself. She couldn't lose him now, not now that they'd cleared away all the barriers to their happiness. She had to know if she had healed him, if he had healed himself. Not of the body but of the soul. She searched his eyes in a moment of anxiety, fretful of finding the familiar caution in their dark depths. Fearing the insurmountable scars.

But his gaze was steady. He, too, was seeking reassurance, some sign that she would allow him inside her guarded circle so he could share his strength. All he'd ever wanted was to share that which he was, to give of himself, to embrace the completing sphere of love and family. Would she let him?

"And I didn't mean to say quite so much. He's your

434

boy, Ora. I got no call to shoot my mouth off when you're doing what you think's right."

"Yes, you do. You have every right. Because you love him, too." She let him absorb that, hoping for some sign of belief. When the rigidity eased from his expression, she ventured, "Did you mean what you told Yellow Bear?"

"All of it," he told her simply and waited for her reaction.

Aurora bit her lip. "It just scares me so."

"What scares you, sweet thing?" His gaze grew very serious, delving into hers. "Me loving you, wanting you?"

"No," she cried, genuinely aghast that he would think so. She came down to him, burrowing atop his chest. "Losing Scotty. Oh, Ethan, the thought of him going back there. I don't know if I have that kind of strength."

"Hell, there ain't nothing stronger than a Kincaid. Or more stubborn," he added to make her smile. His arm curled about her shoulders, hugging her to him, enjoying the softness that so deliciously masked the steel of her character. "And Scotty, he'll be strong, too. You won't need to worry over him. Only he won't be a Kincaid. He'll be a Prescott."

He felt her go suddenly still. And all too silent.

"That all right with you?" he prompted gently.

"Righter than anything I can imagine."

They lay quiet for a moment, enjoying the pleasure of their thoughts, basking in the closeness of their love. It was their first chance to fully believe in the idea of a future together. And it felt—good!

"We'll be living at the Lone Star," he announced and paused as if expecting her to object.

"I'd like that," was all she said.

435

"Well, your daddy's not going to be any too pleased when he has to clear off all his cattle."

"He'll get over it," she declared firmly and Ethan reveled in wonder at her determined faith. "He'll get used to the idea of having a grandson who's related to the Sioux when they quit raiding his livestock. And he'll accept a son-in-law from Texas or he'll never get a visit from his daughter and her brood of Lone Star babies."

Laughter rumbled beneath her cheek. "You planning on raising a cash crop between us?"

"Would you mind?" She lifted up and looked long and lovingly into his simmering dark eyes.

"No. It'll give me something to do on those cold Dakota winters." From his lazy grin, she could see he was imagining them already. "That is, if your daddy don't come up with some reason to hang me first."

"Then he'll just have to string us up together," Aurora claimed fiercely. "Or get used to the idea that he can't always get what he wants. Nothing stands in the way of Kincaid. And I'm my father's daughter."

"And what is it this Kincaid wants?" he asked her with a sultry smile of confidence teasing about his lips.

"This Kincaid wants to be Mrs. Ethan Prescott. Tomorrow. You got a problem with that, sweet thang?"

"No, ma'am," he drawled. "Suits me jus' fine."

"Than hush your mouth and commence to kissing me."

"Yes, ma'am." No argument there.

Epilogue

"The buffalo we call *pte* or uncle. To you, it would be father. He provides our people with all we need to live. From his flesh, we eat; fresh for our cook pots, dried meat and fat to make pemmican. His thick hide makes heavy robes for winter covering. When tanned by our women, it covers our beds in summer, makes our leggings, hunting shirts, moccasins and women's clothing. Tipis of dressed cow hide are light, warm and easy to move as we follow the path of our uncle. The hide of the old bull is stretched tight over a frame of green willows into a boat to carry our families. The thick hide from the neck is shrunken into a shield that will turn the sharpest lance or arrow. Runners for the dog-drawn sleds come from rib bones, hoes and axes from shoulderblades, tools for dressing hides from cannon bones. The hoof is boiled for glue used in feathering arrows. Hair becomes soft cushions and padded saddles. The *pte's* long beard adorns our clothes, our shields and quivers. Bone is used for needles, sinew for thread and bowstrings. Horns are peeled and polished for spoons and ladles. Green hide is used to hold meat as it boils. The lining of the paunch makes water buckets. The skin of hind leg makes a tough boot or moccasins. Brushes come from the tail. From our uncle, we also get our saddle cloths, knife sheaths, quivers, bow cases and gun covers. Nothing goes to waste, *takoja*. That is part of the universe's design."

Yellow Bear paused to look down into the bright eager face of his grandson and smiled. He saw his son sitting before him listening with rapt attention to the legends of their people. His heart felt light but sad, too.

"In the spring," he continued, "the males and females separated over the long winter came together in great herds. The roaring of the bulls, the battering of their horns, skulls and forefeet as they battled at the time of breeding echoed into the hills like thunder. The stamping of their hooves and the scent of their bodies made their presence known tens of miles away. Then at The-Time-when-the-Wild-Plums-Ripen, the herds would separate into groups of male and female and roam south, and our people would go to their winter camp."

"I've never seen a herd of buffalo as big as the cattle my grandfather runs," the boy remarked in innocence.

"Nor will you, *takoja*. The *washachu* and his spindly animals on the hoof have driven them from the land as they have driven off your father's people."

"Is that why your tipi is made from canvas instead of hide?"

Yellow Bear nodded then said, "At one time, when I was a youth as you, a man could ride an entire day in an effort to find the edge of a buffalo herd. One could look out in every direction to see them covering the land like a great black blanket."

The boy's golden eyes shown with excitement and dreams. The time of the buffalo had become just another legend to be passed down through the generations, taken on faith and existing only in the mind's eye. It was an unhappy truth that the boy would have to imagine such a sight. Just as he would have to imagine the Lakotas as proud, free people. That heaviness of spirit caused a sharpness in the old chief's voice.

"Now the buffalo are gone. The old ones would say it is because our women lost their virtue that they are no more and our people starve."

"If the people are hungry, why don't they go to the agency for food? My grandfather supplies them with plenty of beef."

Anger was so rare in the stoic chief that Scotty was alarmed by its appearance on the seamless face. That single, cold look was more admonishing than the sternest slap. Scotty recoiled in confusion. Alarmed and aghast that he had said something to provoke such a response. He paled, golden eyes growing huge and anguished.

Seeing the boy's undeserved distress, Yellow Bear relented. It was his duty to instruct, not to judge. That, the boy would have to do on his own, from the truth in his own heart.

"Have you ever seen a reservation, my son?" The dark head shook from side to side and the old man put his hand upon it gently. "When you have seen, you will know."

Yellow Bear saw other questions gather but suddenly, he was tired. Weariness was something unknown to the young. He held up his hand to halt the words anxious to tumble from the boy's lips.

"It is time, *takoja*. You must change your clothes and be ready to go."

The boy caught the undercurrent of tension and

wrongly assumed he was the reason. With head lowered, he murmured, "I am not ashamed of how I look."

Yellow Bear assessed the young form with proud eyes. For all his lack of years, his grandson possessed a promising figure of manhood. In the brief breechcloth, his limbs were long and lithe, already molded with clumps of muscle from hard days of riding and wrestling. His boyish chest displayed a powerful breadth. Nothing to be ashamed of. The girls of the *tiyospaye* eyed him with coy interest and the boys respected his wiry strength. His features were chiseled like the wind-sculpted buttes into intriguing hollows and sharp edges with all the handsome arrogance of his age. No, there was nothing lacking in the man he would become, in the graceful, quick creature he already was. His form and face were fine. It was the outside trappings that offended.

"Hold up your head, boy. Do not look at the dirt when you speak of yourself."

The boy's eyes lifted. They were filled with a dampness that shimmered like a hot sunset over water. Ordinarily, Yellow Bear would chide him for tears but these were not signs of weakness. Rather of confusion and anger. And the older man's heart softened. He took the proud chin in his palm.

"You are the son of a great Lakota warrior. Carry that knowledge with pride. Always. Never let another shame you for what beats in your heart and flows through your veins. It is the blood of chiefs. You do not leave that behind you when you ride from this camp."

The boy's shoulders squared and an embarrassed hand swept his eyes. "My mother would have it so if she could," he said sullenly. His grandfather could feel the pain behind that admission. And the unvoiced fear that it would come to pass. That he would be denied the joys he found among his father's people. "She'd keep me at home and fuss over me like a prairie hen."

"*Wadutah* does not understand what moves in a man's heart. She is woman but she is also of a brave spirit. You dishonor yourself when you speak of her without respect."

"I am sorry, *tunkasila*," he murmured with a genuine humility. Yellow Bear was pleased. It was easier to teach a body strength than a soul sincerity. It was a praised virtue in one so young.

"And your white father. What does he say? Would he, too, keep you within his walls?"

The youthful features lit with a proud affection as he claimed, "No. He'd have me learn all I can. He speaks of my real father to me. He insists I be allowed to visit with you. Mama doesn't like it. It makes them fight sometimes." Sadness and a guilt too old and understanding for his years flickered in his eyes then was gone. "I'm glad he lets me come but I wish it wouldn't make my mother cry."

"Never give her reason for the tears, *takoja*. As a man, you must protect her and show her tenderness. You walk in two worlds and it cannot be an easy journey. When in your mother's world, embrace it with your arms but never with all your heart. Do not let her see the part of you that dwells with the Lakota people if it brings her pain."

"Why, *tunkasila?* Why is she so set against me being here? You're my family, as Grandfather Kincaid is my family."

"Such questions," the old man murmured. His gnarled hand fit against the boy's smooth bronze cheek. "Had I that answer, we would all live together instead of some of us inside and some of us outside the fences. Only your mother can tell you of her reasons."

"But she won't." His face screwed tight in frustration and Yellow Bear ached for his adolescent pain.

"In time, my son. Go to your father with your questions if you cannot find the patience within yourself. He has great wisdom and he will understand. Now go. Shed your buckskins and await your family with a smile in your soul."

"I wish I could stay," he mumbled.

"Someday, you will have that choice. For now, you owe obedience to others."

"As you say, *tunkasila*.

And so, it was a freshly scrubbed eight-year old who waited at the edge of the camp, his freedom restricted by stitched boots, crisp denims and a chambray shirt. His black hair had been slicked back behind his ears and covered with a new Stetson hat that was a size too big. As he glumly toed the dust to make circular patterns on the ground, none would have mistaken him for one of the Indian youths engaged in a noisy mud-and-willow fight near the stream meandering behind the camp. And, from the stoic expression on his face, none would guess his desire to join them. None but his grandfather, who could read his dejection like signs on a trail — or his white father as he drew the wagon up in front of him.

The boy needed no prompting to run to his family, nor was there any pretense in the way he launched himself into the big Texan's embrace. He was swept up to a great height; almost to the sky he'd thought when he was younger.

"Howdy, little pard. Got some good stories to tell?"

Scotty wound his arms about Ethan's neck and hugged hard. His father never asked the silly things his mother dwelt upon, like did he eat well, did he remember his prayers, did he miss them? He answered those loaded questions the way he thought she'd want him to, but Ethan always knew the truth. It was a secret they shared. And Scotty loved him fiercely for it.

"Go give your mama a kiss," Ethan whispered. "She's been a-jawing my ear off the whole way here. And if you've been running buck naked or eating dog, for the love of God, don't go a-telling her about it."

Scotty leaned back and grinned. "Yes, sir."

He clattered obediently in his heavy Cuban-heeled boots to the side of the wagon where his mother sat frowning. He could see the flaming red of his brother Rory's hair as he tried to peer around her.

"Howdy, Mama. I shore been a-missing you." He climbed up on the wheel so she could pull him close against her, just a minute too long, just a tad too tight. He fought the desire to wiggle in embarrassment. The fact that she smelled better than anything made it easier to endure.

"Why, Scotty Prescott, you're nothing but bone! Haven't you been eating anything?"

"Everything what's put in front a me, 'cepting dog, of course."

"I should hope not," she gasped, sounding properly shocked. He was old enough to wonder if she'd tasted dog in the time she'd lived with the Sioux. She never talked about it and if he asked, there was a funny sort of distress in her vague replies. So he stopped asking. He wouldn't hurt his mama for the world. But he still wondered.

Aurora made herself release him. She hated to admit it, but he looked wonderful, like a healthy young

443

boy full of life and animation. Yet, she noticed, too, the quiet reserve in him that strengthened with each visit to the Lakota camp. As if he was shutting her out from a part of himself.

She glanced up to see Ethan watching her, gauging her expression. She managed a smile that was both gay and false, hoping Scotty wouldn't know the difference. But he did. How could she expect an eight-year old to understand the hell these trips put her through? The nightmare of worries that plagued her each time she let him amble away in innocence into the Sioux camp? The agony she suffered until he was returned to her care? How hard she fought not to remain in his room long after she'd tucked him in, just to enjoy the sight of him asleep in his bed? Ethan recognized the desperate possessiveness that settled every time Scotty came home, and he tried hard to laugh or bully or just plain love her out of it. "Let the boy breathe, Ora," she could hear him chiding. And mostly, he succeeded in getting her to relax her vigil.

She forced her fingers to stop their fussing at his hair and collar and simply smiled at him. And Scotty beamed his gratitude.

"I love you, Mama," he said with youthful candor, then leaped down from the wagon and sprinted to his adopted father, not seeing the tears he'd brought to well in his mother's eyes.

Her gaze followed her husband and her son as they sauntered over to speak to Yellow Bear. The old Lakota chief never approached her, and she was knew it was out of respect for her fears. She watched the old man place a hand upon the boy's shoulder and saw his posture square with pride beneath it's weight. Her chest tightened. And she hated the old man for the love her son felt for him.

444

She felt a scurry of movement beside her and reached out to grab onto a thin arm. "Rory Prescott, you stay put."

"Aww, Ma, can't I get down an' play Injun with Scotty?"

Her fingers clenched unknowingly until the five-year old winced and whined in protest. She gentled her grip and told him for the hundredth time, "No, you cannot. You're too little." And if she had her way, he would never, ever run next to naked and wild with his brother 'playing' at being an Indian. The thought of Scotty bounding bare-chested and streaked with paint and grease next to his copper-skinned cousins was an image that haunted her dreams.

Aurora shook off her dark thoughts as her oldest son scrambled up onto the wagon seat. There was a momentary tussle between the two brothers before they settled one on either side of her. She put her arms around them. Rory snuggled close into her side. Scotty sat straight and tall. She wanted to believe it was his age that made him so distant.

"Look what I made for you, Mama," Scotty announced proudly as he produced a stick of wood from his pocket. "It's a *siyotanka*. My *tunkasila* taught me how to make it."

Aurora looked at the satiny finish and smooth bores her son had labored over but she had no desire to take it from him. Like Ethan, he loved shaping wood. She wished fervently that he'd stick to the bird whistles his father showed him to carve.

Scotty was watching her face, searching for a sign of interest, listening for a word of praise. He was confused. "It's a flute," he explained softly. "The Lakota use it to—"

"I know why they use it." It was a courting flute,

445

made to woo an Indian maiden, and she had no wish to be consider her son might someday think of using it in earnest.

"Ora." It was a quiet word from Ethan. He'd seen the way Scotty's face had fallen at his mother's sharp reply. "Why don't you ask him to play something for us."

Aurora looked up at her husband, knowing he understood her dismay and loving him for the tenderness in his gaze. But there was also a warning in his dark eyes. His fingertips brushed along the tense line of her shoulders and paused to knead. Her fears dissolved beneath that sensuous persuasion. With a small smile, she turned back to her silent son.

"Can you actually play something that doesn't sound like the mating call of a wild turkey?"

He gave a slight nod.

"Let's hear something, then. And I don't want to find you playing for any big-eyed little girls for at least another ten years or so."

"Mama!" He sounded pained. "What would I want with some dumb ole girl?"

Over their son's bright head, she and Ethan exchanged a lingering look. Her husband loosed a lazy Texas grin, daring her to elaborate, then clucked at the horses.

"Let's get home."

As Scotty began the first notes of his song, Ethan shook the reins and guided the team down from the hills toward where the summer wheat spread like golden Dakota sunshine. To the home where he and Aurora Prescott made all their dreams come true.

FIERY ROMANCE

CALIFORNIA CARESS   (2771, $3.75)
by Rebecca Sinclair

Hope Bennett was determined to save her brother's life. And if that meant paying notorious gunslinger Drake Frazier to take his place in a fight, she'd barter her last gold nugget. But Hope soon discovered she'd have to give the handsome rattlesnake more than riches if she wanted his help. His improper demands infuriated her; even as she luxuriated in the tantalizing heat of his embrace, she refused to yield to her desires.

ARIZONA CAPTIVE   (2718, $3.75)
by Laree Bryant

Logan Powers had always taken his role as a lady-killer very seriously and no woman was going to change that. Not even the breathtakingly beautiful Callie Nolan with her luxuriant black hair and startling blue eyes. Logan might have considered a lusty romp with her but it was apparent she was a lady, through and through. Hard as he tried, Logan couldn't resist wanting to take her warm slender body in his arms and hold her close to his heart forever.

DECEPTION'S EMBRACE   (2720, $3.75)
by Jeanne Hansen

Terrified heiress Katrina Montgomery fled Memphis with what little she could carry and headed west, hiding in a freight car. By the time she reached Kansas City, she was feeling almost safe . . . until the handsomest man she'd ever seen entered the car and swept her into his embrace. She didn't know who he was or why he refused to let her go, but when she gazed into his eyes, she somehow knew she could trust him with her life . . . and her heart.

Available wherever paperbacks are sold, or order direct from the Publisher. Send cover price plus 50¢ per copy for mailing and handling to Zebra Books, Dept. 3597, 475 Park Avenue South, New York, N.Y. 10016. Residents of New York, New Jersey and Pennsylvania must include sales tax. DO NOT SEND CASH.

THE BEST IN HISTORICAL ROMANCES

TIME-KEPT PROMISES (2422, $3.95)
by Constance O'Day Flannery

Sean O'Mara froze when he saw his wife Christina standing before him. She had vanished and the news had been written about in all of the papers—he had even been charged with her murder! But now he had living proof of his innocence, and Sean was not about to let her get away. No matter that the woman was claiming to be someone named Kristine; she still caused his blood to boil.

PASSION'S PRISONER (2573, $3.95)
by Casey Stewart

When Cassandra Lansing put on men's clothing and entered the Rawlings saloon she didn't expect to lose anything—in fact she was sure that she would win back her prized horse Rapscallion that her grandfather lost in a card game. She almost got a smug satisfaction at the thought of fooling the gamblers into believing that she was a man. But once she caught a glimpse of the virile Josh Rawlings, Cassandra wanted to be the woman in his embrace!

ANGEL HEART (2426, $3.95)
by Victoria Thompson

Ever since Angelica's father died, Harlan Snyder had been angling to get his hands on her ranch, the Diamond R. And now, just when she had an important government contract to fulfill, she couldn't find a single cowhand to hire—all because of Snyder's threats. It was only a matter of time before the legendary gunfighter Kid Collins turned up on her doorstep, badly wounded. Angelica assessed his firmly muscled physique and stared into his startling blue eyes. Beneath all that blood and dirt he was the handsomest man she had ever seen, and the one person who could help beat Snyder at his own game.

Available wherever paperbacks are sold, or order direct from the Publisher. Send cover price plus 50¢ per copy for mailing and handling to Zebra Books, Dept. 3597, 475 Park Avenue South, New York, N.Y. 10016. Residents of New York, New Jersey and Pennsylvania must include sales tax. DO NOT SEND CASH.